She lifted the receiver, but didn't get a chance to say hello. "Sarah." She barely recognized her brother. "God…" His voice was weak, breathless.

Sarah gripped the phone hard. "Rob? What's wrong? What—"

"I made Nate call you. I…*damn*."

"Are you in New York?" She could hear sirens in the background, people shouting, and felt panic rising in her throat. "Rob, talk to me! What's going on? Who's Nate?"

A fat bumblebee landed on the rim of her tea glass. She couldn't breathe, couldn't think as she waited for her brother to answer.

"I've been shot. I'll be okay."

"Rob!" She jumped to her feet. "Rob, where are you? What can I do?"

Another voice came onto the line. "Miss Dunnemore? Nate Winter. I work with your brother. Is someone with you?"

"No. No, I'm here alone. Rob—"

"He wanted you to hear the news from him. A paramedic's with him now. We've got to go. I'll call you as soon as I can with more information."

"Wait—don't hang up! Where was he shot? How bad is it?"

"He took a bullet to the left upper abdomen." Nate Winter's voice was professional, unemotional, but Sarah thought she heard a ripple of something else. Pain, dread. "Paramedics are coming for me. Sorry, I've got to go. We'll get you more information. I promise."

His words sank in. "Have you been shot, too? My God—"

The line went dead.

CARLA NEGGERS

NIGHT'S LANDING

ISBN 0-7783-2038-3

NIGHT'S LANDING

www.MIRABooks.com

Printed in U.S.A.

ACKNOWLEDGMENTS

Many thanks to Christine Wenger, Glen Stone, Paul Hudson and Dr. Carla Patton for answering all my questions and thinking up a few I didn't know to ask.

A special thank-you to my Southern in-laws, Jimmy and Estelle Jewell, whose Tennessee roots literally go back to Daniel Boone. Writing this book gave me the opportunity to get them to talk about the Cumberland River and some of the changes in it and middle Tennessee over the past century—I love to listen to their stories! Although…no, I never do want to get eyeball-to-eyeball with a water moccasin.

Thanks also—always—to Meg Ruley and everyone at the Jane Rotrosen Agency, and to Amy Moore-Benson, Dianne Moggy, Donna Hayes, Katherine Orr, Tania Charzewski and everyone at MIRA Books.

As I write this, I've put away my hiking boots (I'm determined to hike all forty-eight peaks over 4000 feet in the New Hampshire White Mountains) and I'm deep into my next book, *The Rapids…* Rob Dunnemore's story. For an excerpt (and pictures of our ongoing house renovations—yes, we were warned!), and to get in touch with me, visit my Web site, www.carlaneggers.com.

Take care,

Carla Neggers

To Lynn Katz...I love your photography
and your sense of humor!

One

After ninety minutes, the press conference dribbled to a close. As far as Nate Winter was concerned, the whole thing could have been wrapped up in fifteen minutes, tops. Announce the results of the joint fugitive task force. Outline its future. Answer a few questions.

Done.

But reporters had an uncanny ability of coming up with another way of asking what they'd just asked and politicians of saying what they'd just said. And the FBI, U.S. Marshals Service and New York Police Department brass wanted their fair share of credit. Deservedly so, maybe, but Nate just wanted to get back to work.

He cleared out of the airless meeting room on the ground floor of a fancy Central Park South hotel—the choice of the mayor's office—and made his way out to the street, welcoming the blast of chilly New York air.

It was midday. Traffic was bad. Some of the pedestrians had unfurled their umbrellas, but it wasn't really raining. Just misting, not even drizzling. People were craving real spring air—it was the first week in May—but it felt like March again.

Rob Dunnemore, a fellow deputy U.S. marshal, stood next to Nate and hunched his shoulders against the cold. "My southern blood is protesting."

Nate glanced at his younger colleague. They both had on their best dark suits, plus their nine-millimeter semiautomatics, their cuffs, their badges—the hardware wasn't visible, but Nate doubted they could pass for New York businessmen, either. "Air feels good to me."

"It would. I'll bet the snow hasn't melted where you come from."

Cold Ridge, New Hampshire, in the heart of the White Mountains. Nate hadn't been home since his sister Carine's wedding in February. "My uncle tells me there's still snow on the ridge. It's melted in the valleys."

"The frozen north." Rob gave an exaggerated shiver. He had the kind of blond good looks and southern charm tinged with danger that had an irresistible effect on the female support staff—and more than one female marshal. "New York's plenty cold enough for me. Come on. I need a dose of springtime. Let's check out the tulips in Central Park."

"Tulips? Dunnemore, what the hell are you talking about?"

"I saw about a million tulips when I was in Holland a couple weeks ago visiting my folks." He gave

Nate an unabashed grin. "I'm kind of into them right now."

Before Nate could respond, Dunnemore seized on a break in traffic and jaywalked across Central Park South. Nate, who was taller and lankier, followed at a slower pace, still unaccustomed to his fellow deputy's wide range of interests. He had no idea how or why Rob Dunnemore had ended up in the U.S. Marshals Service, never mind being assigned to its southern New York district. The Dunnemores were a prominent Tennessee family—Rob had been educated at private schools in Nashville and Washington, D.C., and graduated from Georgetown. He'd done a year abroad. Paris. He'd been everywhere and spoke six or seven languages, including Arabic and Farsi. Sooner or later, someone in Washington would reel him in and put him to work in intelligence.

After just four months in New York, Rob noticed everything. After five years, Nate didn't even notice the noise and grime anymore. He liked the city, but he didn't delude himself. He wasn't staying there. There was talk of sitting him at a desk at USMS headquarters in Arlington, Virginia. It would be a major promotion after more than a dozen years in street law enforcement.

He and Rob walked down the steps at Fifth Avenue and Fifty-ninth Street and entered the normally busy southeast corner of the park. But on such a miserable day, it was quiet, the noontime traffic above them almost distant, as if they'd entered an oasis in the middle of the tall buildings and millions of people.

The grass was lush and green, the spring leaves thickening on the trees and brush on the steep bank along the Central Park South fence and the famous elliptical-shaped pond. There was just enough of a drizzle to cause pinpricks across the pond's gray water.

"The tulips are something, aren't they?" Rob walked up the gently curving path along the edge of the pond. "My sister says they're done for in Tennessee."

"Rob, Christ. I've got work to do. I can't be wasting time looking at flowers."

"What's the matter? We hard-ass marshals can't appreciate tulips?"

Nate made himself take in the thousands of tulips that blossomed in waves on the sloping lawn to the right of the path, opposite the pond. Dark pink, light pink, white—they added a cheerful touch of color against the gloom. "All right. I've appreciated the tulips."

"When do tulips bloom in New Hampshire? July?"

"We're a couple weeks behind New York."

Probably more than a couple weeks this year, according to his uncle. Even for a tried-and-true northern New Englander like Gus Winter, it had been a long winter. More snow than normal, more days with temperatures that fell below zero—and a Valentine's Day wedding in the middle of it. The second of Nate's younger sisters, Carine, and her childhood friend, Tyler North, had finally married. They'd almost made it to the altar the previous Valentine's

Day, but called the wedding off at the last moment. It had taken a murder in Boston and a dangerous showdown with a madman on infamous Cold Ridge in the White Mountains before they came to their senses and finally married.

The previous October, Nate's other younger sister, Antonia, had married Hank Callahan, now the junior U.S. senator from Massachusetts.

No one had said, "Two down, one to go," but Nate had heard the words in his mind. He had no intention of getting married while he was still working on the streets. He'd been orphaned as a little boy. He liked not having anyone worrying about whether he'd come home that night. A wife, kids. A dog. He didn't even own a cat.

Gus, at least, left him alone. His uncle was in his fifties now and had never married. He was just twenty when he'd ended up raising his nephew and two nieces after their parents died of exposure on the ridge that loomed over their small New Hampshire town of the same name.

Nate had left Cold Ridge at eighteen and never went back to live.

He never would.

"I caught the dogwoods when I was home in April," Rob said in his amiable southern accent. "You don't see so many dogwoods up here."

"Dunnemore? Are you going to keep talking about goddamn flowers all afternoon?"

"Dogwoods are a flowering tree—"

"I know. Give me a break."

"You should come to Nashville. My sister—" Rob flinched suddenly, his body jerking back and up, his knees stiffening as he grabbed his upper left abdomen and swore. "Fuck. Nate…*shit…*"

Nate drew his Heckler & Koch, but told himself Rob could just be having a back spasm or a heart attack. The guy almost never swore. Something had to be wrong. Maybe a bee sting. Was he allergic?

Rob staggered back a step, his suitcoat falling open.

Blood.

It seeped between his fingers and spread across his white shirt on his upper left side.

A lot of blood.

"I've been shot," he said, sinking.

Nate caught him around the middle with his left arm, still holding the HK in his right hand, and glanced around for cover, spotted a rock outcropping near the pond on the other side of the path.

The shooter—where the hell was he?

Rob tried to keep his feet moving, but Nate more or less dragged him toward the rocks, then realized he hadn't heard any gunfire. Apparently no one else had, either. People were going about their business. Two elderly women with Bergdorf Goodman bags, a middle-aged man jogging on the path, a park worker inside a fenced area near the far edge of the tulips. They were all potential targets.

"Get down!" Nate yelled. "Federal officers! Get down *now!*"

The park worker dove for the ground without hesitation. The women and the jogger were confused at first, then did likewise, covering their heads with their hands and going still, not making a sound.

The rocks seemed a million miles away. Nate had no idea where the shot had come from. Fifth Avenue? Central Park South? The undergrowth along the shore of the pond presented a number of places for a shooter to conceal himself.

A trained sniper could be within hundreds of yards.

A bullet tore into Nate's upper left arm. He knew instantly what it was. He swore but didn't let go of Rob, didn't let go of his semiautomatic.

Definitely no gunfire. Even with the street noise, he should have been able to hear a shot.

The asshole was using a silencer.

"Put pressure on your wound," he told Rob. "Don't let go. You hear me? I'll get help."

But before Nate could get to his feet, a mounted NYPD police officer rode toward them. "What's—"

"Sniper," Nate cut in. "Get off your horse before—"

He didn't need to finish. The NYPD cop saw Rob's bloody front, saw his badge on his belt and dismounted, shouting into his radio for help. Officers down. Sniper at the pond in Central Park.

Nate knew the cavalry would be there in seconds.

The young NYPD cop stayed calm and crept toward the rocks. "You both hit?"

Nate nodded. "We're deputy marshals. The shooter's using a silencer."

"All right. Stay cool."

Rob moaned, his arm falling away from his wound.

Nate took over, applying pressure with his hand, as he'd learned in his first-aid training. He could feel his own pain now. His suit jacket was torn and bloody where the bullet had ripped through the fabric. What caliber? Where was the bastard who'd shot him?

Who was next?

The NYPD cop yelled instructions to bystanders.

Sirens. Lots of sirens on the streets above them.

Nate looked at the thousands of tulips brightening the dull landscape.

What the hell had just happened?

Two

Sarah Dunnemore jammed a cinnamon stick among the ice cubes and the slice of orange in her tall glass of sweet tea punch and sat back in the old wicker rocker on the front porch of her family's 1918 log house. The air was warm, no hint yet of the heat and humidity that would come with the middle Tennessee summer, and the sky was washed from yesterday's rain. A gentle breeze floated up from the river and brought with it the faint scent of roses.

Somewhere nearby, a mockingbird sang.

Sarah had warned herself to be prepared for the worst when she came home. Leaks in the roof, unmowed grass, bats, mice, food rotting in the refrigerator—her parents had last been in Night's Landing in early April, though they wouldn't necessarily notice such things or have them tended to. But they'd hired a new "gardener," as her mother called the property manager, and he seemed to be working out. He hadn't disappeared yet, as so many of his predecessors had, and he was good at his job. The lawn was manicured, the flower and vegetable gardens were in top shape, and the house was in good repair on what was a perfect early May afternoon.

The Dunnemores had arrived on the Cumberland River in the late eighteenth century and had been there ever since, sometimes eking out a living, sometimes managing quite nicely—always having adventures and too often dying young.

After just one sip of her tea punch, Sarah resolved not to drink the entire pitcher by herself. It was even sweeter than she remembered. She'd come home last at Christmas, but tea punch was a summer treat. She'd only made it to Night's Landing once the previous summer, a whirlwind visit that did not involve a leisurely afternoon on the porch.

The porch was shaded by a massive oak that she and her brother, Rob, used to climb as children, but even the lowest branch was too high now. They'd sneak up there and spy on Granny Dunnemore and their father, arguing politics on the porch, or their mother as she snapped beans and hummed to herself, thinking she was alone.

Sarah had made the tea punch herself, dunking tea bags into Granny's old sun-tea bottle and setting it out on the porch for an hour, then adding the litany of ingredients—frozen orange juice and lemon juice, mint extract, spices, sugar. She knew not to ponder them too much or she'd never drink the stuff. She never had an urge for sweet tea punch except when she was home in Tennessee.

Her friends in Scotland had made faces when she'd described Granny's recipe. "Do you waste proper tea on it?"

Well, no. She didn't. She used the cheapest tea bags she could find.

She took her friends' chiding in stride. It wasn't as if they didn't have oddities in their comfort cuisine.

She'd spent two weeks in Scotland in the fall and then the past three months straight, working nonstop, completing—yes, that was the word, she told herself—the final project in a series of projects under one huge heading: the Poe House. How dry and ordinary it sounded. Yet it had consumed her since high school, before she even knew what historical archaeology was.

The Poes had arrived on the Cumberland River not that long after the Dunnemores. Sarah knew their family history, the history of their post–Civil War house just downriver, of the land it was built on, better than she did her own. She'd written articles and papers, she'd done interviews and research; she'd organized archaeological digs on the site; she'd preserved documents and artifacts; she'd scrambled for grants; she'd helped create a private trust that worked with the state and federal government to preserve the Poe house as an historic site; and now she'd produced a documentary that took the family back to its roots in Scotland.

It was time to move on. Find something else to do.

She had no idea what but pushed back any thought of the possibilities before it could explode into a full-blown obsession, as it had on the long trip home from Scotland. What would she do *now?* Teach full-time? Work for a foundation? A museum? Find a new project?

Have a life?

Sarah yanked her cinnamon stick out of her glass and licked the end of it, watching the dappled shade on the rich, green lawn. She wondered if her grandfather, who'd built the log house in order to attract a bride, had ever imagined that dams would raise the river and bring it closer to the front porch, if he'd ever pictured how beautiful the landscape would be almost a hundred years later—if he'd ever guessed that his family would become so attached to it. Sarah had never known him. He'd died an early and tragic death like so many Dunnemores before him.

When she was a little girl, she'd believed stories that the logs for the house had come from trees cut down, blown down or otherwise destroyed when the U.S. Army Corps of Engineers dammed up the Cumberland for flood control and hydroelectric power, until she realized that the dams had been built decades *after* the house.

More than most in middle Tennessee, her family had a flare for storytelling and would go to great lengths, including embellishment, to make an already good story better.

She was convinced it was one of the reasons her father was such a natural diplomat. He didn't necessarily believe anything anyone told him, but at the same time, he didn't condemn them for stretching the truth, exaggerating, tweaking and otherwise making what they had to say suit their ends. To Stuart Dunnemore, that was all perfectly normal.

Sarah had no intention of making researching her own family her next career. It was enough to have researched her Night's Landing neighbors—especially when the last of the Poes had just been elected to the White House. She'd promised John Wesley Poe—President Poe—that he could be the first to view her documentary, which was finished, edited, *done*. But he couldn't ask her to change anything. That was the deal.

A mockingbird was singing somewhere nearby. Sarah smiled, watching a boat make its way upriver along the steep bluffs on the opposite bank, and drank more of her tea. Maybe it wasn't too sweet, after all.

Maybe, despite having nothing particular to do, this time she wouldn't get herself into trouble. She'd never done well with time on her hands. She hated being bored. She liked the independence her work afforded her, being her own boss, making her natural impulsiveness a virtue rather than a liability. Some of her best work had started out as wild-goose chases. But when she had no focus, nothing to anchor her, her impulsiveness hadn't always served her well. Once, she'd tried building her own boat and nearly drowned. Another time she'd tried her hand at frog-gigging and came up with a leg full of leeches. Then there was the time she'd ended up, on a whim, in Peru with nowhere near enough money to get by.

No affairs, anyway. She'd learned not to be impulsive with men.

The telephone rang, interrupting her mind-wandering. She set her glass on a rickety old table and reached for the ancient, heavy dial phone that had been wired up for use on the porch for as long as she could remember. It would never die. The phone company would have to come for it and tell them they couldn't use it anymore.

It was probably a solicitor. Not many people knew

she was home. Her parents, but they were in Amsterdam. Rob, but he was on duty in New York—she'd promised to get up there soon to see him. Her Scottish friends.

The president, except Wes Poe didn't call that often.

Virtually none of her Tennessee friends and relatives knew she was back in Night's Landing. It had only been a week—she had only just recovered from jet lag.

She lifted the receiver but didn't get a chance to say hello. "Sarah." She barely recognized her brother. "God…" His voice was weak, breathless.

Sarah gripped the phone hard. "Rob? What's wrong? What—"

"I made Nate call you. I…*damn.*"

"Are you in New York?" She could hear sirens in the background, people shouting, and felt panic rising in her throat. "Rob, talk to me! What's going on? Who's Nate?"

A fat bumblebee landed on the rim of her glass. She couldn't breathe, couldn't think, as she waited for her brother to answer.

"I've been shot. I'll be okay."

"*Rob!*" She jumped to her feet. "Rob, where are you? What can I do?"

Another voice came on the line. "Miss Dunnemore? Nate Winter. I work with your brother. Is someone with you?"

"No. No, I'm here alone. Rob—"

"He wanted you to hear the news from him. A paramedic's with him now. We've got to go. I'll call you as soon as I can with more information."

"Wait—don't hang up! Where was he shot? How bad is it?"

"He took a bullet to the left upper abdomen." Nate Winter's voice was professional, unemotional, but Sarah thought she heard a ripple of something else. Pain, dread. "Paramedics are coming for me. Sorry, I've got to go. We'll get you more information. I promise."

His words sank in. "Have you been shot, too? My God—"

The line went dead.

Sarah's hands shook so badly she had trouble cradling the receiver. Was Nate Winter another deputy U.S. marshal? She knew very little about her brother's work. He knew even less about hers. Historical archaeology—he'd say he didn't even know what it was. *Traditional archaeology studies prehistoric people and cultures. Historical archaeology is a subdiscipline of archaeology that studies people and cultures that existed during recorded history.*

She'd given Rob that explanation dozens of times.

He chased fugitives. Armed and dangerous fugitives. She knew that much.

Had one just shot him?

Her teeth were chattering, and she was pacing. Gulping for air.

"Ma'am?"

Ethan Brooker, her parents' new property manager, walked slowly up the porch steps, his concern evident. He had on his habitual overalls and Tennessee Titans shirt, his dark hair pulled back into a ponytail, at least a two days' growth of scruffy beard along his square jaw. He was tanned and muscular and had a black graphic tattoo on his huge right arm.

"Miss Sarah, you don't look so good." He spoke in an easy, heavy West Texas drawl. "Is there anything I can do for you?"

"I need—" She took in another breath, but couldn't seem to get any air. It was as if her entire body was trying to absorb the shock of Rob's call. "I need to wait for a phone call. My brother..." She couldn't finish, just kept trying to get air into her lungs.

The old porch floor, painted a dark evergreen, creaked under Ethan's weight. He was a year or two older than she was at thirty-two and taller. Her parents had found him down on the dock fishing when they were home for a few days. Trespassing, really, but he'd explained that he'd just moved to Nashville and was looking for work. Since they'd come home to a leaky ceiling in the living room and an overgrown yard, they offered him a job. He'd worked hard every day since Sarah had arrived in Night's Landing a week ago. He lived in Granny Dunnemore's old cottage down by the river, close to the woods between the Dunnemores and the Poes.

Granny had lost a husband in a logging accident, a son in World War II. Her surviving son's first wife had died after a long struggle with multiple sclerosis. Granny had built the cottage for herself after insisting he and his very sick wife move home.

Sarah knew the story of how her father had almost withered away here in Night's Landing after his wife's death, until he met her mother, twenty-two years his junior, the young and vibrant Betsy Quinlan, a woman even Granny Dunnemore had come to believe had changed the Dunnemore luck.

Sarah could feel her heart thumping in her chest.

Not another Dunnemore tragedy...not Rob...

"What about your brother, Miss Sarah?"

Ethan was invariably polite and deferential. She suspected he was a country-western musician looking for his big break in Nashville. She'd heard him playing acoustic guitar on the cottage porch early in the morning and late in the evening.

"Ma'am?"

"Rob—he's been shot."

The words felt no less surreal now that she'd said them herself.

Biting back tears, trying to breathe normally, she told Ethan about her brother's call from New York, Nate Winter, his promise to call her as soon as possible.

"What a shame, Miss Sarah. What a crying shame." He shook his head and exhaled forcefully, as if it would ease his own tension. "Who'd want to shoot two people like that?"

"Rob's a deputy U.S. marshal. They're called deputies. I didn't know that when he first started. A U.S. marshal heads up each district—they're not deputies. They're appointed by the president. I—" She didn't know what she was saying. "I don't know what Rob was doing."

"The marshals must have an office in Nashville. They'll send someone out here. You just sit tight." Ethan spoke with confidence as he withdrew a faded red bandanna from his back pocket and wiped away the dirt and grease stuck between his fingers and under his fingernails. "You're your brother's closest kin in the country, aren't you? The marshals will take good care of you."

Sarah's stomach twisted. "My parents. They're in Amsterdam. Oh, God. Who's going to tell them?"

"Let the marshals do it. You don't have enough information yet. If you try calling now, you'll just scare them, maybe unnecessarily."

Ethan's steady manner helped her to regain her composure. She felt as if someone were standing on her chest—she couldn't get air—and made herself breathe from the diaphragm, counting to four as she inhaled through her nose, then to eight as she exhaled through her mouth.

"Rob was able to talk," she said. "That's a good sign, don't you think?"

"Don't get ahead of yourself. Why don't you go inside and throw some cold water on your face? That always helps me when I've had the rug pulled out from under me."

Cold water. She wondered if she looked as if she was going to pass out.

"Go on," Ethan said calmly. "I'll go down to the cottage and get cleaned up, then come back here and stay with you until the marshals get here or this deputy you talked to calls back."

"You don't think he will, do you?"

"Not if he was shot, too, ma'am. Doctors and FBI will have him sewn up. Now, go on. One step at a time, okay?"

Sarah nodded. "Thank you. Rob and I are twins. Did you know that?"

"I think your mother told me that, yes, ma'am."

"She almost died when she had us."

Supposedly. It could have been another in a long string of Dunnemore enhancements. Although not a blood Dunnemore, Betsy Quinlan had fallen right in line with that particular Dunnemore tradition. Even letters and diaries from the nineteenth century that Sarah had uncovered in her Poe research had mentioned the Dunnemores and their zest for drama and adventure. They'd made so many bad, romantic, impractical decisions that had led to disaster—which was exactly how their father had viewed Rob's decision to become a marshal. A bad decision that would lead to disaster.

But Sarah didn't know why she'd mentioned that their mother had almost died in childbirth—why she'd even thought of it.

Ethan didn't comment and walked back down the porch steps with the same deliberateness as he'd mounted them. He paused, glancing up at Sarah as if to make sure she hadn't fallen apart in the few seconds he'd had his back turned. She couldn't smile. She couldn't do anything to reassure him.

"A splash of cold water, Miss Sarah," he repeated. "It'll help. I'll be back in a few minutes."

She managed to pull open the screen door and step into the front room with its walls of squared logs and thick, white caulking, with its old furnishings and frayed knitted afghans, its threadbare rugs, its wall of framed photographs. Her gaze landed on an oval portrait of Granny Dunnemore at eighty, in her pink sweater and cameo pin, a woman who'd endured so much sorrow and tragedy, who'd nonetheless stayed strong and kept her spirit, her faith.

Sarah ran back to the kitchen and turned on the faucet in the old sink.

"I've been shot. I'll be okay."

Crying, she splashed her face with cold water and prayed those wouldn't be her brother's last words to her.

An hour after Sarah's brother took a bullet in Central Park, two deputy marshals arrived at the Dunnemore house in a black government car. They came all the way around to the front porch, which afforded Ethan Brooker the opportunity to wish her luck, ask her to give her brother his best and slip out the back door.

He didn't need to be introducing himself to a couple of feds.

As pretty as she was, Sarah looked like hell. Pale, frightened, splotchy-faced from shock and tears. The other fed shot with her brother—Nate Winter—hadn't called her back. Understandable. The cable news channels reported that both he and Rob Dunnemore were in surgery. Winter was stable. Rob Dunnemore was critical and unstable.

If the reporters got it right. There was a lot of confusion, and the feds weren't releasing much information.

Ethan had talked Sarah into shutting off the television. CNN, MSNBC and FOX were all carrying the story live, with helicopter shots of Central Park and the manhunt for the sniper. They'd brought in experts to talk about what kind of person would do such a thing and explain what the U.S. Marshals Service was.

They repeated footage from the news conference that had preceded the shooting and showed Nate Winter and Rob Dunnemore standing behind the mayor, the U.S. marshal from their district, the chief deputy marshal, the assistant director in charge of the FBI, the NYPD commissioner—an impressive gathering of state, federal and local law enforcement types.

Winter was tall, rangy and all business.

Dunnemore looked like a frat boy.

Every time she saw the footage of her brother, Sarah went a little paler.

A joint FBI, NYPD and U.S. Marshal's Service news conference was scheduled for later that night and would, Ethan suspected, tell people nothing. The feds would be playing it close to the vest when two of their own had just been picked off in Central Park in broad daylight.

The all-news networks promised to carry, live, any briefings from the hospital where the two deputies were being treated.

As he made his way down to his cottage, Ethan stayed out of sight of the porch and any windows that could offer the feds a view of him. The breeze had strengthened into a stiff wind, damp and earthy smelling.

He entered through the back door, not making a sound. The cottage was made of the same rough logs as the main house and had an old-lady feel to it. Hand-crocheted afghans in bright, wear-ever yarns, doilies on the end tables, pink tile in the bathroom. When she'd shown him the place, Betsy Dunnemore had explained that her mother-in-law had built the cottage for herself after insisting her son live in the main house when he returned to Night's Landing with his dying first wife. Even after her daughter-in-law died, Granny Dunnemore, as she was known by everyone, had stayed on in the cottage until her own death fifteen years ago.

The place had a small kitchen, two tiny bedrooms and a front room and small porch that looked out at the river.

It could have been a tent for all Ethan cared.

A fishing boat with two old men talking loudly at each other puttered upstream, and Ethan had to fight an urge to find a boat and get the hell away from Night's Landing.

Charlene would want him to. *Get on with your life. You can't change what happened.*

She wouldn't be fooled into believing it was justice he was after.

It was revenge. Absolution for his own guilt.

He pulled himself away from the front window. Charlene would have loved it here. She'd never been a grasper—she'd talk about quitting the military and getting a little place in the country, having a couple of kids. He was the one who wasn't ready to stand down. *A couple more years, Char. A couple more.*

She hadn't had years the last time she'd brought up the subject.

She hadn't had months.

Only days.

And he wasn't with her when she died.

When she was murdered.

Ethan grabbed the pair of clippers he'd tossed onto the kitchen counter earlier and headed back outside. He didn't know as much about gardening as he'd claimed to Stuart and Betsy Dunnemore, but they'd never bothered to test his knowledge of flowers, trees and shrubs or even check his phony references. He'd made sure he so looked the part of a disarming, hardworking good ol' boy that they'd let it go.

He was from West Texas, but the rest was pure fiction.

Concealed behind a cedar tree, he watched the two marshals leave via the back door, one of them carrying a small suitcase, presumably Sarah's. But instead of following them, she came out onto the porch and trotted down the steps and across the yard to the cottage. "Ethan?" Her voice sounded tight but more composed. "Ethan, I'm going to New York to see Rob. Where—''

He ducked out from his hiding place. "That's good, ma'am."

She almost smiled. "You were right about the marshals looking after me. I don't know how long I'll be gone. A few days, at least, I would think."

"You just go on and don't worry about a thing here."

She seemed relieved, as if she'd expected him to evaporate on her. "I left my cell phone number on the refrigerator in case you need to reach me. You were right about the marshals getting in touch with my parents, too. They just called. They're waiting to get more information after Rob gets out of surgery before they decide what to do."

How much information did they need? Their son had been shot. He was in surgery. As far as Ethan was concerned, they should get their butts on a plane.

But Stuart Dunnemore did important work. He was

in Amsterdam negotiating world peace or some damn thing. And he was old. A lot older than his wife— eighty or close to it. It couldn't be easy at that age to drop everything and fly across the Atlantic, even in an emergency.

Ethan put aside his disapproval. He didn't know what, if any, role the Dunnemores had played in his wife's death, only that Char had met them in Amsterdam two days before she was killed. He wasn't even sure if the Dutch authorities knew. Or if it mattered. The Dunnemores had returned to the States the day after they met with Charlene, the day before she was killed. That was eight months ago. Ethan had arrived at Night's Landing in early April to check them out. They'd ended up hiring him.

He hadn't bothered using an alias. The Dunnemores showed no sign that Brooker was a name they ought to know. Maybe Charlene had used an alias with them? Maybe they didn't remember her name? They'd returned to Amsterdam in February and rented an apartment on a canal. Hiring Ethan on a quick trip home in April was supposed to give them peace of mind while they were away—it wasn't easy for them to get back to Night's Landing to check on their place. Maybe they didn't know about Charlene's death.

Since coming to Tennessee, Ethan had learned that the president of the United States was a family friend who'd grown up next door. He had no idea if that had anything to do with Charlene's death or what he'd do if the Secret Service decided to check out the Dunnemore's new gardener.

He'd also searched every inch of the Dunnemore house.

He gave Sarah a reassuring smile. "I'll take care of the place while you're gone. You just take care of yourself and your brother."

"Thanks, Ethan. No wonder my parents were thrilled when you agreed to work here. Thanks for everything."

He didn't feel even a twinge of guilt. All Ethan needed to do if he felt guilty about duping the Dunnemores was picture his wife lying in a pool of her own blood. There'd be no civilian life for them. No quiet place in the country. No babies. The investigation into her murder kept hitting brick wall after brick wall. Ethan hadn't had an update in weeks. In the meantime, he had his own sources, his own methods. So far, they'd brought him to Night's Landing and the Dunnemores.

He hadn't anticipated Rob Dunnemore getting shot in New York.

Who? Who was responsible? Did the shooting have anything to do with Char's murder?

He could hear her voice. *You're grasping at straws, Ethan. Let the authorities do their job.*

There wasn't necessarily a connection between what had happened to Charlene Brooker in Amsterdam eight months ago and what had happened to Rob Dunnemore and Nate Winter in New York that afternoon.

Ethan watched the fed sedan pull out of the long, curving driveway.

Yeah, right. He didn't believe in coincidence.

There had to be a connection.

He snipped a dead branch off some kind of white-flowering bush. An azalea, probably. He wasn't sure. Some gardener.

He wasn't an investigator by nature or training. He was a search-and-destroy specialist. His wife was the plotter, the thinker, the analyst.

She'd want him to call the police when he found her killer.

But he had a feeling he wouldn't do that.

Three

Nate climbed off the exam table and continued his argument with his doctor—her badge identified her as Sharon Ling, and she was all of five feet tall and *maybe* thirty years old—about getting his pants and shoes back and clearing out of the E.R. He'd heard that the news reports had him in surgery, but he'd only needed a few stitches. But apparently that was plenty for Dr. Ling. She wanted him admitted.

"Pants, shoes, whatever paperwork I need to get out of here," he said. "A couple of Tylenol and I'll be fine."

She shook her head not for the first time. "No way. You can go home in the morning."

He'd turned his weapon and cuffs over to Juliet Longstreet, another marshal who'd arrived on the scene before he and Rob were whisked away. The paramedics had shredded his shirt and jacket. Nate figured he could tuck in his hospital gown and change when he got home. But it was hard to look commanding and tough with a gown flapping on his back end. Dr. Ling had explained that he had a perforating, not a penetrating, wound, meaning she hadn't had to dig out the bullet that had struck him. The FBI investigators were undoubtedly looking for it somewhere in Central Park. Maybe it was at the bottom of the pond. Maybe the ducks had made off with it.

Nate didn't give a damn. He just wanted to get out of the hospital.

Dr. Ling didn't seem to consider the armed deputy posted at the exam room door anything out of the ordinary, probably because she'd treated plenty of wounded criminals. Nate knew from his E.R. doctor sister, Antonia, that it was her job as a doctor to treat the patient in front of her. Period. Meaning Dr. Ling would do her job whether he was a murder suspect or a federal law enforcement officer with fifteen years experience catching bad guys.

She sighed through her teeth. "You are a very determined man, Deputy Winter. At least let me get you into a room for a few hours. You can sit tight until your local anesthetic wears off."

"Doesn't it make more sense to get out of here while it's still working? I can have my feet up in front of the television before I start hurting."

She seemed singularly unimpressed with his argument. She crossed her arms on her chest and gave him a firm look. "You're a very lucky man, Deputy Winter. I don't think I'd be pushing my luck any more today."

What she meant, Nate knew, was that the bullet that had ripped into the fleshy part of his upper arm had caused a superficial wound that would heal fast. No permanent damage. No surgery. A couple inches one way, the bullet would have missed him entirely.

A couple inches another way, it could have nicked an artery or shattered bone.

Luck.

He agreed to sit tight for a few hours.

Dr. Ling handed him his pants and shoes—he'd track down Longstreet for his weapon—and an orderly and the deputy guard wheeled him upstairs.

Nate noticed the dried blood on the knee of his pants and the tops of his shoes.

Rob's blood.

When he got to his floor, he understood the subtext of Dr. Ling's stubbornness. Control and security. No media allowed, more armed deputies and a private waiting room for family members and any political, FBI, USMS, ATF and NYPD brass who wanted to check on the two wounded deputies.

No family members had arrived yet.

Thank God.

Nate didn't think he could deal with Gus and his sisters right now. The politicians and law enforcement types in the waiting room stayed put when he was wheeled past the open door.

They wouldn't want him off on his own too fast. A sniper had just tried to take out two federal agents in Central Park. All hell had to be breaking loose.

A nurse greeted him in his private room. Nate asked about Rob.

"He's still in surgery."

"Any word on his prognosis?"

She shook her head.

After she left, Nate ducked into the bathroom and put on his pants. He dampened a paper towel and scrubbed the blood off his shoes. Nothing to be done about the blood on his pants.

He checked his reflection and winced. "Hell."

It wasn't just pressure from his bosses that had compelled Dr. Ling to want to admit him. It was her medical judgment. He looked like shit. He was pale, he had dark circles under his eyes, he'd cut his lip from biting down too hard—no wonder she didn't want him going home right away.

He washed his face, felt his stomach turn over, almost barfed and decided, okay, maybe he should take it easy. He staggered back out of the bathroom.

FBI Special Agent Joe Collins was waiting for him. "Thought I was going to have to go in there and scrape you off the floor. How you feel?"

"Like I look."

"I was afraid of that. Up to talking?"

Nate knew Collins, although they'd never worked together. The shooting of two U.S. marshals was a federal crime that fell to the FBI to investigate, with the assistance of the Marshals Service, ATF and the New York Police Department. The marshals handled fugitive investigations and apprehension, prisoner transport, witness protection, the security of the federal judiciary and special operations—evidence gathering in federal criminal investigations was up to the FBI.

Nate nodded. "Sure. Excuse the outfit."

"You've got someone bringing you a change of clothes?"

His uncle Gus and sister Carine would have been contacted by now in Cold Ridge, about a six-hour drive to New York unless they got a shuttle flight from Manchester. Antonia was in Washington. Closer. But she was almost eight months pregnant. Maybe she'd stay put.

Not a chance.

And his brothers-in-law would be at their wives' sides.

Collins looked tired, but he always did. He had the kind of laid-back demeanor that made people think he wasn't quite with it—their mistake. He was in his mid-forties, his wedding ring too tight on a knuckle-swollen finger, his stomach pushing against the buttons of his button-down blue shirt. He had a friendly face filled with broken capillaries.

Another FBI agent, straight backed, tense looking, maybe in her mid-twenties, stood silently in the corner by the bathroom.

"Any word on Rob?" Nate asked.

"He lost his spleen," Collins said. "You can live without a spleen. It's the blood loss the doctors are worried about. It's still touch-and-go."

Nate remembered the paramedics talking about internal bleeding at the scene. He didn't respond. What was there to say?

"How're you doing?" Collins asked.

"Fine."

The FBI agent gave him a look that said they both knew better.

"We walked down to Central Park after the news conference. Rob—Christ, he wanted to see the tulips. Someone shot us." Nate sat on the edge of his hospital bed. "That's it. End of story."

Except he knew it wasn't. Collins would want to ask why they went into the park, who knew they'd be at the news conference, what they saw—and that was just for starters.

At this point, Nate doubted anyone thought it was a random shooting, a guy concealed somewhere in or around the park with an assault rifle and a silencer, waiting for the right moment, as opposed to the right victims, to shoot.

"He had to have an escape route," Nate said.

"One thing at a time."

Collins took him through the shooting step by step, minute by minute. Nate could feel his anesthetic slowly wearing off, the bandage heavy on his arm, the reality of what had happened earlier in the day hitting him. He'd been taking down fugitives for a long time, guys wanted for murder, carjacking, drug dealing, torture, rape and every other manner of violent crime. He'd been shot at before, but never like this—never a sneak attack, never with a fellow deputy collapsing, maybe dying, at his side.

"Deputy Dunnemore called his sister before the paramedics arrived?" Collins asked.

Nate pulled himself back to the matter at hand. "That's right."

"You dialed?"

"He had her number in memory. He wasn't in any condition to talk. I think he just wanted her to hear what happened from him."

"Then you talked to her?"

"That's right. Rob couldn't hold on to the phone. I took it." Nate related his brief conversation with a shocked, frightened Sarah Dunnemore. "I told her I'd call her back, but I haven't been able to. I'd need Rob's cell phone. I don't have her number."

Collins wanted to know what Rob said to his sister. Nate told him.

There were more questions. The guy wasn't leaving a stone unturned.

Nate's head throbbed, and Special Agent Collins was getting on his nerves. Anyone would. He felt woozy from whatever crap Dr. Ling had pumped into him. A couple of Tylenol and directions to the exit would have suited him fine.

"They're twins," Collins said, "Deputy Dunnemore and his sister. You have two sisters, right? You call them?"

"Not yet, no. What the hell, Collins? You suspicious because Rob called his sister? For God's sake, *she* didn't shoot him."

Collins ignored him. "Okay, you rest. Doctors say they might spring you later on, let you sleep in your own bed tonight. That must sound pretty good right now."

"Just find the damn shooter. Never mind me."

"Yeah. We're on it. You're not going to get in the way, are you?"

Nate said nothing.

"One last thing," Collins said. "What were you and Deputy Dunnemore talking about before you got hit?"

"Tulips."

The FBI agent managed a small grin before he left. Even the stone-faced female agent in the corner had a twitch of a smile.

Nate had his bed cranked up to a sitting position and was lying back against his skinny pillow, his shoes still on and his ankles crossed, when his family descended.

Gus, Antonia, Carine and their new husbands, Hank Callahan and Tyler North.

Collins had left almost an hour before. Since then, Nate had refused all company and stared at the ceiling, seeing Rob's body jerking up as the bullet hit, hearing his sister's shocked, frightened voice when Nate had talked to her. He saw the blood on the phone. Heard his own calm voice, as if he wasn't really there, in the middle of chaos, shot, trying to save his colleague, trying to find the shooter. So much happening at once, but certain things stuck with him, wouldn't recede.

He hadn't called the sister back. He couldn't—her number was on Rob's cell phone.

Someone must have contacted her by now.

Twins. Nate couldn't remember Rob ever saying much about her.

The image started replaying itself, like a movie, but Nate pulled himself out of it and sat up straighter. He tried to smile at his family. "I feel like Dorothy in *The Wizard of Oz.* All I need is Toto to show up. They let you all in here at once?"

His white-haired uncle, built like Nate, grunted. "It's Antonia's fault. She told your doctors you could handle all of us."

Nate eyed his out-to-there pregnant sister, wearing what at a guess was one of her husband's shirts. "I can handle the stress, but can you, Antonia? You look like you're going to have that baby any second."

"Not for a few more weeks." Always the doctor,

she picked up his chart and scanned it, sighing. "How's your arm?"

"Anesthetized. I can't feel a thing. Rob Dunnemore's the one in rough shape."

She nodded. "So I understand."

Tyler North, Carine's air force pararescueman husband, spoke up. "A wound like that. Chances are he's either going to make a full recovery or he's going to die. There's not much in between."

Antonia winced. "Ty, for God's sake—"

But North wasn't one to pussyfoot around. They'd all been friends since childhood, and Nate appreciated his straightforward assessment. Carine leaned over his bed, the stress of the past hours evident in her drawn, pale look, in the blue eyes all three siblings shared. Carine was the youngest. Her auburn hair was lighter than Antonia's, Nate's own hair so dark the red streaks were barely noticeable. Carine had been shot at. She knew what it was like. "I'm glad you weren't killed," she whispered.

"Me, too."

Hank Callahan, Antonia's husband, slipped an arm around his wife and eyed Nate. "Is there anything I can do?" Once a helicopter rescue pilot and now a junior senator from Massachusetts, Hank, like the rest of them, was used to taking action.

"Get me a shirt. I feel like an idiot in this gown."

Antonia hissed. "I knew you'd be impossible. Didn't I tell you, Gus?"

Their uncle stared out the window with its view of the street. He was in jeans and a hiking jersey. He was one of the best outfitters in the White Mountains, content to stay home in Cold Ridge and hike, cook and redecorate the house he'd inherited from his older brother. But Gus had been shot at more than any of them. He'd served a year in combat in Vietnam before coming home, only to end up raising his orphaned nieces and nephew.

He glanced back at Nate. "Why don't you drive home with me? The mountain air'll do you good."

Nate shook his head. "Last time I was home, you served orange eggs."

"They're not that orange. You're just used to New York eggs."

"I'm used to yellow eggs."

"It's what Moon feeds them."

Moon. Moon Solaire. She was a newcomer to Cold Ridge. People called her the egg lady because she had dozens of chickens in a variety of breeds. She and Gus had been seeing each other for a couple of months. "Moon's really into chickens, isn't she?"

Nate was starting to feel sluggish and achy, some of his earlier adrenaline rush wearing off. Or maybe now that his family was there, he could allow himself a letdown.

"Who knew there were that many different kinds of chickens?" Gus said. "I thought she might be one of your people, with a fake name like Moon Solaire."

"What do you mean, one of my people?"

Gus shrugged. "You know, some lowlife you're protecting so they can testify against some bigger lowlife you're not protecting."

He meant WITSEC. The Witness Security Program. Gus's rendition of its mission of protecting government witnesses and their dependents was over-simplified and biased, but Nate was in no mood to argue. "Not all protected federal witnesses are criminals, and I'd be surprised if we ever gave one a name like Moon Solaire—"

"I know, I know. She made it up. Ex-hippie. Real name's Linda."

Nate didn't know about the ex.

Antonia touched their uncle's arm. "We should go."

Gus didn't budge, his blue eyes pinned on his nephew. With just a thirteen-year age difference between them, Gus was in some ways like an older brother to Nate, in other ways like a father. "I turned on CNN before the marshals called, and I knew it was you. I'm telling you. I just knew."

"I'm sorry, Gus. It's my job—"

"It's not your job to get shot by some asshole in Central Park."

Antonia groaned. "Gus! Now's not the time." She shifted her attention to her older brother. "You'll do what your doctors say, won't you? And don't be stingy with the pain medication. Take what you need."

"Got it."

She wasn't convinced. "You do not. You're itching to get out of this bed and go find who shot you."

"And you wouldn't be?"

She didn't answer. No one did, because his uncle, his sisters and the men they'd married were all cut from the same cloth when it came to waiting patiently for others to do what they wanted to do themselves. They simply didn't.

Nate felt bad about what they'd been through today. He knew what it was like—he remembered how he'd reacted when he learned about the close calls his sisters and brothers-in-law had had last fall. ''Where are you guys staying tonight?''

No one wanted to answer that one, either, but finally Ty did. ''Your place. Hank and I are heading out tonight, but your uncle and sisters are staying. Gus took a lasagna out of the freezer and brought it down.''

The thought of Gus's rich, uncompromising lasagna made Nate nauseous. Spending the night in the hospital suddenly didn't look so bad. Armed guards and medical types hovering over him—or his family.

When his nurse entered the room, his entourage retreated, but Nate could hear them out in the hall. If his bandaged arm hadn't forced the reality of his situation to sink in, their presence did.

He'd been shot.

He'd damn near been killed.

And Rob Dunnemore—it could go either way with him.

After the nurse left, Nate tried to get the deputy at his door to find who he needed to see about checking himself out.

No dice.

He'd just have to wait.

Four

Juliet Longstreet made herself dump the last of her latte in the water fountain next to the elevator that had dropped her off on Rob and Nate's floor. It was her seventh latte of the day, and she had acid burning up her throat. Not a good sign.

She ran the water to clean the drain but didn't take a sip. She didn't like drinking out of hospital water fountains.

She didn't like anything about this whole damn day.

The chief deputy had turned the care and feeding of Rob Dunnemore's sister over to her, probably because they were both female and blond. Any comparison ended there. Sarah Dunnemore was just about the prettiest woman Juliet had ever actually met in person. Long honey-colored hair streaked with pale blond highlights, gray eyes, slim build, elegant even in her jeans and dark gray silk twin set. She wore two delicate little rings on her fingers. Juliet still had Band-Aid scum on her thumb after jamming it in the weight room. She was a lot taller. And her hair. Nobody could do a thing with it. A friend had dragged her to a trendy New York salon, and she'd learned about hair wax and identified every one of her cowlicks—she'd spent a fortune and looked good for about three days.

Christ.

Rob was in there dying, and she was thinking about her hair.

"Dr. Dunnemore?" Faking a calm professionalism, Juliet pretended her throat wasn't burning and motioned toward the waiting room recently vacated by the Winter family. "Let's go in there. It'll be quiet."

It seemed to take a few seconds for her words to sink it, but Sarah Dunnemore nodded and mumbled something about calling her by her first name, then walked into the little room. Juliet had already kicked out any loitering law enforcement types. All the armed marshals in the halls were enough to agitate her, never mind a Ph.D. who'd just learned her twin brother had been seriously wounded in a sniper attack. A New York hospital on a good day was hard to take. This was not a good day.

Juliet had no idea what to say. None.

"Can I get you anything?" she asked finally.

Sarah shook her head. "When can I talk to Rob's doctor?"

"Soon. Your brother's just out of surgery."

The gray eyes were steady, but Juliet could see the fear in them and realized that Sarah couldn't speak.

"He's holding his own," Juliet said, guessing Sarah's question. "I understand that the next twenty-four hours are critical."

Sarah took a moment to digest Juliet's words, then

breathed in through her nose and nodded. "What about the deputy who was with him? Nate Winter. How is he?"

"He's fine. Someone forgot to chain him to his bed, so he got out of here about an hour ago." It was seven now. Juliet had returned his weapon to him and, like everyone else, futilely told him to go home and take it easy. "The bullet that hit him just grazed his upper arm. He was never in surgery."

"That's good," Sarah said absently. She remained on her feet—she was wearing sandals that would not be adequate for the miserable weather New York was having. "I don't know much about guns. Shots like that—would they be difficult shots? Do you think the shooter meant to kill my brother and Deputy Winter outright?"

"No answers yet. FBI's investigating."

"There must be witnesses. Central Park at midday—someone must have seen something. Are there places for a shooter to hide? How would he escape? If the police arrived quickly—"

"Look, have a seat." The chief deputy had warned Juliet to try to keep Rob's sister from dwelling on, dissecting, the shooting. It wasn't good for her. It wasn't good for any of them. "At least let me get you a cup of coffee."

"I don't drink coffee, but thank you. I'm okay. I just want to see my brother."

"I know, but it might not be tonight." He was in intensive care, on a respirator. Juliet didn't want to be the one to tell Sarah Dunnemore that. "Let's just wait and you can talk to his doctor."

Sarah nodded, saying nothing, and lowered her

head, fiddling with one of her rings, as if to keep
Juliet from seeing that she was on the verge of tears.

Hell. Juliet took in a steadying breath. Now her
stomach was burning. She had no idea what to say to
this woman. "Where are you staying?"

"I could stay at Rob's. I haven't visited since he
was assigned up here, but I could—I'm sure I could
get the key."

"That's not a good idea, not tonight. FBI could be
going through his place for all I know, but you
shouldn't stay there on your own. Forget about it,
okay? Trust me. You can stay at my place if you don't
mind my fish and plants, or I can book you into a
hotel."

"That's very nice of you, Deputy—Longstreet,
right?"

"Juliet'll do."

"Juliet. That's a pretty name."

"Yeah." She smiled. "I used to think I should
change it to something meaner sounding."

Sarah raised her eyes. "You and Rob..." But she
trailed off, not finishing.

Juliet understood what she was trying to say. "We
used to see each other."

"Not anymore?"

"No. Not anymore."

The noise and lights of the city—the crush of people—struck Sarah as oddly reassuring as she and Juliet Longstreet climbed out of the back of the government car that had driven them to the Marriott
Marquis in the heart of Times Square. It wasn't that
far from the hospital, but Rob's bosses didn't want

her walking. They'd made that clear. They didn't say it was because a sniper was on the loose in the city and they were afraid Juliet or even Sarah might be his next target—they said it was because Sarah was obviously exhausted, emotionally wrung out and on edge.

But they all were tired and on edge, she thought. A steady stream of law enforcement and political types had stopped at the hospital to check on Rob and Nate and to greet her, to offer to do whatever they could for her. She'd sensed not only their concern for the injured officers, but their worry about the situation itself. The chief deputy, the district U.S. marshal, the FBI agent leading the investigation, the FBI assistant director in charge of the New York FBI office, the mayor—they'd all attended the news conference that had preceded the shooting. The shooter could have been after one of them instead and seized on Rob and Nate as a second choice, targets of opportunity—get someone, anyone, who'd been at the news conference.

The bottom line was clear. Two federal agents had been gunned down in daylight in Central Park, and the gunman was still at large.

"I'll check you in," Juliet said, briskly leading the way up the elevators to the eighth-floor lobby of the huge conference hotel.

She'd insisted on carrying Sarah's bag, saying it was part of the job. Sarah wanted to ask about Juliet's relationship with her brother, who'd only mentioned in one e-mail that he'd been seeing another deputy and it hadn't worked out—but Juliet had cut off that topic.

When they arrived at the lobby, Sarah waited off

to the side while Juliet checked her in. She'd never seriously considered imposing on her marshal escort—she liked the anonymity of the large hotel. She needed time to herself. Space. Rob's doctors were guarded but not discouraging in their assessment of her brother's condition. He'd lost a lot of blood but the surgery had gone well. The bullet could have done far more damage than it had, although the damage it *had* done was considerable. They'd watch him closely for complications from blood loss, a recurrence of bleeding, infection—he had a long way to go.

Without her having to plead, his doctors had allowed her peek in on him.

He was intubated and attached to a ventilator, hooked up to a myriad of IVs and tubes and unconscious. But he was alive, and that was what Sarah had tried to focus on as she touched him gently on the forehead and told him she was there and would see him in the morning. She hoped that on some subconscious level he could hear her, knew she was rooting for him and he wasn't alone.

But when she left the I.C.U., she burst into tears and almost threw up. Juliet Longstreet had hesitated, obviously awkward and unsure of what to do, but the chief deputy—Mike Rivera, a stocky rock of a man—stepped forward and maneuvered Sarah into the waiting room.

That was when they all decided she shouldn't walk alone to her hotel.

Juliet turned from the front desk with a small key folder. "Tenth floor okay?"

"Anything's fine."

"Elevators are over here."

When they reached her room, Juliet used the card key and pushed open the door, then checked out the place, even pulling open the closet and drawers. Sarah caught a glimpse of her weapon, a reminder that her escort was a federal agent on duty. She wasn't just being kind.

"Place looks clean and safe enough." Juliet turned from the closet and frowned at Sarah. "You look beat. Take a bath and get some sleep. If there's any news, someone will call you. Promise."

Sarah sank onto the bed. Her room was clean and pleasant, a large window overlooking Times Square with its huge, flashing billboards. She was struck by the disconnect between here and her family home in Night's Landing. Not that long ago, she'd been listening to a mockingbird and drinking tea punch.

She doubted she'd sleep, never mind the flashing billboards and sirens down on the busy New York street.

A cell phone trilled, but it took a moment for Sarah to realize it was hers. She fished it from an outer pocket of her tote bag.

"Sarah—Sarah, honey, it's Wes."

Fresh tears welled in Sarah's eyes at the sound of John Wesley Poe's familiar, caring voice. "Wes— I'm so glad you called. It's been an awful day."

"I know, honey. I heard about Rob. I am so, so sorry."

"I saw him for a few seconds. He made it out of surgery. That's a good sign."

Juliet turned from the window, not hiding that she was listening. Sarah knew she couldn't possibly explain that she was talking to the president of the

United States. Deputy U.S. Marshal Juliet Long-street's ultimate boss. Rob's boss. But to her, he was a friend, a neighbor, a man she'd known and adored all her life.

"Ev and I are thinking of you, praying for both you and Rob," Wes said. "If there's anything we can do, please, just say the word."

"Thank you. Thank you for calling. Just knowing you're thinking of him makes a difference. He's—it's tough, Wes. He's on a respirator—the bandages—" Her voice faltered. "But I keep telling myself that at least he's alive. He has a chance."

"He's strong, and so are you." But beneath his soothing words, she heard the undertone of concern and fear, because for all his brilliance and compassion, Wes Poe didn't know if Rob would live, either. "Where are you now?"

"A hotel in New York."

"Alone?"

"I have a deputy marshal escort. Wes, don't worry about me. I'm fine."

"What about your parents?"

"They're waiting until morning their time before they decide what to do."

"God love them. This has to be a parent's worst nightmare."

Wes and Evelyn Poe had no children. That it was a political liability was something Sarah had found distasteful. Evelyn had had four miscarriages and stillbirths before an emergency hysterectomy put an end to all hope of giving birth. Sarah remembered how distraught Wes was after that fourth and last loss. He'd come to Night's Landing alone, so his wife wouldn't see him mourn, so he could be strong for her when they were together. But even before that terrible day, Sarah had become something of a surrogate daughter to them. In some ways, they'd been more reliable and solid—more available—than her own parents.

"Sarah...the media..." Wes hesitated, a rarity for him. "They'll zero in on my relationship with your family at some point. Right now, there's no indication that Rob was targeted because of it."

Sarah nearly dropped the phone.

Juliet Longstreet took a step toward her, her expression tight, alert.

"Wes!" Sarah choked, gripping the phone. "My God, that never even occurred to me!"

"I'm mentioning it only because it could come up as a theory, and I don't want you to be blindsided." The strain in his voice, famous for its ability to soothe yet sound commanding, was evident. "Honey, you just focus on being there for Rob. I'll worry about the rest of it."

"Thank you." She didn't know what else to say.

"Ev sends her love."

"I love you both. Thank you for calling."

After Sarah hung up, Juliet pulled the drapes. "Do you mind if I ask who that was?" she asked.

Sarah's heart thumped painfully in her chest. Her eyes felt squeezed. In Scotland, for weeks—for most of John Wesley Poe's first months in office—she hadn't had to deal with the reality that her closest and oldest family friend had been elected president of the United States.

"Sarah?"

"Wes. Wes Poe. He and my father go way back. My mother went to college with him. She almost married him." Sarah winced, wondering why she'd brought that up. "Supposedly. You never know with my family."

"Jesus Christ," Juliet said under her breath, then snapped up straight, looking every inch the federal agent she was. "All right. No goddamn way am I leaving you to your own devices tonight. Either we switch to a double room and I camp out with you, or you take the futon at my place."

"Would I be sleeping with the fish or the plants?"

She managed a crooked smile. "Both. You'll see."

Since she'd be sleeping in a strange bed no matter what she did, Sarah rose and grabbed her suitcase. She had no intention of making Juliet spend the night in a hotel after the day they'd both had—and there was no way Sarah was going to talk Deputy Longstreet into leaving her alone.

"Rob never mentioned we were friends with President Poe?"

"No."

"He didn't want it to affect him on the job—"

"We weren't always on the job." Juliet bit off a sigh. "We worked out okay before he was transferred to New York. I knew your family was white bread, but—" She tore open the door, grinding her teeth. "You didn't happen to mention your friendship with the president to the FBI, did you? Collins? He talked to you, right?"

"He asked me about my phone call from Rob. Our friendship with the president didn't come up."

"Trust me," Deputy Longstreet said, walking out into the hall, "it will."

Five

Ethan switched off CNN and listened to the crickets out in the dark. He had the windows in his cottage open. The breeze had died down, making the crickets even more noticeable. He almost turned the television back on, but he didn't think he could take one more idiot talking about the possible firearm the sniper could have used. What the hell difference did it make? Two federal agents were in the hospital. Go find the fucker.

He put his feet up on the old flat-topped trunk set up as a coffee table, its wood varnished to a high gloss, probably hurting its value as an antique. The Dunnemores didn't seem to think much in terms of antiques. A different sort of family, for sure. Eccentrics. Ethan's parents were ranchers in West Texas. Hard working, well-respected. They had no idea what their younger son was up to.

Char's father was a widower, career military, who pretty much thought Ethan had killed her.

He wasn't that far off.

FOX News had done a diagram of the kind of

wound Rob Dunnemore might have suffered in his left upper abdomen. Explained how he could live without a spleen. About the risks of blood loss, the strain it put on the kidneys. Luckily, he'd gotten medical attention within the "golden hour."

Char hadn't.

Because Ethan hadn't been there.

He hadn't been there a lot during their two-year marriage.

He jumped to his feet and tore open the small refrigerator, grabbed a glass container of leftover barbecue and popped it into the microwave. It was an ancient microwave. It must have been one of the first ones off the assembly line. The Dunnemores weren't into gadgets.

He got out dill pickle slices and found a dried-up sesame-seed bun in the bread box. He softened it up in the microwave and put the whole mess together and ate it leaning against the sink, wondering what in hell he thought he was doing. Night's Landing. The Dunnemores. President Poe's boyhood home just up river. Ethan knew better than to turn into some kind of nutball loose cannon, but here he was.

He'd read Sarah Dunnemore's dissertation on the Poe house and how the Poe family fit into the post– Civil War South. Thought he'd go blind. She'd just finished producing and directing a documentary. There was talk of her becoming the director of the Poe House and working to open it to the public as an historic site. Now that he'd met her, Ethan couldn't see Sarah Dunnemore spending her time figuring out where the visitors' center should go, doing fundraising, training docents—she needed a new project.

Ethan had taken his own private, illicit, midnight tour of the Poe house downriver from the Dunnemores. It hadn't produced a single thing except a spider bite on his ankle. His search of the Dunnemore house hadn't produced much more. He'd gone through file cabinets, photo albums, old yearbooks. The father had written plenty of boring papers of his own. The mother was into art.

He'd found Sarah's locked diary from when she was fifteen but decided he wasn't low enough to break into it and read it.

But he might yet. He was *that* goddamn frustrated.

He wasn't sure what he expected to find in Tennessee. A connection, a hint, a link. Something that explained Charlene's interest in the Dunnemores. Why she'd contacted Betsy Dunnemore in Amsterdam two days before she was killed. What it had to do with her death.

She'd gone to Amsterdam on her own. On holiday, she'd told her friends and superiors, Euro-style. Ethan had shown up at her base in Germany without notice, found her gone, figured out where she was and headed to Amsterdam to join her. He could track down anyone, so he'd tracked down his ambitious, incredible wife.

He hadn't considered the importance of her trip until she'd turned up dead. Then he wanted to know everything. Why Amsterdam? What had Char been up to?

Weeks of probing, spying and prowling in Europe had landed him on the Cumberland River in middle Tennessee, playing gardener.

Waiting like a damn fool for answers to fall into his lap.

Ten days ago, he'd bought a ticket back to Amsterdam.

But he hadn't yet used it. Because Sarah Dunnemore had returned from Scotland. And now her brother had been shot in Central Park.

Suddenly Ethan realized the crickets had stopped chirping.

He set his plate in the sink and went still, listening, aware of the .38 semiautomatic strapped to his ankle under his overalls.

"Mr. Brooker? It's me, Conroy Fontaine." The accent was distinctly Southern, the voice amiable, familiar. "Would you mind if I had a word with you?"

Ethan stifled a groan. Just what he needed, a bottom-feeding reporter who liked to pass himself off as a legitimate journalist-historian. Before he could respond, Fontaine was at the door. He was working on an unauthorized, tabloid-style biography of the president. He'd set up shop a couple weeks ago at a cabin he'd rented at a fishing camp farther up river from the Poe house. He was worming his way into Sarah's good graces, presumably in an attempt to get access to the president and dig up any dirt he could find— not that she was anyone's fool. As far as Ethan had seen, so far she hadn't told Fontaine much more than what kind of mint extract she used in her sweet tea punch.

He and Ethan were about the same age, but Conroy Fontaine seemed like a throwback to another generation, pre–World War II, maybe even pre–World War I. He was unfailingly polite and tended to dress in penny loafers with no socks, chinos, polo shirts and a retro Timex watch. He wore rimless glasses and his sandy-colored hair was getting thin on top, but he kept himself in decent shape. Nearly every morning, Ethan would see him up on the road jogging what he said was a six-mile route. He must also pump iron, given his muscle mass, but where he did that, Ethan didn't know or care.

He opened up the screen door, then remembered his good ol' boy act. "What can I do for you, Mr. Fontaine?"

"I'm sorry to bother you so late. I've been working all day on my book. I didn't have the radio on. I just heard the news—"

"Yes, sir, it's an awful situation."

Conroy shook his head in obvious despair. He had a broad forehead, a strong jaw—not a bad-looking guy. "It's *terrible*. Sarah's gone to New York?"

"She left a short time after she heard about the shooting."

Fontaine took in a breath. "Good heavens. I simply can't imagine. The FBI just held a press conference—it was carried by all the news channels. Rob Dunnemore's still in critical condition, but at least he's stable. He made it out of surgery. Sarah must be beside herself."

Ethan noted the familiar way Fontaine talked about Sarah and wondered if they'd struck up a real friendship since she'd arrived back in Night's Landing. He turned on the tap at the sink and rinsed off his barbecue plate. "She was pretty upset when she left here, Mr. Fontaine."

"Understandably. Do you know anything? Anything that's not on the news? Are the parents flying in from Amsterdam? Will Rob be brought down here to recuperate—''

"If I knew anything," Ethan said, turning from the sink, "I don't believe I'd tell you. No offense, sir, but you're a reporter. It's not my job to blab family business to reporters."

Conroy's back stiffened visibly, but he smiled. "No offense taken, but you're quite wrong about me. If I were the kind of reporter you obviously think I am, I'd be on the phone to CNN right now alerting them to Rob Dunnemore's connection to the president. But I haven't done that."

"No money in it?"

"Name recognition. That would help me with my book when it goes to press." He sighed, his shoulders sagging. "I've never been very good at selling myself. My interest is always the story. This book—I'm doing a responsible job on it. I want it to be respectable. The most difficult part…" He trailed off, avoiding Ethan's eye. "Sarah. I didn't expect—" He seemed unable to go on.

"You didn't expect to want her approval," Ethan finished for him, then added, matter-of-fact, "She's a beautiful woman."

Fontaine still didn't look at him. He nodded, embarrassed. "That's right. I want to do my best work on this book. I'd like her respect. I've read her dissertation, and I understand the documentary she just finished is stunning. I can't compete with that kind of scholarship. Of course, her work doesn't focus on the president. What I'm doing is quite different."

The guy sounded smitten. Ethan got it, but Sarah

Dunnemore was sisterlike material as far as he was concerned. "Look, Mr. Fontaine," he said, "you don't have to justify yourself to me. What you do is none of my business. I'll tell Sarah you dropped by and let you know if I hear anything. Fair enough?"

Fontaine seemed pleased, even relieved. "Thank you. It's a worrisome situation, isn't it?"

"Sure is, sir."

"Sarah... I wonder how long she'll be up there. If she needs anything—"

"I'll tell her you offered."

After Fontaine left, Ethan got a beer out of the refrigerator and walked down to the dock. It was dark out, not much for moon and stars. Chilly. He could fly up to New York. Ask questions, stick his nose where it didn't belong.

Get arrested.

Bad enough having Conroy Fontaine, would-be presidential biographer, sniffing around Night's Landing. In New York, Ethan'd be facing scores of hard-nosed, cynical reporters who had space and time to fill with whatever they could fill it with, all of them eager for anything that would spin the Central Park sniper story into a new direction for another day or two of audience-grabbing coverage.

He should have used an alias. Never mind Fontaine and a bunch of national and New York reporters—if the FBI and the marshals fed his name into a computer, God only knows what'd pop out.

"Yeah, well," Ethan said into the night. "Whatever."

He finished his beer and went back inside.

Six

Nate woke up irritable and in pain, even before he remembered that his uncle and two sisters were in the next room. He rented an apartment in Queens, upstairs from a New York firefighter he'd met in the aftermath of September 11. Gus had invited him up for lasagna until Antonia intervened and reminded him that Nate had just been shot.

Shot.

Right. He pulled on clothes and popped a couple of Extra Strength Tylenol. No bleed-through on his bandages. Had to be a good sign.

Gus was making omelettes from eggs he'd brought down from New Hampshire in a cooler. "Look at them," Nate said. "They're orange."

"They're not that orange."

They were that orange. They turned his stomach.

His uncle sighed at Nate's obvious lack of enthusiasm. "Okay, so eat toast."

Nate sat at his small kitchen table. The place had come furnished—he didn't have Antonia's money or

Carine's design flare, and, basically, he didn't care. "I'm sorry. I'm not in a great mood."

"Relax." Gus lowered the heat under the frying pan. "You've been griping about my cooking since you were a little tyke. How's the arm this morning?"

"Aches."

Antonia lumbered into the kitchen, rubbing her huge belly. She smiled. "Baby's tap-dancing. How're you doing, big brother?" She checked his bandage and made him check his temperature, then warned him, not for the first time, to take his pain medication. "Just do it."

Fortunately, his brothers-in-law had headed home last night. Nate had room for two guests. Three was pushing it, but five would have driven him over the edge.

Carine, showered and dressed, wandered into the kitchen and sat across from Nate, frowning at him. "You're going to take a bath or something, right?"

"What, do I smell?"

"You just look like death warmed over."

He loved his family. He really did. But he preferred being frank with them versus having them be frank with him, and he was rattled and raw from yesterday's trauma. Dr. Ling had given him the number of a psychiatrist. The USMS had people he could talk to.

He didn't want to talk to anyone. He just wanted the son of a bitch who'd shot him and Rob off the streets. In a perfect world, Nate would be the one who nailed his ass.

Gus flipped an orange omelette onto a plate and set it in front of Carine, who dug right in.

Nate excused himself and beelined for the bathroom in time for a couple of dry heaves over the john.

When he returned to his family, Gus and his sisters were cleaning up the kitchen and packing. "You need your space," Carine said. "You always have. But if there's anything we can do, you know where to find us."

"Guys—"

"Give yourself some time," Gus said. "Don't fight it. You're going to have the yips for a few weeks. It's normal."

Antonia, looking tired and strained, smiled. "By 'yips' he means posttrauma stress symptoms. Nightmares, jumpiness, irritability. They're the body's way of processing a traumatic event. You can also do rapid-eye-movement desensitization and reprogramming therapy—" She stopped herself. "I'm sure your doctor's discussed your options with you."

Nate got through breakfast and afterward almost told them not to leave. But he didn't, and once they were out the door, he headed to the hospital to check in on Rob.

He found Juliet Longstreet slumped in a straight-backed plastic chair in the private waiting room outside the I.C.U. where they had Rob. It was barely nine o'clock in the morning, but her eyes were closed. "Sleeping on the job," Nate said.

She didn't open her eyes. "Go to hell."

"Hey. I was shot yesterday. Be nice." He also outranked her, but she wouldn't care. "How's the sister?"

Now Juliet opened her eyes and sat up straight,

frowning. "She's buds with the president, that's how's the sister."

Nate let her words register. "President Poe?"

"He grew up next to the Dunnemores in Tennessee. Sarah's like a daughter to him. Rob's a pal, too. Did you know?"

"Rob never mentioned he'd even met the president. Did you tell Joe Collins?"

"Oh, yeah. Big time. He's Mr. Cool. Just said, 'Thank you, Deputy.'" She did a perfect imitation of the FBI investigator. "He might have known already, but I wasn't taking any chances."

"Smart move."

"Bet he's got the Secret Service hanging on his shoulder, not that we'll ever know. If the shooter targeted Rob specifically because of his friendship with the president—" She broke off, no further comment necessary. "Sarah wanted me to leave her to her own devices last night, but I gave her a choice of me in her hotel room with her or her on the futon at my place."

Nate gave a wry smile. He'd known Juliet since she'd started with the Marshals Service four years ago. She was tough and ambitious. "You warned her about the fish and the plants?"

"I did. She was fine with them. Me—I didn't sleep a wink. I kept picturing assassins bursting through the window and shooting us both dead."

"You'd have shot them before they shot you."

"What if someone wants to upset the president by—"

"Don't go there."

Juliet clamped her mouth shut. She was thirty and

good at her job, but she'd say anything—and nothing intimidated her. Sometimes it scared senior deputies like Nate, but she'd been an asset since her arrival in New York eighteen months ago. She'd kept her relationship with Rob quiet. Then he ended up in New York, but the two of them working out of the same office had apparently killed their relationship.

Nate poured himself a cup of coffee that smelled as if it'd been made hours ago. He added powdered creamer but didn't stir. He took a sip before the creamer had melted, the little fake milk lumps making the brew even nastier that it might have been.

He eyed Juliet. She had outdoorsy good looks and a direct manner that sometimes took people by surprise. She could be irritating as hell, but she'd earned Nate's respect. "I take it Rob never told you he and President Poe were friends, either."

"It didn't come up." She stretched her arms above her head, yawning. "Knowing Rob, he wouldn't want it to become a 'thing,' get in the way of his work, make other people feel self-conscious. I gather the sister's closer to the president than Rob is."

"Makes for a hell of a fly in the ointment. What's the word on Rob this morning?"

"He's doing better. They've got him off the respirator. What about you? Should you even be here?"

The Tylenol had kicked in, but Nate still could feel the ache. He didn't want his brain fuzzed up with prescription painkillers. He swallowed more of the lousy coffee. "I won't be doing push-ups for a couple weeks, but otherwise I'm fine."

"What about your head?"

He set his cup on the edge of the coffee station.

He couldn't drink another sip. "I didn't get shot in the head."

Juliet scowled. "You know what I mean. Everyone says you should go home to New Hampshire, at least for a few days. Why don't you?"

He didn't answer. Gus and his sisters had asked him the same question, and he hadn't answered them. He wasn't that close to Juliet Longstreet.

But, of course, she had no instinct for when she was pushing up against her boundaries. "Christ, you are a case, aren't you?" She got up and poured herself a cup of coffee, taking it black. "I hope you don't plan to go into the office today and start pissing people off."

"Juliet—"

"Someone's going to tie you up and toss you into a trunk, drive you to New Hampshire." She took a big gulp of coffee, no sign she thought it was old and near rancid. "It's hard to stand on the sidelines. Can't be easy seeing the FBI working the case."

"It's their job to investigate the shooting of two federal agents—"

"So? Doesn't mean you have to like it."

He reminded himself that she'd had a shock yesterday herself—arriving on the scene in time to see the paramedics working on her ex-boyfriend. Rob was still in rough shape. Nate figured he could cut her some slack.

She grinned feebly at him. "I'm overstepping, huh? At least you can go home and climb mountains. I'm stuck here baby-sitting Rob's twin sister. She's— oh, shit." Juliet groaned, nearly spilling her coffee. "Damn. Now I've done it."

Nate glanced behind him and saw a pretty blonde in slim jeans and a black sweater turn about-face and retreat down the hall.

"Sarah Dunnemore?" He shook his head. "Good one, Longstreet."

"*Crap.* At least Rob and I ended it on a positive note or this'd be even worse." She set her coffee on the small refreshment cart. "Sarah's really nice. Why don't you come meet her?"

"You dug your hole. I'm not going to help you dig yourself out of it."

She snorted at him. "I could tell you what people say about you behind your back, you know."

As if he didn't know. As if he cared. Nate grinned at her, but she squared her shoulders and headed out into the hall. He had the feeling she'd rather face the sniper who'd shot at him and Rob rather than have to make amends to Rob's offended twin sister.

The armed deputies securing all access to her brother—medical, professional and personal—underscored for Sarah the gravity of his situation and the cold fact that the shooter was still at large.

The deputies let her pass without explanation of why she'd returned so soon. She'd just left the private corner of the I.C.U. where Rob lay with his tubes and monitors, asleep. She thought she'd step into the waiting room and collect herself before her next visit. Now she wished she hadn't. Juliet's words, which she obviously hadn't meant for Sarah to hear, had stung.

Rob stirred when she approached him, as if sensing her presence, and any thought of her embarrassment receded. "Hey, kid," he said without opening his eyes, his voice hoarse from the respirator. "How ya doing?"

It was the first time he'd managed to speak to her. "I'm fine. Don't worry about me. Rob—oh, God, Rob, you've been through absolute hell, haven't you? But your doctors say you're doing well."

"Yeah." He moved his fingers, and she took his hand, his skin moist and pale. His eyes fluttered open—they were bloodshot, glassy looking—but the effort was too much and he shut them again. "Sarah, listen to me..."

"Sure, Rob. What can I do for you?"

"You're on vacation." He coughed, and she noticed spots of some kind of brownish ointment on his gown, the fresh bandage on his abdomen. He was weak, heavily medicated, exhausted. His attempt to talk—to make sense—had to be a struggle. "I don't want you here if I've got someone shooting at me."

It wasn't what she'd expected to hear. "Just relax, okay? It'll be all right."

"If this guy sees you..."

"Nobody's going to see me." She tried to sound cheerful, but his fear was palpable, unnerving. "Rob, please don't worry—just concentrate on getting better."

His eyes still closed, he mustered his energy and squeezed her hand. His hair was matted, dirty. "You're too trusting."

She wanted to reassure him, but she had no intention of going back to Tennessee, not until he was more himself. "I'll go home. Of course I will. I can't wait to go home. *After* I know you're better."

"What time is it?"

"It's a little after nine in the morning. You were injured yesterday around lunchtime."

"Tonight. You can catch a flight back to Nashville tonight. Promise me."

She didn't know if he was entirely lucid or if the trauma of his injury, the lifesaving surgery and the medications he was on were making him a little crazy. Paranoid. She had a friend whose father, suffering complications after heart surgery, kept insisting he saw waiters in tuxedos delivering him pheasant under glass in the I.C.U.

Or was her brother simply projecting his own fears onto her? If she were drinking tea on the front porch at home in Night's Landing, he'd feel safer.

"I don't…" His voice was barely a rasping whisper now. "I don't remember anything."

He looked so vulnerable, so out of his element. Sarah could picture him yesterday in Central Park— strong, vital, a professional but also a man with a sense of fun. Why would someone shoot him? *Who* would do something like that? She'd lain awake much of the night on the futon in Juliet Longstreet's, surrounded by plants and fish tanks as the questions repeated themselves. And over and over, until she finally gave up on sleeping at all, she kept hearing Rob on the phone, telling her he'd been shot.

She found herself having to choke back tears. "I'll let you sleep. I'll see you soon."

But her twin brother had already drifted off.

Brushing her tears off her cheeks with her fingertips, Sarah stepped backward toward the exit and stumbled on someone's feet. Before she could fall flat on her face, a firm hand caught her by the elbow, steadying her.

"Whoa, there. Easy."

She spun around, straight into Nate Winter, the deputy who'd been shot with her brother. She recognized him from the photo they'd shown on TV. He was tall, lean, his dark hair softened with just a hint of auburn, and he had, Sarah thought, the most incisive, the most no-nonsense blue eyes she'd ever seen. He wore black jeans, a black T-shirt under a dark plaid flannel shirt and scuffed running shoes.

The blue eyes settled on her. "Sarah Dunnemore, right?"

She nodded. "Deputy Winter—I hope I didn't hurt your arm."

She realized she was about to cry. She'd held her tears in check since the marshals had arrived in Night's Landing yesterday, but now, with her brother lying a few feet away from her, hurting, begging her to go home, with the lingering sting of Juliet's words, she couldn't hold back. "I should go."

Nate Winter didn't say a word, didn't try to stop her as she pushed past him and ran out of the I.C.U. into the hall, sobbing, tears streaming down her face. She couldn't stop herself, couldn't bring herself under control. She *hated* crying in front of anyone.

Juliet shot out of the waiting room. "Sarah—wait."

Sarah broke into a run, charging past startled law enforcement officers. She squeezed by doctors and nurses getting off and onto an elevator and pushed her way to the back wall, sinking against it, bracing her knees as she focused on her breathing in an attempt to calm herself.

Nate Winter had been *shot* yesterday, and he was a rock. Steady, unemotional.

She had no business falling apart.

"You're too trusting."

Maybe. Maybe she shouldn't have told the truth about who'd called last night. Maybe she shouldn't have let Juliet Longstreet insist on moving her out of the hotel.

Maybe she shouldn't trust her brother's colleagues to have her best interests at heart.

They were all in shock themselves. They wanted to find a sniper, not be burdened with a wounded deputy's archaeologist sister.

She had to get a grip.

Had Winter overheard her brother urging her to go home? Would he take it as his duty to put her on a plane back to Nashville?

She didn't like the idea of being a nuisance, having these people think they were responsible for her. Before her flight to New York, her deputy escorts had offered to arrange for a counselor to be with her, but she'd turned them down. Maybe if her brother had been killed.

But he was alive. He'd be all right. She'd been so determined not to tempt fate by agreeing prematurely to counseling. She just had an ordeal to get through.

She hadn't expected, though, that Rob wouldn't want her in New York.

The elevator doors shut. An elderly doctor frowned at her in concern. "Are you all right?" he asked softly.

She nodded and brushed at her tears, relieved to be getting off Rob's floor, away from the able-bodied deputies. She needed something to eat, a break. She didn't want to feel sorry for herself. She wasn't the one lying in the I.C.U. And what kind of compassion did she expect from a bunch of armed federal law enforcement officers? They were doing the best they could.

The elevator doors opened again, suddenly, and Juliet Longstreet stepped in. She put up a hand to Sarah, stopping her before she could get started. "I'm a jerk. I'm sorry. What I said in the waiting room—it was stupid."

The older doctor moved to the front of the elevator car, letting Juliet take his spot. Sarah felt an immediate urge to ease some of Juliet's obvious guilt. "It's a difficult time for everyone."

But Juliet refused to cut herself any slack. "For *you*. You're Rob's twin sister. I'm only a colleague." She didn't mention their past relationship. "I was just trying to look tough in front of Nate. I'm sorry I mouthed off at your expense."

"No harm done."

"Sure there was. You must have felt like the kid sister at the big kids' party." She smiled crookedly. "I'd say belt me one, but you'd probably have a half-dozen marshals jump on the elevator and pin you against the wall in two seconds flat. We're all in rotten moods. But, hey, you see some of those guys? Very buff."

Sarah fought a smile of her own, her first, she thought, in many hours. "Nate Winter—I just met him."

"Yeah. I can tell. Most people run when they meet him. You're not the first. He's a total hard-ass."

"You're very irreverent, aren't you?"

Juliet smiled, relaxing some. "Helps in dealing with things like two marshals getting shot in Central Park. At least the news on Rob is positive. Barring complications, he should be back on the streets before too long."

Sarah tried to let Juliet's optimism sink into her psyche, tried to visualize Rob back on his feet, with that lazy grin of his, that way he had of making people think he was a hundred percent on their side. "What about Deputy Winter?" she asked. "How's he doing?"

"He'd like to get his hands around the neck of whoever shot him."

"But physically?"

"Just enough of a wound to piss him off."

The medical personnel all got off at the cafeteria floor, leaving Sarah and Juliet alone in the elevator. "I keep picturing the two of them leaving the news conference yesterday and walking into the park," Sarah said. "Why did they do that? Do you know?"

"No, I don't."

"The news conference—did a lot of people know about it in advance?"

"The world. That was the whole idea. It wasn't thrown together at the last second." Juliet frowned at her, then smiled gently. "Now, come on, don't you start. The best investigators in the country are on this thing. In fact, Joe Collins called me while you were in with your brother. He wants to talk to you."

"Why?"

"Are you kidding? After the bombshell you dropped?"

Sarah winced. "President Poe was calling as a friend—"

"Exactly."

"I almost wish I'd told you it was another Wes on the line."

"Nah. It's better this way. Get it out in the open. Your relationship with the president isn't something you'd want Joe Collins stumbling over on his own. He's in a private meeting room down the hall from your brother. He'll have food. Collins *always* has food." Juliet hit the button for Rob's floor and sighed. "And you look as if you could use something to eat."

Neither of them had been in the mood to eat that morning at Juliet's apartment—actually, an apartment she was borrowing from a well-heeled friend, because, she'd explained, even as small as it was, she couldn't afford Manhattan's upper west side on her government salary.

"All right," Sarah said. "I'll talk to Agent Collins. Then, please, go back to your normal duties. I can book a room at the hotel where we were last night. Tell your boss it's what I want."

"You just don't like my plants and my fish."

Juliet hadn't exaggerated—her apartment was a jungle of plants and had at least four fish tanks. But Sarah shook her head. "Your apartment's great. I'm just used to being on my own."

"Now that I understand."

She sank back against the cool wall of the elevator and closed her eyes. *"I don't want you here if I've got someone shooting at me."*

But how could she go home? She imagined herself on her front porch, drinking her sweet tea punch and feeling the soft breeze as if nothing had happened.

Given her family's predilection for not leading quiet lives, she'd been prepared for anything when she returned to Night's Landing—but not this, she thought. Not her brother getting shot in Central Park. Not the possibility that he could become another Dunnemore who died an early, tragic death.

She stopped her negative thinking in its tracks.

Stay positive.

The elevator opened on Rob's floor. "Come on," Juliet said. "Let's go see Special Agent Joe and talk to him about your Tennessee neighbor."

Nate didn't follow Rob's sister, but he was tempted—and duty and chivalry had nothing to do with it. The feel of her slim waist when he'd grabbed her, the blond hair, the gray eyes, the tears.

Damn.

He stood next to Rob's bed. "Your sister's prettier than you are."

He was awake, but not by much. "Smarter, too. What time is it?"

"About nine in the morning the day after the shooting." Which Sarah Dunnemore had told him before she'd stepped on Nate's toes and ran off crying.

"I don't…" Rob's red-rimmed, bloodshot eyes tried to focus. "I don't remember."

The doctors had warned Nate that Rob might never remember the shooting. His body had poured all its energy into keeping him alive, not in remembering what had happened. "That's normal. How're you feeling?"

"Like shit."

"The nurses are going to get you up today if they can. They like to do that."

He wasn't paying attention. "Sarah should go back home." He coughed, shuddering in agony, his voice weaker, raspier, when he resumed. "She doesn't belong here."

His concern for his sister was palpable. "She's with Juliet right now." Nate assumed Longstreet would be trying to make amends for her ill-advised remark. "Just because you were shot doesn't mean she's in any danger."

"It wasn't random. The shooting. I was the target. He was after me."

"Rob—"

"I know it. I have…this certainty." He shut his eyes, and he seemed to sink deeper into the bed. "I'm sorry."

"Get some rest. Don't worry about anything."

Rob was done for. His mouth opened slightly as he fell back to sleep. He looked dead lying there in the bed. Nate checked the monitors, just to be sure. He glanced at the stone-faced guard, felt the dull ache in his arm where he'd been shot. He could have been the one shot in the gut.

But he wasn't. Rob, just four months in New York, was.

Nate had to stifle a wave of guilt and regret—he should have prevented this. Somehow, some way. He should have kept his and Rob's presence at the news conference quiet. They shouldn't have gone at all. He should have seen something in the park, sensed it, known they were in danger.

Dead-end thinking.

Better to concentrate on his anger. It was sharp, focused, explosive, not a slow burn, not a simmering kind of fury—and yet there wasn't a damn thing he could do with it, except go home to Cold Ridge and climb mountains and eat Gus's orange eggs.

He thought instead he'd check on the gray-eyed sister and see if she'd forgiven Longstreet for being such an ass.

Seven

Betsy Dunnemore's daughter was attractive, but she, the mother, was beautiful—and she always had been. As he sipped his espresso and watched her coming up the cobblestone Amsterdam street, Nicholas Janssen remembered the day he met her more than thirty years ago, when they were both freshmen at Vanderbilt University in Nashville. She was beautiful, shy and nervous, although the campus was less than ten miles from her home in Belle Meade.

It was all such a lifetime ago.

She was pale now, clutching her red leather handbag as she threaded her way among the scatter of tables at the streetside café. She'd tied a red silk scarf over her hair and secured it with a knot to one side of her throat, and she wore black pants and a lightweight black-and-white sweater.

Every man at Vanderbilt had wanted her. Nicholas had been just one among many. They'd never dated, had only attended a few classes together before he'd had to leave in the middle of his sophomore year.

Family problems, he'd told people, but that wasn't the reason. Money was. Always money.

When he'd transferred, everyone still assumed that Betsy Quinlan would end up marrying handsome, likable John Wesley Poe, who wasn't the best student or the worst but was, by far, the most ambitious. Instead, a month after graduation, Betsy married brilliant, eccentric Stuart Dunnemore, a childless widower twenty-two years her senior.

She inhaled sharply when she saw Nicholas and almost stumbled backward. He had deliberately chosen her favorite café not far from the apartment she and her husband had shared since agreeing to participate in a special commission at the International Court of Justice at The Hague.

For a moment, Nicholas thought Betsy would run in the opposite direction, but she regained her composure and proceeded to his table.

She sat across from him and looked at him as if she might have just found a disagreeable insect on her table. But he could see the fear in her gray eyes, the strain of the past twenty-four hours. Amsterdam was six hours ahead of New York—it was late afternoon now. This time yesterday, she would have been just getting the news of the shooting in Central Park.

"Did you have anything to do with what happened to my son?" she asked, her voice low, intense, accusatory.

"Betsy. How could you think—"

She didn't back off. "*Did* you?"

Nicholas sipped his espresso and took a small bite of the cookie that came with it. It was a cool, windy afternoon. The café was uncrowded, although bicycles and people moved about in the streets. He was dressed casually in a brown silk sweater and trousers, trying not to call attention to himself, although he doubted a federal agent would jump out of an alley and kidnap him back to the United States. They had bigger fish to fry. Or so they believed.

People often underestimated Betsy Dunnemore. Because she'd married a man so much older, because she'd devoted herself to him and to raising her children. An educated housewife, an amateur art historian. The condescension had to be hard for her to take at times. But Nicholas had known her at eighteen, and he had never underestimated her—her intelligence, her determination, her grit. It was her steady devotion to her aging husband that had taken him by surprise. He'd seen it when he'd first contacted her last fall— another "chance" meeting—with the hope of maneuvering himself into her circle, the dream, even, of having an affair.

He remembered how much he'd wanted her at eighteen.

"I had nothing to do with the shooting." He kept his tone mild. "I've made my share of mistakes, but I'm not a violent man. You're upset. I understand that."

"Don't patronize me. *Don't*." She didn't yell, but she was tight with anger, an easier emotion for her, he thought, than fear. "You should turn yourself in to U.S. authorities and go home to stand trial. You're a fugitive, Nicholas. I don't want anything to do with you."

"My status is a complicated legal matter."

"It's not complicated. You're charged with felony

tax evasion. You were supposed to appear for trial in a U.S. court of law. Instead you fled.'' She looked away from him, her lower lip quivering, a weakness she wouldn't want him to see. ''You slipped out of the country to Switzerland—''

''I have a home there.''

''You knew it would be difficult if not impossible for you to be extradited for tax evasion. I don't know about the Netherlands.'' She shifted, her gray eyes on him. ''Is it safe for you here?''

''Don't get carried away. It's a trying legal matter. Nothing more.''

''Did Rob see you at the Rijksmuseum last month?'' She kept her voice low, but her sarcasm was knifelike. ''Did he recognize you? Did you have him shot because of it?''

The Rijksmuseum. Nicholas recognized now that intercepting her at the renowned Amsterdam-museum had been bad timing. He hadn't realized her son the U.S. marshal was in town. A critical oversight. But he'd only dared surface in the Netherlands for a short time—he wanted to strengthen the bond between them now that he'd reestablished contact with her. It had been a long, trying winter. Seeing her had renewed his sense of hope.

Yet when they'd stood together three weeks ago in front of Rembrandt's massive, famous painting, *The Night Watch,* Betsy had told him—again—that she wanted nothing to do with him.

''Betsy. Please. I'm not here to argue with you. I made an effort to see you because you were a familiar face, an old friend.'' That was the truth, as far as it went. Nicholas smiled tenderly. ''We had a pleasant visit when I was here last in November. A cup of coffee. A nice chat about old times. It was a chance encounter—''

''It wasn't chance. You arranged it. You manipulated me so that I'd run into you. I wasn't aware of your legal status, but I am now.'' She didn't soften. ''And we were never friends.''

He attributed her coldness and sarcasm to her desperate fear for her son. He let his gaze drift to the swell of her breasts, the soft shape of her hands. He'd accepted that the chance of a sexual affair was remote, at least while her husband was still alive. Nicholas was a vital man, wealthy, his hair silver now but his body taut, well-conditioned. Stuart Dunnemore was old. Just plain old. He was in his late seventies, but still a force in diplomatic circles, an expert—a visionary—in international conflict resolution. A realist, not a romantic. A pragmatist, not an ideologue. And a good man. He had humility, and he was kind. He'd endured terrible losses, a father dead in a logging accident at thirty-two, a brother killed on the beaches of Normandy, a wife he'd watched slowly waste away from multiple sclerosis.

Betsy would never leave him. But he wouldn't live forever, either.

Right now, Nicholas needed to play on her emotions—her sympathy for him as a former classmate, for the struggling eighteen-year-old she must remember. He was a self-made man. He'd worked hard. He had so much to offer the world. But he couldn't contribute if he was behind bars.

The Dunnemores were known for their compassion.

And they had the ear of the new president of the United States.

Betsy was right. It wasn't just friendship that had drawn him to her. Nicholas wanted to convince her to tell her friend, Wes Poe, that their old classmate deserved a break. He'd paid a price for his mistakes. He would use his wealth for good.

He wanted her to get him a presidential pardon. It would stop the legal proceedings against him dead in their tracks. A pardon wouldn't exonerate him, but it would keep him out of prison and buy him time to distance himself from his other activities before they, too, caught up with him. Time to take his profits and move on.

"How is Rob?" Nicholas asked quietly.

Her eyes glistened with sudden tears—a mother's tears. They made her seem vulnerable, even more beautiful. He'd wanted Betsy Quinlan for a long time. He had wanted the girl she'd been at eighteen, and he wanted what she could do for him now, as a woman, as a friend and confidante of President John Wesley Poe.

"Oh, Nicholas. Damn. I must be out of my mind. I don't approve of what you've done, but tax evasion—" She collapsed back against her chair. "It's not a violent crime."

"You're upset because of Rob. I understand."

Even in her early fifties, her skin was translucent, smooth and barely lined, her delicate bone structure the stuff of a man's dreams. Nicholas wanted to take her hand and comfort her, but he knew better, resisted the instinctive reaction to her tears. A mother's grief.

She gulped in a breath. "He's holding his own. I want to be there now—" She broke off, biting back a sob.

"When will you go?"

"As soon as we can. I told Sarah—" She stopped herself, as if she realized she was venturing into territory that was none of his business. "Travel isn't as easy for Stuart these days, and he's in the middle of critical meetings. If Rob were in danger—we'd be there now."

"Of course you would."

"But his doctors tell us that each day—each hour—that passes without complications is a good sign. They expect him to make a full recovery." She held her purse close to her chest and got to her feet. "Sarah's in New York. My daughter. She was at the Rijksmuseum, too."

Nicholas had seen her. Pretty, smart. One of his men had delayed her to give him time to speak to her mother—who'd promptly told him she didn't want him to contact her again.

"I hope Sarah didn't see you," Betsy said. "I hope no one saw you."

He leaned back, studying her as he had when he'd sat behind her in a dull philosophy class, wondering if she were a virgin. The word in the dorm halls said she was. The Quinlans were well-to-do, classy people who gave a lot of money to Vanderbilt.

He sighed, pushing his coffee aside. "Betsy, please believe that I had nothing to do with the shooting yesterday."

"I wish we'd never run into each other." She seemed tired now, spent. "Call the U.S. embassy.

Turn yourself in. If you're innocent, trust the judicial system—''

''My attorneys—''

''I don't want to hear about your damn lawyers!'' She took a breath, her tears gone now. ''You should have told me right from the start you were on the lam. I shouldn't have had to find out on my own.''

He narrowed his gaze on her. ''How did you find out?''

She averted her eyes. ''That doesn't matter.''

But it did. Charlene Brooker had told her. Betsy had to wonder why an army captain stationed in Germany had contacted her to discuss her relationship with him.

Did Betsy know that Captain Brooker had been murdered in Amsterdam, two days after the meeting about him?

''Stay away from me,'' Betsy whispered tightly. ''Stay away from my family.''

With a spurt of energy, she jumped up, almost turning over a chair as she made her way back out to the narrow cobblestone street, then quickly disappeared past a cheese-and-bread shop. She was smartly dressed, but she wore shoes that could handle Amsterdam's many brick and cobblestone walks and streets, reminding him that she wasn't eighteen anymore.

A large group of American tourists started rearranging tables, calling loudly, cheerfully, to each other about who would sit where.

A street musician fired up his accordion and moved in, playing a cheerful tune. The tourists laughed, loving it.

Janssen paid for his coffee and walked down the street to a small Mercedes that awaited him. The back door opened, and he slid onto the cool leather seat next to Claude Rousseau, his most experienced bodyguard.

"She won't say anything," Nicholas said. "She hasn't told anyone that we've met. She's not going to now that her son's been shot. It would only complicate the situation for everyone—her, her husband, her son. The president."

"Is she afraid?"

"Terrified."

He sighed, his pulse quickening. Yes, terrified. And yet all beautiful Betsy Quinlan Dunnemore knew was that her old *acquaintance* from college was a convicted tax evader.

"Did she believe you?" Rousseau asked.

"About her son? I don't know." That troubled him, because he'd told her the truth. He'd had nothing to do with the shooting. "Have you heard from our man in New York? Does he have any idea what the hell's going on there?"

Rousseau shook his head. He was dark haired, angular, good-looking and lethal. Thrown out of the French army. A mercenary, plain and simple. "Nothing."

"Be prepared. You might have to go to there."

Claude smiled. "All of my passports are in order."

Janssen knew not to ask how many passports, how many identities, Rousseau—if that was his real name—had at his disposal. Even if Claude would tell him, which he wouldn't, there was always, for Nicholas, the question of plausible deniability. Some things he was better off not knowing. His people knew it and sometimes didn't trouble him with details.

Could his man in New York have taken it upon himself to try to kill Rob Dunnemore?

If so, he should have finished the job—done it right and killed both marshals. Now it could look like a botched job, which, if his friends or enemies thought he was behind it, would only make Nicholas appear weak.

The Mercedes pulled out into Amsterdam's tangle of impossibly narrow streets, many indistinguishable from the sidewalks and ubiquitous bike paths. Janssen settled back in his seat and shut his eyes, picturing himself bike riding in the hills of northern Virginia as a boy, picking wild strawberries on a warm spring day, driving north into Pennsylvania with his father and walking up Little Round Top as his father regaled him with details of the Battle of Gettysburg. It had all sounded so romantic. To Father, the soldiers on both sides exemplified duty, honor, integrity and courage. They were men who'd never given up.

Nicholas imagined the federal agents hunting him were much the same. He had no illusions they'd forgotten about him. "Failure to appear" was not a good thing. If convicted of the tax charges, he faced a maximum sentence of five years in federal prison—what would taking off to Switzerland before his trial tack onto his sentence?

Going to trial wasn't an option.

Prison wasn't an option.

But he could never go home.

That was what he hadn't realized, on a soul-deep level, when he'd fled.

He did now.

He opened his eyes, saw a Dutch couple riding bicycles with their blond toddlers in little seats on the handlebars. Everything seemed so foreign to him. He felt the familiar lump in his throat. He was, he thought, so far from home.

Eight

Sarah passed bellmen and limousines on Central Park South and lingered a few seconds under the awning of the expensive hotel where the news conference touting the joint fugitive task force had been held.

She could almost see Nate Winter and her brother walking out onto the street in their dark suits, relieved to have that tedious ninety minutes behind them.

The weather was better today. Cool, partly cloudy.

And it was later in the day. Afternoon rush hour. Sarah made her way across the busy street. There had to be more cars and more pedestrians on Central Park South now than yesterday at midday.

For the first time all day, she was—at last—alone. She walked alongside the stone fence overlooking the south end of the park until she came to Fifth Avenue, which ran north along the huge park's eastern side.

Her interview with Joe Collins had been short and to the point. Sarah had made it clear that President Poe had checked on her simply as a friend. It wasn't that big a deal. She didn't know whether Collins was convinced or not. She spent the afternoon with her brother for five or ten minutes at a time. He was still out of it from his surgery and medications, but when he was awake enough to talk, he told her to go back to Tennessee.

Sarah had finally told everyone she needed to get out on her own for a while. By herself. No marshals, no FBI, no doctors. No seriously injured brother she was upsetting with her presence.

What if Rob got into trouble for being the president's friend? Had he intentionally kept it a secret from his bosses, and now his twin sister had opened her big mouth? In hindsight, Sarah wished she'd taken the phone into the bathroom of her hotel room instead of talking to Wes right there in front of a deputy U.S. marshal. Let Rob be the one to tell his colleagues about their friendship with the president.

She stopped hard at the Fifty-ninth Street entrance into Central Park, the same one her brother and Nate Winter had used yesterday. Across from her, the Grand Army Plaza split Fifth Avenue. She noticed the bright gold statue of William Tecumseh Sherman on his horse. The "Grand Army" was the Union Army of the Potomac, the plaza named in its honor after the Battle of Gettysburg.

She'd read about it in a New York guidebook Juliet had thrust at her during a long wait at the hospital while doctors were in with her brother.

The new leaves on the trees were a fresh spring-green, not as thick as the leaves in Night's Landing, and when Sarah started down the stone steps, she saw the stretches of lush grass and the thousands of tulips that had been shown repeatedly on the television coverage of the shooting.

The crime scene tape was gone. Sarah didn't notice any FBI agents or reporters, but she did see two uniformed NYPD officers on foot.

Her breathing was shallow, her stomach tight with tension.

Ducks floated along the pond's edge. An elderly woman with a cane settled onto a bench as if nothing had happened there, and three animated women in sneakers fast-walked north into the park.

Normalcy.

People must have accepted that the sniper had specifically targeted the two marshals, and yesterday's shooting wasn't a random act likely to be repeated, at least not with regular New Yorkers in the crosshairs. Maybe with another deputy.

Maybe with a deputy's sister.

Sarah pushed the ridiculous thought out of her mind and continued gingerly down the steps.

There'd been no warning—no man seen running with a gun, no shouted demands from the bushes. Just Rob jerking with the impact of the first shot, Nate Winter seeing the blood and getting them both to cover.

She spotted the rock outcropping and realized for the first time that the park was well below street level here at its southeast corner.

Was the shooter hiding somewhere in the bush now, watching, waiting?

She warned herself not to succumb to her family penchant for drama and instead tried to absorb some of the get-on-with-life spirit of the tourists and New Yorkers around her.

But her hands were clammy, and her vision seemed

constricted, as if her mind was resisting taking in the details of her surroundings, mixing them with those of what she'd seen on television on the shooting, what she'd been told and had heard in the hospital corridors.

According to news reports, witnesses hadn't heard shots fired or noticed anything out of the ordinary, certainly no one crouched in the bushes with an assault rifle. They'd only seen the two men falling, the tall one helping the more seriously injured one to cover behind the rocks, his gun drawn as he shouted instructions to onlookers, then the New York City police officer arriving on his horse, and finally dozens of paramedics and federal, state and city law enforcement officers descending.

The undergrowth along the pond and on the hillside below Central Park South conceivably could hide a shooter, but how could he get away with a near-instantaneous dragnet dropping on the surrounding area? How could he have avoided being seen crawling under the brush, setting up his weapon? The Pond—that was its name, just *The Pond*—was a wildlife sanctuary in the heart of the city.

Sarah reminded herself she wasn't an investigator or firearms expert. She ran her fingertips along the smooth granite face of the rock outcropping.

As she forced herself to take a deep breath she noticed a man standing at the stone fence above her on Central Park South. He seemed to be watching her. He wore a black turtleneck and black leather jacket that were a little too warm for the conditions.

She couldn't move. She couldn't breathe.

The clothes. The dark hair that was long in the front.

She squinted—yes, the angular features.

She'd seen him before.

Not in New York. He wasn't a reporter, a doctor, a marshal.

Where?

Amsterdam.

Sarah expelled the air from her lungs and tried to gulp in more, but her head was spinning. How could it have been Amsterdam?

The Rijksmuseum.

Now she remembered. She'd flown to Amsterdam from Scotland three weeks ago to visit her parents while Rob was there on vacation.

They'd all gone to the Rijksmuseum together.

You're being dramatic again.

What difference did it make if it was the same man she'd seen at the museum?

The man above her on Central Park South made eye contact with her briefly, then turned and disappeared across the street.

Sarah started for a bench, but her knees buckled under her. She felt herself sinking. *Damn. I can't faint.*

"Hold your breath." Nate Winter walked up behind her, speaking firmly, even sternly. "You're hyperventilating."

"I'm not—I can't breathe."

"It just feels that way."

She nodded, doing as he said. He slipped an arm around her middle and stood motionless, silent, for the minute or so it took for her to get her breathing back to normal.

Feeling foolish, she stepped back out of his arm. "I'm okay now. Thanks." She was too far away to have made a credible, positive identification of the man—of anyone—up on Central Park South. Thinking she recognized him had to have been a trick of her imagination. A product of the stress of the past two days. "I hope you didn't hurt your arm."

Winter seemed even taller than he had at the hospital. "I didn't grab you with my injured arm, although I could have. It's doing fine."

"I wouldn't have fainted."

He half smiled. "Of course not."

Sarah had no intention of telling him that she may have recognized someone up on the street. New York had a population of eight million—it had to be a common experience for people to think they saw someone they knew and have it turn out to be a perfect stranger. She didn't even know why she remembered the man from Amsterdam. Because he'd stopped to look at a Dutch painting with her while she waited for her mother?

Not entirely, she thought. She also had wondered if he might be with the silver-haired man who'd stopped to say hello to her mother in front of Rembrandt's *The Night Watch.*

But that happened all the time. Her parents knew many people that Sarah had never met.

"I didn't expect to have that reaction," she said, covering for her embarrassment. "I've never fainted. I thought—I guess I didn't think. I just ended up here, and I assumed I was prepared." She directed her gaze at Nate, met his blue eyes with an incisive look of her own. "Did you follow me from the hospital or are you here for your own reasons?"

"Both."

"Shouldn't you be resting?"

"Probably. There's a hotel bar I like between here and the hospital. I can get a drink and take a breather, and you can get something to eat before you really do pass out. When's the last time you ate?"

She thought a moment. "I had a candy bar at lunch."

"No wonder you're wobbly. Your blood sugar must be in the cellar." He nodded toward the steps back up to Fifth Avenue. "Let's go."

"Deputy Winter—"

"You can call me Nate."

"Okay." She made herself smile. "It's still hard for me to think of my brother as Deputy Dunnemore. When I think of marshals, I tend to think of Bat Masterson and Wyatt Earp."

One corner of his mouth twitched, but he said nothing as he led her up to Fifth Avenue, then back along Central Park South to the Avenue of the Americas and a hotel with a sprawling ground-floor bar that looked out on the street. They sat at a small round table near a window. He ordered a beer, and she ordered a beer and a quesadilla, wondering if she'd have pegged him as a federal agent if she were just meeting him.

More likely as someone here to rob the place, she thought.

Maybe if he were in a suit.

"You okay?" he asked.

She checked her thoughts. "Yes, fine. Thank you."

He settled back in his cushioned chair, his so-blue eyes narrowed. Although he gave off an air of nonchalance, nothing about him was relaxed. "I can see why your brother wants to get rid of you. You don't belong here."

"I was hoping you hadn't overheard that."

She scooped up a handful of peanuts and tiny pretzels from a small bowl their waitress had dropped off and noticed the strain in his face, the shadows under his eyes. He'd been out there yesterday. Getting shot, trying to save a colleague. He wouldn't have known if the sniper meant to mow down everyone within his sights.

"Rob's just scared and frustrated," she went on. "It can't be easy for him to lie in that hospital bed, hurting, unable to chase after whoever shot him."

"He wouldn't be able to chase after the shooter, regardless. It's not his job."

"Or yours?"

His gaze settled on her. "That's right."

The man had zero sense of humor, at least right now—or humor wasn't something he used to defuse his own anxiety. Or anyone else's. Like hers. "Rob and I are twins."

"So I hear. Fraternal twins, obviously. He doesn't wear sweater sets."

There. A touch of humor. It threw Sarah, especially when he looked at her in her twinset the way he did. "We're very close. I'm sure he's just projecting his own feelings onto me. I think that's what I just did in the park. I could imagine him out there yesterday— it was so real. On some subconscious level, Rob wants to be safe in Night's Landing himself, so he wants me to be there.''

"He's worried about you."

"Projection. He's dealing with his own fears by worrying that I could be the shooter's next victim."

"I've learned to pay attention to my instincts."

"I'm not talking about instincts." She decided she should just stop talking, trying to explain. Nate was a concrete thinker. Give him the facts, skip the bullshit, the loosey-goosey bond between fraternal twins, brother and sister. "I'm sure instincts are fine when they're not clouded by medications, surgery and blood loss."

Their beers arrived, and Nate took a sip of his, eyeing her. "There's nothing else?"

She didn't touch her beer. "What do you mean?"

"There's no reason for Rob to be worried about you?"

"No, of course not. Is this a friendly drink or an interrogation?"

His smile caught her completely, totally off guard. "Neither."

She felt the heat rush to her cheeks.

"I promised your brother we'd look after you," he added.

"Oh."

Their waiter brought her quesadilla. Nate nodded to her. "You should eat some of that before you belt down your drink."

"What about you? Aren't you on pain medication? I didn't think it mixed with alcohol—"

"I'm on Tylenol."

Sarah lifted a triangle of the hot quesadilla, realizing something about him made her feel so self-conscious. He'd seen her in weak moments twice in one day. It was a thing with her, she knew—she didn't like men seeing her when she was vulnerable, thinking they had to take over her life because she was small and blond and book-smart. And impulsive, she thought. It was impulsiveness that had taken her to Central Park and put her in the position where she was having a beer and a quesadilla with this man.

She noticed that the sleeves of his flannel shirt were rolled up to his elbows. He had taut muscles in his forearms. She assumed he was armed but couldn't see his weapon under his shirt. She'd never gotten used to the idea of her brother walking around armed. What was it he carried? A Glock, she thought.

She pulled herself from her thoughts. "Rob's just freaked out by what happened," she said. "Don't try to read anything into his concerns."

"Right, Deputy Dunnemore. I'll remember that."

There was a slight edge to his words. She swallowed her bite of quesadilla. "I don't mean to tell you how to do your job."

"Forget it. I've been in a bad mood all day." He paused, the incisive gaze settling on her again. "Sorry if I'm making you feel uncomfortable."

She licked her lips. "I have a feeling you make most people feel uncomfortable."

He winked at her. "You look as if you can handle it."

She took another triangle of quesadilla, the hot cheese oozing out onto the plate. She realized how hungry she was. "Aren't you hungry? You're welcome to a piece—"

"Beer's fine. You're an archaeologist?"

"Historical archaeologist." She was aware of him watching her and wondered if he could see the strain of the past two days on her. Did she look drawn and tense? But she hadn't been shot, she reminded herself. She'd had bad news. There was a difference. But, once more, she forced herself not to let her thoughts drift too far astray, not to let Nate Winter have that kind of an effect on her. "It means I deal in the historical period—people and societies that left behind some sort of historical evidence. Letters, diaries, books and so on. Historical archaeology is an interdisciplinary field. It incorporates archaeology, anthropology, history, folklore—the idea is to try to piece together what everyday life was like in the past."

He took a drink of his beer, in a tall, slender glass. "You don't dig up bones?"

"I can. I'm more likely to dig up a family dump— what we'd call the material remains of a site. We put them together with any written record and oral history." She smiled, aware of her southern accent amid her fast-paced urban surroundings. "It's rather like quilting. There are all these pieces that make up a fascinating whole."

"You could go on forever, couldn't you?"

"I almost have, haven't I?"

"No. I'm not bored." He held up his glass. "Helps to have a beer. I understand you've spent most of your career working on President Poe's childhood home."

That brought her up short. "Rob told you?"

He shook his head. "Juliet. She checked you out." Taken aback, Sarah abandoned her quesadilla.

What she'd thought was a casual, friendly conversation about what she did for a living was obviously something else entirely. She wondered if Nate Winter allowed himself casual, friendly conversations or if he was all work, all the time.

Then again, they were just a few blocks from where he'd been shot a little more than twenty-four hours ago. Under the circumstances, she could cut him some slack.

And herself, she thought. She didn't have to get everything right, not today.

"I suppose that's to be expected," she said, trying to hide how upset she was. "He wasn't president when I became interested in the Poe House. He wasn't even the governor of Tennessee. I was in high school. Leola and Violet Poe, the sisters who raised him, were our neighbors and very dear friends."

"They're the ones who found Wes Poe on their doorstep?"

Suddenly Sarah could picture them in their rockers as elderly women, reminiscing, wandering from one topic to another and back again as they talked about neighbors, family, friends, people they'd met on the river—and, always, their fight to keep and raise the infant boy they'd found one Sunday morning on their porch overlooking the Cumberland River.

Now he was the president. It was the sort of story Americans loved. Some were already placing it alongside George Washington's cherry tree and Abe Lincoln's log cabin.

"He was in an apple basket," Sarah said. "Dr. Jimmy—Jimmy Hankins, Leola and Violet's doctor—said he wasn't more than two days old."

"Do you have a theory about who his mother was?"

"Theories, rumors and hints are easy to come by."

She laid on her southern accent, although she wasn't sure why. To mark her territory to this hard-nosed New Englander? To give weight to her own claim to the topic of the Poe sisters? It had consumed her for so long. But she knew she had to let go. She wasn't Wes Poe's biographer—she'd hardly touched on his life. It was the Poe house, the Poe family, the site itself and its development along the river that had excited her. Wes was a neighbor and a friend. He was complicated, driven, ambitious and compassionate. And, now, he was the president—not exactly an "ordinary" person.

Nate seemed, finally, to sense her ambivalence and changed the subject. "Rob said you two grew up in D.C. more than you did in Tennessee."

"We went to school in Washington. Home is Night's Landing."

He smiled. "Do you speak seven languages like your brother does?"

She shook her head, her unexpected tension easing. "French and a little Spanish. Rob's always had a gift for languages."

"You and your family weren't prepared for him to become a marshal, were you?"

"I didn't even realize marshals were still around."

His eyes sparked with unexpected humor. "Thought we went out with Bat Masterson and Wyatt Earp?"

"I still don't know exactly what you all do."

He swallowed more of his beer. "Some days neither do I. How's the quesadilla?"

She hadn't touched another bite. "It's good. Have some."

"My family left me with a refrigerator full of food."

"Parents, brothers, sisters?"

"An uncle, two sisters and two brothers-in-law. No parents. They got killed hiking in a storm on Cold Ridge when I was seven."

"You're the oldest?"

"My sisters were five and three."

"So they don't really remember, and you do."

His eyes were distant. "You're quick, Sarah. Most people don't get that right away."

"I'm sorry. I didn't mean—"

"No need to be sorry."

She thought he meant it. "Sometimes I can be too impulsive. It's been known to get me into trouble."

"You don't look like a troublemaker."

She laughed. "That's why it surprises people when I do something I shouldn't." She stared at the rest of her quesadilla, no longer hungry. "My parents are still in Amsterdam. It's not that easy for my father to travel these days. Flying to New York and back to Amsterdam again would be hard on him. And, no," she added, "I'm not making excuses for him or my mother. It's just the reality we all have to deal with."

"Does he advise the president?"

"As a friend, if asked."

"He was an assistant secretary of state—"

"For about five minutes for an administration that was not John Wesley Poe's."

"They get along?"

"Very much so." She sat back, studying the man across from her. "Special Agent Collins asked me many of these same questions, you know."

Nate surprised her again by smiling. "But he was asking them because he's conducting an investigation. I'm asking because I'm curious."

"I think you're looking for distractions."

"Maybe. I've worked with your brother for four months. I didn't have a clue he was pals with the president. I need a little time to adjust."

Sarah doubted he'd needed more than a half second to adjust, but she didn't call him on it.

"Rob visited your folks in Amsterdam a few weeks ago. Were you there?"

She thought of the man in the park and felt her stomach tighten, even as she reminded herself it had to be a case of mistaken identity. "I flew in from Scotland. We don't get that many opportunities to be together as a family."

"I've never been to Amsterdam." Nate finished the last of his beer. "What's it like?"

"Narrow streets, a mix of old and new buildings, crowded, fascinating, more diverse than you might think. *Lots* of bicycles. The canals are beautiful—we all did a canal tour."

She didn't mention the Rijksmuseum, because if she did, her anxiety would show, Nate would see it, and she'd have to tell him about the man in the park and what a nutcase she was for thinking she'd recognized him from the museum. But that had been such a strange day, her, Rob, their parents, playing tourist, trying to be a family in that foreign city because that was where they'd found themselves together.

She couldn't eat any more and took one last sip of beer, her glass still half-full. She offered Nate money for the tab, but he refused. As he pulled out his wallet, she noticed that he favored his injured arm and saw him wince in pain. She regretted how close she'd come to losing it in the park, to the point that he'd obviously felt he'd had to whisk her off for a beer and something to eat. However bad the past day and a half had been for her, they'd been so much worse for him and her brother.

The evening air had turned chilly, but Sarah felt hot, agitated. Nate was watching her closely—too closely, as if he believed she was trying to hide something from him. Not a pleasant position to be in. But she didn't consider herself to be hiding anything. She'd been mistaken about the man in the park.

And Nate was recovering from a bullet wound and a shocking attack that could have killed him.

She had no business reading anything into his actions, his questions, the way he looked at her.

"I should get back to the hospital," she said. "It really was serendipity that you followed me. Thanks."

He stepped off the curb to flag a cab. "I don't believe in serendipity."

She smiled at him. "Of course not."

When they arrived back at the hospital, Rob was out for the night—and Nate was done for. Sarah could see it in the dark smudges of fatigue under his eyes, the hollow look to his cheeks. "Do you have a car?"

she asked him when they returned to the waiting room. "Do you want me to drive you home?"

"That bad, huh?" He grinned at her, a sudden spark in his eyes. "You can drive me home another time, Dr. Dunnemore. When I don't look and feel like death on a cracker."

Her mouth snapped shut.

He laughed, and although he sounded exhausted, she felt a tingle of pure sexual awareness dance up her spine.

After he left, Juliet Longstreet put down the magazine she'd been staring at and shook her head. "That man. Total hard-ass, married to the job and absolute hell on women. They all fall for him."

"Did you?"

"No way." She grinned. "I go for the southern frat-boy types."

Sarah laughed.

"I think Nate liked following you. Gave him something to do. He does not tolerate idleness well." Juliet got to her feet and stretched her arms over her head. "Which should be a warning to you."

Not knowing what to say, Sarah peeked in on her brother. He looked better. Not well, but better. She wondered if he wanted her out of town not so much because of snipers in the park, but because of the reputation of his senior deputy—but that was a lot of silliness. She rejoined Juliet in the hall and set out to her apartment for another night with the fish and the plants.

Nine

John Wesley Poe had heard that the junior senator from Massachusetts, elected in November along with the new president, was one impressive cuss, and it was true, even more so in person. Hank Callahan strode into Wes's private study—Wes wanted to keep this visit as quiet and unofficial as possible—with the confidence of someone who'd come under fire in more ways than one in his forty-something years. Even his enemies said he was a man of the highest integrity, a retired air force rescue helicopter pilot whose first wife and young daughter were killed in a car accident while he was serving overseas.

Last fall, he'd stumbled into the headlines twice, once before the election, once after—and both times in dangerous incidents involving the Winter family of Cold Ridge, New Hampshire. His now-wife, Antonia, when she encountered a stalker. Then his sister-in-law, Carine, when she stumbled upon a murder.

Now, here was another Winter in trouble. This time it was the brother, Nate.

"Mr. President," Hank Callahan said, remaining

on his feet, his military bearing evident. "It's good to see you."

Wes rose from the sofa and shook hands with the younger senator. "Thank you for stopping by. Here, have a seat. I won't keep you. I understand that one of the marshals shot yesterday in Central Park is your brother-in-law."

Callahan took the most uncomfortable chair in the room, his signal, Wes thought, that he didn't plan to stay long. "Nate Winter is my wife's brother, yes."

"He's doing all right? You've seen him?"

"He's in good shape. The other marshal—"

"Rob Dunnemore is a family friend."

Wes didn't mince words. The story had just broken. It was all over the news now, but from his blank reaction, either Callahan hadn't heard of Wes's relationship with the wounded deputy or was pretending he hadn't. "I didn't realize he was a friend. I'm sorry."

Wes had just issued a statement through his press secretary. It was a balancing act. He didn't want to give the impression, no matter how unintentionally, that anyone in his administration—anyone in law enforcement—believed that the shooting in Central Park yesterday was in any way connected to him.

"I understand Rob's had a rough time of it," Wes said. "We came close to losing him yesterday."

"Antonia—my wife—says his chances for a full recovery grow with every hour he goes without complications, especially from blood loss."

"Did you see him? Rob—how did he look? Under the circumstances, it's difficult for me to go up there myself. There's nothing political here, by the way. This is an entirely personal conversation.''

But their surroundings begged the question—was anything personal, was anything private, when one was president?

Callahan stayed unreadable. ''Of course, Mr. President. No, I didn't see Deputy Dunnemore myself.''

Wes nodded, wondering why he'd bothered to invite Callahan over to the White House. To assuage his own guilt at having neglected Rob in recent years? Wes hadn't approved of him becoming a marshal. Rob's own father hadn't approved, although Stuart Dunnemore's reasons were different and he'd have been more subtle about his objections. The kid was smart, well connected, personable. He could do anything with his life. Why spend it in the gutter catching criminals? Now that he was in the Oval Office, Wes thought, he had a different view. The work the USMS did was vital, and it needed good people like Rob Dunnemore.

And that was what scared Rob's father, Wes knew. He wasn't worried so much that Rob could do better—he was worried his only son was a throwback to the wild Dunnemores of the past, a mix of loggers and riverboat workers who lived hard and died young. To his own brother, who'd died a hero on Omaha Beach.

''You and your wife are expecting a child?'' Wes asked casually.

His question seemed to catch Callahan off guard. ''Just a few more weeks to go.''

''That's wonderful. Nervous?''

The young senator didn't answer at once, but he

obviously understood the subtext. In light of the tragedy of losing his firstborn, was he nervous about this baby? Wes's own wife had lost all four of their babies. They'd almost saved the last one, a baby girl. People told him, or at least implied, it wasn't like losing a three-year-old, as Callahan had. Wes knew it was probably true. But miscarriage and stillbirth were their own special pain, their own special hell.

And the effect it'd had on Ev. She'd tell him he hadn't done anything wrong—it was her, all her. She'd let go some of the self-blame and self-pity since he'd entered public service and she'd taken on her own issues, devoting herself to children's health, poverty and underachievement.

They both considered the Dunnemore twins as close as they would come to having children of their own. They'd watched them grow up, attended their birthday parties and graduations, took them out on the river—and they'd gone to funerals together. Granny Dunnemore's. Leola's, Violet's. Thank God he and Ev hadn't had to face Rob's funeral.

Callahan managed a brief smile. "I guess a little nervousness is to be expected, Mr. President."

"Good luck to you. Let me know, will you?"

"I'd be glad to. Mr. President—"

"I don't know anything more about yesterday's shooting than you do," Wes said, anticipating the senator's question. "Did you happen to see Sarah Dunnemore, Rob's sister?"

Callahan shook his head. "As soon as we realized Nate was all right, we got out of his way."

"She's an historical archaeologist. She doesn't have a background in law enforcement, the military, politics. She's just back from a research trip in Scotland. She's spent years researching the house where I grew up and the family that raised me.'' He sighed, picturing her hearing the news about her brother. ''But she's tough. I keep telling myself that.''

Callahan maintained his correct bearing. ''I'm sure it's a difficult time for all of Deputy Dunnemore's friends and family.''

Wes nodded, sighing heavily. ''It's strange how we go through these times in our lives when it's as if we're under siege. I can't imagine how you all must have felt when you found out your brother-in-law had been shot, even if he was only slightly wounded. After what you went through last fall—''

''It hasn't been easy, but we're relieved he's okay.''

''Deputy Winter—he's solid?''

''Rock solid, Mr. President.''

''We don't know yet if he was the target, or if Rob was—or if they both were. Well, the FBI and the marshals won't leave a stone unturned in searching for whoever did the shooting. That much we know for sure.''

Wes pictured Granny Dunnemore, as everyone called her, at her stove in the beautiful log house on the Cumberland River that her late husband had built just to attract a woman. They'd owned a sawmill that went out of business in the Depression. Not long after, Web Dunnemore died in a logging accident. Pearl Dunnemore always preferred her simple ways and said she never missed the mill. She remained a widow, without self-pity, for over fifty years. She made the best white beans in middle Tennessee. Even now, Wes could smell them simmering on her stove.

She was Leola and Violet's contemporary, just a few years younger than they were. But they were all gone now. Some days, it was hard to believe. They were strong women, survivors determined to do what they believed was right. Granny Dunnemore had lost her husband young, then her firstborn son in the war, and she meant her second son to live a long and happy life. She encouraged Stuart to study hard and got the application to Vanderbilt herself, then cheered him when he went off to Washington, D.C., to begin his long, illustrious career as a diplomat and an advisor, a brilliant thinker. It was a life that, to Wes as a boy, seemed so far away, so beyond his grasp.

Reach for the stars and you might hook the moon, Pearl Dunnemore would tell him. You could be president one day.

Yet he knew Stuart's departure from Night's Landing had been another kind of a loss for his mother. Wes had seen her sitting out on her porch, crying after her son's visits and she was alone again. When he moved back with his first wife, Pearl couldn't hide her joy at having him home, despite the tragic circumstances.

And when Stuart remarried and the twins were born, Granny was the happiest woman in Tennessee. Even when Stuart took up traveling again, she understood that Night's Landing was in his blood, that it was his home, his anchor.

Leola and Violet didn't have it in them to encourage Wes to stretch his wings. They'd loved him without condition, and he them, but they'd feared the outside world. Become a schoolteacher in town, they'd say. Get a job at the local bank. Don't walk away from your home, your roots.

But what home did he have, what roots?

Hank Callahan cleared his throat in the awkward silence. "If anything," he said, "Nate might step on toes to get answers. I imagine Rob Dunnemore would, too, once he's on his feet. They're not going to sit back." He tried to smile. "Well, they're not going to *like* sitting back."

"Rob's twin sister has the makings of a loose cannon, especially where her brother is concerned." But people never guessed it—they'd look at her and see the pretty face, the gray eyes, the sweep of blond hair and think good girl, not realize that she came from a family tree filled with scoundrels and adventurers. Wes smiled. "I hope the marshals are keeping an eye on her."

Callahan angled a look at him, respectful but at the same time curious, even suspicious. "Mr. President, the attack yesterday—are you certain it had nothing to do with you?"

"There's no evidence of that whatsoever."

The young senator seemed satisfied, and in another minute, they bid each other good-night. After Callahan left Wes sank back down on the sofa. He'd spoken with such assurance, but did he know, beyond the shadow of a doubt, that yesterday's shooting had nothing to do with him? No one had given him that assurance.

But it couldn't.

He'd never be able to live with himself if something happened to Rob or to Sarah because of him, because of his position. Neither would Ev. She'd lost too much already.

He glanced at his watch. Just nine o'clock. He'd work for a couple more hours, make sure Ev was asleep and unable to ask questions, unable to articulate her fears, before he ventured to bed.

Ten

Sarah awoke to the gurgle of fish tanks and the spiked end of a spider plant tickling her nose. She'd acquiesced to another night on the futon in Juliet's front room and slept better, but not much better, than she had the night before. When Juliet suggested they get breakfast somewhere, Sarah jumped at the chance.

They walked to a diner and tucked themselves into a small booth with cracked red vinyl seats. Sarah ordered a cheese omelette and iced tea. She didn't feel as trapped, as hemmed in and claustrophobic, as she had yesterday and realized it had been her own fears at work, not anything her brother's colleagues had done to her.

At least she'd had the good sense not to mention the man at the park to Juliet or especially to Nate Winter. Thinking she'd recognized him from Amsterdam seemed even more ridiculous this morning. It was simply her nerves playing on her, ratcheting up the stakes and the tension. Her Dunnemore genes kicking in.

The omelette was hot and perfectly cooked, and

Sarah ate every bite, determined not to let low blood sugar affect her thinking—she'd had a shock. Even if Rob's situation was far worse than her own, she had to give herself time to adjust to what had happened.

Juliet had a bagel and three cups of black coffee.

"Did you sleep okay?" she asked Sarah.

Sarah nodded. "The aquariums and the street traffic are like white noise after a while, aren't they? I haven't lived in a city in so long." She drank more of her tea. "Where are you from originally?"

"The boonies of Vermont." But Juliet was obviously uncomfortable talking about herself and picked up the bill, heading for the cash register. "Come on. We'll take a cab to the hospital. I'll figure out a way to bypass the media if they look like they're going to pounce."

They'd watched the news last night and heard Wes Poe's statement about his friendship with the Dunnemores. It was no secret—it'd been covered in his campaign. Just no one had thought the deputy shot in Central Park was a member of *that* Dunnemore family.

Wes hadn't called, but Sarah told herself that she couldn't expect him to.

When they arrived at the hospital, over a dozen reporters had gathered at the ambulance entrance not far from the main door. Video cameras were rolling, photographers snapping pictures, reporters asking questions. Sarah got out of the cab, then noticed Nate Winter in the middle of the throng.

"Ouch," Juliet said, coming up next to her. "He doesn't look very happy, does he? Hell. They've got him surrounded. He should pull a faint or something and get out of there.''

A young female reporter thrust a microphone in his face.

"Deputy Winter, Hector Sanchez was a known informant. Did you or Deputy Dunnemore tell him that you would be at the news conference?''

Then more questions, coming all at once.

"Do you believe he was the shooter?''

"Sources say he died of a drug overdose—do you think he was celebrating the Central Park attack?''

"Can you confirm that the rifle allegedly used in the shooting was found at his side?''

"What about the president? Has he talked to Rob Dunnemore?''

Nate held up a hand. "Sorry. No comment. If you'll excuse me.''

That was it. He was done.

Juliet huddled close to Sarah and maneuvered her toward the main entrance. "Let's get you out of here before they recognize you.''

"What about Nate?''

"He can take care of himself.''

Once past security and into the hospital lobby, Sarah shuddered as if she'd shaken off a swarm of bees. She turned to Juliet. "What was that all about? Does the FBI have the sniper? It sounds as if he's dead—''

"I'll see what I can find out.''

"Who's Hector Sanchez? Did you realize he was a suspect?'' She took a breath, but Juliet didn't respond, simply banged the up button for the elevator.

Sarah felt a stab of dread. "It sounds as if the media think someone screwed up—"

"It's the FBI's investigation," Juliet said tightly. "Let's go—"

Sarah shook her head. "I'm fine on my own today. Really. Tell your bosses I appreciate the moral support."

"Sarah—"

"I'm used to being on my own, and I'm not in any danger."

Juliet sighed. "I'll see you upstairs in ten minutes."

She headed back through the lobby toward the main entrance and the reporters, presumably, Sarah thought, to find out what was going on.

The elevators churned and groaned inside the empty shafts. She didn't feel nearly as raw and exhausted as yesterday. She'd showered, put on fresh clothes—black pants, a blue silk sweater, shoes that could handle New York walking. Her quick, early-morning call to Rob's nurse had left her feeling optimistic. He'd had a good night and was more alert today. They'd be getting him up and moving.

A trio of medical students floated toward the elevators in an intense discussion.

Nate Winter walked past them at a fast, deliberate pace.

There was no sign of Juliet behind him.

Where was he off to?

The elevator dinged. Sarah watched its doors open, then bolted down the corridor, going after Nate at a half run.

He had a decent head start on her—she almost

missed him retreating through a side door. It was an "exit only," not an entrance, and she went through it without hesitation.

When she reached the street, Nate was climbing into the driver's side of a black sedan parked about fifty yards up from the ambulance entrance and the throng of reporters.

With an outward calm, Sarah stepped off the curb and stuck her hand up in the air, flagging a cab before she had seriously considered her options. She opened the rear door and climbed in. "Can you follow that black car just in front of us? He left his wallet."

"I can flash my lights—"

"No, that's not necessary. I'll just give it to him wherever he stops."

She knew what she was doing was wrong. Impulsive, insane. Even dumb. She was following a deputy U.S. marshal who'd just been shot and undoubtedly was in no mood to find her on his tail. Nate didn't seem to have a lot of patience on a good day. And, given the journalistic onslaught he'd just faced and the possibility that a USMS informant was the shooter, this couldn't be starting off as a good day.

Not that he'd looked upset or irritated. He'd looked focused, as if he were on a mission.

Possibly doing something he shouldn't be doing?

She'd sensed his bridled energy last night. As exhausted as he was, he was a man of action. He didn't take to being on the sidelines.

Wounded, still experiencing the shock of what had happened to him, he could easily go off half-cocked.

Maybe today was *his* day to fall apart, to feel trapped and hemmed in by events, and if she could keep him from doing something he'd later regret, why not?

It was her version of catching him before he fell flat on his face.

Payback for saving her brother's life.

She stared out the window, her cab speeding north. She knew she was rationalizing her behavior.

But she didn't tell her driver to turn around, and tailing Nate proved easier than she expected.

They ended up in a run-down section of the city on a mixed bag of a street, some buildings neat and clean, even boasting window boxes, others complete wrecks with nasty graffiti, broken windows, people loitering on the steps. Fortunately, Nate's car stopped in front of one of the neat, clean buildings.

He mounted the front steps at a trot and disappeared inside. No one had buzzed him in, and he hadn't used a key—which meant there was no lock on the main door.

Sarah paid her cab driver. "I'll only be a minute. Can you wait for me?"

He didn't answer, but the moment she shut her door, he was hurling up the street, leaving her on the curb.

Okay, so she'd have to find another cab back.

Or ask Nate for a ride.

She winced at the thought. Preferably, she wouldn't even have to see him. She just wanted to make sure he hadn't gone off the deep end.

Who was she kidding? *She* was the one who'd gone off the deep end in following him.

A stout, elderly woman wearing a wild hat mounted the steps to an adjoining building, more run-down than the one Nate had entered, and two young women in white uniforms rushed along the sidewalk, talking in Spanish—Sarah made out something about an exercise class they were taking. Their casual attitude helped her feel safer, although she had no idea where she was.

The front door was, indeed, unlocked, creaking loudly when Sarah pushed it open.

The entry smelled of a strong cleaning solution. She could hear music playing somewhere above her. The ordinariness of the scene helped her to relax slightly. Nate had followed her to Central Park yesterday. Even if her motives weren't entirely pure, why shouldn't she follow him?

Because he's a federal law enforcement officer.

But she was an historical archaeologist, and that took a certain amount of curiosity, guts and drive—a willingness to take risks.

Not that she'd thought through the particular risks, whatever they might be, of following a wounded deputy marshal.

She had no idea where Nate was. Upstairs, down the hall. Was there a basement? Should she start knocking on doors?

Feeling less smug about her tailing abilities, Sarah stood at the bottom of the stairs and contemplated her options. Just wait for him here?

"You're going to be a problem, aren't you?"

She almost screamed and spun around so fast, her hair whipped into her face. Nate had materialized behind her. Sarah caught her breath. "Scare me to death, why don't you?"

His blue eyes bored into her. "It's a thought."

Sarah told herself he had a right to be irritated with her. But she didn't let it get to her. "Where were you?"

"Let's go."

"This isn't your apartment, is it?" She glanced around the tidy, worn entry. "I thought you were going home. Juliet and I saw you with the reporters and I was concerned—"

"Bullshit."

She sighed. No **way** was she worming herself out of this one. "Okay, fine. You think the FBI has the wrong shooter, don't you? This guy, Hector Sanchez—"

She was out the door before she realized what was happening. Her feet were touching the ground, but she wasn't walking on her own—he had her by one arm and was marching her down the stairs and out to his car.

He opened the passenger door with his injured arm, apparently by mistake, and swore, then shoved her inside. "Watch your head."

"Going to cuff me, too?"

"I could. You're interfering with a federal investigation."

"Me? What about you? Last I checked, you were a wounded deputy U.S. marshal who was supposed to stay on the sidelines—"

He banged her door shut and walked around the front to the driver's side.

Sarah felt a wave of guilt when he climbed in. "Do you want me to drive?"

He didn't answer.

"Your arm—is it bleeding?"

"Doesn't matter."

"You didn't need to haul me out of there. You could have asked politely, and I'd have left."

He started the car engine. "I'm not in a polite mood."

"Are you ever?"

"Sure." He smiled at her then, a smile that reached his hard eyes and was so unexpected and so sexy, so *deliberately* sexy, it curled her toes. "I can be very polite."

Juliet had spotted Sarah jumping into a cab and following Nate's car and almost went after her—then she figured Nate could handle Rob's pretty southern Ph.D. sister all by himself.

She wasn't surprised when Nate dropped Sarah off at the private waiting room. "Don't let her out of your sight," he said through gritted teeth, then disappeared down the hall.

Sarah's cheeks were slightly flushed, but otherwise, she didn't look as stricken as most people would after pissing off Nate Winter. And she didn't look particularly guilty for having done it. But why the hell wasn't he home in bed? Juliet couldn't muster a lot of sympathy for him.

She crumpled up her paper water cup. "Dare I ask what happened?"

"Nothing. I followed him." Sarah sighed and sat in one of the plastic chairs. "It seemed like a good idea at the time."

Juliet tossed the paper cup and poured herself more coffee. It smelled fine to her, but people had been complaining about it all morning. "Most people kind of wilt for a bit after getting chewed out by Nate. He's not exactly your warm and fuzzy marshal.''

Sarah managed a smile. ''Is there such a thing?'' But she didn't wait for an answer. ''Did you learn anything about Hector Sanchez?''

Juliet had no intention of getting into the scuttlebutt on Sanchez. ''Just what's in the media. Turns out two witnesses identified him. Said they saw him crouched in the bushes on the bank just below Central Park South. He had a rifle.''

''Does the FBI believe he's their shooter?''

''There's been no official comment—''

''Tell me unofficially then.''

Juliet thought a moment. Sarah was upset, if not about Nate catching her following him, then about her brother, the whole situation. She deserved what answers Juliet could give her. ''It's hard to say. Nobody's talking right now. Everyone's being tight-lipped around here. We can't afford to screw up. No one wants the shooter to have another crack at Nate and Rob—or anyone else.''

''Why doesn't Nate have a security detail?''

Juliet smiled. ''He *is* a security detail.''

Sarah didn't seem satisfied with that explanation. ''Rob has guards just because he's more seriously injured?''

''Correct.''

With both hands, she raked her fingers through her hair, then made an abrupt change in the subject. ''I've been in Scotland on and off for months, working non-stop to finish a major project. I saw Rob briefly in Amsterdam last month, but it wasn't nearly enough time to get caught up with each other. What happened to the two of you?"

Juliet shrugged. "We did great when we were working out of different district offices—not so great when we both ended up in New York."

"You were here first?"

"That wasn't the problem. I'm more ambitious than your brother."

Sarah smiled. "Rob can be very driven, but he's not ambitious."

Juliet nodded in spite of her own urge to give Sarah Dunnemore hell for following a marshal. "I should find myself a nice guy who doesn't know how to shoot. Why on earth did Rob become a marshal? I never figured that one out."

"I've always thought he watched too many Bat Masterson reruns as a kid."

"Yep. We marshals tamed the Wild West."

But Sarah, rising suddenly, shook her head. "I think Rob just liked the idea of doing something that made a tangible difference. Catching fugitives and escaped prisoners, protecting the federal courts—it's more straightforward than what our father does. It's more like what our ancestors did."

"He told me some of them were bank robbers."

"Trains and riverboats, mostly. Not that many banks. And it was only one—Jesse Dunnemore. He ended up going west and getting killed."

"Probably by a marshal from the sound of him."

Sarah picked up the coffeepot, but seemed oblivious to how old and nasty its contents were. "Nate— does he hold a grudge?"

Juliet tossed her crumpled cup into the trash. "For-ever."

To her credit, Sarah seemed neither surprised nor distressed at the prospect of having fallen out of his good graces. She set the coffeepot down, obviously having reconsidered the merits of pouring herself a cup—Juliet figured it was rough enough coffee even for a committed coffee-drinker like herself.

"I'm going to check on Rob," Sarah mumbled.

Given her track record, Juliet followed her down the hall and made sure Sarah was inside the I.C.U. before retreating back to the waiting room.

Juliet was fidgety and jumpy from too much bad coffee and her prolonged high state of tension. She knew Hector Sanchez. Most people in the district office did. Rob had reeled him in as an informant three months ago. He'd provided good information that had led to several high-profile arrests, ones the news conference yesterday had underscored. There'd been rumors Rob had tried to get Hector into the witness protection program, but Hector had balked. He didn't want to leave behind his neighborhood. Someone had told Juliet that Hector was a peripheral figure who was too chicken to be a real criminal and too stupid to be a real player.

And he was a drug addict who always vowed he was going to stay clean.

The idea of Sanchez figuring out that Nate and Rob were at the news conference, where it was being held, where he should hide to get a couple of shots off—the idea of him even owning a rifle that could do the job—

None of it washed.

Juliet cleaned up the beverage area and found herself staring into a half-filled mug of cold coffee, gray and filmed over, seeing a dead Hector Sanchez, an AR-15 and a stash of cocaine next to his body. The cocaine she could believe. A drug overdose. Hector dead at twenty-nine. All that made sense. But the AR-15? The silencer? Executing the difficult shots to hit Rob in the gut and even Nate in the arm?

She dumped the coffee into the trash.

Not a chance.

Eleven

❧❦❧

Rob looked better and sounded more alert, less hoarse and confused, but he was still tethered to various tubes and monitors. He gave Nate a weak grin. "I can't believe Sarah followed you. Holy shit. What was she thinking?"

"She wasn't thinking." Nate hadn't ratted Sarah out to his younger colleague—she'd done it herself before Nate got in there. But if he were in Rob's position, he'd want to know what was going on. Even if he were at death's door, he wouldn't tolerate anyone coddling him. He expected Rob was of a similar mind. "We can get her a counselor if you'd think that'd help."

"Nah. She's just like this. Where did you go?"

"I checked in with someone I know in Spanish Harlem."

It was all he could give Rob. Nate had already talked to Joe Collins about his visit with Maria Rodriguez, a Puerto Rican ex-nun who'd moved to New York three years ago. Within a month of her arrival, she contacted Nate with information that had exonerated a man the USMS was looking for. She'd become a regular informant, but only on her terms, only when she could save someone.

She knew Hector Sanchez, not as a street thug or the confidential informant who'd helped Rob Dunnemore take down a USMS Top Fifteen Most Wanted fugitive—Rob's biggest coup as a deputy—but as a young man who was trying to put his life back together. Sister Maria, as she was known on the street, had encouraged him to listen to Rob and talk to the U.S. attorney, pursue entry into WITSEC. But Hector couldn't bring himself to fully give up the life he'd known since he was thirteen.

Now he was dead.

Sister Maria insisted he hadn't tried to murder Rob and Nate in Central Park. That he couldn't have. She was adamant, and her certainty had nothing to do with her faith in him as a person. She was a realist—she knew Hector would have setbacks, would lie, would disappoint her. He'd done it before. But she was convinced he hadn't committed the sniper attack two days ago because he couldn't. He'd cut a tendon in his right hand a year ago and couldn't pull a trigger, much less manage a sniper rifle.

Hector Sanchez was physically unable to fire an AR-15.

Nate had suggested Joe Collins make sure the autopsy on Sanchez included a check of his right hand. Not that Collins needed any advice—and he sure as hell wasn't thrilled when Nate refused to tell him his source.

But that was the way it was—he wasn't putting Sister Maria through an FBI interrogation. She worked in her neighborhood and believed in its people, and no matter how many times one or another of them betrayed her trust, she would never betray theirs.

The FBI had the wrong man. In her mind, it was that simple.

Except Joe Collins wasn't yet convinced. He had solid witnesses who put Hector in Central Park with an AR-15 at the time of the shooting.

He had the weapon.

He had the silencer.

Collins, in his mild-mannered way, had reminded Nate that he was supposed to be recuperating, not meddling in an FBI investigation.

Rob tried to sit up. "I'm supposed to be blowing in that air thing more. For my lungs. Keeps me from getting pneumonia. It wears me out." He sank back against the bed. "Christ. I'm a mess."

"Give it time."

"Hector was my guy. Is this going to come back and bite me in the ass?"

"I don't know." Nate didn't bother with niceties, but there was no point in Rob dwelling on what he couldn't change. "I think you were right about getting your sister out of here."

"She's pretty, isn't she?"

She was pretty. Very pretty. Nate had come in contact with her three times in less than twenty-four hours, and he wasn't immune to the feel of that slim body. But talk about a mustn't touch. A seriously wounded marshal's twin sister, the president's surrogate daughter—an attractive academic who wanted answers to the shooting as much as any of them.

"I'm lowering the boom on her before she does

something stupid,'' Nate said. "She's upset about you. It's making her reckless.''

"Send her back to Tennessee.''

Rob obviously hadn't changed his mind now that he was more lucid. "Why do you want her out of here?''

"Because she does things like follow senior deputies.''

"Rob, if there's something else, now's the time—''

"My parents,'' Rob said weakly. "They're coming?''

"That's what I understand. I don't have the specifics. Rob—''

"They can take over family duty. Get Sarah out of here. Wes Poe—that's out, right? That he and my family are friends?''

"It's out.''

"Sarah can't stay here. At home…'' His eyes were half-closed, and he was fading fast, sinking into the bed. "Tell her I'll be there soon. Tell her she can make me a prune cake.''

A nurse came over and checked Rob's IV line, glancing meaningfully at Nate. He took the hint. "Take care of yourself, Rob. Don't worry about anything else. I'll look after your sister myself.''

He managed a wry smile. "Why am I not reassured?''

Nate found Sarah chatting with Juliet Longstreet in the waiting room. He thought he heard his name mentioned, and when he walked in, even Juliet went red. "Looks like I should have eavesdropped,'' he said. "What did I miss?''

"Don't mind him,'' Juliet said to Sarah. "You

have to pass a jackass test to become a senior deputy."

Nate pointed at her. "One day, Longstreet, someone's going to take exception to that mouth of yours."

She gave him a big, phony smile. "Just kidding, Deputy Winter." She shifted her attention back to Sarah. "I'll see you in a bit."

Sarah made a move to go after her—to escape, Nate thought—then gave it up and cleared her throat, fixing her gray eyes on him. "I apologize for following you."

"Apology accepted." He decided not to waste any time on niceties. "Here's the deal. I've talked to Rob. You're going home to Tennessee. I'm putting you on a plane myself."

She didn't seem surprised and just shook her head at him. "I'm staying here until Rob's better."

Nate could feel himself responding to her obstinacy with a touch of his own. If they were going to get into a power struggle, he planned to win. Plus, he knew he was right. Rob was right. The woman needed to get out of the thick of things.

"I told him that," she added.

"Your brother wants you out of here. I want you out of here. So guess what? I can pack your bags, or you can. Make up your mind."

"It's not like I committed a federal offense—"

"Actually, yes, it is. Interference in a federal investigation."

"You're not investigating—" She stopped herself. "Anyway, Juliet says you had to have known I was following you. You could have stopped me, and you didn't.''

Leave it to Juliet to open her big damn mouth. ''Deputy Longstreet is welcome to her opinion.''

Sarah tilted her head back, the gray eyes cool now, intelligent and not particularly apologetic—she didn't regret what she'd done. ''I'm not always that impulsive.''

Nate didn't give her an inch. ''From what I've seen so far, I'll bet you are.''

His conversation with Sister Maria—Hector's death—had thrown him. Rob's certainty that he was the shooter's target, his determination to get his sister out of New York, her friendship with the president and Nate's own growing conviction that Dr. Dunnemore, with her pretty eyes and blond hair and her sexy southern accent, was trouble.

It made sense to put her on a plane.

''You don't know anything about me,'' she said stiffly. ''I thought I was following a man who'd gone through a terrible ordeal and had just heard some upsetting news. I wasn't thinking about you as a federal agent.''

''Your mistake.''

''What, are you going to arrest me?''

''I might.''

She didn't seem especially intimidated. ''You eat, sleep and drink your work, don't you, Deputy Winter?''

''And you don't, Dr. Dunnemore?''

''My work doesn't involve guns and bad guys.''

''Precisely why you're going home.''

She bristled. ''I want to see my brother.''

"Go ahead."

She walked stiffly out of the room, but Nate was impressed. He'd done his best to wither her, and she hadn't withered. People far more accustomed to him in a kick-ass mood would have.

He'd have to make sure he didn't touch her again. Catching her when she'd tripped on his feet yesterday, then when she started to go down in the park, this morning when he'd marched her out the door at Sister Maria's—no telling what would happen if he got hold of that slip of a body again.

He told himself it wasn't the reason he was sending her home.

Sarah rode up front with Nate with her knees pressed together, her hands on her thighs and her eyes straight ahead, making no pretense that she liked one damn thing about being sent home. But it was what Rob wanted—it seemed to be what he needed—so she was going.

She didn't care what Nate wanted. His threat to arrest her was a lot of hot air—he wouldn't dare. Like Rob, he needed a place to put his anxiety over the shooting and Hector Sanchez's death, and it was on her shoulders.

Having reporters shouting questions at her about her relationship with the president as she and Nate had left the hospital hadn't helped her case, either.

Rob was fully on board in the conspiracy to get her out of town.

And maybe it did make sense. He was improving, at least physically. Their parents would be there soon and could help get him back to Night's Landing to complete his recovery. In the meantime, Sarah would make him a prune cake and fix up the downstairs bedroom for him.

When he got home, she'd take him out on the river in the boat. They'd read books on the porch and drink gin and tonics and catch up with each other. It'd been ages since they'd had a good stretch of time together. She was between projects. She didn't know what to do with herself—she could easily stay in Night's Landing until Rob was back on his feet.

But she'd made it clear to her brother that she was returning to Night's Landing to put his mind at ease, and for no other reason.

He'd been amused. "I can just see you going toe-to-toe with Nate, but I'd put money on Nate. You still care what people think. He doesn't. He's a good guy, but you're not going to win with him."

She didn't want to win. She just wanted her brother safe and well, and if going home helped him in his recovery, even in a small way, then she'd go home.

Nate negotiated the city traffic with no indication that his injured arm bothered him in the least. "Mad?" he asked, unconcerned.

"Resigned to my fate."

His laugh surprised her. "Is that a touch of the infamous Dunnemore drama?"

Sarah glanced over at him and saw that his color was off slightly. He had to be in at least some pain. "You've been researching my family?"

"Ten minutes on the Web last night. If all those reporters can do it, so can I. I found some paper you wrote on southern historical archaeology sites."

"Did you read it?"

He gave her a quick, wry smile. "I only had ten minutes." He made a turn into LaGuardia Airport, impervious to the crush of traffic. "Anyone else in Night's Landing?"

"The property manager. Neighbors, friends. I won't be alone."

"This property manager lives in your house?"

"In a separate cottage."

"Fancy."

She smiled. "My grandmother used to live there. The place is lovely, and it's very special to my family, but I wouldn't say it's fancy."

"My uncle's redecorating the house I grew up in. He did up the half bath like it's a tropical paradise. It's god-awful."

Sarah laughed in spite of her determination to stay irritated. She didn't want to let him off the hook for pressuring her, threatening her with arrest. "Why don't you go up there to recuperate?"

He turned to her without warning, his eyes almost a navy blue in the afternoon light, then shifted his gaze back to the congested traffic ahead of him. "I wasn't seriously injured."

"But the trauma of being shot—"

"I've been shot at before."

She didn't push her point further. "The distinction being that the bullet didn't actually hit you."

"I don't need to recuperate."

"You want to find the real sniper before he tries again," she said quietly, without any hint of accusation.

"Everyone does."

"But you're one of the victims. The FBI and your

bosses can't want you intruding—any more than you wanted me following you this morning.''

He kept his eyes pinned on the road. ''I'm not worried about getting into trouble with the FBI or anyone else.''

''In a way, we're in the same position.''

''No, we're not.''

She decided to abandon that approach. ''Does Special Agent Collins believe Hector Sanchez is their man?''

Nate didn't answer. She started to point out the signs directing them to her gate, but he'd already made the turn.

''I see. Wrong question. You're not going to or you can't tell me. If the shooter, whoever it is, actually targeted you and Rob, he had to know you were going to be at that news conference. You can't just pull off a sniper attack in Central Park without advance planning. Was Hector Sanchez capable of that kind of detailed planning?''

More silence.

''Then the real shooter—the guy who set up Mr. Sanchez—must have known he was one of Rob's informants, manipulated him somehow because of it, and then killed him when he no longer needed him.'' Sarah thought a moment. ''No one's going to think Rob slipped up, will they? Blame him because the real shooter found out about Sanchez?''

''Sarah, I'm not discussing the investigation with you.''

''Why not? I'm about to fly to Tennessee and spend the next few days baking prune cakes and fluffing pillows in anticipation of my brother's arrival. I'm not going to meddle in the FBI's and the Marshals Service's business. Even if I wanted to, how could I?''

Nate glanced at her. ''Time to change the subject.''

She wasn't getting anything out of him. ''How far did I really get before you were onto me this afternoon?''

''Not an inch. I saw you get into your cab.''

Sarah believed him. She told herself she wasn't surprised and had no reason to be embarrassed, but felt a jolt of heat that, after he parked, prompted her to try to talk him out of escorting her to the gate. ''I've got an hour. There's no chance I'm not going to make my flight.''

''That's right,'' he said. ''There isn't.''

''You know, I'm not a prisoner you're transporting.''

''It'd be a hell of a lot easier if you were,'' he said, getting out of the car.

Sarah decided not to pursue that one.

In spite of the bullet wound in his arm, he insisted on carrying her bag, and bought her a bottle of water for her flight. He was a federal officer, and thus allowed to escort her all the way to her gate.

When her flight started to board, she felt a prick of panic at the idea of leaving. ''If there's any change in Rob's condition—''

''I'll let you know myself. I promise.''

She had the feeling Nate was a man who didn't make many promises. ''I'll be on the first flight back to New York.''

''Understood.''

''All right. Fair enough.'' She straightened, sighing, awkward. "Well. I guess that's it. Take care of yourself, okay, Deputy Winter?"

He gave her that toe-curling smile. "Just get on that damn plane."

She blew him a kiss, hoping to throw him off his hard-ass game and assert some control over her situation, but he grinned and winked at her, sending hot sparks right through her.

Just as well she was getting out of town. Another day with him, and they'd be in bed.

The thought propelled her down the jetway.

When she took her seat on the plane, the realization that she was alone hit her. Her throat tightened.

But wasn't this what she was used to? Never mind that she'd been all but run out of town on a rail, she was on her own with no one to answer to, no one to rein in her impulses—and no one beside her, she thought with an unexpected rush of emotion. When she got to Night's Landing, she could do as she pleased. Wasn't it the way she liked it?

Whether she liked it or not, it was the way it was.

Twelve

Nicholas Janssen waited until after midnight Amsterdam time for the call from Claude Rousseau, who should have arrived in New York yesterday afternoon. Janssen was still in the Dutch city, isolated in a suite of rooms in a seventeenth-century gabled house that had been converted into a very small, very private hotel along picturesque Herengracht, one of the finest canals in Amsterdam.

He was surrounded by men he paid well to protect him. He had no other relationship with them. Nicholas didn't delude himself. They weren't family, they weren't friends.

Even at his chalet in Switzerland, he was isolated, his fugitive status in the United States hanging over him. His international jet-setter neighbors distrusted him. Swiss natives wanted nothing to do with him. He knew about the dubious origins of the fortunes of some of the people who snubbed him. Tax evasion was the least of what their fathers and grandfathers had done.

But it was the least of what he'd done, too.

Finally the call came. "Rob Dunnemore is improving and should make a full recovery," Rousseau said. "His sister is on her way back to Tennessee."

"The second marshal? Winter?"

There was the slightest hesitation. "He could become a problem."

"But the FBI have their shooter, don't they?"

"Maybe. Maybe not."

Janssen sat forward in his leather chair next to an open window. The low ceilings in the old building made him claustrophobic. The call was secure—the owner of the hotel, who understood his clientele, had the best technical people in Europe regularly sweep for bugs, check with their sources for any attempt to tap the phone lines, legally or otherwise. But, still, Janssen was careful with what he said. "You'll do what needs to be done, won't you?"

"Of course." Rousseau had arrived in New York only yesterday but exhibited no sign of jet lag. "I'm in touch with your man here. We're working together on the problem."

"No ties back to me. None." Janssen didn't need to remind Rousseau that he had access to Rousseau's family—his mother, his ex-wife, his two teenage daughters. "Is that clear?"

"Very," Rousseau said calmly.

"Keep me apprised."

After he hung up, Janssen lit his pipe and lifted his feet onto a leather ottoman. His dogs, two Rhodesian ridgebacks who always traveled with him, lay atop a thick Persian carpet. They were his best, most trusted companions. Like him, they had learned discipline, patience.

But they were of a kind, and they had each other. He had no one.

The wealth he could reveal openly wasn't particularly impressive—it was the wealth he concealed that one day he would blend with his legal fortune, that would widen eyes and open doors. Then he could lead the life he'd always imagined for himself. He'd have the woman he wanted, the position, the power, the respect.

By then, perhaps Stuart Dunnemore would have died in his sleep, and Betsy would be free.

She'd need time to mourn, of course, but not that much. She had to know she'd outlive Stuart—she'd had to be preparing herself, even now, for going on without him.

But first, Janssen knew he had to get her to help him deal with the fact that he couldn't return to his own country without facing prosecution and the certainty of a prison sentence. Betsy would eventually see that it was unfair. That he'd paid for whatever mistakes he'd made and could offer the world more as a free man.

No, his legal status wasn't first. He tightened his grip on his pipe and controlled a wave of irritation.

Dealing with the situation in New York was first.

He prayed that the Dunnemore twins hadn't seen him in Amsterdam—that the shooting in Central Park in no way involved him and any of his people.

But if they had, if it did, Nicholas was prepared to act. Too much was at stake for him not to.

Thirteen

It was after dark when two deputy marshals dropped Sarah off at Night's Landing. Ethan waited until she'd reassured them she was fine there on her own and their car had pulled out of the long, curving driveway. Then he knocked on her kitchen door.

Sarah opened it, looking drawn and tired, but she attempted a smile. "Hey, Ethan."

He adopted his stereotypical good ol' boy demeanor. "I didn't expect you home so soon, Miss Sarah."

"Rob and his marshal buddies basically kicked me out. A classic case of projection. Really they're worried about themselves and their own safety, but instead they say they're worried about me."

Ethan doubted it was projection—the marshals probably had damn good reason to worry about her. She was an attractive academic with no experience in law enforcement and sniper attacks. In their position, he wouldn't want her underfoot, either.

"Anything I can do for you?" he asked.

She shook her head. "I'm going to take a bath and

go to bed. Thanks. Tomorrow—I don't know.'' Her eyes brightened for all of half a second. ''I might just go fishing.''

''I didn't know you liked to fish, Miss Sarah.''

''I don't particularly, but it's better than sitting around here worrying about Rob and feeling sorry for myself.''

Ethan smiled and managed to shuffle his feet. ''I know it's a hard time for you. The neighbors stopped by to give their regards. Mr. Fontaine, Miss Prichard, Mr. and Mrs. Kidd. They wanted to bring casseroles and flowers, but I told them I didn't know when you'd be back.''

''That's sweet of them.'' She seemed to take pleasure in the concern of her neighbors. ''I'd love to have a few more casseroles in the freezer for when Rob gets here. He's coming down to recuperate as soon as his doctors allow him to travel. What about reporters?''

''A few. I let them pound on the door, then came out and looked scary when they started peeking in the windows.''

That brought on a genuine smile. ''Good thinking.''

He left her in the big empty house, the ground soft under his feet as he walked back to his cottage. He could smell the wetness of the river, hear it lapping the limestone along its banks. The stars and half-moon created enough light for the trees to cast dark, wavering shadows. He hadn't grown up near water and trees.

He opened up all the cottage windows. The curtains fluttered in a cool breeze. Quickly, routinely, he checked his weapons. He had two Browning single-action 9 mm semiautomatics, as well as the Smith & Wesson .38 semiautomatic he used as an ankle gun.

The two wounded deputy marshals in New York. The archaeologist sister. The elderly statesman and his younger wife in Amsterdam.

The president of the United States.

Charlene Brooker, murdered army captain.

Ethan couldn't see how they fit together. Maybe they didn't. Maybe only some did. But he'd never been a big plotter, one to agonize over every why and wherefore. Establish the mission, then accomplish it. He figured if he got in these people's faces, something would start clicking.

In the meantime, he had nothing solid to take to the FBI, the U.S. Marshals Service, the Secret Service, army investigators, the Dutch police or anyone else.

Not that he would go to any of them when he did.

He wanted Charlene's killer all to himself.

Fourteen

    A fine mist rose off the river, sparkling in the early-morning sun that would burn it off within the hour. Sarah had walked down to the dock and up along the riverbank to the edge of the fields, aware of the tightness in her muscles after so many hours of worry, fear and tension. But she felt less conflicted about being back in Night's Landing, less guilty for having left her brother. It was what he wanted. He had friends, colleagues—armed guards—who'd look after him.

    And she was home, away from the guns, the investigation, the angry and concerned federal agents.

    When she returned to the house, she put on water for hot tea and settled at the round oak kitchen table, piled with mail Ethan must have brought in while she was in New York. She flipped through it, hoping for a good catalogue to occupy her while she drank her tea. There were cards and notes from well-wishers—most were people she knew, but some were strangers who'd heard that her brother had been shot and wanted his family to know they were thinking of him.

She made her tea and read the cards and letters one by one, appreciating the good thoughts from friend and stranger alike. *I know I haven't seen you in several years, but I had to write...*

"Nice," she said aloud, lifting a larger envelope off the pile.

No return address. New York postmark. One of Rob's associates?

She opened it and unfolded the single white eight-and-a-half-by-eleven paper inside. Several lines were centered on the page in large, bold, computer-printed italics.

A poem, she thought.

No.

The first words registered.

If I can get to your brother, I can get to you.

Unable to breathe, Sarah shoved her chair back, its legs screeching on the wood floor. She lurched to her feet.

The paper fluttered in a breeze from the open window, the words plainly visible in at least twenty-eight-point italic type, glaring up at her.

If I can get to your brother, I can get to you.
Do nothing. Tell no one.
The marshals, the FBI, your local sheriff.
Your parents in Amsterdam.
I'll know if you talk.
Wait.

She was aware of herself gulping in air without expelling any. Aware of her tea mug teetering on the edge of the table, of her hand holding tightly onto the back of the old oak chair. It was as if she was looking down at herself. She couldn't make herself stop.

What was going on? Was someone trying to take advantage of her situation for their own jollies, to terrify her, to get attention—to *what?*

Was it a serious, credible threat?

From the shooter?

From someone else?

She didn't dare touch the offending letter again for fear of further contaminating any forensic evidence it might contain. The envelope was front-down on the table. Was the address printed, or handwritten? She couldn't remember.

But what difference did it make? She wasn't an investigator, a handwriting analyst.

She picked up her mug, careful not to spill tea all over the letter, and staggered to the kitchen counter with it and set it down. She grabbed the old telephone, immediately dialing her parents' number in Amsterdam. She had it memorized, just as well because she doubted she'd have been able to look it up. Her hands were shaking, her head spinning—she remembered Nate ordering her to hold her breath in the park. She'd been hyperventilating. That was what she was doing now.

She didn't want to pass out.

She held her breath, but somehow, it made her want to cry.

Her mother answered.

"Hi—it's me." Sarah winced at the sound of her own voice. She felt as if she were back in school, calling and pretending all was well when she was homesick, exhausted, anxious, miserable. "I just wanted to check in. I made it back to Night's Landing okay. I haven't talked to Rob yet this morning. It's still early. How're you and Dad?''

"We're hanging in there." Her mother's voice sounded almost as strained as her own. But that was to be expected under the circumstances—it didn't mean she'd received an anonymous letter of her own. "We're making plans to leave for New York, I hope tomorrow. I can't—neither of us can stand not seeing Rob another day."

"Is anyone there with you?"

"Not right now. The Marshals Service sent someone over yesterday to check in on us." Her mother hesitated. "Sarah? What's wrong?"

She sank against the counter. She was still shaking, but she had her breathing under reasonable control. "Why don't you let the marshals take care of you? Two deputies met me at the airport when I got back last night and drove me home. It was a big comfort."

"You're spooked, aren't you? Being home alone after what happened to Rob. Well, I don't blame you. Frankly, I think you'd have been better off staying in New York. I don't care what Rob says."

"I'll be okay. I just—"

"Call one of your cousins, or your uncle." The Quinlans were all in Belle Meade west of Nashville. "You have enough family and friends in the area that you don't need to be alone."

It was sound advice, but Sarah had no intention of dragging anyone else into her mess.

She couldn't tell her mother about the note. She'd meant to, maybe, but now she realized she couldn't. Her mother was safe and there was nothing she could do from Amsterdam. Whoever had sent her the letter could have her phone tapped, her house bugged.

I'll know if you talk.

How? Was it an idle threat, designed to frighten her?

"I'll be all right," she said. "It's been a stressful few days, but at least Rob's doing well."

"We'll get him down to Night's Landing. This'll be behind us in time." Her mother took in an audible breath. "Sarah, are you sure you're all right?"

She reassured her mother and quickly said goodbye.

The note continued to flutter in the breeze, and she half wished it'd blow out a window and into the river, except the windows all had screens and the river was in the other direction.

God.

What was she going to do?

She spotted Nate Winter's card on the counter. She'd found it in her pocketbook last night before she went to bed and assumed he must have tucked it in there when she wasn't looking. He'd scrawled his home number on the back.

She'd thought about him for most of her flight to Nashville. Most of the night. He was good-looking, sexy, hard-edged, impatient and impossible to figure out, at least in the couple of days she'd known him— and yet she couldn't deny she was attracted to him. It was crazy. Had to be adrenaline.

She splashed her face with cold water at the kitchen sink and, without considering the pros and cons, dialed his home number.

What time was it? She glanced at the stove clock.

Six-fifteen, but she was in Central Time. It was seven-fifteen in New York. Still early, possibly even by Deputy Winter standards.

He answered on the second ring. "Winter."

Sarah took a calming breath. Though he was at home, he sounded as if he was on duty. But she couldn't do it. She couldn't tell him. What if the note was for real and the person who wrote it did have her phones tapped, her house bugged? Or Nate's phones, his apartment?

What if she talked and ended up getting someone killed because of it?

"Sarah? What's going on?"

"I knew you'd have caller ID." She gave a faltering laugh. "Paranoid cops. I'm home, safe and sound. I wanted to let you know." She didn't sound believable even to herself. "It's early, I realize, but you strike me as the crack-of-dawn type."

"You sound like you're coming undone."

"Do I?" She tried another laugh, but it only seemed to make her sound even nuttier.

"What's wrong?"

"Nothing. Have a good day. Sorry if I woke you."

She slammed down the phone and took it apart, then charged into the living room and took apart that phone, and finally ran upstairs and took apart that one.

She didn't find anything that looked like a phone tap, not that she knew what she was looking for.

"You're insane," she said aloud. "Just drive to the police station and hand them the stupid letter."

There. A plan.

What if she was followed?

What if Ethan Brooker had sent her the letter?

From New York?

Okay, so that didn't make sense. But the point was—did she dare risk telling someone, anyone? Did she dare risk *not* telling someone?

At least her parents were safe in Amsterdam, and her brother had his armed guards in New York.

She put the phones back together and made more hot tea, calming down as she sipped it and stared at the note, as if it might make better sense to her now that she'd gotten over the initial shock of it.

If I can get to your brother, I can get to you.

Special Agent Collins would definitely want a look at this little missive. The FBI had profilers, hand-writing analysts, fingerprinters, paper analysts and ink analysts. They'd figure out if it was for real or just some jerk getting off at her expense.

Feeling more in control of herself, Sarah opened the rest of the mail and discovered two obvious crank notes. One was from a woman who wanted a lock of Rob's hair so she could make psychic contact with the sniper—obviously she was not a legitimate psychic. The other was from a man who claimed Rob and Nate had lived only because God was giving them a second chance to renounce their sinning ways.

In that context, the anonymous note from New York maybe *wasn't* for real. The shooting had received maximum news coverage. It had brought out a few nuts, and the writer of the offending note could be just another one of them, someone who wanted to frighten and get everyone stirred up but who wouldn't act on his threats.

Her phone rang, startling her. Her mind leaped in a dozen different directions, but she composed herself enough to answer in a reasonably calm voice on the third ring. "Dunnemores."

"I'm on a midmorning flight to Nashville," Nate said. "Stay put."

He hung up before she could say a word.

Midmorning his time. A two-hour flight would put him in Nashville before noon her time, in Night's Landing thirty to forty-five minutes later. He hadn't asked her to pick him up at the airport. For all she knew, he'd get a ride from another marshal.

Rob would tell her she was on a need-to-know basis and should learn to live with it.

Blowing out a lungful of air, Sarah got a pair of dented aluminum tongs from a drawer and shoved the offending note and its envelope to the bottom of the pile of mail. When Nate arrived, she'd show it to him.

Problem solved. He was the law enforcement professional. He could help her figure out what to do.

He'd be on his way back to New York by tonight.

In the meantime, she'd make her prune cake.

Fifteen

━━━━━∞⟳∞⟳∞⟳∞━━━━━

Nate bought a map and rented a car at the Nashville airport and drove east until he came to Night's Landing, basically a wide bend on the Cumberland River. It wasn't even a town, really. He pulled into a gas station and started to call Sarah for directions to her house, but there was no cell service. Before using a pay phone, he asked inside.

"I thought Sarah was still in Scotland," the skinny old man at the cash register said. "I've been telling the reporters that. She and Rob used to like to come in here and buy red licorice. I told them it'd rot their teeth." He eyed Nate suspiciously. "Why should I tell you where they live?"

Nate was in no mood to screw around and showed the man his badge.

Directions involved a cornfield, a country church and a back road he wasn't supposed to take and one he was.

The back road brought him down toward the deep, slow river, and he turned left, as the old man had instructed, onto a long driveway that led to a log house nestled among shade trees and gardens, its sprawling lawn ending at a dock on the riverfront. On one side of the property were more fields, on the other, thick woods that seemed to go on forever. Spring was further along in middle Tennessee than in New York, the leaves full and dark, a huge pink azalea growing close to the house, a tangle of white roses creeping up one side of the front porch.

Nate parked behind an old pickup with Tennessee plates and climbed out of his car. He could smell freshly mowed grass tinged with the sweetness of flowers and heard a small boat puttering on the river.

In the side yard, a ponytailed man in overalls stabbed a pitchfork into a pile of compost and dumped it onto a plowed vegetable garden. One end had sprouts growing—spinach, onions, loose-leaf lettuce. The man shooed a horsefly with one hand. "Can I help you, sir?" he called to Nate.

Nate walked down to the garden. "I'm looking for Sarah Dunnemore."

"And you would be?"

"Deputy U.S. Marshal Nate Winter. I work with her brother."

The man—presumably the property manager Sarah had mentioned—had a black bandanna tied around his forehead. Sweat dripped down his face nonetheless. "You're the other marshal who was shot with him, aren't you? Doing okay, sir?"

"Yes, thanks, and you're—"

"Brooker, sir. Ethan Brooker." He grinned amiably, not breathing that hard from his work. "Chief manure spreader. Composted or not, horse manure stinks, don't it? I take care of the place."

Nate noticed the tattoo on the man's tanned, muscular right arm. He had on a dirty T-shirt under the overalls. By contrast, Nate had put on a suit for his travels south. His bandaged arm had given him some discomfort on the flight, but he'd taken a couple of Tylenol when he landed.

"Dr. Dunnemore's in the house," Brooker said. "Is she expecting you? She's got company."

Nate didn't like the idea of her having company, not after her early-morning phone call. She'd tried to hide her stress and fear, but they were obvious. He nodded to Brooker. "Yes, she's expecting me."

He left Brooker to his manure spreading and took a half gravel, half stone path to the back steps. It seemed more like the main entrance than the one on the porch that faced the river. Through a screen door, he could hear Sarah talking to a man with a pronounced southern accent.

They were discussing prune cake recipes.

"My granny always made a three-layer prune cake," the man said. "She insisted it was best the next day, after the flavors had time to settle and blend."

Sarah laughed, but Nate could hear a lingering strain in her voice. He wondered if the guy with her noticed. "I like prune cake anytime, anywhere, provided it's not hard as a rock."

Nate peered through the screen door. Sarah's visitor was sitting at a round table. He looked to be in his early thirties, with glasses, close-cropped sandy hair and regular features. He wore a polo shirt, khakis and penny loafers. Sarah was at the counter in a flour-covered pink apron.

She spotted him, her eyes connecting with his, widening, and Nate knew that whatever had prompted her to call him in a panic was still a factor. He wasn't going to have prune cake and coffee and turn around and head back to New York. Something was up.

The man at the table leaped to his feet. "Sarah?"

"It's okay," she said quickly, moving toward the screen door.

Nate pulled it open. "How are you, Sarah?"

"I didn't hear your car—" She smiled nervously. "Conroy and I have been busy talking prune cake recipes. Here, come in. Conroy, this is Nate Winter, one of Rob's colleagues from New York. Nate, Conroy Fontaine, a journalist and temporary neighbor."

Fontaine put out a hand, then pulled it back. "Sorry, sir. I forgot you were hit the other day. The arm, right?"

"It's fine. Why are you a temporary neighbor?"

The man seemed taken aback by Nate's directness, but he recovered and smiled. "I'm renting a cabin upriver a piece while I work on a book."

"He's working on an unauthorized biography of President Poe," Sarah said neutrally, then stepped from behind the counter. "Thanks for stopping by, Conroy. Come back anytime for your slice of prune cake."

He lifted a lightweight jacket off the back of a chair. "I'll see you later, Sarah. Deputy, very nice to meet you. I'm so sorry about what happened."

He slipped out the back door.

Nate glanced around the country kitchen and its squared-off log walls with thick layers of white caulking between them. The oak table and chairs were worn and cracked with age, the simple linoleum floor spotless, the cabinets and countertops timeless and functional. A cross-stitched sampler about friendship hung above the table.

The window next to the table looked out on the side yard with its azaleas and vegetable garden. Ethan Brooker had abandoned his pile of horse manure.

The place was more isolated than Nate had expected.

"Whose truck?" he asked.

"The family's. Ethan uses it, too. Conroy walked down from the fishing camp where he's staying." Sarah returned to her mixing bowl and cutting board of what presumably were chopped prunes. "You were expecting Tara, weren't you?"

"Well, not Daniel Boone."

"My parents have lived all over the world," she said, lifting handfuls of chopped prunes into her mixing bowl. "But this has always been home."

"I met your gardener. He almost stuck me with his pitchfork. Conroy's a buff guy, too." Nate settled on a stool across from her at the counter, noticed the slight tremble in her hands. "How come you don't have any scrawny old guys hanging around you?"

"Conroy runs to keep in shape—apparently he has a grueling deadline for his book. I met him last fall when he was still deciding if he wanted to take on the project. He wants to interview me, but I keep putting him off."

"By bringing up prune cake recipes?"

"Watch, he'll find some way to use it in his book." She picked up a wood-handled spatula and folded the prunes into the brownish batter. "And Ethan's the nicest guy. Anyway, a pitchfork's no match for whatever you're carrying.''

Which Nate had no intention of discussing with her. She lifted her bowl and started spooning the thick batter into one of the square pans she had set out on the counter. She took a breath, setting down the bowl quickly, as if she'd been about to drop it. The tremble in her hands was noticeably worse.

She avoided his eye and spoke as she stared down at her cake batter. ''You didn't have to come here. I should have stopped you. I'm sorry you've wasted your time.'' She picked up her bowl again, stubbornly folding batter into another pan. ''I'm not in any danger here.''

Nate didn't respond. She set down the bowl once more, batter spilling down its sides, then tore open the oven door and shoved the pans inside. She turned on the timer with more force than was necessary.

''I need air,'' she said, pulling off her apron and tossing it onto the counter.

She moved down a hall toward the front of the house, at a fast walk at first, then a run. Nate could hear her footsteps on the wood floor. He eased off the stool and followed her out to the porch, overfurnished with old rockers and chairs, even an iron daybed.

Sarah had made it down the steps and was well on her way to the river and the small, well-kept dock.

He wondered if she'd run right into the water and try to swim away from whatever was bothering her. It wasn't him. Or not just him. He was a reminder, tangible evidence that she wasn't just home on vacation. That was an illusion, a ruse that had helped get her through the morning.

She stopped at the very end of the dock.

Nate walked out to her. An ancient fishing boat bobbed in the dark water. He didn't blame her. He felt an urge to grab her and jump in the boat, go wherever the river took them and forget about shootings and whatever had frightened her. In an image that felt real, that rocked him to the point his knees almost buckled, he saw them stopped at a quiet clearing, a blanket spread, the sun on them as they made love. It was as if her body were under him now, soft and yielding, their lovemaking tender, slow, as if they didn't have a care in the world.

Christ. What the hell was wrong with him?

Sarah glanced back at him. She had on jeans and a lightweight zip-up top in a dusty blue-gray that matched her eyes. "How's your arm?"

The air seemed cooler, damper, on the river. His arm ached. His whole body ached. "Doctor rebandaged it this morning before I left. It's healing well. Doesn't bother me that much." He glanced at the undergrowth and the rocks along the riverbank, upriver, toward the Poe house. "You swim in the river?"

"All the time. The Corps of Engineer dams backed up the river so that it's wider and deeper here than it used to be. It's more like a lake nowadays, so the current's not bad."

He shifted back to her. "Snakes?"

"Oh, sure, but they leave us alone. Sometimes you can see a water moccasin sunning on the rocks. They're poisonous. You don't have them up north." She looked back at him, her words almost rote. "People often confuse them with water snakes that aren't poisonous.''

Nate decided to let her talk about snakes and prune cake, until she was calm enough to tell him what was going on, why she'd called him at six her time—why she hadn't called him again and dissuaded him from coming down here. ''You can tell the difference?''

She nodded. ''Water moccasins are a kind of pit viper. They swim on top of the water with their heads above the surface—water snakes tend to swim under the water. They're not as fat as the cottonmouths— that's what people call water moccasins—and they're more likely to hang from trees and slither off when they're startled. A cottonmouth will stand its ground.''

Like her, Nate thought. Like her brother. Even in the short time they'd worked together, Nate had done enough arrests with Rob to know he didn't like to back down. ''Ever run into a cottonmouth?''

''All the time. Rob and I used to catch them when we were kids, but Granny Dunnemore told us to leave them alone. None of the snakes will bother you if you don't bother them. It's when they're startled or fool threatened that they bite.''

He smiled. ''I'll try not to startle or threaten any snakes.''

She didn't smile back, seemed barely aware that he'd spoken. ''Even most cottonmouth bites aren't fatal.'' She stared into the water, as if she were looking for snakes. ''Thank you for coming down here. It was a decent thing to do. I know I must have sounded awful on the phone this morning. I'm sure I overreacted to something.''

"Tell me about it."

She shook her head. "I have to show you."

But she didn't want to show him. Nate could see her reluctance in her body language. Tight, closed, afraid. Showing him meant that the "something" that had prompted her to call him was real.

She dropped her arms to her sides and pushed past him with sudden energy, almost knocking him into the river.

He followed her back to the house, into a country-style living room with quilts and afghans in odd colors piled onto overstuffed furniture and shelves bearing an eclectic collection of books, including scholarly works and what had to be every mystery Rex Stout and Agatha Christie had ever written.

"Wait here," she said, her tone more tired than commanding, and retreated back to the kitchen.

Nate debated going after her, but decided to do as she'd asked. He stood in front of the stone fireplace, noting a wedding picture on the mantel. The parents, Stuart and Betsy Dunnemore. He was handsome, she was beautiful—startlingly beautiful. And very obviously much younger.

Sarah returned with an envelope and a sheet of paper that she laid on the marble-topped coffee table. "Here. I've already touched them, so they have my fingerprints on them."

Nate took in the words in a single glance.

If I can get to your brother, I can get to you.

"Jesus Christ," he said under his breath.

She seemed almost relieved at his reaction. "I didn't know what to do. It was in with a bunch of cards and letters, some of them kind of nutty." She sank onto a chair and took a breath. "It's amazing what some people will stoop to. I don't want to take any chances, but I don't want to send you all on a wild-goose chase, either."

"This was in your mail?"

"Ethan piled it on the kitchen table, unopened. It was here when I arrived. I opened it this morning." She leaned forward and stared at the paper, her cheeks pale, but she seemed calmer now that she'd told him about it. "After I called you, I checked all the phones for bugs. I don't even know what one looks like, and I imagine there are ways for someone to tap a phone line that I'd never find."

"Sarah."

"I couldn't make myself tell you on the phone. I was really spooked. I let my thinking run wild."

She was upset, uncertain, a capable, intelligent woman not used to being out of her element—not used to having to trust someone, count on someone, besides herself.

But Nate knew there was more. Something else.

She twisted her hands together, working one of her delicate rings up to her knuckle, then back down again. "I don't want anyone else to get hurt."

"None of us does."

"Rob, my parents. If something happens to them because of something I did or didn't do..." She trailed off, not finishing.

"Your parents are still in Amsterdam."

She nodded, taking in a small breath. "I know. I called them, too. I didn't tell them about the note." She stopped abruptly and lifted her eyes to him. "I really don't like being afraid, you know."

Nate sat on the edge of the couch and folded his hands. His head ached now, too. But his thinking was clear, sharp. After he'd left her last night, he'd thought about finding her collapsing in Central Park—thought about her body language and how similar it was to when he'd caught her following him to Sister Maria's.

Sarah Dunnemore wasn't a bad liar. But she wasn't a good one, either.

"What happened in Central Park?" he asked her.

She almost slid off her chair. "What? Rob—" She took a breath. "You know what happened. You were there. It's where you and Rob were shot."

"To you. What happened to you in Central Park? Why did you almost pass out?" He settled back on the couch. "Don't tell me it was the 'twin thing.' That won't wash twice."

"Nothing happened, at least, nothing that relates to the note."

"Sarah, you're a smart woman. I'm sure you're a hell of an archaeologist, not that I'd be able to judge. It's not my area of expertise, like law enforcement isn't yours."

She was silent, still twisting one of her rings.

"You're feeling isolated," he said, "and you don't need to."

"I don't want to send you all off on some wild-goose chase. If I tell you what happened, which was nothing, you'll investigate." She shook her head. "No, it's crazy."

"Guess what, Dr. Dunnemore. You don't get to decide."

That brought her up short. "All right. Fair enough. I'll let that be your job."

He smiled, trying to take some of the edge off his demeanor. But his arm hurt, and he still had an image of the two of them on the blanket. "That *is* my job."

She didn't relax. "I saw a man I thought I recognized. He was up on the street, on Central Park South, looking down into the park."

"Recognized him from where?"

She hesitated. "Amsterdam."

Hell.

Nate didn't speak. He wanted her to do the talking.

"I'm sure it was just my mind playing tricks on me. He reminded me of a man I saw at the Rijksmuseum. We were all there—my parents, Rob, me." Sarah jumped up abruptly, turning away from him and gazing out a window onto the porch, down to the river. "I was on my own. Waiting for my mother, actually. Rob and my father were off looking at the Delftware. It's a huge museum—we limited ourselves to the Dutch collection."

"Where was your mother?"

"Viewing Rembrandt's *The Night Watch*. It's an incredible painting—it's in its own rotunda. I was in an adjoining gallery. I don't even remember what I was looking at. Earlier Dutch works, I believe. This man approached me, and we chatted for a minute or two about the paintings, the museum. He was friendly. French, I think. My parents know so many people, I assumed it was one of their friends or acquaintances."

"Did you ask them about him?"

"No. It didn't occur to me. It's not as if he said outright that he knew them."

"Describe him."

She didn't hesitate. "About five-ten, angular features, dark hair that's long in front. Nate, he can't be the same man as the one I saw at the park. It'd been a long, stressful day. I couldn't swear—"

"What was he wearing?"

"Black leather jacket and black turtleneck. So was the man at the park. That must be what made me think I recognized him."

"Rob didn't see the man who approached you at the museum?"

"I don't know how he could have."

She turned from the window, her arms crossed on her chest, a way, Nate thought, for her to keep him from seeing that her hands were still shaking. She was a woman accustomed to staying in control. She wouldn't want him to see just how the events of the past few days had rocked her. "You're going to tell Agent Collins, aren't you?" Her tone was cool now, almost resigned. "About both the letter and the man in the park."

"Damn straight."

She nodded and let her arms drop to her side. No shaking hands now. "I wasn't holding back on you. I was convinced—I *am* convinced the man isn't the same man I ran into at the museum. Even if it is, so what? It doesn't mean he had anything to do with the shooting. It could just be one of those weird coincidences. If I hadn't gotten the letter…" She didn't finish.

"We'll get to the bottom of whatever's going on."

"Maybe it's nothing." She tried to smile. "I should show you my letter from the psychic."

Nate got to his feet, feeling the silence of the place, the isolation on this quiet stretch of river. Obviously Rob hadn't expected his sister to come home to a threatening letter.

It was postmarked the day of the shooting. Whoever sent it hadn't wasted any time.

"What goes on prune cake?" Nate asked.

Sarah seemed to have no idea what he was talking about. "What?"

"Frosting." He wanted to pull her out of her spinning thoughts, just as his uncle had done with him with his talk of his orange eggs. "Does it have a frosting, or do you eat it plain like gingerbread?"

"It has a caramel glaze. You put it on when the cake's still warm."

He could hear the southern roots in her words, a soft lilt that seemed to match the breeze off the river. "You can probably finish making it before the FBI gets here. I'll call Joe Collins in New York and find out what he wants to do."

She nodded, her breathing shallow, then started for the kitchen. She paused in the hall doorway and glanced back at him. "I'm glad you're here." Then a quick smile, a welcome flash in her eyes. "I think."

Nate glanced at the note.

I'll know if you talk.

Wait.

She'd waited—she'd waited to tell him.

Everyone assumed the answers to the sniper attack were in New York, embedded somewhere in what he and Rob did for a living. Nate was no longer so sure.

He had a feeling they could be here, in Night's Landing, in the lives of a well-known, progressive southern family who happened to be friends and neighbors to the president of the United States.

He dreaded making the call to Joe Collins in New York.

And Rob—what to tell him about his sister's letter?

Nothing, Nate decided. At least not until he knew more.

He could smell the prune cake baking, filling the house with warmth and the scent of cinnamon. Cozy, homey smells. She'd imposed normalcy onto herself as a way to cope. He pictured Sarah racing around that morning, pulling apart phones, trying to talk herself into believing the note didn't mean anything, that she'd been right about the man in Central Park, after all, and he was no one.

Maybe she had a point. Maybe the wide coverage of the shooting and something about the Dunnemores themselves had brought out the head cases.

But Nate didn't think so.

Sixteen

❧᠊᠊᠊᠊᠊᠊᠊᠊᠊᠊᠊᠊᠊᠊᠊᠊᠊᠊᠊᠊᠊᠊᠊᠊᠊᠊᠊᠊᠊᠊᠊᠊᠊

It was late afternoon before all the federal law enforcement types left—except for Nate. He obviously had no immediate plans to go anywhere. Sarah retreated to the kitchen and made the caramel glaze for the prune cake, pouring it between the layers and on the top while it was still hot. She hadn't had time to really cook in months. Now it helped her control her racing thoughts, center her as she considered her options. And the old-fashioned southern recipes helped her feel more rooted and less isolated, as if she could draw on her grandmother's strength.

She'd taken the FBI agents, the deputy marshals and the one guy who was probably Secret Service but never said so through her house, answered all their questions and offered them iced sweet tea punch, which they'd refused. She held her temper and her tears *and* her nerves.

She thought she'd done all right, but now, in the immediate aftermath of their search, she wished she'd simply thrown the note into the garbage.

The agents had whisked it away.

They'd told her nothing. No theories, no assessments, no hint of what they thought of the anonymous note.

Nate had kept his distance. After the last car pulled out of the driveway, he drifted out to the front porch. Sarah had a feeling he wasn't going to be on an evening flight back to New York.

She didn't know what to do with him besides feed him prune cake.

She set it to cool on a pink Depression-glass plate and washed her hands, then dialed the hospital.

Her brother was awake. He could talk to her.

"Joe Collins just left here," he said, sounding tired but agitated. "Christ, Sarah. What the hell's going on?"

"I don't know. Maybe I'm just going off the deep end."

"The letter's for real." He took in what sounded like a painful breath. "You didn't make it up. The guy in Amsterdam—I'm no help. I didn't see him. I'm still fogged in from the meds, but I'd remember."

"It was probably just a regular guy in Amsterdam and a regular guy in New York and all the adrenaline—" She sighed, sinking against the counter. "Rob, it's been an awful few days. I haven't been at the top of my game. I didn't get a close enough look at the man in the park to be positive it was the same guy. If I hadn't gotten the letter, I'd never have mentioned him. Part of me still wishes I hadn't."

"I'm sorry, Sarah. If I hadn't got shot—"

"Don't go there."

"Why don't you go back to Scotland for a week or so? Hang out with your friends. Buy me a kilt."

She shook her head as if he could see her. "I can't. Not now. Rob—"

"I don't remember the shooting. I don't even remember calling you. I just remember hoping Nate wouldn't die because of me."

"Maybe you were dreaming on the operating table."

"No, Sarah. I was the shooter's target."

"But why? Because of your work?" She hesitated, focusing on the old kitchen, every corner of it familiar to her, although she hadn't lived here in years. "Or because you're a Dunnemore?"

"There's never been anything dangerous about being a Dunnemore."

"You're right. Crazy, maybe, but not dangerous." She could feel the weight of his depression, his fear that he was responsible for what was happening—and his disgust with his inability to do anything about it. "I've been thinking. What if all this has nothing to do with you? What if I picked up an enemy in Scotland? Maybe the guy in Amsterdam and then in Central Park was following me."

"Come on, Sarah. You don't have enemies. Maybe the ghost of some bones you dug up haunt you, but otherwise—no way."

She'd known her theory would perk him up. "I don't deal much in bones."

"I'm fading," he said. "Nurses had me up today. God, I'm so weak. I thought you'd be better off in Night's Landing. Out of the fray. Now, I don't know. Nate…make sure he knows you're tougher than you look."

"There's still time for him to fly back to New York tonight."

"Dream on. Hang in there, okay?"

"You, too."

The kitchen seemed quiet and still after she hung up. She cut the prune cake in two chunks and wrapped half, carefully placing it in the freezer in anticipation of Rob's return home, then headed out through the back door. She was restless, her head spinning.

She found herself on the narrow trail to the Poe house. It wound along the river, on the edge of the woods of cedar trees, limestone pits and small caves, a route she'd taken hundreds of times since she was a child.

Within five steps, Nate fell in behind her.

Sarah almost smiled. "I knew I wouldn't get far without you."

"Rob's right. You are tougher than you look."

His words registered, and she whipped around at him, furious. "You eavesdropped on my conversation with my brother?"

"Picked up the extension on the porch. Piece of cake."

"*Damn* it, don't I have any privacy?"

"Not when the same guy who shot me could be after you."

"No one's after me," she said, picking up her pace, pushing aside low tree branches on the damp path. The river oozed below her on her left. The path would take her higher, onto impressive limestone bluffs.

"I didn't listen to the entire conversation. That help?"

"Not particularly."

"Where are we going?" he asked.

"*I'm* going for a walk."

And without any warning—without even breathing—he caught one arm around her waist and drew her to him.

She gulped in a breath. "What are you doing?"

"I'm thinking about kissing you. I've been thinking about it for a couple of days now."

"You've only known me a couple of days."

"Plenty long enough to think about kissing you."

His mouth found hers, and she didn't resist, didn't even consider it—she shut her eyes and felt the softness of his lips, the coolness of the breeze against her bare arms. She remembered his injured arm and grabbed the other one instead, holding him tightly as his mouth opened to hers, his arm dropping lower, drawing her more firmly against him. He was all hard muscle and bone, not an easy man, not the sort she'd ever imagined herself wanting to kiss. Well, wanting to, maybe. He was sexy, the kind of sexy she'd been taught to resist. Didn't *need* to be taught to resist.

Only when he set her down did she realize he'd lifted her off her feet.

She cleared her throat and ran her fingers through her hair. "Well. I guess that excuses you for eavesdropping."

"I'll remember that."

"We should head back. You have time to make an evening flight—"

"I checked out the upstairs while you were frosting

the prune cake. I think I'll take the blue room." He motioned up the path with one hand. "Lead the way."

"I had a feeling I wasn't getting rid of you tonight. We used to get bats in the blue room."

He grinned at her. "I'm not afraid of bats."

"You've got flour on your jacket." She brushed at the spot with her fingertips. "That would never do for a marshal, would it? Against all your dress codes, I imagine. Did I hurt your arm?"

His eyes went very dark, smoldering dark. "Sarah…"

She caught her breath. "Yes. I should lead the way."

The Poe home was an 1868 brick Greek Revival set on three acres of yard and gardens high on a bluff above the Cumberland River. Nate remembered seeing pictures of it when Wes Poe was campaigning for the White House. On the walk over, along the river, Sarah had explained that the house was a state and national historic site, not only because of her pal the president, but because of its own unique history and near pristine condition.

"It represents almost a hundred and fifty years of middle Tennessee history," she said. "Leola and Violet Poe made very few improvements in it over the years. There's still no central heat and only cold running water."

"President Poe's a wealthy man—"

"It wasn't about money. Leola and Violet didn't embrace change."

Nate followed her onto a stone path that led

through the overgrown grass to the porch. "I like my hot water."

"They had hot water. They just had to boil it."

"Wes Poe didn't have a typical baby boomer up-bringing, did he?"

"He was born during the war, so technically he's not a boomer, but, no, the Poe sisters weren't exactly Ward and June Cleaver."

Sarah trotted up the steps onto the porch, more at ease than Nate had seen her since he'd arrived in Night's Landing. It wasn't just being on familiar turf—it was having told someone else about the letter, calling the bluff of the asshole who'd written it. He joined her on the porch, feeling as if he'd just stepped back in time.

"When I was growing up," she went on, "I'd sneak up here every chance I got and sit out on the porch and listen to Leola and Violet tell stories. When I was in high school, I started videotaping them."

"Did you include some of the footage in your documentary?"

She nodded. "They're incredible, so natural and real. Every story is priceless, whether it's something ordinary like picking blackberries and going to church suppers, or something melodramatic, like hiding in the cellar during a tornado, or finding my grandfather dead. They were elderly by the time I was a teenager, but they had such vivid memories. Their stories helped me get to know them as children and teenagers themselves, as young women." She gazed out at the knee-high grass and weeds popping up through the rosebush. "I miss them."

Nate knew she was seeing more than an empty historic house. "I imagine people will be most interested in what the Poe sisters have to say about the president."

"I'm not his biographer. I don't focus on him. His is a fascinating and unique story, but it's not the only one." She straightened her spine and seemed to make an effort to return herself to the present. "I've been working on one aspect of the Poe house or another since high school. But I'm done with it now."

"What's next?"

"I'm supposed to be taking a break and figuring that out."

"What happens to this place?"

"It'll open to the public at some point. There's still a lot to be sorted out. Parking, visitors' center, rest rooms. Who does what. The trust, the state, the federal government."

"Wes Poe didn't want it?"

She shook her head. "He thinks Leola and Violet would have approved of its fate in their own way. Imagine. They opened their door one morning and found him right here on this porch."

"In an apple basket," Nate said, remembering their conversation from the other night in New York over beer and her half-eaten quesadilla. He leaned against the porch rail, still feeling their kiss, the eagerness of her mouth on his. But she was off in Poe land, the house a living and breathing entity to her. "Think one of the sisters had him and just didn't want to admit it?"

"It's possible, but very unlikely. They were both well into their forties when they found him."

Conroy Fontaine rounded a mass of red roses.

"And our Dr. Dunnemore no doubt knows more than she'll ever tell," he said pleasantly. "I should practice my eavesdropping skills and see what I can learn."

Sarah's laugh struck Nate as polite more than heartfelt. "I had a professor who often said that one can tell a good paper as much by what's not in it as what is. I imagine I know more about this land and the people who've lived on it than anyone in their right mind would ever want to know. But, everything I have, I've turned over to the Poe House Trust."

Fontaine leaned on the rickety rail of the porch steps. "I've heard you picked through the Poe family dump."

"The word is excavated."

He grinned at her. "Find any old diaries?"

"You are hopeless, Mr. Fontaine," she said in an exaggerated Scarlett O'Hara accent.

Fontaine looked at Nate, then motioned vaguely up the river. "My fishing camp's just up the road. It has a tricky gas stove. I almost blew myself up just now trying to light the pilot and decided to take a walk to calm my nerves. I heard you two out here."

Sarah sat on the top step. "What were you planning to cook?" she asked.

"Your prune cake got me hankering for real southern food. I was going to try my hand at fried apricot pies."

"Fried apricot pies—oh, Conroy! I adore fried pies."

She was into the southern thing. Nate watched her cheeks go from dead-pale to rosy. Next time, he thought, amused, instead of kissing her, he'd bring up southern food. But he understood—it was a distraction.

Conroy was having fun, too. "I like them still warm, sprinkled with confectioner's sugar—"

"They're not easy to make. I tend to burn them."

"If I bring you fried apricot pies for breakfast, will you get me an interview with your friend the president?"

"You are incorrigible, Mr. Fontaine." She was good-natured about his relentless, open push for her to trade on her friendship with John Wesley Poe—it seemed to be a conversation they'd had before. "It used to be that not many people even knew we were friends. Now—well, that's changed, hasn't it?"

"People knew," Conroy said, suddenly serious. "They just have such enormous respect for your family that they didn't want to intrude. Even nosy reporters like me." But his seriousness didn't last. "Deputy Winter, you work for the president, don't you? Technically. The Marshals Service is part of the Department of Justice. Your boss is the director, his boss is the attorney general—and *his* boss is the president. There. *You* could introduce me."

Nate didn't respond. He'd never met any of the presidents in office during his years as a deputy, and he didn't joke about them.

"Ah. I see I stepped over the line. Well, I don't want to get anyone into trouble, least of all me." Fontaine patted his stomach. "I think I'll go wrestle with my stove and try my fried pies again. I'll bring some by if they come out."

"I hope you will," Sarah said.

After he was gone, she leaned into Nate and whispered, "I know where there's a key."

Great. He was going to get a tour. "What about the alarm system?"

"I have the code. If I told Conroy, he'd want a personal tour. At this point I think most of what he has on President Poe is off the Internet, although I understand he's interviewed most of the neighbors, even ones who moved in long after Wes left."

"Your family?"

"He's tried. My parents don't give interviews about President Poe."

"What about Rob?"

"He doesn't, either. Nor do I. We made that decision a long time ago, before Wes went into politics. He had an unusual background, and we all adored Leola and Violet—we knew sooner or later someone would take an interest in his story."

"I think your buddy Conroy has the hots for you."

She blushed. "Not everyone thinks that way."

Fontaine did. Nate didn't know yet about the property manager.

The house was cool and elegant, furnished in a mix of country and Victorian antiques, as if the two maiden sisters had just stepped out. Not much dust. Sarah explained that it was cleaned and the yard mowed on a regular, if not totally adequate, basis.

On a marble mantel, there were pictures of Leola and Violet Poe, two ordinary-looking women who'd raised a president, and of John Wesley Poe as a little boy, a teenager, a college graduate—and as the governor of Tennessee.

"They never wanted him to leave Night's Landing,

but they were proud of him,'' Sarah said. ''They and my grandmother died within two years of each other when I was in college. You passed the little church cemetery where they're buried.''

Nate wandered with her through the drawing room and the library, the kitchen, the butler's pantry, and upstairs to the bedrooms. ''Did the family have money?'' he asked.

''When they built this house, they did. It didn't last. Leola and Violet weren't ashamed of it. They had a small inheritance, but they both worked in a local bank for years. They were very pragmatic when it came to money.'' She caught herself. ''I'm sorry. I'm boring you.''

''Not yet. You're passionate about your work. I can see that.''

''This house, Leola and Violet—'' She glanced around the small room, not seeing what was there now, Nate thought, but what had been there. ''It really is hard to believe I'm done with all this.''

''Did you interview your father?''

''Definitely. He's between the Poe sisters and Wes in age. People have even speculated that he could be Wes's father, but—'' She shook her head. ''He's one in a long, long line of possibilities. There's just no evidence. It could have been anyone.''

''There's DNA these days.''

She smiled slightly. ''Yes, there is. Shall we go, or do you want to hear more? I hope it's been a distraction, at least.''

''I could do worse for distractions.'' And better, he thought, noting the curve of her hip. ''My uncle would have me wallpapering my sister Carine's old room.''

''Wallpapering could be therapeutic.''

''You haven't seen Gus's taste in wallpaper.''

She headed across the lawn and back onto the path along the river, warning him about mosquitoes, chiggers and ticks, telling him how the river was higher now, because of the dams, than it had been when the Poes had built the house after the Civil War.

No more pleasant, exaggerated southern accent. No more charm and laughter and relaxed talk.

Something about him had gotten under her skin. Nate had no idea what.

Finally she spun around at him on the narrow path, her face flushed with exertion and emotion. ''Has it occurred to you that the letter from New York has nothing to do with me and everything to do with you? That it's a ruse—the shooter or whoever sent it saw me in New York and decided to throw you off the scent.''

''I'm not on the scent. I'm one of the victims.''

''You don't expect me to believe that, do you? You're not here just out of a noble concern for my safety, or to put Rob's mind at ease. You're here because you think Joe Collins and his team are on the wrong track.''

Nate hated to see the fear back in her gray eyes. ''I don't know what track they're on.''

''Hector Sanchez. Agent Collins hasn't given up on him.''

''Because witnesses place him—''

''It doesn't matter. You think the answers to the shooting are here.''

''It's not that clear-cut,'' Nate said. He found himself wanting to see her smile, to ease her tension and fear—maybe because it would help ease his own. He smiled. ''Except for one thing. I doubt I'm putting Rob's mind at ease. He thinks I'm here because you're pretty.''

She gave him a direct look. ''Are you?''

He met her gaze, one she'd probably used to wither more than a few men by now, and shrugged. ''It doesn't hurt.''

She sighed. ''I see now why Juliet warned me about you.''

''Juliet? What did she say?''

''That you're hell on women.''

She turned and started back down the path, the late afternoon sun catching the pale highlights in her hair.

He grunted. ''And exactly what are you on men?''

She glanced back at him and smiled. ''Nothing. I've been too busy for men.''

Afraid of men, maybe. At least distrustful. She must have had a man or two who'd wanted her because of her looks and never saw beyond them to the woman underneath. Nate wasn't so sure he wasn't one of them—although the past few days had been a crash course in what made Sarah Dunnemore tick. The trauma of the attack on her brother had stripped away her defenses. Nate didn't know what the hell it had done to him.

''You're not busy anymore,'' he said to her back.

She stumbled, but grabbed a thin tree and righted herself. And pressed on without so much as a backward glance. Which was a good thing, because Nate didn't think he could hide just how much he wanted her. But she was a smart woman. She probably knew that.

Seventeen

~~~~~~

Even before Claude Rousseau spoke, Janssen realized the news from New York wasn't good. "Nate Winter left for Tennessee this morning," Rousseau said without preamble. "I don't know why."

Nicholas sat back in the black leather chair in the sitting room of his Herengracht suite. It was time to leave Holland and go back to Switzerland. But the Dunnemores were still here. Betsy.

"Sarah Dunnemore's a pretty young woman," he said.

"Agreed." But Rousseau, a meticulous though unimaginative man, would be merely stating a fact, not extrapolating from it any reason for Winter to head south. "Do you want me to go down there?"

"If you have to. What's Rob Dunnemore's condition?"

"Improving."

Why had someone shot him? Janssen stood up under the low, slanted ceiling and looked out his window at the street, bicyclists pedaling past the picturesque canal. His instincts seldom lead him astray.

"The FBI agent in charge of the investigation went to see Deputy Dunnemore again today," Rousseau went on. "I doubt it was a courtesy call."

"You think something's up?"

"I don't have any additional information. Until I do, it's my advice that you go back to Switzerland and lay low until this thing gets cleared up."

Always the thundercloud. It was why Rousseau would never be a real player. Nicholas opened an expensive humidor and lifted out a fat, fragrant cigar. "Find out why Sarah Dunnemore went back to Night's Landing. Find out why Deputy Winter is there. I don't want any interference in what you have to do. Again, no footsteps back to me. None. Understood?"

"Of course."

Janssen hung up and lit his cigar. Europeans, at least, weren't as fixated as Americans were on tobacco as one of the world's great evils—a small consolation to living in exile.

He had to trust that Rousseau was up to the job. Tax evasion was a nonviolent crime, one for which many people had at least some sympathy, but the attempted murder of two federal agents and the fear generated by a sniper attack in Central Park weren't something he wanted tied back to him in any way, even peripherally. He was under enough federal scrutiny as it was.

Rob Dunnemore and his sister were children of privilege and position, if not of immense wealth. Nicholas didn't know what to make of them. They'd never had to struggle. Neither had Betsy, but she was naturally gracious and well-mannered.

It was possible Sarah had seen him at the Rijks-museum. Likely, even.

Did it matter?

He was a fugitive simply because he'd failed to turn up for his trial on tax charges.

But the Dunnemores were friends with the president. They had their own reputations to protect. Having a wanted man turn up out of Betsy's past *would* be a cause for concern.

Nicholas savored the flavor of his cigar as he put his questions out of his mind. He debated whether he should take the risk of hiring a prostitute tonight, then envisioned himself with Betsy, beautiful Betsy.

Oh, God.

Choking on a mouthful of smoke, he ran into the bathroom and stabbed out his cigar in the sink. He drank from the faucet, pushing back the image. Even now, he could see her at eighteen, smiling at him, taking an interest in him. What a misfit he'd been. An outsider.

The tension of not knowing what was happening in New York was getting to him. He hated waiting.

A prostitute, even in permissive Amsterdam, brought with it certain hazards, to his health, to his mental well-being—to his freedom if he had the wrong prostitute, one who recognized him, who talked. It had happened once. But he'd dealt with the problem before it had got out of hand. As he had Charlene Brooker.

As he would deal with any problem in New York.

His phone rang again. It wouldn't be Rousseau. He had his orders. But few people had Janssen's number in Amsterdam.

He picked up the extension but said nothing.

"I'm going to have something you want within forty-eight hours," the voice on the other end, indistinguishably male or female, said. "Be prepared to wire five million U.S. dollars into my account. I'll call with the number when I have what you want."

Janssen sank back onto the leather chair. "Brooker?"

But the person on the other end had already disconnected.

Nicholas tensed the muscles in his hands to keep himself from throwing the phone across the room, instead carefully, quietly cradling it. Control was essential. He had to maintain his grasp of the situation at all times, or he'd never win.

What did the caller expect to have that was worth five million dollars?

Nicholas regretted having blurted a name. His men had lost track of Ethan Brooker weeks ago.

Was he responsible for the Central Park attack?

Was it a trap he'd set?

In hindsight, Janssen knew he'd handled the former Special Forces officer badly. By not presenting authorities with a suspect for Brooker's wife's death, Nicholas had put his entire operation—he'd put himself—in jeopardy. The only answer now was to have Ethan Brooker killed. The sooner the better.

Five million dollars. It was ridiculous.

Janssen didn't call Rousseau back to tell him about the anonymous call. It wouldn't affect his orders. He knew what he needed to do. If the trail in New York led to Ethan Brooker, distraught widower, army officer bent on revenge, then Rousseau would deal with it.

Leaning back in his chair, Janssen listened to the noise of the street below him. While he wanted to recapture the urge to have a whore, he couldn't. He could only imagine his mother on her death bed in northern Virginia, calling for her only son—her only child—as she sobbed herself quietly into the grave.

He let the tears flow unchecked. There was no one to see them, no one in his life who cared or understood that he'd loved his mother.

"Why?" she'd cried to him over the phone. *"Why didn't you just pay your taxes like everyone else?"*

But his life was so much more complicated than his mother had ever been able to grasp.

Now he didn't even dare send money for her headstone.

The federal government would hound him forever. They'd never let him come home. They'd slap him in cuffs at his poor mother's grave and stick him in jail until he stood trial. He'd added how many years to his maximum sentence by running? Five years, ten years? He didn't even know.

His lawyers had urged him to surrender to U.S. authorities. They'd have been relieved if he'd turned himself over to Rob Dunnemore at the Rijksmuseum.

But Janssen knew if he went to trial, he'd be convicted, and if he went to prison, he'd never get out.

If his enemies didn't rat him out, his so-called friends would. One way or the other, the feds would figure out that tax evasion was only the tip of the iceberg when it came to his crimes.

And once he was vulnerable, friend and enemy

alike would find a way to kill him. He wouldn't last a month in prison. The federal authorities couldn't protect him.

No one would care that he planned to do good with the fortune he'd amassed. If the ends didn't fully justify the means, he knew he wasn't a bad man. Look at Rockefeller, Vanderbilt, J.P. Morgan, Hearst. Had they led exemplary lives? They all had skeletons in their closets.

"Mama, Mama," he whispered. "What do I do?"

But there was no answer. She was dead, gone forever.

Eighteen

~~~~~~~~~~~~~~~~~~~~~~~~~~~~

Juliet carried a monstrous spider plant to her kitchen sink and wondered when and where this weird, irritating conversation with Joe Collins would end. She turned on the spray faucet, aware of the senior FBI special agent watching her from the table. The doorman, none too happy, had called ten minutes ago to announce her unexpected "guest." Collins had requested a bit of her time to ask her a few questions, and when she'd said okay—what other choice was there?—he'd parked himself at her table and told her to continue with what she was doing.

Watering plants. Lots of plants.

The life of a real, live deputy U.S. marshal.

Since Collins was from New York, he had to know that even a small apartment on the Upper West Side was still an expensive undertaking, well beyond what she could afford. It wasn't so great by suburban standards. The bathroom had a view of a brick wall. The living-room windows were constantly blackened by soot. There was no garbage disposal. But the building had a fantastic location, it had an elevator, it had a doorman—what was not to like?

And, for her, it was damn near free thanks to a generous friend who was in L.A. on some theater project for at least six months.

Then Juliet, her plants and her fish would have to find a new home.

She'd explained the friend in L.A. before Collins even asked, which she regretted. It made her sound defensive, as if he had reason to think she was on the take or something.

He fiddled with an unlit cigarette. "All these plants are yours?"

"All mine."

"You like New York?"

"I like the work I'm doing here."

"You were here first, before Deputy Dunnemore."

She wanted to ask Collins what the hell her relationship with Rob had to do with who freaking shot him in Central Park, but decided that wasn't the way to go. Stay cool. Answer the agent's questions. She squirted more water down into the spider plant's roots. "I've been in New York eighteen months. Rob got here in February. It was hard to pretend I'm not as driven as I am when we were working out of the same district." Using her fingers, she wiped dust off the dampened variegated spikes. "We called it quits in March."

"Not that I asked," Collins said.

She glanced around at him. "You were going to."

"How did you two meet?"

"Rob came up here from Baltimore to collect a prisoner."

"It'd be tough, I think, being married to someone doing the same job as me. My wife's a high-school guidance counselor."

Juliet sighed. There'd never been talk of marriage with her and Rob. "Good for her."

"Hardest job in the world. These kids—you just hurt for some of them. Shit lives, shit choices." Collins rolled his cigarette between his fingers. "Dunnemore. He was born with a silver spoon in his mouth."

"Silver plate, not pure silver. The Dunnemores aren't rich. They're not poor, either, but the father doesn't come from money. He was assistant secretary of state once, but, hell, I don't think he made much more than we do."

That drew a half smile from Collins. "You ever make it to the family home in Tennessee? Night's Landing. Sounds like a nice place, doesn't it?"

"No." She gave the spider plant a final, hard spray. "Never made it."

"Sore subject?"

Rob had invited her down for a weekend in March, a month before his vacation in Amsterdam. Said they could get a jump on spring. She'd worked instead. She could have gotten off—they both knew it.

End of romance.

"Not at all," she told Collins. "Just didn't work out."

"Nate Winter's down there with the sister. You get a feel for her when she was up here?"

"Nice. Smart. Pretty. Impulsive. Agent Collins—"

"She got an anonymous letter in the mail."

Juliet grabbed another plant, an orchid she was sur-

An Important Message
from the Editors

Dear Reader,

Because you've chosen to read one of our fine books, we'd like to say "thank you"! And, as a special way to thank you, we're offering you a choice of two more of the books you love so well, and a surprise gift to send you — absolutely FREE!

Please enjoy them with our compliments...

Pam Powers

Peel off Seal and
Place Inside...

THE EDITOR'S "THANK YOU" FREE GIFTS INCLUDE:

▶ 2 Romance OR 2 Suspense books

▶ An exciting surprise gift

YES! I have placed my Editor's "thank you" Free Gifts seal in the space provided above. Please send me the 2 FREE books which I have selected, and my FREE Mystery Gift. I understand that I am under no obligation to purchase anything further, as explained on the back and opposite page.

PLACE FREE GIFTS SEAL HERE

▶ DETACH AND MAIL CARD TODAY!

Check one:

ROMANCE
193 MDL DVFJ   393 MDL DVFL

SUSPENSE
192 MDL DVFH   392 MDL DVFK

FIRST NAME

LAST NAME

ADDRESS

APT.#

CITY

STATE/PROV.

ZIP/POSTAL CODE

BUSINESS REPLY MAIL

FIRST-CLASS MAIL   PERMIT NO. 717-003   BUFFALO, NY

POSTAGE WILL BE PAID BY ADDRESSEE

THE READER SERVICE
3010 WALDEN AVE
PO BOX 1341
BUFFALO NY 14240-8571

NO POSTAGE
NECESSARY
IF MAILED
IN THE
UNITED STATES

prised wasn't dead yet. As much as she loved plants, they had to be hardy to survive her lifestyle and the tough conditions of her borrowed New York apartment.

Collins carefully returned his cigarette to his pack, but she noticed it was bent, bits of tobacco spilling out onto the table. She'd let him smoke. She didn't care. But it broke house rules. For all she knew, her friend had little cigarette smoke alarms all through the place.

She set the orchid in the sink. She forgot what kind it was, but it wasn't that pretty when it was blooming and was truly ugly when it wasn't. She gave an audible sigh. "Okay, is this where I'm supposed to ask 'what anonymous letter'?" But she immediately regretted her irritable remark. "Sorry. I guess I'm as nerved up about this whole business as anyone."

"Feel like you're next?"

"No, goddammit. What a thing to say."

He shrugged, then told her about the letter. Sarah's call. Nate's flight to Tennessee. How she said she'd torn apart the phones looking for taps. Juliet smiled at that one—she had a feeling that, never mind the delicate gold rings and blond good looks, Sarah Dunnemore would do just about anything.

"You think this letter's for real?" Juliet asked.

"Lab guys are checking it out. It was postmarked New York."

"What, you think one of us sent it? Rob, Nate, me? The chief deputy?"

Collins didn't answer.

Juliet groaned. Her and her mouth. "Any more questions?"

"Nah." He got heavily to his feet. "Thanks for your time, Deputy."

After he left, she banged her head on the door a couple of times just to see if she could knock some sense into herself. *Jesus.* How not to handle an FBI interrogation.

That was what it was, too. Collins had asked her if he could talk to her. She'd said yes.

It wasn't a courtesy visit. He was an FBI agent in charge of a high-profile investigation. The man was just doing his job.

And he'd been very deliberate about it. No slipups. He'd told her only what he'd wanted her to know—what he wanted to see her reaction to.

He'd played her beautifully.

But who cared? She had nothing to hide. He had to work all the angles of the investigation at once. Crazy ones, even. Like maybe Rob or Nate had screwed up and done something that'd gotten them shot. Like maybe she had a vendetta against Rob and had hired someone to take him out.

Except he hadn't died, and neither had Nate.

Maybe dead wasn't the point. Maybe dead *or* wounded was the point.

Why?

The letter Sarah had received...what was *that* all about?

"Not your problem."

Juliet flipped all the locks on the door and picked up an ivy plant with crispy leaves. She must have missed that one her last go-round with the spray faucet. But it still showed signs of life. Her brothers would tell her she was losing her touch—she'd always had a green thumb.

She noticed a little goldfish belly-up in one of the tanks.

Damn.

She set the ivy on the sink and found a slotted spoon, scooped out the dead fish and flushed it down the toilet, then flipped the lid and sat down.

"Oh, shit."

But she couldn't stop the tears. For the first time since she'd heard the news about the shooting, she sat and cried. She'd loved Rob. Totally. And it hadn't worked out, just like all her other relationships. Then he'd almost died. He was still in rotten shape. Miserable, in pain. He had to be scared out of his mind for his sister.

Would he turn to *her* for help?

Hell, no.

She looked out the window at the brick wall and listened to the gurgle of her aquariums. This was it. She was going to spend the rest of her life with a bunch of plants and fish for company.

And her work. God knows she'd have her work.

Nineteen

❧⟨∞⟩❧

Ethan lit his first cigarette in eight months. Charlene used to harp on him for smoking, but he'd always believed something would get him before smoking did.

Something got her, instead.

Someone.

It was dusk, the sky muted and purplish against the darkening landscape of trees as he walked up the path from the river and across the overgrown lawn of the Poe house. The mosquitoes were out. One buzzed around his head. He heard crickets chirping in the tall grass, boats puttering down on the river. He had his Smith & Wesson strapped to his right ankle and one of his Brownings tucked in a belt holster under his Titans shirt. No damn overalls tonight.

He didn't plan on killing anyone, but that didn't mean he wasn't prepared.

There were rumors on the river that the Poe House Trust was considering selling off some of the acreage lots to country-western music stars, to raise money for a visitors' center. But even understated development would change the isolated, rural character of Night's Landing, make it harder to visualize the kind of lives the Poes had led there since the Civil War. The rumors weren't true, but if they were, Ethan figured Sarah Dunnemore would have a fit. Yet locals also said she couldn't stay steeped in the Poe house the way she had been for some years. She had to leave its future to other people, people who were more objective, who didn't have such a personal involvement.

Leola and Violet Poe had died within two years of each other more than a decade ago. They'd lived to see the boy they'd raised move into the Tennessee governor's mansion, but not the White House. People said they'd had mixed feelings about John Wesley— that was what the sisters had always called him— entering politics, even leaving Night's Landing.

Ethan ducked past twin dogwoods in the front yard and headed up the back road that led to a down-on-its-luck fishing camp. After a hundred feet the pavement turned to gravel. He could hear his running shoes crunching, but stealth wasn't an issue, not tonight. He didn't care who the hell saw him, who heard him.

It was an old-fashioned camp with a row of a half-dozen, one-room cabins with shed roofs and no frills. Conroy Fontaine struck Ethan as a frills type. But maybe he was saving himself for when he hit it big with his book. Maybe he'd do damn near anything, including sleep on a moldy horsehair mattress, to get what dirt he could on President Poe.

Poe hadn't lived in Night's Landing in years. He and his wife had a place in Nashville. Nothing huge. A Victorian they'd fixed up. The Poe House wouldn't be open to the public for another couple years, at least. By then, maybe someone would have torched the fishing camp up the road. Each cabin had its own rusted lawn chair and ancient charcoal grill. The smell of smoke and trout hung in the air, fishy, not anything Ethan would want to eat.

He stopped at the main office and asked a very overweight woman with a long, greasy gray braid which cabin Conroy Fontaine had rented. She didn't hesitate. "Last one on the left."

Ethan passed three empty cabins before he reached the last one on the left. A light was on. The front door was open. He could see Fontaine sitting at a table in the front window. Ethan threw down his cigarette, stamped it out and kicked in the screen door.

He grabbed a stunned Fontaine up off his chair, twisted his right arm around to the small of his back and shoved him face first into the refrigerator. "Who the fuck are you?"

"All right. Calm down." Fontaine's voice squeaked, but he still had the southern accent, which meant it was probably for real. "We can talk."

Ethan patted him down. No weapons, but the guy was fit as hell. "Sit. Move any way I don't like, you lose teeth. Come at me, you're in the hospital. Try to hurt me, you're dead."

"Heavens, man. You're some gardener."

Bravado. Fontaine gave himself a little shake, as if to loosen himself up, and sat back at the table. It was rickety, covered with a cigarette-burned yellow vinyl cloth.

Ethan reached over to a stack of papers on the table

and lifted out a picture of a silver-haired man. A mug shot, pulled off the Internet.

Nicholas Janssen.

Ethan shoved the picture at Fontaine. "Who's this?"

"You know already, don't you?"

Janssen was an international fugitive, a rich idiot who was supposed to be in prison for tax evasion by now. Three weeks after Charlene's murder, Ethan had followed Betsy Dunnemore to an Amsterdam café where she'd run into Nicholas Janssen. Accidentally, on purpose—Ethan didn't know which. She and Janssen had coffee. Talked. Heatedly. Then went in separate directions. Before her death, Charlene had met with Betsy Dunnemore. It was one of the pieces Ethan had. He knew it fit into his puzzle—he just wasn't sure where.

"I ask the questions," he told Fontaine.

"When we're done here, I'm calling the police."

"Fine with me. Your interest in this guy?"

"Journalistic. I think there's a connection between him and President Poe."

Ethan sneered at the guy in disgust. "You really are a bottom feeder."

Fontaine rubbed the elbow that Ethan had jerked. "Why are you picking on me? I've done nothing. Are you upset over the feds who were crawling through the Dunnemore house today? I was going to stop by and talk Sarah into sharing her prune cake, but when I saw them, I thought better of it." He made a face. "I'm not proud of myself, I have to say. A better friend would have made sure she was all right."

Ethan had made himself scarce when the feds were

at the house, but only after he'd figured out what was wrong—Sarah had received a threatening note. He could picture it, the letter with the New York postmark. He'd pulled it out of the mailbox himself and set it on the table.

He should have opened it.

Sarah hadn't come to him for help—why should she? He was the mild-mannered, songwriting good ol' boy.

The feds hadn't talked to him. They hadn't talked to Fontaine.

Not yet, anyway.

Ethan glanced at Janssen's handsome face. "Does Sarah Dunnemore know this guy?"

"I don't know. I'm trying to find out, but it's—" He paused, choosing his words. "It's a sensitive subject. He and her mother..." He drifted off.

"You think they're having an affair? You really are scum."

"He's a lonely man. Janssen lives in Switzerland surrounded by bodyguards—he's afraid federal agents will drop out of nowhere and kidnap him back to the U.S. to stand trial. His mother died over the winter. He couldn't come back for her funeral." Fontaine stretched out his legs, folded his hands on his stomach as if he had nothing to fear. "I don't believe Mr. Janssen thinks things through, do you? He'd fit in around here."

"You've been sniffing around Janssen and the Dunnemores for this book of yours?"

"I made a whirlwind trip to Europe in April. A tax-deductible research trip. Rob Dunnemore was in Amsterdam visiting his parents. He snubbed me.

Sarah hadn't arrived yet.'' Fontaine spoke matter-of-factly, as if this sort of thing was par for the course in his line of work. ''I decided to try my luck again here in Night's Landing. I was here briefly last fall, trying to decide whether or not I even wanted to take on this project. Now, Mr. Brooker, I believe I've answered all the questions I'm going to. Whatever angles I'm pursuing are my business. I'm a legitimate journalist.''

''Bullshit. What are you, a political hack looking for dirt on the president?'' Ethan didn't wait for an answer. ''A bounty hunter? Is there a reward for reeling in Nicholas Janssen?''

Fontaine glanced up at him. ''What's your interest in Mr. Janssen?''

''None. I read the papers.''

''I've told you what I know. You have no reason to behave this way, barge in here, threaten me—''

''I haven't threatened you. I've just scared the hell out of you.'' Ethan gave him a cold grin. ''There's a difference, you know.''

''Please, leave, Mr. Brooker. Don't make me call the police.''

Ethan was tempted to toss the place, but he doubted he'd find anything that would lead him anywhere but down more blind alleys and to more dead ends. Whether Conroy Fontaine was a legitimate journalist, a bottom-feeding journalist or something else entirely, he had his own agenda in Night's Landing. He wanted Ethan to find the picture. Fontaine expected one of them to confront him at some point. Sarah Dunnemore. Nate Winter. He was prepared. Stir the pot a little by having Fontaine's pictures at the ready. See how people reacted. It was a tactic Ethan understood.

Fontaine fingered one of the cigarette burns on the tablecloth. "I won't call the police this time. I understand you're protective of our fair-haired Dr. Dunnemore. Who wouldn't be? I've been trying to soften her up so she'll talk to me, but I have to say, I've come under her spell myself." His affection for Sarah seemed genuine. "She's a lovely woman, inside and out."

"She's got a marshal with her. I'd mind my p's and q's if I were you."

Ethan took the picture of Janssen with him and almost ripped the damn door off its hinges on his way out.

Sometimes he wasn't direct. This time, he was.

Fat lot of good it did him.

On his way out of the camp, he threw his pack of cigarettes to a wiry old guy with a lit cigarette hanging off his lower lip. "Quitting?" The old man coughed. "Good luck to you, fella. I've quit every New Year's for the past thirty years."

Ethan kept walking, getting himself back under control, one muscle—one cell—at a time.

Charlene...

Conroy Fontaine could be a reporter unraveling the same story Ethan was, finding the pieces and shreds that kept eluding him. He just had to be patient, to think things through. As evidenced by his behavior tonight, he thought, neither was his style.

He could almost see his wife smile in agreement.

Dinner was a chicken-and-vegetable casserole Sarah dug out of the freezer and prune cake, which reminded Nate of Gus's applesauce spice cake, for dessert. But Sarah didn't eat a bite, just stared at her plate, then bolted from the table and ran down the hall and out the front door.

Post-trauma stress. The past few days had just gut-punched her.

Nate knew the feeling. His mind would drift off, and he'd see Rob jerk up with the impact of the bullet. He'd feel a pain in his arm and his heart would race. His training helped, his experience and knowledge of the mind and body's normal reactions to a trauma.

He gave Sarah a minute, then followed her down to the dock.

The evening air was cool and the breeze smelled, tasted, of the river. Sarah was sitting at the end of the dock, her shoes at her side, her feet dangling in the water.

The last red rays of the dying sunset hit her hair, making it look golden, almost fiery.

Nate walked onto the old wood dock. She splashed water with her feet. "Not worried about snakes biting your toes?" he asked.

She shook her head, not looking around at him.

He'd never done WITSEC work. He didn't think he could stand the emotions of witnesses who had to take on new identities because of what they knew. Some of the witnesses were unsavory characters themselves. But they were human beings. Their families, who also had to give up the lives they knew, were human beings. It was what Nate always tried to remember as a professional law enforcement officer— that regardless of what they'd done, what punishment they were due for their actions, the people he dealt with were human beings. He'd had that conversation with Sister Maria a dozen times. He'd have had it again yesterday about Hector Sanchez if Sarah hadn't followed him. Sister Maria would have served him strong coffee and had him sit for a while, talk to him about the young man who was now dead, whom she believed with all her heart and soul—which was saying something—hadn't shot anyone in Central Park.

Not that Sanchez wasn't incapable of being used, bribed, set up and discarded. Just that he hadn't shot anyone.

Nate sighed. He shouldn't have kissed Sarah earlier. He should have resisted. They both had too much on their minds.

"Sarah…"

"I held up on the plane to New York." Her voice was quiet, steady, her accent hardly detectable. "I held up in the hospital. I held up more or less in Central Park when I recognized the man from the Rijksmuseum. Even when I got that note—I didn't go completely to pieces."

"It's okay to go to pieces."

"You don't."

"I almost did last fall when my sisters got themselves into messes. It's different when it's people you care about who are hurting, when it's not just the job."

She kicked her feet up out of the water and stared at her toes, painted a pretty lavender. "Is being here just 'the job' for you?"

He felt awkward, out of his element, but she had a way of cutting to the heart of matters, a directness he seldom encountered in the women he dated. "No, actually, I'm probably the last person who should be here, seeing how I was with your brother when he was shot."

"You were shot, too."

"Barely."

"Barely counts." She glanced up at him again, the fading light catching the shine of tears on her cheeks, in her eyes. "It was an awful day for you, too. More so than for me."

"It's not a competition."

He kicked off his running shoes and pulled off his socks, hoping his damn feet didn't stink. He rolled up his pant legs and sat next to her. "Water cold?"

She managed a smile. "Not by New Hampshire standards."

Indeed, the coppery river was refreshing, not nearly as cold as a midsummer New Hampshire stream. "We're lucky the water ever gets this warm at home."

"I've never been to the White Mountains." Strands of hair had caught in her tears and matted to her cheeks, but she didn't seem to notice. "I understand they're beautiful. Or aren't they beautiful to you because of your parents?"

That natural directness again. Nate shook his head. "No, they're still beautiful. And still dangerous. It can be hard to predict conditions these days. Thirty years ago—there was no way my parents could have known they'd fall and get stuck in freezing rain."

"So it wasn't their fault—not that fault matters to a child."

"It was an accident. It was traumatic, but they weren't murdered. They didn't have any enemies."

"Is that why you became a marshal? Because you could make sense of going after fugitives?"

He smiled at her. "I became a marshal because they gave me a job."

She took an audible breath. "I'm sorry. I'm being too intense—"

"My parents led the lives they wanted to lead. They didn't mean to leave my sisters and me orphans. It just happened. My uncle did a good job raising us. We had happy childhoods. We'll always feel the loss and wonder what might have been, but it worked out okay." He let his feet drop deeper into the murky water. Unlike Sarah, he thought about snakes. "A part of you must be ticked off at Rob for getting shot."

She jerked around at him. "How could you say such a thing? That's absurd. It's not as if he got shot just to upset me."

"But he has a dangerous profession. He wants the tough assignments. He's known for it. That's why he's in New York." Nate didn't let her off the hook. "You've only been home for a week—"

"I'm not angry with my brother for putting me in this position."

She jumped up, splashing him with water. She scooped up her shoes and stomped off the dock, leaving wet footprints behind her and walking barefoot through the grass.

Nate lifted his feet out of the water. He should have had a second piece of prune cake and let her have her cry. He'd never been good at any kind of debriefing.

She spun around at him. It was almost dark now,

her slim figure a silhouette against the background of her home. "Anyway, you think Rob was shot because he's a Dunnemore, not because he's a marshal."

"Maybe both. And it doesn't matter what I think."

"That's right," she snapped, "it doesn't."

Her emotions were raw, and she was on edge. *Don't let things fester,* Gus used to tell him and his sisters as kids. *You need to cry, cry. You need to throw something, throw something. Just don't hurt anyone.*

Nate had seldom cried, and he'd never thrown anything.

He pulled his feet out of the water, stuffed his socks into his shoes and followed Sarah onto the cool grass. "When I was a kid," he said, "I'd see my sisters crying for my parents, and I'd want to fix it. I held back my own grief and anger because I didn't want to upset them." He sighed, wincing at his lame words. "Christ, this is stupid. I'm sorry. I never could do a damn thing to make Antonia and Carine feel better, either."

"You don't have to make me feel better." There was no sting in her words. "Some things no one can fix. You just have to go through them. I'll get through this mess. So will you." Her sudden smile took him by surprise, lit up her eyes. "More prune cake?"

"I won't make myself sick?"

"No one's ever made themselves sick on Granny Dunnemore's prune cake."

She practically ran up to the house.

Nate watched her in amazement, then warned himself to be careful. To go slow, to remember his own raw state. But as he followed her in the house, all he could think of was the feel of her mouth on his, her soft skin under his hands, her body pressed up against him.

Fortunately, Conroy Fontaine was at the back door.

Twenty

～ꙮ～

Sarah went straight to the sink, turned on the faucet and got out the dented aluminum dishpan, squirting in detergent as she tried to pull herself together. "Come on in," she called to Conroy. "The door's open."

"I'm sorry to bother you."

"No, it's okay. I'm just doing dishes. My parents have never seen fit to invest in a dishwasher." She manufactured a smile. "But Dad has a state-of-the-art computer upstairs. He *loves* computers."

She wondered if her cheerfulness sounded phony, if Conroy would excuse or even notice that she'd been crying. She had no idea how she'd get through the night alone with Nate in the house. She was convinced he was half the reason she'd lost it. Being around him had a way of bringing her emotions to the surface—even ones she wanted to hold at bay. She was usually more reserved around men, always believing she was destined for quiet, civilized relationships.

"I suppose our not having a dishwasher is a tidbit

you can use in your book,'' she added as Conroy
stepped inside.

He stayed close to the back door, not sitting down.
Sarah detected a strain in his normally easy manner.
''Where's your deputy?'' he asked.

''He was just down on the dock. I imagine he's
right behind me.''

''Sarah—'' Conroy narrowed his gaze on her,
wincing. ''Oh, dear. I see I've come at a bad time. Is
it Rob? He hasn't take a turn for the worse, has he?''

''No, no, it's nothing like that. He's okay. Doing
much better, in fact.'' She dumped dishes into the hot,
soapy water. She had to look like a wreck. ''And I'm
okay. The stress of the past few days just got to me,
that's all.''

''I understand.'' He seemed awkward, shoved his
hands into the pockets of his loose-fitting khakis. He
wore a button-down blue oxford cloth shirt, the
sleeves rolled up to his elbows, a sports watch on his
wrist. He looked as if he'd been at his book all day.
''Look, I know my timing couldn't be worse, but I
need to talk to you about your property manager.''

''Ethan? Why, what's up?'' She decided to let the
dishes soak and grabbed a knife out of a drawer.
''Here, sit down. I'll cut you a piece of prune cake.''

''I can't stay.'' He smiled nervously. ''But I'll take
a piece with me.''

Nate materialized in the hall doorway, leaning
against it.

''Evening, Deputy,'' Conroy said.

''Mr. Fontaine.''

''Oh, just Conroy will be fine. I'm going to sample
a piece of Sarah's prune cake.''

"It came out okay." She cut the cake, easing the fat slice onto a plate. "So, what's the story with Ethan?"

"Having the authorities here today must have unnerved him. I don't want to pry—"

"It's all right." Sarah found a square of tinfoil in another drawer and laid the cake slice on it. "My brother's situation is receiving a lot of media attention. Consequently, I had mail here when I arrived. Some of it was kind of bizarre, and the FBI wanted to take a look."

"I see. No Secret Service?"

She sensed, more than saw Nate stiffening, but she reminded herself that Conroy was a journalist—and possibly not a very reputable one. She didn't want him selling the story of her anonymous letter to the tabloids. "I have no idea, there were so many. I know this situation must be upsetting for everyone around here. It certainly is for me."

"Some of the old-timers around here are saying President Poe would drop everything on your say-so and fly down—"

"I doubt that, Conroy. And I have parents. They're heading to New York tomorrow."

He smiled. "The point is, the president is that fond of you."

"No. That's what people are telling you. You don't know it for a fact."

"Ah, the Ph.D. at work."

She handed the wrapped cake to him. "President Poe has been like a second father to me. I'm very, very lucky in that regard."

"I'm sure you are," Conroy said softly.

Sarah climbed onto a stool at the counter. He was just two feet in front of her, one hand on the screen door. It was dark out now, a cricket chirping loudly nearby. "Are you going to tell me about Ethan?" she asked.

"I will. Look—" He shifted, sighing uncomfortably. "I don't want to be the bearer of bad news, but the guy's out of control."

"Ethan?" Sarah couldn't conceal her surprise. "What did he do?"

"He barged into my cabin earlier and interrogated me about who I am and what I'm doing here. I think he was just being protective of you, but it was unsettling. I was going to call the police." He shrugged. "I decided you don't need that."

Nate stepped into the kitchen and went over to the sink, lifting a sopping dishrag out of the suds. That seemed to bring Conroy up short. She had an armed federal agent on the premises. But Nate said nothing, and Sarah took a breath and eased off the stool. "What exactly happened?"

Conroy hesitated, then continued. "He kicked in my front door while I was working and asked questions. I was shocked. I'm just doing this simple pop biography of the president." He gave a ragged smile. "Which is what I told Mr. Brooker."

"Ethan seems so mild mannered."

"He wasn't mild mannered when he slammed me against the refrigerator."

Nate silently washed dishes, no visible indication he was even listening to her conversation with Conroy. But Sarah knew better. "I apologize. I imagine he's just rattled by what's been going on. He was here when I got the call from Rob in Central Park. It was very upsetting, and perhaps he overreacted.'' She stopped herself there, because she didn't really know Ethan Brooker and couldn't vouch for him. "I'll speak to him.''

"If you don't mind, I'd rather you didn't bring my name up with him. He makes me nervous. If you could just reassure him that he's supposed to take care of the property, not you." Conroy broke off with a shrug. "It might help."

"I'll do that.''

He held up the foil-wrapped prune cake. "Thanks. I'll let you know how it compares to my granny's recipe.''

After he left, Sarah didn't say a word to Nate and marched up the front hall, fully intending to head to Ethan's cottage and confront him about his behavior.

He was already on the porch.

And Nate was right behind her, drying his hands with a dish towel.

She pulled open the door. "Ethan, Conroy Fontaine was just here—"

"I know, ma'am. I saw him. I'm sorry, ma'am." He spoke directly to her, ignoring Nate. "I lost my head. Mr. Fontaine has been sneaking around the area, asking everybody questions, and with your brother getting shot and everything, I went over to check him out. He wasn't very nice." Ethan shrugged his big shoulders. "Usually it takes more than that for me to lose my temper.''

"We've all been under a lot of stress," Sarah said. "I'll apologize to him.''

"I'd stay away from him," Nate said. "Let him

cool off before you end up in a holding cell at the local jail.''

Sarah nodded. ''We all need a few days to calm down.''

''All right, Miss Sarah. If you say so.''

He said good-night and shambled back down the porch steps.

Nate stiffly shut the front door, his eyes as intense as she'd seen them yet. But he smiled suddenly, surprising her. ''Now, aren't you glad I'm here?''

''In their own ways, they're both looking out for me.''

''Don't count on it.''

''Such a cynic. What are you going to do?''

''Finish the dishes. Unpack.'' He looked at her, then touched a finger just under her eye, where it was still moist from her crying jag. ''You okay?''

She nodded. Just that slight touch had her reeling, but she tried not to let it show. ''You know, I think—'' She smiled, starting back to the kitchen. ''I'm going to make fried pies.''

There had to be dried apricots in the pantry. Fried apricot pies were one of her father's favorites. Even her mother, who was no cook, had learned the tricky art of making them.

Nate didn't say a word, just followed Sarah back to the kitchen. She rummaged around the pantry's open shelves.

There. Dried apricots, unopened.

She reached behind bags of dried beans and pulled out the box of apricots, then returned to the counter. Nate had rolled up his sleeves and was up to his forearms in dishwater.

"Let me do those," she said. "Your arm—you were shot, you know."

"I can handle doing dishes."

The telephone rang, and Sarah froze. She didn't know why. Did she think it was the bastard who'd sent her the note, calling to tell her he knew she'd blabbed to the feds? She had no idea what she was thinking. Rob. Had something happened to him?

Nate dried off one hand and picked up the kitchen extension. "Dunnemore residence. Yes, sir, she's right here." He handed the phone to Sarah, his blue eyes piercing, unyielding, no hint of a smile now. "It's President Poe."

Sarah took the phone, delighted—relieved—that it was a friend. "How are you? Thank you for calling."

"I'm well. How are *you?* And who was that who answered?"

"That was Nate Winter, the other deputy who was shot with Rob. He flew down here this morning."

"So I heard. I should have said something to him. Please give him my best, will you?"

"Of course."

"I was told about the note, Sarah," Wes Poe said, his tone serious now, not just that of a family friend checking on her. "I'm worried about you. I'd put a Secret Service detail on you—"

"No, please, don't."

She could sense his smile. "I knew that's what you'd say. At least Deputy Winter is there with you. They say he's one of the best. Rock solid."

"He's not really here in an official capacity. He's just—" She glanced at him watching her. "Here."

"Well, it's reassuring that he is there. I understand

your parents are heading to New York sometime to-morrow. That'll do you and Rob good. I know you're both grown and tough as nails, but, still, it's always nice to see your folks. Ev and I can't wait to see you ourselves.''

"Same here."

He was a natural politician in the best sense, gen-uine, able to make people feel at ease in his presence but still aware that he was president—and he was straightforward. Nonetheless, he had a gift for em-bellishment, a flare for story, that sometimes made Sarah wonder if it were more a Night's Landing trait than just a Dunnemore trait. He didn't employ it in policy decisions, only in playing the political game. But who could blame him? He was the self-made man who was found on a doorstep as a baby and raised by two maiden sisters. He wasn't without fault. He'd fight for what he believed in.

"I've got to go. Good night, Sarah. Ev and I love you dearly."

"I love you both, too. Give her my best."

After she hung up, Nate grunted. "I didn't expect him to dial his own damn phone."

"He said he's heard you're rock solid."

Nate didn't look thrilled. "I didn't necessarily want to pop up on the president's radar screen. He must be hoping this situation doesn't end up biting him in the ass."

"At this point I don't think he cares. He's as wor-ried about Rob as any of us."

"He offered to put a Secret Service detail on you?"

"I turned him down." She smiled. "I've got you."

She didn't know why she said it, why she said it

the way she did, so quietly, with her eyes on him. Before he could react, she tore open her box of dried apricots.

Dump them into a pan, add a little water, cook them until soft.

Then mash them.

Add spices.

Which spices? Cinnamon. For sure, cinnamon.

I can't think...

She grabbed her apron, realized her hands were shaking.

Nate slipped in behind her and took the apron from her hands, setting it on the counter, then catching her fingers into his and pulling her toward him. "If I'm complicating your life..."

"You are. But I don't mind." She smiled, relishing the feel of his hands in hers. "I can't be doing a whole lot for your life."

"More than you know. I thought your brother was dead the other day. I'd never met you. I'd never seen you cry. If I'd imagined you here when he called you, I don't know if I'd have made it through that day."

"You would have. You did your job."

"I'm not doing it now." He scooped one hand up her bare arm. "I'm breaking all the rules."

"But you're not here officially. You're recuperating."

He gave her a dubious smile. "Recuperating. Right."

She didn't want to hear more and placed her hands on his shoulders. He was tall, and she almost had to stand on her tiptoes to reach him. Stretching upward, she found his mouth with hers, felt his instant response—she hadn't surprised him as much as she might have thought. She wondered if he could see into her and recognize her desire for what it was, a physical yearning, an unresolved tension, a need she'd felt building from the moment she'd spotted him in the hospital, maybe even from the moment he'd picked up Rob's cell phone after he'd collapsed, after they'd both been shot.

Their kiss deepened, eliminating any thought she might have had that he'd want to hold back. He dropped his right arm—his uninjured arm—to her hips and lifted her onto him, pressing her against the counter, her shirt lifting. She could feel his arm hot against her bare skin.

The lights were off in the kitchen. It was fully dark now.

He drew back from their kiss and raised her shirt, easing it off, exposing her to the cool night air.

''Sarah…''

His fingertips skimmed over her breasts, her nipples hard inside her flimsy bra.

She tried to undo the buttons on his shirt, but she didn't get very far. Her movements were awkward, fumbling. Too much, she thought. She'd done too much today.

He kissed one breast, lingering there as he unbuttoned his own shirt, pulling it off, casting it to the floor. She marveled at his skill even as she went breathless at the feel of his tongue.

His chest and shoulders were muscular, his stomach flat. His arm was still bandaged, but there was no sign of blood.

He shifted to her other breast, and she heard his

belt unbuckle, his pants unzip, and her head spun with the reality of what they were about to do. But she wanted the release, had never been so desperate for sex. That was all this was, she warned herself. Sex. A physical release.

She didn't care.

Somehow, he got her pants off, and she was impatient now, panting, a little shocked at her own behavior. "We can't—are we going to make love on the kitchen floor?"

Without answering, he lifted her off the counter, oblivious to any pain he might be feeling in his arm, and lowered her onto him. She gasped, falling back against the counter, but he didn't let go, plunged himself deeper into her.

She'd never in her life done anything like it.

A half-dozen hard thrusts, and she couldn't stand it anymore. She came in one great wave, moaning as he kept thrusting, going limp, spent, as he kept pulsing into her, until he shuddered, his body tensing, then going still.

He remained inside her, holding her. She could feel his heart beating. They both were sweating. "Never on the kitchen floor," he whispered, then kissed her softly and set her back down.

He had the grace to gather up her clothes and hand them to her before scooping up his own, pulling on his pants.

"Your arm?" she asked.

"Throbbing." He smiled back at her. "But it's a good kind of throb."

She felt herself blushing, but tried to stop it. She

was thirty-two years old, a Ph.D., a woman not completely inexperienced in relationships.

But Nate was different, and it wasn't just the headiness of the moment at work. He was hard-edged, impatient, no-nonsense—it was easy to find him sexy. A hard-ass federal agent. A Yankee mountainman.

Yet she'd seen his concern, his kindness, his humor. With Rob, with his family. With her.

Don't fall for him. You're in no state of mind.

He left the kitchen without another word or a backward glance. She took it to mean he was giving her privacy, not that he wanted to go hang himself for having had sex with an injured deputy's twin sister.

But how did she know what he was thinking?

She slipped into her clothes and washed her hands and face in the kitchen sink—she could hear Granny Dunnemore clucking with disapproval, nothing, of course, compared to what she'd have thought of her granddaughter screwing herself blind against the counters.

Oh, God…

Drying her hands, Sarah flipped on a light. She was exhausted. Spent. But she'd just toss and turn if she tried to go up to bed. She tore off the top of the apricots and dumped them into a saucepan. Flour—she'd need flour for the turnover-like crust. And oil for frying the pies. Brown paper sacks for letting them drain and cool.

She and Nate could have fried apricot pies for breakfast.

Twenty-One

John Wesley Poe gave up on trying to get to sleep. He switched on the bedside lamp and sat up, haunted, even now, by the memory of taking fair-haired Betsy Quinlan to Night's Landing for the first time.

It was more than thirty years ago. Hard to believe. He'd done so much since then. Yet he still could feel his awkwardness, his sense of inadequacy, around brilliant, gentlemanly Stuart Dunnemore.

And he could see the look in Betsy's eyes when Stuart stood up to greet her on the front porch of the log house. He was a widower, no longer sad but so alone. He'd gone back to Washington by then but would come home for holidays, the occasional weekend. And he'd tend the family graves. His grandparents, his father, his brother, his wife. Granny—she wasn't an actual grandmother until the twins were born but people called her Granny, anyway—hated going to the cemetery. She'd tap the side of her head and tell Wes that the people she'd lost were there, not buried deep in the earth.

Wes had lost his virginity to Betsy Quinlan. She'd

lost hers to him. Their college romance had been brief, not that well-known even among their friends. It was before Stuart, and nothing like the kind of love he and Betsy had for each other, the kind of love Wes had eventually found with Ev. Devastated when he and Betsy drifted apart, he had kept his pain to himself, but Leola and Violet had seen it—and they'd told him, these two elderly sisters who'd never married, that there was someone out there for him.

That he and the Dunnemores had remained steadfast friends all these years was as much an accident of geography as anything else—they were neighbors. They had Night's Landing in common.

And Stuart, Wes thought. He owed so much to his longtime friend and neighbor. They'd sit on the porch late into the evening and listen to the crickets, talk about politics and international affairs, the economy, social justice, personal and public accountability, terrorism—and fishing, varieties of tomato plants, the weather. Wes remembered when the twins were born, how shocked and happy Stuart was to be a father at last, and Wes had known that Betsy had married the better man.

Evelyn slipped into bed. She often stayed up late reading. She was a small, shy, attractive woman, more up to her role as First Lady than anyone had anticipated. People empathized with her awkwardness, the losses she'd endured.

"You can't sleep?" she asked.

Wes shook his head. "No."

"I keep thinking about poor Sarah and Rob. What a nightmare this must be for them. To have had that wonderful visit together in Amsterdam, and just a few weeks later—'' She shuddered. ''It's hard to think about Rob suffering. And Sarah's only just home from Scotland. Don't you just hate to think about what they're both going through?''

''Sarah's back in Night's Landing.''

Ev shuddered. She'd always been ambivalent about Night's Landing. She'd never been a part of his life there or had any interest in making the Poe house her own. She appreciated Wes's devotion to Leola and Violet, but to Evelyn, the sisters were remote, quaint, a little unreal. She was from an upper-crust Belle Meade family—she ran in loftier circles than the Quinlans. Her connections had helped propel him to the governor's mansion, not that it mattered. Wes had fallen hopelessly in love with her in his late twenties, years after Betsy Quinlan had married Stuart Dunnemore and had born twins.

But Evelyn was no longer secure in his love for her—he didn't know if she ever would be, if he ever could make her believe that she hadn't let him down by not being able to bear children.

''Wes.''

''What is it, Ev?''

''If you had it to do all over again, would you still marry me?''

''Of course! Oh, Ev. Don't think like that.''

''I love Sarah and Rob as if they were our own, but I know they're not. I've never discouraged you from being a part of their lives. The Dunnemores are almost as much your family as Leola and Violet were. But you can't let your affection for them cloud your judgment.''

"There's no judgment to cloud. I'm on the side-lines."

She looked at him as only she could, with a frank honesty he'd come to expect and appreciate—to need in his life. "Do you really think so?"

He didn't answer, knew he couldn't convince her.

"You'd do anything for Sarah and Rob. Anything. I'm not the only one who knows it."

"Ev…"

"Our love for them makes us both vulnerable, but especially you. Just promise me you'll be careful."

Wes sighed. She was the worrier, the conspiracy theorist, in many ways, more tough-minded than he was. He could lead and inspire, but he was the last to recognize an enemy. "I promise."

She rolled over, her back to him. Wes turned out the light. He listened to his wife take in sharp, fearful breaths, and he could almost feel her mind racing ahead, imagining terrible scenarios, working herself up into an anxious frenzy. So often, her instincts were on target.

But not this time, Wes told himself. This time, she was worrying over nothing.

Some thug in Central Park had tried to take out two federal agents.

That was it. There was nothing more.

Twenty-Two

$\sim\!\!\textbf{e}\textbf{g}\textbf{o}\!\!\sim$

Sarah woke up early and alone in bed, a mockingbird singing outside her open window and the air smelling faintly of roses. But the familiar sounds and smells did nothing to soothe her after her night of unsettling dreams and images. She slipped into jeans and a light-weight hiking top and tiptoed down to the kitchen, the fried apricot pies where she'd left them on a brown paper sack.

When she'd gone up to bed last night, Nate was in the shower. She'd slipped into her room and crawled under the covers, listened to the water turn off, the bathroom door shut, then his door shut, and she wondered if he was furious with himself for what had happened in the kitchen. If he regretted it because they both were under such stress, because he was a law enforcement officer and she was Rob's sister—because, basically, he should know better.

Then again, he might not regret anything.

She poured herself a glass of iced tea and dialed Rob's room at the hospital.

She pictured them as little kids running through the

house, their laissez-faire parents only vaguely aware of what they were up to most of the time. They'd catch frogs and snakes and explore the limestone caves and sinks along the riverbank, and in winter, they'd wait for an ice storm so they could get out their orange plastic flying saucers and try to make it as close to the riverbank as possible—not that they ever went into the water. Once, Rob had slid off his saucer and cut his face and hands on the ice that covered every blade of grass, every exposed twig. It was the first time Sarah remembered seeing him in real pain.

He answered his phone himself.

"Am I calling too early?" she asked cheerfully.

"Yes. What're you up to?"

"I'm about to eat a fried apricot pie for breakfast. I made them last night before bed."

"Where's Nate? Is he behaving himself?"

She sipped her tea, welcoming the jolt of sweetness. "I think he's still in bed."

"Stay on your toes with him. I know you like those old fusty academic types, but the guy has a hell of a reputation with women."

"What old fusty academic guys?"

"Come on. You don't trust hard-ass guys like Nate. You figure they're just after your body not your mind—"

"Rob! You must be feeling better."

"Yeah." He sounded relieved, as if he couldn't quite believe it himself.

"Don't worry about me, okay? I can take care of myself."

"Nate's married to the job, but he's got total focus—he's the best at what he does, no matter what little tootsie he's got on the side.''

"Little tootsie?'' Sarah made herself smile, hoping it'd reflect in her voice. "Thanks for the warning, but maybe it's time I let a hard-ass type have his way with me.''

"Oh, man. I don't even want to go there. Have you talked to Mother and Dad? They're heading to New York.'' He didn't sound enthusiastic. "They'll be here in time to tuck me in tonight.''

"Aren't you lonely?'' She was half kidding.

Rob scoffed. "Not a chance. All the brass will roll out for them when they get here. Just what I need. I hate for Dad to make the trip when it's not necessary.''

It was more than that, Sarah knew. He hated for their father to see him in the condition he was in, seriously injured on a job both parents thought he wasn't suited for. To them, Rob was a fun-loving charmer, an average student who excelled at languages because he liked them. They didn't really believe he had the backbone to be a federal agent. They feared he was a throwback to the Dunnemores of old, adventurous but without their tough recklessness, their ability to truly not give a damn.

"Dad'll be fine,'' she said. "He'll probably live to be a hundred. Rob, you know he's proud of what you do.''

"He'd rather I were secretary of state.''

She tried to laugh but hated how low he sounded. "But then you'd have to answer to Wes, and that'd never work. It's not like getting shot proves Dad right—it was never a question about being right, anyway. It's about his hopes for you.''

''I know.''

But there was something in his tone. Sarah frowned. ''You're not getting depressed on us, are you?''

''Dreading seeing the old man with my spleen in a garbage disposal and a scar—'' He broke off, and she could hear that he was in a slump. ''There's something I'm missing. I don't know. This guy you saw in Central Park—''

She picked at the browned edges of a fried pie. ''I'm sure it's a case of mistaken identity. I almost wish I hadn't mentioned him.''

''You should have told Nate about him right from the start. Have you told anyone else about him?''

''Only you feds.''

''What about this note you found?''

''It was in the same pile as a note from a psychic.'' She could hear the frustration building in her brother's voice and decided to give him something new to think about. ''Have you met the new property manager yet? Ethan Brooker?''

''No.''

''This reporter working on a bio of Wes, Conroy Fontaine?''

Rob was silent.

Sarah's heart jumped. ''Rob?''

''Is he in Night's Landing?''

''He rented a cabin at the fishing camp a few weeks ago. I met him last fall—''

''Last fall? Where?''

''Here. I was on my own for a few days. He was

in the area trying to decide if he wanted to do this book. Rob? Do you know him?''

''He was in Amsterdam in April before you came over from Scotland. He wanted to interview Mother and Dad and got me instead. I ran him off. I didn't think to say anything to you. I was going to check him out—what's he got to do with this Brooker character?''

''Nothing. Ethan went over to Conroy's cabin last night to check him out, and they got into a bit of a scuffle. Nothing to worry about. Ethan—'' She hesitated. ''He's a good ol' boy from West Texas. I think he's trying to break into songwriting.''

Rob gave a long-suffering sigh, almost sounding like himself. ''Another of Mother and Dad's three-legged puppies?''

''They caught him fishing on the dock.''

''Trespassing.''

Sarah smiled. ''They hired him on the spot.''

''Nate's checking out both of these guys?''

''I wouldn't be surprised.''

''I don't know, maybe I shouldn't have been so quick to run you out of here. I was thinking you'd be home on your own. I didn't figure on a weird letter, all these guys—''

''Just concentrate on getting better. I'll be fine.''

She could feel him making the effort to be cheerful. ''Not if you're eating fried apricot pies for breakfast. Put one in the freezer for me, okay?''

''Hurry home.''

''I'm trying.''

The doctors had warned her that as the anesthesia got out of his system and he started weaning off the heavy-duty painkillers, he could have an emotional letdown. Sarah hated to say goodbye.

She broke one of the half-moon-shaped pies and took it with her as she ducked out the back door, letting it shut quietly behind her so as not to wake Nate. She wanted to postpone the inevitable "morning after" awkwardness for as long as possible and hoped he didn't regret what they'd done right to his bones. She didn't. She'd never done anything like it, but she didn't regret it.

At least not to her bones.

Sarah spotted Ethan working on the wood rail fence along the edge of a field they rented to a local farmer for haying and headed in that direction, taking a bite of the pie, relishing how good it tasted. Prune cake, casseroles and tea punch yesterday, and now fried apricot pies. They all tasted of home and, with the azaleas in bloom and the river coursing in front of her, the grass thick and soft underfoot, she was caught up in a wave of nostalgia that brought a tightness to her throat. As accustomed as she was to coming and going, living in different places, Night's Landing had always been her anchor. She couldn't imagine not having it to come back to.

When she reached him, Ethan was sweating from digging a post hole to fix a length of fence that had been rotting and sagging for as long as Sarah could remember. He stood up and leaned against his shovel. She noticed his black tattoo, the tanned muscles in his shoulders and arms. Probably, she thought, her parents should have checked him out before they gave him keys to the house.

"Good morning, Miss Sarah," he said, ever amiable.

"Hi, Ethan." She'd finished her fried pie on the walk across the yard and wished now she'd taken a whole one. "You have a minute?"

"You want to talk to me some more about Conroy Fontaine."

She nodded. "It sounds like you're lucky he didn't call the police. What happened? What made you go over there?"

"You're too trusting, Miss Sarah. You need to watch yourself." He paused, his dark eyes on her, as if he were trying to tell her it was a mistake to trust him, too. "You don't like to think there are bad people in the world."

"Nobody does."

He shrugged his powerful shoulders. "I don't think about it one way or the other. It's just the way it is." He peeled a black bandanna from around his neck and used it to wipe the sweat off his face. "You'll excuse my language, ma'am, but Fontaine's a bottom-feeding piece of shit."

Sarah took no offense at his language or his frank assessment of their temporary neighbor. "He's a reporter trying to make a buck. Nothing's going to come of his book. I haven't told him anything except that my Granny Dunnemore was a good cook."

"He'll twist your words."

"What would you have me do?"

"Refuse to talk to him. Go back to Scotland." He tilted his head and looked down at her, his eyes sparking with sudden humor. "Take your deputy friend with you."

She shifted, wondering how obvious the sparks between her and Nate had been yesterday, and felt the rich, sweet apricot pie heavy in her stomach. Ethan's deferential manner didn't seem as pronounced this morning—or as genuine.

"I went over to Fontaine's cabin early this morning to apologize," he went on. "He wasn't around."

"He hasn't cleared out, has he?"

"I don't think so."

"Maybe he just wants to give you a chance to cool down."

Ethan tucked the bandanna in a back pocket of his overalls. "I wasn't upset. I was just checking up on him. Maybe I made him nervous."

"He said you rammed him against his refrigerator."

He picked up his shovel, as effortlessly as if it had been a switch. "Mr. Fontaine has a gift for storytelling, ma'am. He exaggerates. Imagine what kind of book he'll write on President Poe."

It was a fair point—not that good storytelling and exaggeration were unheard of in Night's Landing—but Sarah could see only trouble ahead if Ethan decided to make Conroy his problem. "We have to put up with him for as long as he's here. It's not like we have a choice. What he's doing is not illegal. We can be cordial."

"You don't have to let him onto the property."

"That's true, I don't." At least Ethan understood that letting Conroy—or anyone else—onto the property was her decision, not his. She hadn't seen this protective side of him in the week she'd been home, but, then, there'd been no brother shot in Central

Park, no feds at the door. "Conroy knows by now that I'm not going to be telling tales on an old friend." But she could, she thought—her whole family could, and Wes on them; it was the nature of their long, close friendship. She smiled at Ethan. "He's not unpleasant to be around. So, okay? No more ass-kicking."

He grinned at her. "That was hardly a good ass-kicking, Miss Sarah. But don't you worry. I'll behave. And you'll be careful?"

"I will. Promise."

"Don't be so trusting. Even that marshal friend of yours—who knows about him? He wasn't hurt that bad in the sniper attack. That'd make me suspicious."

"Ethan, please—"

"Hell of an alibi, ain't it?"

"He did everything he could to save Rob's life."

"So he wanted to be the hero, I don't know." Ethan's tone was matter-of-fact; Sarah had no idea if he was making a serious point or exaggerating to underline his point about her being less trusting. "I'm not accusing him of a thing, Miss Sarah. I'm really not. I'm just saying you shouldn't always be thinking people have your best interests at heart."

"Including you?"

"I've been here a month without causing trouble, stealing, burning the place down. That's saying something."

"I appreciate your concern."

Ethan nodded toward the house. "Here's your fellow coming after you now. He's not the trusting type, Miss Sarah, I'll say that for him."

She spun around. Ethan wasn't kidding—Nate was

walking up from the house. He had on jeans and a black jacket, probably to hide the weapon he was carrying, and his expression was unreadable as he approached the fence. "I didn't realize you were up," she said, pushing back any sense of awkwardness at seeing him. "I left a fried pie for you in the toaster oven."

"Pies for breakfast. That a habit here?"

She shook her head. "I'm just not in much of a mood to resist."

She immediately regretted her comment, felt the heat rising to her cheeks, but Nate had already shifted back to Ethan, who, if he noticed the tension between his boss and her company, made no comment. "I want to talk to you later," Nate told Ethan. "Stay where I can find you."

"Yes, sir, Deputy Winter."

Sarah thought she detected a hint of sarcasm in Ethan's tone, another surprise from him, but she supposed lawmen elicited different reactions from people. But Nate didn't linger or argue, and she chose not to ask more questions—or to remind the two men that they were both on Dunnemore property at her sufferance.

She walked past Nate and felt a blast of damp, chilly air off the river as she headed back to the house, pounding up the porch steps, her heart racing, her cheeks flushed from awareness and anxiety. She tore open the porch door and marched down the hall to the kitchen. Using a dish towel as a pot holder, she pulled a fried pie from the toaster oven, put it on a plate and dusted it with confectioner's sugar.

Nate came into the kitchen, and she shoved it at

him. "Fried apricot pies might even be better than prune cake."

"Better than sex?"

She stared at him. *There. Throw down the gauntlet, Deputy.*

He wasn't letting her off the hook. He wasn't going to pretend last night hadn't happened. She leaned back against the counter, twisting her dish towel in both hands, and decided not to let him get to her, even if he was more accustomed to "morning afters" than she was.

Her brother was wrong. She wasn't afraid of hardass types who wanted her just for her body and didn't much care about her as a person. She just knew she should avoid them.

Or she used to know it.

Not that Nate *didn't* care about her as a person.

"I guess it depends on the sex," she said airily. "Last night was right up there with fried pies, I'd say. But, I imagine it broke every rule in the deputy U.S. marshal rule book—"

"There are no rules that cover you. Twin sister of a wounded deputy, friend of the president, daughter of a diplomat, southern academic. Pretty." He smiled and sat at the table with his pie. "Very pretty."

"Well, my life would be easier if it'd been someone else with Rob, or someone else who flew down here—"

"Someone you're not so attracted to?"

"God, you can be direct."

"It's a quality we share."

And she was attracted to him. Never mind what he

wanted from her or what he cared about, she hadn't objected to sex with him in the kitchen.

Not even a little.

She decided to change the subject. "Ethan said he checked on Conroy this morning. I wish he hadn't, but at least Conroy wasn't around. And I talked to Rob. Our folks are arriving in New York tonight. I told him about Ethan and Conroy. Turns out he met Conroy in Amsterdam. Conroy was there trying to get interviews with my parents. Nice business write-off." She sat across from Nate, trying to calm herself down. "My family attracts a lot of drama on a good day. These haven't been particularly good days."

Nate didn't answer. He picked up a pie semicircle and examined it as if it might have ants. "What's in it?"

"What? Oh. Apricots and spices."

"So, it's like a turnover."

"Better."

He smiled. "Better than a turnover, maybe or maybe not better than sex." He broke the pie in half, the warm cinnamon-apricot filling oozing out. "Another stick-to-your-ribs southern recipe."

"They're one of Wes Poe's favorites. I don't think he tells many people. And, no, it's not something I shared with Conroy."

Nate tried a bite. "Not bad." He sat back in his chair, his incisive eyes on her. "I don't trust Ethan Brooker. I don't trust Conroy Fontaine. Hell, I don't trust myself." He sighed. "You do bear closer watching, Miss Sarah."

"You're not responsible for me."

"Yes, I am."

"Not officially." She had no intention of backing down with him. "I'm not letting you or anyone else force a security detail on me in my own home. I won't have it, not unless there's just no other choice."

His eyes were flinty. "We'll see what comes in the mail today."

She ignored him. "I suppose what happened last night wouldn't have happened if you were here 'officially.'"

"I love the oblique way you put it. You mean indulging in prune cake or—"

She pushed back her chair and threw her dish towel at him, which he caught with one hand, laughing unexpectedly for the first time since she'd met him, at least like that. He had a great laugh. Sexy. But she was in a frame of mind and all her nerve endings were such that they had her thinking everything about him was sexy.

"About last night." She cleared her throat and made herself go on. "I shouldn't have taken advantage of you that way. You've experienced a recent trauma, and I should have been more sensitive to that."

He almost choked on his apricot pie. He had to get up, go to the sink and get water before he could speak again.

Sarah frowned. "What? *I* started things rolling last night. *I'm* not the one who was shot the other day. It was up to me to stop things before they went too far." She had a feeling she was making a mess of things. "I'm just saying, if you have any regrets this morning, I understand."

He waved one hand and choked out, "No regrets."

He took another drink of water, then turned and leaned back against the sink. "God, you're a trip, Dr. Dunnemore. You tell me how the hell you could possibly have taken advantage of me when I'm the one who was standing, holding you, when we—" He shook his head. "Never mind."

"I'm talking about emotional advantage more than physical advantage. If I'd simply gone about making my fried pies—"

"You'd just have had more flour on you when we made love."

She was getting nowhere. She wasn't sure she wanted to and smiled. "And dough on my hands. Sticky dough."

"Jesus." He grinned at her. "You're right. You did take advantage of me. I hope you will again soon." But he went still and swore under his breath, drawing his weapon. "Don't move."

Sarah followed his gaze, stifling a yell of surprise when she saw the fat, black snake slithering up the hall toward the kitchen.

"Water snake or cottonmouth?" Nate asked in a low voice.

She noted the triangle-shaped head and stout body. "Cottonmouth."

It was at least three feet long. Nate kept his eyes on it.

Sarah took a breath. "Slowly move toward the back door."

"And what? Let it find its way under my bed? Not a chance."

"Well, you're not going to shoot it!" She took a step toward the counters, the snake moving quickly now. "Try to get behind it if you can. Rob and I used to catch cottonmouths all the time, but outside. I think they might be faster on a floor."

"Oh, good."

He didn't sound scared at all. Sarah realized that getting behind the snake, which was coming toward them in the kitchen, wasn't going to be easy. "I'm going to the pantry, okay? Granny used to catch snakes with the mop handle." She moved deliberately, as quickly as she dared, to the pantry in the corner of the kitchen. "Distract it if it goes after me."

"I'm going to shoot it if it goes after you."

She grabbed the rag mop from the open pantry and detached its metal head. "We just need to get it outside. Remember, most water moccasin bites don't end up being poisonous. They don't release their venom willy-nilly. Anyway, I have an antivenom kit. Of course," she added, walking slowly back toward the hall doorway, "I've never had to use it."

Nate glanced at her. "Want me to do it?"

She shook her head. "I watched Granny catch snakes with the mop a dozen times, at least. Usually grass snakes, though."

The snake slithered under the table. Nate still had his gun pointed at it. Careful not to do anything sudden, Sarah came up behind the snake, then, in a swift, one-chance-only move, she pinned it down within the hardware that usually held the mop head in place, just as her grandmother had done so many times.

She didn't hesitate. She grabbed the snake just behind its head, removed the mop handle and stood up straight, the black body wriggling in front of her. "This was a lot more fun when I was a kid."

Nate stepped forward and took the mop from her. She ran out the back door, the snake's thick three-foot body hanging past her knees. She kept going, all the way down to the dock.

She flung the cottonmouth as hard as she could into the river.

It disappeared in the brown water.

She was breathing hard, aware of Nate behind her on the dock.

Ethan eased in behind them. "I'd have shot it if I were you, Deputy."

Sarah spun around at him. "Did you put that snake in my house? Because I got on your case about Conroy—"

"Not me, Miss Sarah." Ethan was unruffled. "I grew up in West Texas. I'm not that big on snakes."

She glanced at Nate and saw that he'd returned his gun to its holster. She turned back to Ethan, who just watched her calmly. She was still on edge. "We haven't had a snake in the house in years, and I don't remember *ever* having a cottonmouth in the house."

Ethan shrugged. "If I were your granny and had to fetch a snake out of the house, I don't know as I'd tell a little kid it was poisonous."

Sarah expelled a breath. "I'm sorry. I have no business accusing you of anything. I'm sure it was an accident." She tried to smile. "At least I know how to catch a snake. I wonder if that poor snake knows I saved its life."

Nate shook his head. "I'm with Brooker. Easier just to shoot it."

"You'd clean up the mess?"

Ethan gave an exaggerated shudder, his eyes sparking with unexpected humor. "You know, Miss Sarah, I could have gone all day without that picture in my head."

"Sorry. But the snake didn't do anything wrong. It's not like it wanted to be in the house—it just found itself there."

"Next time you find a snake in the house," Ethan said, "you call me, okay? That's what I'm here for."

"You won't shoot it?"

"No, ma'am, how could I shoot it? I don't carry a gun."

He ambled off the dock and back toward the fence. Nate stared out at the water. The sun broke through the clouds and played on the ripples of coppery water. A bright red male cardinal flew into the low brush along the river, and Sarah could hear a mourning dove with its intermittent, almost plaintive song.

So quiet, so peaceful.

But her heart was thumping, and she couldn't stop thinking about the snake and how it had gotten into the house.

"About last night," Nate said. "It shouldn't have happened."

She nodded.

"Your brother's trusting me to look after you—"

"I can look after myself."

He half smiled. "You did all right with that snake."

She glanced up at him and forced herself to smile. "I did, didn't I?"

"You're pals with the president. For all we know, a dozen Secret Service agents are camped out here."

"And saw us last night? I don't think so. Nobody saw anything."

His eyes sparked. "There was plenty to see."

She thought of diving into the river. The snake was probably halfway to Nashville by now. Nate's words had brought back all of last night. She could feel her body quaking with him inside her, remembered how she'd resisted screaming out—how uninhibited she'd been with him. He was not an inexperienced lover. She warned herself not to expect anything more.

She ran her hands through her hair. "I think we should check the house for more snakes, don't you?"

"Damn straight."

But when they reached the house, he stopped in the front hall and curved an arm around her middle, kissing her softly. "Last night wasn't just opportunistic," he whispered. "When this thing gets settled—" But he didn't finish, just stood back and sighed. "We'll see."

He didn't trust himself right now on any level— she guessed that was what he was trying to say. Which made sense to her, because she didn't trust herself, either.

Twenty-Three

~~~

Betsy Dunnemore looked even more drawn and stressed-out than she had the other day when Nicholas had intercepted her at the café. She stood in the elegant living room of his hotel suite as if she were his captive. In a way, she was. His orders to his men had been precise—bring her to him without fail, but voluntarily. Persuade her. Create a sense of urgency that she couldn't ignore.

Anything could happen in New York. Anything at all.

He needed to speak with her before she got there. He wanted her on his side. He wanted her at least to understand his position.

And if he could get it, he wanted information from her. What did she know about the sniper investigation? Did anyone realize he'd contacted her? Were the feds trying to pin the Central Park attack on him? Rousseau was drawing blanks in New York. He was useless.

"Who were those men?" Betsy tossed her head in an obvious effort to look outraged, but she was too upset, too frightened, to pull it off. "Your hired thugs?"

"Bodyguards. In my position—"

"As a fugitive," she cut in coldly.

"As a wealthy man who not only my enemies but my own government want to bring down."

She snorted. "Spare me your self-pity. What do you want?" Her tone was slicing. "Your 'bodyguards' made it clear they'd drag me here if I didn't come on my own."

"I'm sure you're reading into their manner. I apologize for any—"

"Just tell me what you want. My husband and I are flying to New York later this afternoon." She had on her travel clothes, a smart black suit with her fashionable but comfortable shoes. "A car is picking us up in half an hour. I have to be back."

Nicholas sipped a glass of a Belgian beer he was fond of. "You'll be back in plenty of time. Won't you sit down?"

"No."

She was strong willed, a beautiful woman in her prime. According to Janssen's sources, Stuart Dunnemore was still a vital, interesting man, but at almost eighty, he wasn't the man she'd married. He was increasingly dependent on her. But Betsy would never let people think she had any regrets about having married a man so much older than she.

"Can I offer you some lunch?" Nicholas asked mildly.

She shook her head, her hands clasped firmly on her handbag. The way she was dressed, the way she carried herself, her hair, her grooming—she looked as if she belonged in the tasteful surroundings. Janssen had to work at looking the part, although his wealth far, far exceeded that of the Dunnemores. But inside, Janssen felt like a phony. A thug, a common criminal.

That, he thought, would change.

"You're free to leave. It's not as if you're my prisoner." He spoke with wry amusement, but Betsy didn't relax even slightly. He set his beer glass down on a small, antique table. "I have contacts in New York who tell me that the FBI's spinning its wheels in its investigation into the shooting. They haven't made any headway since they found that drug addict dead—"

"What contacts?"

"That's not important. What's important is that you and your husband are walking into a very tense situation. My contacts also tell me that the FBI and the Marshals Service are bracing for another attack."

"I want to see my son," she said tightly. "That's all."

"Of course. I understand."

She leveled her unflinching gaze on him. "I'm going to tell Rob—and the investigators—that you've approached me several times since last fall. As soon as I learned of your legal status I've asked you not to contact me."

It was the truth, as far as it went, but she wasn't saying how she'd learned he was a fugitive. Charlene Brooker. Either Betsy was deliberately not mentioning her meeting with the young army captain or didn't think it was important. But the FBI would want to know how Betsy Dunnemore had found out her old college classmate was a fugitive—they'd want to know everything murdered army captain Charlene Brooker had told her. Janssen knew now he should have acted sooner, *before* Char Brooker had contacted Betsy.

"I've done nothing wrong," Betsy said. "What you're up to—"

"I'm not up to anything. I'm just a man in legal limbo who ran into an old friend—" He smiled, remembering her previous stinging words on that subject. "An old acquaintance."

Her gray eyes narrowed slightly. "My son's situation and yours had better be coincidence and nothing more."

Or what? Nicholas almost asked her, almost called her bluff—fought an urge to threaten her and demonstrate just how dangerous he was. "I'm sure they will. In the meantime, they could cause us both problems. You're not only the mother of a wounded marshal, you're a friend of the president."

"Don't bring Wes into this."

Janssen shrugged, rising so that he was a few inches above eye level with her. "Betsy, I'm an innocent man. I want to put my legal problems behind me and do good in the world. You can help me."

She gave a small gasp that she must have wished she could have held back. "I have no intention of helping you!"

He smiled gently. "You already have. Just seeing you has made a difference to me."

She took a breath. "Nick, please. Stay out of my life."

"I had nothing to do with the attack on your son.

It's insane to think I did. But if you tell the authorities about me—''

"Are you suggesting I don't? What, are you going to threaten me?''

But she regained her self-control and tilted her head back, studying him a moment through those half-closed eyes. They were beautiful eyes. Stormy and vivid, with just enough mystery.

"Why did you seek me out in the first place? The FBI's going to want to know, if they don't already.''

"Betsy, remember. I knew Wes Poe in college, too. He was my friend, too.''

She inhaled through her nose. "Don't you even think—''

"Why, because he complicates everything for you? Or because you know you should have married him?''

"That's it. I'm leaving. I don't ever want to see you again. If your men come near me, I'll call the police.''

"I'm a decent man, Betsy.'' He ached to reach her, to convince her. "If I made a mistake in fleeing my country, it was because I wasn't thinking. I want to go home. I want to see my mother's grave.''

She stared at him, and he wondered if she was seeing him at eighteen, a misfit intellectually, socially and culturally. She'd tried to help him make more friends. She'd felt sorry for him then—she'd had sympathy for him.

But all that was gone.

He couldn't count on convincing her to want to step in on his behalf with the president by being nice. He saw that now.

"A presidential pardon would clear my name.'' He

spoke softly and met her eyes, saw the shock in them. "You could make it happen."

"Bastard," she said through her teeth and ran for the door, pushing past a bodyguard who could have snapped her neck without breaking a sweat. Janssen motioned for him to let her go. She gave him one last, scathing look and started for the steep, curving stairs. "Don't you *ever* try to contact me again."

"Betsy. Don't leave. Not just yet." He lifted an envelope from a small side table. "There's a picture of a woman in here."

"I'm leaving." But her voice faltered, and she didn't move.

Janssen withdrew the photograph Charlene Brooker he'd cut out of an Amsterdam newspaper. "You recognize this woman, don't you? She's an army captain. You two met last fall."

Betsy gasped. "What—Nick, what's going on? Why was her picture in the paper?"

"She was found dead two days after you met with her. Shot in the chest. Point-blank range. Hookers found her in the red-light district." Janssen set the picture faceup on the table. "Amsterdam's a safe city, but—" He didn't finish. "It's a very sad story."

"She's dead? Murdered? My God, I had no idea. Stuart and I left for home a day or two after I saw her. She told me about your fugitive status." Betsy spoke in a tight, rapid voice. "I didn't mention her because I didn't think it was any of your business. I never heard from her again."

"Perhaps because she was dead." Janssen eased back onto his chair, aware of how brittle with tension she was. He had to play this moment very carefully. "Another coincidence."

Her eyebrows arched. He could see her fear now. "How do you know I met with her?"

"It's not important. But if I know, Betsy, other people know. The FBI will want to know. The Dutch police."

"I'll tell them everything, of course, but I don't even remember the poor woman's name."

Nicholas decided not to tell her. He leaned back, crossing one leg over the other.

In the silence, she bit her lower lip and grasped her stomach, as if she might vomit. "Do you believe her killer is also responsible for Rob—for shooting my son and the deputy who was with him? Nick, please. Tell me what you know."

"Your captain was in army intelligence. Just because she told you about my situation doesn't mean she was investigating *me*." But, of course, that wasn't true. "Betsy, I don't need to remind you that your husband is an important man. He has important enemies inside and outside the government."

"But not *violent* enemies."

"Everyone's violent these days, one way or another. People listen to your husband. The president listens. That makes him powerful."

"I'm leaving. You're deliberately trying to scare me."

"This can all spin out of control, Betsy, if you aren't careful. I know you want to protect your family. Let me help you." He let his gaze connect with hers. "Then you can help me."

But she fled, taking the steep, curving stairs as fast as she possibly could.

Janssen flopped back against his chair and stifled a moan of pain and despair. His head throbbed. He was so tired. But while their meeting could have gone better, it had gone about as well as he'd expected. He'd planted the seed. Soon she would realize that the only way to get him out of her life and to save her family was to use her influence with President John Wesley Poe and persuade him to pardon an old college classmate.

Before his other activities came to light.

When he returned to his beer, there was a call for him. "Is the money ready?" the voice on the other end asked. "You'll have your presidential pardon within twenty-four hours."

"What? Who are you? Stay the hell out of my affairs!"

"The clock is ticking."

"Wait—"

But the caller had already disconnected.

Twenty-Four

Rob was sitting up in bed, picking at a plate of hospital food, when Juliet arrived. She was relieved to see him in a private room. She didn't like being around sick people. The doctors and nurses had him up walking as much as possible, but he was still weak—and he still had his marshal guards. They weren't going anywhere, not with the investigation still ongoing, his sister receiving threatening letters and Rob unable to pick up a gun much less fire one.

That he couldn't defend himself didn't sit well with him. "I can't wait to get out of here. What's going on that nobody else will tell me?"

"Nothing," Juliet said. "You're a hundred percent in the loop."

He snorted. "Right. Liar."

"Joe Collins is covering all the angles, even the cranks." His unsettling visit to her apartment last night was still fresh in her mind. "I think deep down he believes Hector's our guy. Even if he had a handicap, he could have pulled off those two shots. People *saw* him—"

"Is that what you believe? That Hector Sanchez was the shooter and he overdosed celebrating his handiwork?"

Juliet sighed. One of Rob's doctors had cornered her in the hall and warned her not to discuss the shooting with him. But, if she was the one bandaged up and stuck in the hospital, she'd want every damn detail she could get. She'd do all she could to get out of there so she could go catch the shooter herself. Rob was laid-back, but he wasn't *that* laid-back.

"I suppose someone could have set him up, made sure people saw him to draw attention away from the real shooter, then paid him off with a drug overdose. Collins isn't saying—"

Rob tried to give her the high sign, but it was too late. "Do I hear my name being taken in vain?" the FBI agent asked behind her.

Juliet spun around. "Rob was just asking a normal question. Damn." She grinned at him. "You FBI types are sneaky."

"We prefer 'stealthy.'"

He had a good-natured manner, but Juliet sensed his underlying seriousness.

"How're you doing today, Deputy?" he asked Rob.

"Not bad. They've got me eating regular food. I'm starving."

"That's got to be a good sign. Your doctors tell me you're making an amazing recovery. All that triathlon training must be helping." He shook his head and patted his gut. "Me, I wouldn't have made it out of the park."

"I almost didn't," Rob said softly.

"Don't be thinking like that. Deputy Longstreet? A word?"

Rob immediately looked suspicious and Juliet didn't blame him. She ran one hand through her hair. "Here or—"

"Out in the hall, if you don't mind."

"What's up?" Rob asked.

"Nothing for you to worry about," the FBI agent said. "I'll be back in a minute to talk to you."

It was clear Rob objected, but there was nothing he could do.

Collins led Juliet into the unoccupied waiting room and shut the door. He shoved his hands into his pants pockets, rattling loose change, a gravity overcoming him that she hadn't seen in him before, even in the first hours after the shooting. "The Dunnemores didn't make it onto their plane in Amsterdam."

"What do you mean, didn't make it? Did something happen to them or did they just miss their flight?"

"We don't know. They refused an escort. They're a stubborn lot, the whole damn family." He sighed through his teeth. "I'm putting someone on them. I don't give a good goddamn if they don't like it—" He broke off with another angry, frustrated sigh. "As soon as we find them."

"Are you going to tell Rob?"

"No. He's the reason I just put you in the loop on this one."

Juliet saw his awkwardness and realized what he was getting at. "Oh, great," she said without enthusiasm. "I get to tell him. Are you shoving it off onto Nate to tell the sister?"

Collins nodded with at least a small measure of guilt.

"Can we give it some time?" Juliet asked. "Wait and see if the parents show up?"

He poured himself a cup of stale coffee. "If you were in Rob Dunnemore's position, would you want us dancing around the truth, or would you want to know straight out what was going on with your folks?"

She knew she didn't need to answer.

Joe Collins stared at his grayish coffee. Juliet wondered what else he knew. What he wasn't telling her. Today he had the look of a man preoccupied with unraveling what was increasingly *not* looking like a simple case of a drugged-out snitch going bad. Whatever was going on was more complicated—and possibly even more dangerous.

Juliet took a breath. "I'll go tell him."

Nate's arm throbbed. A wonder he hadn't killed himself making love to Sarah last night. He watched her stirring her tea punch with a cinnamon stick. He'd had two sips and decided it was too sweet for his taste. They were alone on the property, out on the porch waiting for word from her parents. Ethan Brooker had taken the truck and gone to town, and Conroy Fontaine wasn't at the back door looking to discuss old southern recipes, currying favor with Sarah to get access to the president.

Nate assumed the FBI agents looking into the anonymous letter were checking out both the gardener and the journalist, but he'd made a few calls himself. So far, nothing back. He assumed Collins and his guys were doing the same.

The tea punch, Sarah had told him tonelessly, was another of her Granny Dunnemore's recipes.

Nate supposed he should feel like a heel for taking advantage of her last night, but he couldn't. He didn't know if it was the shooting, the bullet wound or the river and the roses and azaleas around him—or if maybe he really was falling for her—but all he could think about was making love to her again. And then again.

Not a good situation. Probably he should call Longstreet and tell her to get her butt down here.

He sighed. "Maybe it would be better if we put an official security detail—"

"No," she said. "Thank you, but no. And you don't have to stay."

He knew a part of her wasn't on the porch with him. She'd already gone upstairs and dug out her passport to head to Amsterdam and hunt for her parents herself. If Nate hadn't been there, she might already be on a plane. Impulsive. He'd seen some of that in her brother when he'd charged into the park to look at the damn tulips, but not on the job.

She broke her cinnamon stick into little pieces and lined them up on the porch rail. "Do you feel New York's your home, or Cold Ridge?"

"I don't think about it."

"Ah. I was warned you're pretty much a workaholic." She glanced at him. "And something of a rake."

"A rake? That's an old-fashioned term."

"I'm drinking tea punch in my grandmother's rocking chair. I'm in an old-fashioned mood."

"Did you miss this place when you were in Scotland?"

"It's home." She leaned forward, rearranging her pieces of cinnamon stick. "I missed walking in the fields and woods, boating on the river—just sitting out here listening to the crickets. But I haven't lived here since college."

"I cleared out of Cold Ridge after high school. I didn't even go home for summers in college. Not to stay, anyway." He tried more of the punch, just to see if he liked it any better, but no, it was too sweet. "I have a good relationship with my family. I just had things I wanted to do that I couldn't at home."

"Do you hike the ridge?"

From her tone, he guessed she was remembering that his parents had died on the ridge. "Every year since I was seven. My uncle took my sisters and me up in the beginning, before we could go on our own. He didn't want us being afraid of it. It looms over the valley where we lived."

"He never considered moving you out of there?"

"Gus?" Nate smiled, shaking his head. "He'd just gotten back from Vietnam. He wasn't going anywhere."

"My grandfather died when my father was young, but he had Granny. I've had both my parents for so long."

"You still do," he said quietly.

She didn't answer.

"Every few years, I hike Cold Ridge on the day my parents died." He didn't know why he was telling her this but didn't make himself stop. "It was in November—the weather's always cold. Sometimes there's snow, ice, freezing rain. They were prepared. If they hadn't fallen, or if the forecast had held, it might have been different."

Sarah seemed to rally with the distraction. "There've been a lot of advances in meteorology since then."

"The forecast still can be tricky. Cold Ridge has its own mini-weather system. It can be warm and sunny in the valley, and snowing on the ridge." He smiled at her suddenly. "I didn't mean to go on like that. I can picture you eking information out of the Poe sisters, getting them to tell you all their stories, all their secrets."

She tried to return his smile. "We're good at stories and secrets here in Night's Landing."

But her lightness didn't quite work, and Nate changed the subject. "I should have taken you out for a candlelight dinner before hitting on you in the kitchen."

That at least brought some color to her cheeks. "We can pretend we stuck candles in the prune cake."

"We got the cart before the horse." But he decided to abandon that subject, too. "More tea, or would you just like another cinnamon stick to break apart?"

Her smile was underlined with tension, fear, and Nate knew she had to be questioning whether the man she'd spotted in Central Park had something to do with her missing parents. She didn't want to believe it was the same man who'd approached her at the museum in Amsterdam, but he'd watched the doubt creep in.

Nate put up his feet and tried to concentrate on some bird chirping in the rosebushes. But he kept seeing Rob grinning over the damn tulips in Central Park, then jerking with the impact of the bullet and grabbing his upper abdomen as blood seeped between his fingers. The blood got worse. The pain. The fear. The certainty he would die. Nate had seen it in Rob's gray eyes, the same as his sister's gray eyes.

"Nate?"

With a deliberate effort, he pulled himself out of the image before it could repeat itself again. It would wake him up in the night. At least he'd had the sense not to try to spend the night with Sarah. He was attracted to her. No question. But he couldn't say for sure whether or not their lovemaking in the kitchen hadn't just been to keep the images at bay. His, hers.

He inhaled through his nose, focusing on his breathing. "Sorry. My mind was wandering."

Sarah nodded. "I understand. You have a lot to think about."

"We both do. You okay?"

But the phone rang before she could answer. She started to pounce on the extension on the porch, but Nate got there first in case it was bad news and he needed to serve as a filter. "Dunnemore residence."

"You must be Deputy Winter." The voice was soft and female with a pleasant southern accent. "Hello, I'm Betsy Dunnemore. Is my daughter there?"

"Right here, Mrs. Dunnemore."

Sarah gasped in relief, and Nate handed over the

phone. He wanted to stay—he was tempted to listen in on an extension in the house—but he made himself get to his feet and walk down to the river, letting mother and daughter talk.

Twenty-Five

Sarah couldn't remember ever hearing her mother sound so close to losing all control. She was hanging by threads, but, of course, she wouldn't admit it. "We're all right," she said. "We had an unexpected delay—we couldn't get hold of anyone. I was afraid you'd all be frantic. I'm so sorry."

"What happened?" Sarah asked.

"I ran into someone I know. It's a long story. I'll explain when we get to New York. We're scheduled for an early-morning flight. Right now, I just want to go to bed. Your dad's exhausted, too."

"I understand, but—"

"I tried to call Rob," her mother cut in, obviously reluctant to go into more detail. "He was asleep. I'll try again in a minute, but if I don't reach him, will you call him later on and let him know we talked?"

"Of course." Sarah hesitated, glancing at Nate down on the dock. Not one inch of him looked relaxed. "But there's something I need to ask you. It can't wait."

Her mother inhaled. "All right."

"When we were all at the Rijksmuseum together in April, a man spoke to me. Dark hair, angular features. He had just a slight accent. French, I think. He approached me while you were at *The Night Watch*. Did you happen to see him?"

"No. No, I didn't."

Sarah sighed. "I thought not. You were talking with another man. I thought they might be together. The man you were with had silver hair—"

"I know. He's—" Her mother broke off, sounding ragged, even afraid. "He's someone I used to know in college. It's a long story. What about this man you were with? Why are you asking about him now?"

"I might have seen him in Central Park the other day. I'm not sure."

Her mother didn't respond.

"The FBI and the marshals are looking into it," Sarah added.

"Dear God." Her mother seemed ready to crack with tension. "The marshal who was shot with Rob— Nate Winter. He's staying in Night's Landing with you?"

"Yes, but—"

"Then you're out of harm's way. Whatever's going on, you and Rob are safe." She gave a fake little laugh. "All this drama. We're all tired and freaked out by this senseless shooting. Let's just stay cool. We'll get everything sorted out when we get to New York tomorrow."

"Mother, *was* the silver-haired man with the guy who approached me?"

"I don't know. Sarah, please. I'm exhausted. Stay safe, okay? I love you very much."

She said good-night and hung up.

Sarah cradled the phone and got to her feet, feeling unsteady, shaken.

Nate appeared on the porch steps. He glanced up at her, his expression more law enforcement officer than friend or lover. "Where are you going?" he asked.

"The kitchen. I think there's another casserole in the freezer. Whatever it is, we can have it for dinner."

But he mounted the steps and caught her by the elbow, turning her to him, not ungently. She felt how rigid she was, not awkward so much as incredibly aware that her mother hadn't wanted to talk about the silver-haired man—that she was hiding something and intended to for as long as she could.

And that Nate wanted whoever had shot him and Rob more than anything else.

It was why he was in Night's Landing. That they'd made love last night was an accident of timing and a product of chemistry. Even if he was genuinely attracted to her, it didn't mean he'd let his feelings interfere with his duties as a marshal and his determination to find out what had happened in Central Park.

She wouldn't expect him to.

"What all happened in the Rijksmuseum?" he asked.

"I thought you weren't listening in."

"I didn't hear everything. You looked like you were going to pass out. I was coming to your rescue."

"Ah. More projection. *You* were on the verge of passing out."

"I've never passed out."

"Nothing happened at the Rijksmuseum. My

mother didn't see the man who approached me. She was still at *The Night Watch.* She's something of an art historian—she takes forever to wander through a museum.''

"Where were she and your father today?" Nate didn't let up on his intensity, didn't release his hold on her. "Why did they miss their flight?"

"She ran into someone she knew. She didn't get into details." Sarah fought to control her emotions. Was her mother hiding something? *Why?* Nerves, fear, drama? "She's the mother of a deputy marshal who's got a long recovery ahead of him. We're all crazed right now. This is why I didn't want to mention the guy in the park—I knew you'd all seize on it, when I'm sure I was mistaken."

"Do your parents often miss planes?"

She jerked back out of his grip, angrily, then saw his face pale, the pain register at the edges of his mouth. "Your arm—oh, my God, I'm so sorry."

He waved her off, visibly absorbing the pain.

"What can I do? Tylenol? A fresh bandage? Should I call an ambulance?"

He managed a thin smile. "A shot of some kind of Tennessee bourbon would be nice."

"That I can manage."

She ran into the front room and found a dusty bottle, a glass that she held up to the light and decided definitely needed rinsing. She brought both into the kitchen, swirled water into the glass, added ice and splashed in the bourbon. Her emotions were all over the place. How could she have forgotten about his arm even for a split second? What was wrong with her?

She returned to the living room with the glass.

He didn't gulp. She had a feeling Nate Winter didn't do much that didn't show total control. Even last night making love to her. As wild as it had been, he'd known precisely, exactly what he was doing. "Go ahead." He waved the glass at her. "Call your brother and tell him you've heard from your mother."

"I'm really sorry."

"I deserved it."

She dialed her brother's room at the hospital, but Joe Collins picked up. "Is that you, Dr. Dunnemore? Your parents are safe."

"You talked to my mother? She just called here, too."

"I didn't talk to her. Juliet Longstreet answered Rob's phone." His tone was difficult to read. "Your brother's knocked out. I'm waiting for him to wake up. Nurse said it probably won't be long. He was in a lot of pain this afternoon. They're working him pretty hard."

"I should be there."

"You should be where you are. Nothing more out of your letter writer?"

"No, sir."

"Quiet day?"

"We had a cottonmouth in the house, but other than that—"

"A snake? Hell, I hate snakes. What'd you do with it?"

"I caught him and released him back in the river."

Collins chuckled, surprising her. "I don't know why your brother worries about you. We'll stay in touch, right, Dr. Dunnemore?"

She nodded at the phone. "Yes. Yes, of course."

Whatever he knew—whatever her mother might have told Juliet that she hadn't told her daughter—Joe Collins was keeping it all to himself. He hung up, and Sarah almost poured herself a glass of bourbon. "Sometimes I wonder why Rob couldn't have become a house painter." She sank onto the couch, aware of Nate standing in the shadows in front of the stone fireplace. "He used to paint houses in college. It was a good job. You might fall off a ladder, but usually people don't shoot house painters."

Nate set his glass down. "You asked your mother if a silver-haired man was with the man who'd approached you at the museum. Why? Who is he?"

"You're relentless, aren't you, Deputy Winter?"

He didn't answer.

"I don't know who he is. My mother said he was somcone she knows."

"Then you didn't recognize him?"

"My parents know a lot of people I wouldn't recognize." Sarah angled a look at him. "Do you want to strap me down and shoot me up with truth serum?"

Not even a flicker of a smile.

She tried to smile, just to ease some of her own tension. "I wouldn't want to be someone you're interrogating."

"That's right. You wouldn't."

She quashed a flare of irritation. "You're known for being the hard-ass of hard-asses, aren't you? Rob didn't tell me that. Neither did Juliet. But it's obvious from the way people treat you. They say it's because you're the best at what you do, but I think they know you're harder sometimes than you need to be."

''Figured that out all by yourself?''

''Don't patronize me.''

He drank more of his bourbon. ''You don't like it when the shoe's on the other foot, do you?''

''I wasn't patronizing you. I was just—''

She didn't know what she was doing. Picking a fight so she didn't have to confront her own fears and worries about her parents? What the *hell* was going on in Amsterdam? How could anything her parents were involved with possibly have spilled out into New York and damn near gotten her brother killed? More Dunnemore drama, embellishment, exaggeration. It had to be. But she blinked back tears and jumped to her feet, heading for the kitchen.

Do nothing. Tell no one.

Had whoever sent her that hideous letter realized she'd talked and gone after her parents? Was that why her mother was so tense?

Sarah shook off that train of thought before it could get started.

''I just had this upsetting conversation with my mother,'' she shot back at Nate, ''and you can't give me five damn minutes to pull myself together.''

''Take ten. Then tell me what happened in Amsterdam.''

''Nothing happened!''

''It stuck out in your mind or you wouldn't have remembered the man who approached you. I've been to museums. I'm trained to remember faces, and I doubt I'd remember anyone who stopped and chatted with me for a few seconds, especially not three weeks later.''

Sarah stormed down the hall to the kitchen.

"Maybe he was good-looking. Maybe that's why I remember him."

She ripped open the freezer, grabbed a frozen dish marked "squash casserole" and slammed it onto the counter, swearing under her breath, her chest tight with anger and a kind of fear she'd never known— as if people were out to kill her, kill her brother, kill her parents. But that was *insane*.

Nate was standing in the kitchen door. She pushed past him, not even looking at him. "Help yourself. I'm not hungry."

He didn't stop her from walking down the hall and heading upstairs.

He didn't say a word. Nothing.

She shut the door to her room.

Five o'clock. Hours left before she could go to bed, but she was exhausted—and feeling guilty, because she knew she'd picked a fight with him in order to keep herself from thinking about her mother and what she was hiding.

It was terribly like her mother to have secrets. The Quinlan side of the family were all big on secrets. They treated them as currency.

Sarah tore open her bedroom door and stormed back into the hall, but all the fury had gone out of her. She hung over the stair railing. "I'm going to take a bath. I'm sorry I'm not better company."

No response.

"And I'm sorry I almost ripped your arm off."

"My arm's fine."

He was behind her. She turned around so fast she almost lost her balance. Her heart was pounding—it was as if all her nerve endings were raw, exposed, responding to him in a thousand different ways. She pushed her hair back with one hand and gave a self-conscious laugh. "I think Wyatt Earp could do that, couldn't he? Materialize out of thin air."

"I think that was Captain Kirk."

"I'll cooperate," she blurted. "So will my mother. You know that, don't you? It's just unnerving to think that we might have any connection to a shooting that almost killed Rob—you—"

"Later."

"But if you've got a bee up your nose—"

He wrapped both arms around her and lifted her off the floor, kissing her, tasting of bourbon and a kind of intensity she'd never known. He carried her back into her room. "I want to feel the breeze off the river while we make love."

"Nate—"

"You and I both have a million things to think about. Let's think about all of them later."

He laid her down on her bed. She could, indeed, feel the breeze off the river. "I've neglected this part of my life," she whispered.

"You don't have to anymore. Neither do I."

"But you—"

"There's sex," he said, "and there's lovemaking. I want to make love to you."

"Why?"

He smiled. "No more questions."

He stripped off his shirt—she could see that his arm had bled slightly through the bandage, but he didn't seem to notice. His pants came next, and it was obvious he'd been anticipating this moment for at least a few minutes. But, instead of rushing, he said, "I want to take my time with you." And he slid in next to her, taking her hands when she started to lift her shirt. "Allow me."

"As you wish."

"And you?" he asked, raising her shirt. "What do you wish?"

He touched his thumbs to her nipples through her bra, and she couldn't answer. Slowly, without any obvious sense of urgency, he lifted her bra and exposed her breasts to the cold breeze and the wet heat of his tongue. He took his time easing off her top, smoothing his hands and tongue over her throat, between her breasts, down her abdomen. He caught his fingers in the waistband of her pants and took them and her underpants off at the same time, exposing her to the same slow, erotic play of hands, teeth and tongue.

"I wish…" She couldn't breathe, couldn't talk. "I wish this could go on forever."

With his fingers still on her, inside her, he took her hand and placed it on him. He was hot, throbbing. He thrust himself against her palm, a promise of what was to come. But she couldn't last another second and moved under him, and he pulled back his hand, then entered her, pushing in hard and deep, his eyes locking with hers. "How long do you mean by forever?"

He took her to the precipice, then fell back again, over and over, until she couldn't speak, couldn't think, could only feel her own blinding need for release. When it came, he stayed with her, spun into a freefall with her, tumbling, picking up speed, but she kept pace with him until his own release overcame him. Afterward, completely spent, she wrapped herself around him so that she could feel the entire length of his body, the taut muscles, the hot skin as the chilly wind blew across them. He was real. So very real. She hadn't imagined one second of what had just happened.

"A Yankee marshal," she whispered, not sure if he could hear her, and smiled. "Dear God."

She could easily fall in love with him.

She might have already.

And there wasn't a damn thing she could do about it, any more than she could stop the river outside her doors from flowing—not that she would if she could.

Finally he stirred. "What's in squash casserole?"

"Summer squash, Ritz crackers, onions, cheese and butter." She sat up, untangling her hair with her fingers. "Lots of butter."

He threw his legs over the edge of her bed. "Another of Granny Dunnemore's recipes?"

Sarah nodded. "One of my favorites."

He grinned at her. "They're all your favorites."

He pulled on his pants and stood up, and when he turned to her, he winced and gave a mock shudder. "I wish I'd seen that before I carried you in here."

She followed his gaze and realized that it was fixed on the picture of her and John Wesley Poe at her college graduation, in front of a table of strawberries and champagne. "He was running for governor then. My parents were out of the country—my father was serving as a special envoy to Indonesia during hard times."

"There are always hard times somewhere."

"I told them it was okay for them not to come."

"You had Wes Poe," Nate said.

"Yes." She pretended not to hear the note of criticism in his voice. "And Rob. He came, too."

"Did your parents make it to his graduation?"

She shook her head. "We had a grand party afterward here at Night's Landing. We've learned to seize the moment, make up for lost time when we're together." She collected her clothes and held them close to her. "Why don't I get dressed and make us some homemade biscuits to go with the squash casserole?"

He pulled on his shirt. "I thought you weren't hungry."

She threw a pillow at him and remembered his injured arm too damn late again, but he caught the pillow with his right hand and tossed it back at her. And in another minute, they were making love again, all thought of biscuits and squash casserole, of loving but neglectful parents—of the family friend who was now in the White House—vanished, which was, Sarah thought, just what Nate had intended.

"Leola and Violet used to tell a story about a Huck-Finn-type boy who lived on the river," Sarah said as she led the way to the Poe house, the river on one side of the narrow trail, the thick woods on the other. It was after dinner, the sun low in the sky, but she had a restless energy that Nate, as tired as he was, understood. "They said he camped in the caves. I'm not sure when it was. I never asked. It's one of a thousand questions I wish I could go back and ask them."

They were on a section of trail that wound over the

top of a near-vertical limestone bluff. One wrong step, and he'd be in the water. The river was quiet, no waves, no boats. "What'd he do, live off the land?"

"They claimed he'd fish, catch frogs and snakes. They liked frog's legs themselves. I think Wes did, too." Sarah paused atop the bluff and caught her breath. "I never developed a taste for them."

Nate smiled next to her. "I've never eaten frog and have no plans to start. What about snake?"

"Oh, no. I'm not eating snake. Leola and Violet claimed they tried it once, when they were little girls." She breathed out. "Hard to believe that was before World War One."

Nate saw that talking about the Poe sisters and her friendship with the president relaxed her. He regretted having pushed hard earlier with his questions, but he'd never been a patient man. A patient lover, sometimes. This afternoon. His doctor probably wouldn't be pleased with him, but, on the other hand, he felt fine. "Isn't there a story about the president and a snake? I don't remember the details. It came out during the campaign."

She shuddered. "I don't know how anyone stands a political campaign. I really don't."

"Do you know the story?"

She glanced at him, her eyes cool, their color matching the churning gray sky. "I was there."

In spite of her seriousness, he smiled. "After this morning, I suppose I shouldn't be surprised. You and your snakes."

"Wes—President Poe—came to Night's Landing not long after he and his wife had lost their fourth and last baby. A little girl, stillborn. They knew there wouldn't be more. I was still in high school. Almost seventeen.''

Nate tried to picture her at almost seventeen. Pretty, intense, dragging her video camera down the river to interview her two elderly neighbors. And direct. She'd have been direct, too.

''I was walking back from the Poe house along this same path, not that far from here. It was a sticky summer day, oppressively hot.'' Her accent seemed more pronounced. ''Wes was standing below me on a narrow, treacherous ledge that leads to a cave just above the water.''

''He was there alone?''

''Ev stayed in Nashville. She was out of the hospital—her mother was with her. I've always thought Wes just needed some time to himself. He was grief-stricken—''

''Do you think he meant to jump that day?''

She shook her head but didn't seem shocked by the question. ''It was just such a hard time. Wes prides himself on getting things done, making things happen. But some things you just can't control. I just think he wanted to be here, on the river.''

''Who saw the snake first?''

''He did. It must have come from the cave. I've seen them out on the ledge, sunning themselves.''

''Water moccasins?''

''Oh, yes.''

Nate remembered some of the story now. ''He saved someone's life, didn't he? Yours? Isn't that the story?''

''That's the story.''

She continued along the trail. When they reached

the Poe house, she led the way through the tall grass to the road, then down to the fishing camp and the cabin Conroy Fontaine had rented.

He was sitting out on a rusted lawn chair, chatting with an old man with a cigarette hanging out of his mouth, and he squinted up at Sarah, then at Nate. "Evening. Sarah, your prune cake was fantastic. I almost sneaked into your house in the middle of the night to steal me another piece, but then I decided that probably wasn't such a good idea." He grinned lazily. "You did your granny proud."

"Thanks. I'm glad you enjoyed it."

"Let me introduce you to my friend Hiram Jones. Hiram, this here is Sarah Dunnemore and her friend, Deputy U.S. Marshal Nate Winter."

Sarah mumbled something about being pleased to meet him. Nate just nodded, and the old guy rolled back in his lawn chair and blew out a lungful of smoke. "I knew Leola and Violet back in the war. Used to come out here to fish. They was real ladies."

Conroy gave Sarah a pointed look. "Hiram was here not long after they found President Poe on the doorstep."

"He wasn't president then," Sarah said, a little sharply. "He was just a baby."

"Cute little fella," the old man said.

Sarah sighed. "You don't let up, do you, Conroy?"

"No, ma'am. I don't give up, either. Anything I can do for you? How's your brother today?"

"He's doing well, thanks. I wanted you to know I spoke to Ethan, and he apologizes. He said he stopped by earlier to apologize to you in person, but you weren't around."

"Out for my run, probably. Water over the dam." He laid on the charm. "Tell him apology accepted."

Sarah thanked him, but he didn't invite her in—and she didn't invite him back to her place to eat the last of the fried apricot pies. The old man puffed on his cigarette.

"It's not a serious interview," Sarah said to Nate on the way back out to the road. "Conroy doesn't have a notepad or a tape recorder."

Nate made a face. "I think you'd have to be a serious journalist to have a serious interview."

"At least he's pleasant."

"Too bad he didn't invite you in for a little nip of something. I'd love to see his notes for his book."

She cut a look at him. "You don't think he's legitimate?"

"I don't think anything one way or the other."

"My opinion? Ethan's right. Much as I hate to say it, Conroy's a bottom-feeder, positioning himself to be in the right place at the right time for a bombshell." She squared her shoulders and picked up her pace. "But my family doesn't have anything to hide, about ourselves or anyone else."

Nate hung back, watching her walk down the road with sudden energy. Caves, snakes, frogs, a baby on a doorstep, an historic house, an old fishing camp, a well-respected diplomat, the president of the United States—if he wanted secrets and lies to drop into his lap, Nate thought, he'd park himself in Night's Landing, just as Conroy Fontaine had done.

Twenty-Six

Juliet changed into her running clothes for her regular five-thirty-in-the-morning, three-mile run. Some days she did five or six miles, but at least five days a week, she did her minimum of three miles. Today was not a strength-training day. No sweating it out in the weight room later.

Thank God.

She stooped in front of her tropical fish tank and said goodbye to a rainbow-colored fish staring at her. Her brothers in Vermont had threatened to fry her fish. They thought she needed to do something about her social life, like get out of law enforcement. It was fine for them to be cops, but not her. And not a *fed.*

Cops and landscapers—an odd combination, but that was her family.

She took the stairs down to the lobby and said a cheerful hello to the doorman. In her next life, she wanted her own Upper West Side apartment in a building that had a doorman.

In *this* life, she couldn't even afford an Upper West Side apartment with no doorman.

Her family didn't have money. That was for damn sure.

She pushed open the glass front door and trotted down the steps to the street.

Crap.

She'd missed the part about rain in the forecast. She'd let herself get too preoccupied with Rob and with what Collins and his team of investigators *weren't* telling her about the shooting. Were they going down blind alleys, barking up the wrong trees, going off on wild tangents? Hell if she knew. No question about it, it'd be easier for everyone if Hector Sanchez was their guy and he'd acted alone. She'd warned Collins not to go off half-cocked because the Dunnemores had missed their plane. Drama tended to follow them around. It would have been surprising, maybe, if they *hadn't* missed their plane. Not that Collins had appreciated her advice.

And Nate. What was going on with him and the twin sister in Tennessee? There'd been nothing more on the anonymous letter.

At least nothing anyone had mentioned to Juliet. She was not assisting in the investigation. She was not doing *anything* anymore. Well, the parents would be arriving later today. That should take her off the hook. Time to get on with her own life.

She glanced up at the overcast sky. It was more of a misting rain than a real downpour. She sighed and jumped off the curb, heading across the street toward Riverside Drive and her regular route along the Hudson. She went at a light jog, warming up her muscles, letting her body get in sync with the idea that, yes, it was a running day, not a rest day. Once she reached

Riverside, she'd stop and stretch a couple minutes before her three-mile run.

"Gotta keep up with the big boys," she said half-aloud.

Rob was a triathlete; Nate was a mountainman. They both could run forever and kick ass with the best of them. They worked at it and so did she. Running, weights, boxing, tai chi, yoga, karate. She wasn't an expert at any of them, but she figured they all helped.

A black car pulled off the curb and just missed running over her toes.

Irritated, Juliet resisted smacking its passenger window.

It came to an abrupt stop, the back door opening. Instinctively she jumped back—but she was too late. A dark-haired man shot out of the door, shoved a gun in her solar plexus and, using his free hand, jerked her into the back seat. She went sprawling over the smooth black leather and almost hit her head on the opposite door.

"Good," the man said, settling in next to her. "You didn't scream. You'd be dead now if you had."

"I had that feeling." Juliet sat up, her knee already swelling from where she'd banged it getting thrown into the car. It looked like one of the thousands of black Lincoln Town Cars the rich and the super-busy almost-rich hired to drive them around the city. "What do you want?"

"Information."

The man had a slight, indefinable accent and sharp features. Juliet examined her knee. No blood. "What kind of information?"

"The Rob Dunnemore investigation."

"Come on. I'm a lowly deputy marshal. Nobody tells me anything."

He slapped her across the face. Hard. She had to stiffen her neck muscles to keep him from knocking her damn head off.

Her lip swelled almost immediately, and she tasted blood.

She didn't say a word.

The man was going to get his information from her. Then he was going to kill her. The scenario was crystal clear to her.

"The other marshal," he said. "Winter. Where is he?"

"I don't know."

He popped her another one on the mouth. "You will tell me what I want to know."

His accent took some of the menace out of his words—she decided they'd have scared the hell out of her in his native language. But Juliet recognized her reaction for what it was. Bravado.

Let your fear work for you.

Who'd told her that? Her instructors at the academy? Her father?

The car had pulled into the morning rush-hour traffic. The driver was blond, older than the guy beside her in back. There was no one in the front passenger seat. Neither man wore a mask or a disguise. More bad news, since they obviously weren't worried about her providing the police with their description.

Her door was unlocked.

This fact registered almost automatically—she wasn't sure she'd even looked at the locks. It was as if she knew. *This is your escape. This is what you have to do.*

American car. These guys were foreign. Maybe they didn't know how to lock up?

Just then the guy next to her realized his mistake. "The locks! Idiot!"

But Juliet was already making her move. In one swift, well-practiced maneuver, she pushed open the door of the moving car and hurled herself out.

She heard the guy in the back seat swear in another language. French? Italian? Not Spanish. She sort of knew Spanish.

She slammed onto the pavement and used her karate and tai chi skills to control her full-body roll even as she felt the pain tear through her.

Brakes screeched all around her.

She scrambled to her feet. A yellow cab came to a hard, crooked stop so close to her that she had to fall onto its hood to keep from ending up under it. Another car rear-ended it, and it was all she could do not to slide off the hood.

"You stupid, fucking bitch," a man yelled out the window of another car.

She didn't exactly blame him.

"Call the police," Juliet told the cab driver, who was staring at her through the windshield, frozen behind the wheel. "Nine-one-one. *Now.* Tell them a federal officer's been hurt. A U.S. marshal."

The driver nodded, his hands shaking. "You shot?"

"No. Hurt."

God, she couldn't breathe.

Had she cracked a rib?

She felt a searing pain in her upper right thigh and glanced down as she eased off the hood of the cab.

Blood. Road rash. *Nasty* road rash.

A half-dozen other cars and cabs stopped. A young man identified himself as an E.R. nurse and asked if she needed help.

"Yes." Juliet could feel him and another guy helping her off the hood. "Yes, I think I do. I'm a federal agent. The car I was in. Did you get its plate number?"

"No, ma'am. Please, try not to talk. Let's have a look—"

"I'm okay. I need a car. I need to go after those assholes—"

"Ma'am. Please."

They got her to the curb. She heard sirens. She saw a police officer. *I'm fine…I'm fine.* She didn't know what she said aloud and what she only thought, but they all got the idea that she wasn't going to let herself get strapped onto a gurney and stuck in any damn ambulance.

While she was still arguing, Joe Collins pulled up in his black G-man car. It was the first time he hadn't looked amiable. "Get in the fucking ambulance," he told her. "I'll see you at the E.R."

"You don't give me orders—"

"I'm quoting your chief deputy. He'd said you'd be like this."

He rolled up his window and drove off.

Juliet looked at the stunned E.R. nurse who'd helped her in the first moments after she'd leaped out of the car. "So. Okay. I guess I'll get in the ambulance. But I'll walk. No stretcher."

Twenty-Seven

Sarah knocked on the side of the screen door to Ethan's cottage. When there was no answer, she debated a half second, then stepped inside, knowing she was violating the basic trust between them. He wouldn't sneak around in the house when her family wasn't home. But she'd slept fitfully, dreaming of water moccasins, haunted by Rob's warnings and Ethan's own words that she was too trusting.

And she'd slept alone. Her own doing. When they'd arrived back at the house after visiting Conroy, her mind was racing, her body quivering from nerves and fatigue. Nate had touched her shoulder gently, even kindly, and suggested she take a hot bath and fall into bed.

They'd gone too fast. They both knew it.

As she moved into the kitchen area, she fought back a memory of Granny Dunnemore greeting her at the cottage, leaning on her cane, by then a tiny, old woman who'd wanted nothing more in her last years than her own independence. More than a decade after her death, the place still reminded Sarah of her father's mother. Ethan kept it tidy and clean, but it had an unlived-in quality that she couldn't pinpoint. It was if Ethan had only lit here temporarily, superficially, and never intended to dig roots.

His coffee mug was in the sink. Instant coffee. Somehow it seemed to fit.

She had no idea where he was. She'd noticed in her first days home that, like her, he was an early riser. He could be working on the fence or out in the fields, tinkering in the shed—the finicky riding lawn mower was often in need of repair.

She checked the small bedroom. The place was furnished, with all the necessary utensils and linens, but it looked as if Ethan hadn't added anything of his own. She pulled open the bedroom closet and found only his work clothes and one pair of dress pants that looked unworn. That fit with his image of the West Texas good ol' boy.

She did believe he was from Texas. His accent hadn't sounded fake to her. The rest—she wasn't sure. During her troubled night, she'd replayed their conversation at the fence in her head, remembering how cogent and well-spoken he'd been. How he'd warned her not to trust him so easily.

Maybe she shouldn't.

She sat on the small sofa in the living room and opened the trunk that served as a coffee table, then almost let it drop shut on her hand.

Ammunition. Boxes of different caliber bullets. There were four boxes for a .38-caliber weapon, six for a 9 mm.

"Ethan...holy..." Granny's presence kept Sarah's language in check.

Under the boxes was a small photo album, the old-fashioned kind that set the pictures in little black triangles instead of between pieces of plastic. She lifted it out and opened to a picture of Ethan standing on a beach with a slender, dark-haired woman in a bathing suit.

Sarah flipped through the pictures slowly, all of them shots of the couple on the beach—a tropical beach. Florida, the Caribbean. Ethan looked younger, happy, strong and superfit—nothing like the polite, slow-talking gardener in overalls she'd come to know.

He looked more like a man who could slam Conroy Fontaine into a refrigerator and scare the hell out of him.

Conroy had called early. He was coming over for prune cake before lunch.

She glanced at the boxes of ammo. Presumably Ethan had guns to go with the bullets. Where? Did she even want to find them?

Time to get the marshal.

She'd slipped out while Nate was in the shower. She hadn't pictured herself searching Ethan's cottage, never mind finding boxes of bullets and a photo album that didn't exactly show him in West Texas.

Taking a calming breath, Sarah noticed a crumpled computer printout on the end table next to the chair in front of the window overlooking the river. She rose and picked it up, then sat back on the couch and smoothed out the paper with her hands—a man's face. Like a mug shot.

"Oh, my God."

It was the silver-haired man who'd chatted with her mother at the Rijksmuseum.

Without a doubt.

There was no name under the photo, no caption, no indication of the Web site from which the photo had been lifted.

The front door opened, and Ethan shut it behind him as he walked into the small room. "I see you're not above snooping," he said casually.

Sarah didn't bother trying to conceal what she was up to. She waved the picture of the silver-haired man at him. "Where—"

"I found that picture in Conroy Fontaine's cabin. I have no idea who it is."

"Why did you take it?"

"It interested him. Therefore, it interested me."

She noticed Ethan wasn't speaking as slowly, as deferentially—he hadn't yet referred to her as Miss Sarah or called her ma'am. He still had the Texas accent, but this different tone fit better with the man in the beach pictures in the photo album. But it was the tone of a harder, more suspicious man.

Whether this was a new act or the real Ethan Brooker, the sweet-natured temperament and over-reaching good ol' boy act were gone.

Sarah debated grabbing one of the ammunition boxes in case he tried anything, but what would she do? Throw a couple of bullets at him? She walked over and shut the trunk. "And I see you're not above lying. The woman in the pictures—who is she?"

He took another step closer to her. "My wife."

There was something in his eyes. He glanced away. Sarah's heart twisted. "Ethan?"

"She was killed last fall."

"I'm so sorry."

"She always wanted me to try my hand at song-writing." He leaned back against the small dining table, where Granny used to sit and watch the cardinals in the pecan tree and the boats on the river. "Charlene thought I could do anything. I should have told you, but it's not easy for me to talk about her. I wanted a fresh start. I didn't want to answer a lot of questions."

"The bullets?"

"Your parents told me they don't like having guns on the premises. I had a nine-millimeter I liked. Legal, of course. I sold it, but I didn't think to sell the ammo."

"There are bullets for a thirty-eight, as well."

"I got rid of that gun a while ago."

Sarah decided not to ask to frisk him.

"With all that's been going on around here," he went on, "I wouldn't mind having a weapon right now. Your brother getting shot, the feds showing up, reporters snooping around—it's a lot. Legit reporters are one thing, but that Conroy Fontaine's a weasel. You know he is."

"Well, he's a charming weasel." Sarah didn't know what to say—she wasn't the one who'd hired Ethan. "My parents like giving people a second chance. Ex-cons and recovering alcoholics and drug addicts who're trying to pick up the pieces of their lives—some have worked out better than others. A bereaved husband is different."

"Not so different." His eyes seemed to bore right through her. "You're in danger, aren't you? Something happened to bring Deputy Winter down here besides falling for your pretty gray eyes. The feds yesterday. They went through your house. What's going on?''

She didn't answer.

"I live here, Dr. Dunnemore. I have a right to know.''

Dr. Dunnemore. No more Miss Sarah. "Did you go and pound Conroy last evening because you were concerned about me? Or did you have your own reasons?''

He ignored her. "I was in the army for a pretty good stretch. I can tell when someone's hanging by their fingernails. That's you, Sarah.''

Now it was Sarah. "Fair enough. I found a threatening anonymous note in my mail. It's why the FBI and the marshals were here sweeping for bugs and taps. But you know that already, don't you? You've been keeping pretty good tabs on what's been going on around here.''

"That's my job. Think the snake in the house was part of it?''

"Part of what?''

"This campaign to scare the hell out of you.''

"Me? There's no evidence that I'm the focus.''

"You look at it the way you want to.'' Ethan's tone took on an extra edge. "Makes no difference to me.''

She stared again at the picture of the silver-haired man. She'd thought nothing of him or the man who'd approached her until she'd gone to Central Park, until she'd come across the threatening letter. "You're sure you don't know who this man is?''

"Ask your marshal friend. He's standing at the back door.''

Sarah turned abruptly, even as she thought that

Ethan might be trying to distract her, but Nate was there, rigid, alert. She couldn't manage the slightest smile. "I see you're done with your shower."

He put out his hand. "Let's see the picture."

"Ethan said he got it from Conroy."

"I heard."

He gave it a quick glance and dropped it on the table. He shifted to Ethan. "What's Mr. Fontaine's interest in this man?"

"I told Sarah what I know. You heard."

"Was it everything?"

But Ethan wasn't the least bit intimidated. "Fontaine's looking for a connection between the man in the picture and the president. Whether he's a reporter or a political hack, he's a total scumbag." Ethan pulled out a chair at the table and sat down, grabbing an almost full pack of cigarettes and tapping one out. "You recognize the guy in the picture, don't you?"

Sarah took a breath, then spoke. "I don't know his name. He stopped to talk to my mother a few months ago at the Rijksmuseum in Amsterdam."

Nate tensed visibly. "His name's Nicholas Janssen. He's a wealthy businessman from northern Virginia who was supposed to stand trial on federal tax evasion charges last year but took off to Switzerland, instead. He's a fugitive. Failure to appear."

Ethan didn't seem surprised.

Sarah's throat was dry, tight. "My mother said he was someone she knew from college."

Neither man responded.

"Tax evasion—it's not a violent crime. It doesn't mean he's involved in the sniper attack." She felt slightly nauseated. "I can't be sure the man who spoke to me at the museum was with him or even was who I saw in Central Park.''

''Where are your parents now?'' Ethan asked seriously.

''On a plane to New York, I hope.''

Nate shifted to him. ''Show me some of your songs.''

Ethan tapped the side of his head. ''They're all up here.''

''Recite a few.''

''Can't. That'd ruin them. It'd be like picking fruit before it's ripe. But if you wait too long, it rots on the tree. I don't want that to happen, either.'' Ethan stuck a cigarette in his mouth and lifted a book of matches, tore off a single match and struck it. ''I know, Sarah. No smoking in the house. Indulge me this one cigarette.'' He didn't wait for her to respond, just lit the cigarette. ''Look, Deputy, you can lighten up. I'm just mowing lawns and picking bugs off the rosebushes.''

''What do you know about Conroy Fontaine?''

''Nothing. Scumbag looking for dirt on the president.''

''Stay where I can find you.'' Nate turned to Sarah, his blue eyes as no-nonsense and incisive as she'd seen. ''Let's go.''

She started to protest his dictatorial tone, but he was in marshal mode and in no mood. She might as well have been a suspect he was marching off to jail, although she decided his manner was for Ethan's benefit more than for hers.

When he fell in beside her on the way back to the house, he didn't relax. He remained tight, rigid. Sarah picked up her pace. "I figured since you're an official federal law enforcement officer, you'd need a warrant to search Ethan's cottage. I had a feeling he was going to bolt."

"You knocked on his door, you realized he was gone, you slipped inside and had a look." He glanced at her. "You're impulsive. You said so yourself."

"You watched me from the bathroom window?"

"I got to the back door just as Brooker got to the front door. If he'd tried anything—"

"You were there. Thanks." She smiled. "I think."

"Sarah…"

She looked out at the lush spring grass, the azaleas and roses, the first vegetables poking up in the garden, the river glistening in the morning sun. She thought of her father and Granny sitting out on the front porch when she and Rob were kids. Her mother cutting flowers in the garden. "It'll never be the same here."

"Sarah, listen to me—"

But she ran inside, suddenly not wanting to hear what he had to tell her. She wished she could close up the house, shutter the windows, hide—stop time. Stop Nate from telling her anything else that she didn't want to hear.

Only she'd never been one to run from the truth.

She waited for him in the front hall.

He entered the house slowly, and when she saw his expression, the air went out of her. "What? What's happened?"

"Collins called while you were in the cottage. Juliet Longstreet was pulled into a car at gunpoint early this morning. She escaped by jumping out into traffic."

"Is she okay?"

"Scrapes and bruises. She was almost roadkill." He managed a half smile. "Leave it to Juliet to jump out of a moving vehicle."

"If it was her only chance—"

"It was. She was unarmed, out for her morning run. The car got away. There were two attackers. One up front, one in back. The one up front had blond hair—that's all she remembers." He paused, his gaze connecting with hers. "The one in back was dark haired with a slight foreign accent."

Sarah tightened her hands into fists and sank against the wall. "It can't be—Nate, it just can't be the man I saw in the park, the man I saw in Amsterdam—"

"Tell me what happened at the museum, Sarah. Everything. Start to finish."

"Nothing 'happened.'"

"You flew in from Scotland, Rob flew in from New York?"

She stared at an old framed map of Tennessee on the wall opposite her.

"Rob was there first?" Nate prodded her.

She nodded. "He got there a few days ahead of me. I came in for the weekend. I was finishing up my documentary and totally preoccupied, but we don't get many opportunities to be together as a family. I felt I had to seize the moment. I arrived on Friday. Saturday morning, we did a canal tour like every other Amsterdam tourist. Saturday afternoon, we went to the museum. Rob and Dad don't linger. My mother and I do. Especially my mother."

"Where were you and Rob staying? With your parents?"

"Yes. They've rented an apartment on one of the canal streets."

"They went on the canal tour with you?"

"That was the whole idea. We did everything together. It was a great few days. Amsterdam's a beautiful city, especially in the spring."

"Then lunch?"

He wasn't in a mood for distractions. Sarah stood up from the wall. "We had Dutch pancakes at a restaurant near the museum."

"Recognize anyone there? Did your parents talk to anyone?"

"No. No, I don't think so. We walked over to the museum from the restaurant. It was fairly crowded— we just did the Dutch collections. We didn't run into anyone or speak to anyone until we got to *The Night Watch*."

Nate leaned against the wall, studying her. He bit off a sigh. "Sarah—Christ—"

"As I've told you, Rob and my father had already moved ahead to the antique Delftware." She spoke briskly, stating the facts. "My mother can take forever with a painting. The crowds got to me, and I wandered into an adjoining collection. That's when the man I thought I recognized in the park spoke to me."

"What did he say?"

"He just talked about the painting. Something about how he was surprised that the old paintings of Amsterdam didn't look all that different from the new paintings of Amsterdam. I think he was trying to be funny. Then he left. I moved on to another painting. I was getting a little impatient for my mother to join me so we could go find Rob and my father. I finally went back to *The Night Watch* and found her talking to another man.''

"Nicholas Janssen,'' Nate said softly.

"I didn't know. He was handsome, well dressed, silver haired. I didn't think much of it.''

"Did he see you?''

Sarah shook her head.

"Your mother—''

"She didn't mention him. I didn't mention him. There was no reason.'' She looked off, remembering that day. "My mother was a little distracted, but nothing that concerned me. She wasn't sweaty or upset or put out—or excited and happy. I assumed she'd met an acquaintance.''

"What did you do after you caught up with your brother and father?''

"We finished up at the museum and walked back to my parents' apartment on one of the canals. It's a long walk, but it was a beautiful afternoon. We took our time. My father does well, but his stamina isn't what it used to be.''

"How old is he?''

"Seventy-eight. And my mother's fifty-six.'' With a burst of energy, Sarah moved into the kitchen. "I know what you're thinking, and you're wrong. My mother is not having an affair with Nicholas Janssen or anyone else.''

Nate followed her without comment.

She turned on the water in the sink and filled a teakettle. "The people who make judgments about my parents based on their age difference don't know them. They're devoted to each other. It doesn't mean my mother's not aware that she's more than twenty years younger than my father and likely to outlive him.''

"Back to Janssen. Did your mother ever mention him? He was in the news when he skipped out?''

''No. And I didn't see the news reports on him, or didn't remember them if I did.'' She set the kettle on the stove, her movements tense, jerky. "Given the number of people my parents know, it's probably to be expected one's turned out to be a fugitive.''

"Your mother's attractive?''

His question took Sarah by surprise, but she tried not to be defensive. "Yes, I think so. Other people do, as well. What's that got to do with anything?''

He eased onto a stool, those blue eyes never leaving her. "Probably nothing.''

"Anyway, you've seen pictures of her. There are some on the mantel and there's one in your room.''

"Three. As far as I can see, she's downright beautiful. Collins will get a sketch together of the men who attacked Juliet. They must be close to completing something on the guy you saw in the park. We'll see what happens.''

"Do you have *any* idea what's going on?''

He shook his head. "Any of those fried pies left?''

"One.''

"We can split it.''

"Damn right, Deputy. I don't get fried apricot pies that often.''

He got to his feet and came around to her at the

stove, caught her by the elbow. "Your parents will be all right. So will Rob. So will you."

"You can't know that."

He smiled, the incisive eyes not so hard now. "Why the hell not?" He kissed her softly, reminded her of their lovemaking yesterday before dinner. "Good thing I'm off duty."

"There's no such thing as an off-duty fed. Rob says that all the time."

"Think he already knows about us? The twin thing."

She liked the way he said "us," as if yesterday, the night before, had meant something to him. She got two mugs out of the cupboard. "If he knows, he'd have checked himself out of the hospital bed by now. He'd drag his IV down here with him if he had to. He's never wanted to introduce me to his marshal buddies."

"Now you can understand why."

"Nate—" She broke off, setting the mugs on the counter. "I've learned to take things one step at a time with my parents. They've always got a pot boiling. Nicholas Janssen could be a red herring."

"Joe Collins will want to know what he and your mother talked about."

"They talked for two seconds at a public museum. It's not as if she can be accused of harboring a fugitive." Sarah lifted the lid off a canister and dug out a couple of tea bags. "Conroy probably discovered the connection between Janssen and my mother and figures he can tie it back to the president." She stopped still, sighing. "That *weasel*. That has to be what he's up to."

"Didn't President Poe go to Vanderbilt with your mother?"

"They were in the came class."

"Does your mother have a college yearbook around here?"

Sarah hesitated, then nodded. She abandoned the tea bags and retreated to the living room, pulling all four of her mother's college yearbooks off a high, dusty shelf in the living room. She dumped them onto the coffee table and sat on the couch, Nate beside her, and flipped through the pages of the one from her mother's freshman year.

About halfway through, she found one small candid shot from a philosophy class with all of them together: Betsy Quinlan, John Wesley Poe and Nicholas Janssen.

Sarah scanned each of the other three yearbooks, but there were no pictures of Janssen in any of them, including the one from what should have been his senior year.

"He must have dropped out," Sarah said.

But Nate was already dialing Joe Collins's number in New York.

Twenty-Eight

~~~~~~~~~~~~

Juliet hurt all over when she coughed, but she managed to extricate herself from the E.R. and bypass any medical types on her way to Rob's room. She still had on her running clothes, the hem of her shorts bloodied from her short skid across the road. The guys guarding Rob eyed her but didn't say a word. Smart. She felt like punching someone. Not that she could muster up the strength to really nail anyone. But she was in the mood.

Rob was on his feet, off all his IVs and looking like he wanted to escape out the nearest window.

"Watch out," Juliet told him. "Collins is getting cranky about deputy marshals who get out of line."

He gave her a ragged look. "I need to get out of here."

"Not without an armed guard. You're still not fit to protect yourself, and, damn, you need protecting. I'm thinking you've got a big-assed target painted on your back."

His gray eyes seemed to focus on her for the first

time since she'd entered his room. "What the hell happened to you? Juliet—"

"I got shoved into a car at gunpoint by a couple of thugs. One got in a few smacks before I jumped out into oncoming traffic. They wanted to know about the investigation into the shooting." She grinned and limped to his bed. "I think they picked me because I'm blond."

He swept a narrowed gaze over her, presumably taking in her swollen lip, the visible portion of her bloodied upper thigh and the obvious pain she was in. "They picked you because you're a creature of habit and run at the same time every morning." He sat on his vinyl-covered hospital chair. "And you're my former girlfriend."

"There. I've always said you'd make a great investigator." It was weird talking with a swollen lip. The doctor had sent her off with an ice pack, which she'd used on the way up to Rob's room but wouldn't use in front of him and his guards. "I swear, I'd rather get shot than have to jump out of a moving vehicle. You should see the rest of this road rash."

"Done. I'll trade you my bullet wound for your road rash."

"You'd get my right thigh with the deal. You might not like that."

"I like your right thigh just fine."

His comment was that of a friend who'd once been a lover, a man who was facing a long recovery, who hadn't had a chance to fight his own attacker. Juliet sat on the edge of his bed, a hospital no-no, careful to avoid touching anything to her road rash. "It could have been a couple of mad reporters for all I know."

"That's not what you think."

No. She thought it was the guy his sister had seen in Central Park. She tried to grin, but it hurt. "You don't look so good today, Dunnemore."

"You should see yourself, Longstreet."

She laughed. "Collins asked me a bunch of pointed questions. I think he's suspicious of me. Thinks I might have faked my own kidnapping. For all I know, he's got it in his head that I shot you and Nate."

"FBI's suspicious of everyone. Collins is no exception."

"*I'm* suspicious of everyone, but he's carrying it too far. He barged in on me in the E.R. I practically had my ass hanging out—"

"Juliet. Jesus Christ."

"Sorry. I grew up as one of the boys. I can be—"

"I wasn't talking about your language. Collins. He doesn't really suspect you. You got a description of the guys who grabbed you?"

She nodded. "I'm not supposed to discuss the details with anyone."

"Understood."

"You want to get back in bed? You look like you're fading. My God, Rob. I can't believe…" But she stopped herself, knowing it wouldn't do him any good to dwell on how close he'd come to being dead. "Maybe I'll just tell Collins I fell while I was on my run and made up the kidnapping just to cover for my embarrassment."

"This thing, whatever's going on—it's not a marshal's deal. Nate knows about you?"

Although he was up, Rob looked more haggard this morning, with dark circles under his eyes. Maybe the doctors and nurses were pushing him too hard. "Collins called him after he got through grilling me."

Rob sank his head back against his chair and exhaled at the ceiling, his chest bandage peeking out of his hospital gown.

Juliet eased back to her feet. "It's hard to look macho in a hospital gown, isn't it?"

"Hard to look macho with a big goddamn bullet hole in you." She'd tried to make him smile, but failed. He had to know she was holding back on him. "You did great, Longstreet. Getting away. I'm glad you had a chance."

"I should have gotten the plate number. Collins would be happier with me if I had."

"Fuck Collins."

She smiled. "No way. He's got a wife and kids, not to mention that gut—"

That drew something of a smile. "You are going straight to hell, you know that, don't you?"

"Just trying to cheer up a fellow deputy. Think the FBI's got me under surveillance? And Nate—I wonder—"

"You and Nate'd sniff out a G-man within a thousand yards of you."

"They can monitor my calls and e-mails all they want—I don't care. I just don't like the idea of someone tailing me."

"You're unnerved, Longstreet. That's not a good place to be."

"How would you know? You've never been unnerved in your life."

"I'm there now. My parents turning up missing yesterday, Sarah and this anonymous note." He shook his head, his distress at his immobility palpable. "And there's not a damn thing I can do about it."

He shifted in his chair, giving an involuntary moan of pain. Juliet remembered laying her hand on his chest, but all the passion and the romance they'd had for each other was gone now, replaced by a steady, resilient friendship that surprised her. For the most part when men were done with her, they ran like hell.

"Come on, Juliet. Quit beating yourself up."

"I should have gotten more out of these guys before I jumped."

"If the car had picked up speed and you jumped, you'd have broken bones instead of bruises."

Or she'd be dead. "They realized they hadn't locked the doors about the time I did. But still—I could have done better."

"You're too hard on yourself."

"Collins is interviewing witnesses himself. He really must think I staged the whole thing." She blinked back infuriating tears. "God, listen to me. You're the one who almost died."

Rob didn't respond.

Juliet sniffled and pulled herself together. What the hell had the doctor given her to make her so pathetic? "I've decided to fly down to Tennessee and talk to Nate, maybe talk to your sister. Don't worry, I'm not going to step on FBI toes."

"Going to ask their permission?"

"No. I don't answer to them. And it's my damn day off. I can do what I want. Rivera tried to put a security detail on me, but I'm still armed and able to take care of myself."

Rob grinned at her, a spark of his former self shining through his pain and weakness. "Tough as nails Deputy Longstreet." But his humor ebbed quickly, and he tightened a fist, staring at his pale skin. "I really need to get out of this goddamn hospital."

"You will." She kissed him on the top of the head. "I'll call you from Tennessee and let you know if Nate's been behaving himself."

"Juliet—"

"Your sister's really pretty. You know that, right? And her and Nate—whoa, when she followed him—"

Rob made a face. "Sarah's always thought she'd fall for some mild-mannered academic, but, watch, it'll be some hard-ass like Nate."

"Think he could fall for her, or will you kill him if he does?"

"You've seen her. You've seen them together. What do you think?"

Juliet pretended to think a moment, but she didn't have to—she had a fair idea of what Winter and Rob's twin sister were like together. "I think the wolf's guarding the proverbial henhouse."

"Sarah can be tough on men," Rob said. "She's had too many go after her just because of her looks. She's got herself convinced now that she wants someone 'safe.'"

Juliet laughed. "That's what we all think when we see Nate, isn't it? Here's a safe guy. Hang in there, okay? They're both adults. Worse thing that can happen is your sister gets pregnant and has a little Nate— or little Nate twins, since they run in the family."

"I wish I had the strength to throw something at you." Rob settled his gray eyes on her, a reminder that beneath the southern charm and easygoing facade was a serious, experienced federal law enforcement officer. "Be careful."

"Of course."

"Think of me languishing up here while you're eating prune cake and drinking sweet tea punch on the porch."

"Trust me," she said, "I'm not eating anything called prune cake."

"You already have. I made it to celebrate my assignment up here."

"You said it was spice cake with caramel frosting."

"Prune cake. I didn't want to prejudice you."

"Gross."

"You loved it."

She'd loved him. But it hadn't worked, the two of them in the same district. She was more ambitious than he was—hell, a frog was more ambitious. "I'm glad we've stayed friends."

He winked at her in the way that used to make her want to jump his bones. It didn't anymore. It just made her feel good. "Me, too."

Twenty-Nine

Nate left Sarah digging through old pictures and yearbooks and found Brooker on the small front porch of the cottage, a green-painted kitchen chair tilted back as he strummed on an acoustic guitar. It sounded as if he knew how to play.

"You want to tell me who you are?" Nate asked.

"I'm the gardener." Brooker looked up from his guitar, an old one, nothing about him suggesting he gave a damn whether Nate planned to cuff him on the spot. "Go ahead. Check me out."

He already had. "The Dunnemores hired you in early April after they found you trespassing. What were you doing here?"

"Fishing." He tweaked a middle string on his guitar, making a twanging sound, and dropped his chair back down onto all four legs. "I didn't shoot you. I was here with Sarah when her brother called. I didn't hire anyone to shoot you. What other people did or didn't do, I can't speak for."

"You were questioned in your wife's murder."

Brooker kept his stony gaze on Nate. "Well, good

for you, Deputy. You've done your homework. I was questioned. Dutch authorities still don't have a suspect in custody.'' The muscles in his arms tensed visibly, as if he wanted to snap the guitar in two. ''It's been eight months. Nothing's going to happen.''

''Your wife was an army captain based in Germany. She worked in intelligence.'' Nate remained on the grass, still damp from overnight showers. ''You're a West Point graduate and an army major yourself. Special Forces. Your missions are all classified, but you're supposed to be one of the best at what you do.''

Brooker got up with his guitar, holding it by its neck. ''I'm not in the army anymore. I quit in March. I didn't give the Dunnemores my history because it's complicated and they didn't ask. I'm trying to get on with my life.''

''You didn't use an alias.''

''I have nothing to hide.''

''Your wife was killed in Amsterdam. The Dunnemores—''

''I know. Amsterdam. They left town just before Char was killed. The rest is coincidence.''

Nate didn't believe him. Brooker was an adept actor and liar. ''Why Night's Landing?''

He shrugged. ''I had reason to believe the Dunnemores were among the last people to see my wife alive. I wanted to ask them how she was, what they talked about. I never did.''

''Doing a little investigating of your own?''

''Trying to make peace with myself. Char and I— we didn't see much of each other the two years before she died. Twenty-one days total, to be exact. I wanted to find a way to connect with her after she'd died. The Dunnemores took me for a down-and-out type. After meeting them, I realized they wouldn't know anything about Char, her murder. I don't know, I was a wreck. I just started in with the good ol' boy act, and here I am."

Nate didn't know what of what Brooker said was true and what was bullshit. The man had his own agenda, but who could blame him? "Nicholas Janssen?"

"I read the papers, that's all." Brooker opened the front door to the cottage, no sign he was veering out of control, ready to rip it off its hinges; but that could be his military training and experience. "Relax, Deputy, I'm on your side. Whatever's going on, Sarah's up to her eyeballs in it. Look after her. I'll look after myself."

He walked into the cottage and let the door bang shut behind him.

Nate returned to the house, going around to the back where a half-dozen fat bumblebees hovered in a sprawling rosebush thick with pale pink blossoms. He smelled frying onions, heard the sizzle of something Sarah had dumped into her frying pan. When he entered the kitchen, she smiled at him as if he'd just come in from working in the garden and all in her life was normal. A defense mechanism. Her hair was pulled back into a loose ponytail, her sleeves pushed up to her elbows as she broke up raw hamburger into her frying pan.

"I found some hamburger in the freezer, so I'm making a casserole," she said. "Egg noodles, hamburger, tomato sauce, cheese, green olives. It's another of my grandmother's recipes.''

Nate said nothing. He could feel the weight of the bandage on his arm, a steady throb that reminded him he hadn't taken any Tylenol that morning and that nothing about this scene was ordinary.

''She lived well into her eighties,'' Sarah went on. ''I guess her cooking didn't kill her. She worked hard all her life, right up to her last days. She endured so many tragedies.''

The telephone rang, but Nate picked up the extension before Sarah could get to it. ''Dunnemore residence.''

''Nate? Hell, you sound like a butler.'' It was Rob, more alert than he had since the shooting. ''You're the one I want to talk to, anyway. Juliet's on her way down there. Getting snatched this morning threw her.''

''What the hell does she want down here?''

''To talk to you. You might want to sit on her when she gets there.''

No kidding. Nate glanced at Sarah, who was now using a spatula to break up the hamburger in the frying pan. It was smoking, sizzling, but he had no illusions—she was listening to every word he said. He hadn't told her yet what he'd learned about their ''gardener'' from his own sources. He wasn't sure if he would, or if he'd tell Rob. He'd told Joe Collins, not that the FBI agent had returned the favor and told him anything.

''Talk to me about Conroy Fontaine,'' Nate said.

He could see Sarah stiffen, but her brother didn't seem to be caught off guard. ''He checks out as a reporter from Memphis,'' Rob said. ''That's as far as I got. I was going to dig deeper after he tracked my folks down in Amsterdam. Where is he now?''

''Last we saw, smoking cigarettes with an old fisherman.''

''What else?'' Rob asked. ''There's more, Nate. I can tell.''

''Fontaine had a picture of Nicholas Janssen with him. Name ring a bell with you?''

''Yeah, sure. Rich tax evader on the lam in Switzerland.''

''He and your mother and President Poe all spent their freshman year together at Vanderbilt.''

Rob was silent. Sarah turned off the heat under her frying pan and shoved it aside, her attempt to distract herself obviously failing her. Her ponytail had nearly worked itself out of its covered rubber band.

''Sarah?'' her brother asked.

''Hanging in there.''

''My parents will be in New York tonight. Maybe they can straighten this out.''

Nate went ahead and filled him in on what he'd learned about Ethan Brooker.

''This all could be a coincidence,'' Rob said quietly. ''My parents have a way of attracting drama to them. A rich tax evader, a reporter looking for a bombshell, this character Brooker maybe grasping at straws—what a mess. But they don't necessarily have anything to do with the attack on us. I get to sit here and blow into this air thing, and you get to hang out on the river and wait for Longstreet to show up. And the FBI. They'll be back knocking on your door soon.''

''I imagine so. Collins has everything I have. It's up to him now.''

Sarah ran out the back door. Nate tried to smile into the phone, hoping it'd somehow take the edge off his words. ''Take care of yourself. I'll be in touch.''

Thirty

Juliet tried to remember what Rob had told her about Night's Landing. A wide bend on the Cumberland River east of Nashville, rural, picturesque, rolling fields and hills. She pictured the photographs he'd shown her. A John Wesley Poe campaign ad.

Nothing helped.

She was lost.

She turned up a country-western radio station and tapped the steering wheel to the beat of a tune she'd never heard before. She was on some godforsaken back road. The river, wide and slow, snaked below her, intermittently visible through thick woods and fields. She finally pulled over in front of an abandoned brick house with an overgrown yard and, incongruously, white lace curtains in the windows. She needed to get her bearings. Her entire body was on fire with pain. She half wished someone had stopped her from heading south. But no one had. She'd been x-rayed and gooed up at the E.R. She'd answered every damn question Joe Collins snapped at her. She'd visited Rob and told him what she was doing.

He was recovering from a serious injury—he couldn't be expected to knock some sense into her.

She'd stopped at the apartment to feed her fish and put on decent clothes and get her gun, all without anyone hog-tying her to keep her from going off half-cocked.

Well, maybe not half-cocked. Maybe only a quarter-cocked. She wanted to talk to Nate. He was an experienced senior deputy who not only could advise her but would want to know what was on her mind.

Something was off. The shooting, the guy Sarah Dunnemore had seen in the park, the anonymous letter, the parents missing their flight in Amsterdam, those assholes snatching her at the crack of dawn.

Hector Sanchez.

The tone and direction of Joe Collins's questions.

"Yeah," she said aloud. "Something's definitely off."

She switched off the engine of her rented car, a cheap compact—she was down here on her own nickel.

The damn road look like a dead end.

How fitting, she thought, pushing open her door and climbing out.

The air was moist, warmer than New York. Fresher. She groaned in pain, leaning on the door as she gazed down at the river and tried to figure out where she'd gone wrong. God, she hurt. She'd had her ass kicked that morning in the city, and here she was in Tennessee. Her own doing. The truth was, she'd made sure no one dissuaded her. She'd all but lied to Collins, letting him assume she was going home to rest after her ordeal. She'd told him if he had any more questions he could reach her on her cell phone.

She assumed that next she'd get her ass kicked by the chief deputy. Or Nate. She'd be seeing him sooner.

She could just turn around and head back to New York.

Nah. In for a penny, in for a pound. It'd always been her way.

She walked onto the gravel driveway and stood in the shade of a tall oak tree. The ground was damp, the sky clearing with golden sunlight sparkling on a huge, scraggly pink azalea.

"Can I help you, ma'am?" a southern male voice asked behind her.

Juliet turned too fast, a bone-deep stab of pain shooting through her ribs. She almost doubled over, but the man didn't make a move to help her. He had on muddy overalls over a T-shirt, his dark hair pulled back in a ponytail, his brown eyes sweeping over her in a frank, assessing glance. Despite his simple attire and deferential manner, she could see that he was thinking five steps ahead while remaining focused on the moment.

She wore a pantsuit, her weapon, a Glock semi-automatic, concealed under her jacket. But she had a feeling he knew it was there. "I'm looking for the Dunnemore place."

He gave her a dubious look. "Lost, huh? Right. What are you, another reporter? Have fun."

He turned to leave.

So much for deference. "I'm a deputy U.S. marshal."

He glanced back at her, the brown eyes almost amused. "What, you want a quarter to call Washington, or do you have a phone in your shoe?"

She probably wasn't looking very marshal-like. "You couldn't be more obnoxious, could you? I've had a hell of a rotten day."

She started to reach for her badge, but he grabbed her elbow before she'd even realized he'd moved. Normally she was more on the ball. She blamed the pain pill she'd let the doctor give her that morning in the E.R., the fuzzy head she still had from the flight down and her wanderings through middle Tennessee.

She noticed the black tattoo on the man's muscular upper arm. "Relax, okay? I'm just going for my badge."

"Save it." He released her. "You can explain yourself to your buddy Deputy Winter. He's pretty much in a rotten mood."

"That sounds like Nate. And you would be?"

"Ethan Brooker. I'm the Dunnemore gardener."

Gardener? She snorted in disbelief. "Trust me, it's more believable that I'm a federal agent. You always manhandle Dunnemore visitors?"

"Only lately."

"Where is their house?"

"You drove right past it."

"The log house? I guess I was expecting something fancier. Well, I can find my way back. A pleasure, Mr. Brooker."

She didn't bother making it sound like she meant it. She started for her car, but winced, her road rash killing her. She had no reserves. She might have even moaned.

"You going to pass out?" Brooker asked. "Because if you are, give me your car keys. I'll drive you and your car down to the house. Easier than having to haul you on my shoulder. Looks like you carry some muscle."

Had he just called her fat? "I've never passed out in my life."

"Who hit you?"

She automatically touched her swollen lip—she'd given up too soon on icing it. "Long story. Let's just say it wasn't a guy wearing overalls." She pulled on a low branch of the oak. "Nice beech tree. Beautiful area to work."

"Yes, ma'am, it's a real pretty place to work."

He'd amped up the down-home accent and manner, but he was no damn gardener. Then he leaned toward her. "Don't get excited, Deputy. It's an oak tree. You'll have to do better than that to trip me up."

She ignored him. "Is this the house where President Poe was raised?"

"It is."

"I guess you don't keep up this place, do you?"

"No, ma'am."

She rolled her eyes and climbed back into her car, giving a shudder of pain when the wheel brushed against her bruised rib. Brooker frowned at her through her open window, a spark of concern in his brown eyes. "You look like shit, Deputy. Want me to drive you to the Dunnemores'?"

"That good ol' boy act comes and goes, doesn't it?"

He grinned at her. "Two minutes, you'll be talking to Deputy Winter."

"He's not going to tell me a posse's out looking for you, is he?"

"No, ma'am."

She thought he winked. She started the engine and pulled farther into the driveway to turn around. Brooker walked alongside her, toward the river. He was a buff gardener, that was for damn sure. A danger-courting type, never mind the overalls.

He got close to her car and tapped the roof. "Hold on, Deputy." His voice was quiet, serious. "We've got a problem."

She'd seen it at the same moment he had. Two bodies were sprawled on the edge of the bluff above the river.

Juliet stopped the car and drew her weapon. "Keep your hands where I can see them."

Brooker didn't argue.

Ignoring her pain, she got out of the car and had him lead the way through the tall grass to the bodies.

Both were men. Obviously dead. White.

One blond, one dark haired.

Christ.

They were the two men who'd snatched her on the Upper West Side that morning. The blond one was facedown in the grass, one foot hanging over the edge of the bluff, at least forty feet above the river. The dark-haired man—the one who'd stuck the gun in Juliet's gut and hit her when she didn't answer his questions right—was on his back, his chest covered in blood.

They must have dumped their car at LaGuardia, caught a flight just ahead of hers and arrived in Tennessee in time to get shot dead.

"You hear any shots fired?" she asked Brooker.

"No."

Neither had Nate and Rob in Central Park. "These two guys attacked me this morning in New York." *Damn.* "I'm going to pat you down."

"I've got a thirty-eight in an ankle holster. Right ankle."

"How convenient." She confiscated the weapon and finished patting him down. Hard body, lots of muscles. He must have worked his butt off as a gardener. "We're going to the Dunnemore house. We'll call the police on the way. I'd better not find anymore dead people there." Nate. Sarah.

"I didn't kill these men."

She heard something stir in the brush behind her and started to swing around. The cool barrel of a gun touched her right ear. She could see it out of the corner of her eye and went still. "Drop your weapon now."

It was another southern male voice. A county sheriff who'd answered a local's call about the bodies?

"Look, I'm the good guy—"

"You're Deputy U.S. Marshal Juliet Longstreet. I knew you'd come."

She got it now. He wasn't a local sheriff.

"One more time," he said. "Drop your weapon—away from our Mr. Brooker, if you please."

She tossed it lightly to her right.

"Brooker's weapon," the man with the gun said.

She pulled out the thirty-eight and tossed it, too. She felt adrenaline surge through her, obliterating the pain from her injuries.

Brooker stood very still, again with that steely look

that said he was thinking five steps ahead of what was going on. Juliet didn't know what to make of him.

"Don't be a hero, Deputy," the man behind her said. "You're in no condition to take me on and risk Brooker's life, not after what those idiots did to you this morning. Brooker, I'll kill her if you flinch."

Brooker hadn't so much as let an eye flicker. "Did you kill my wife?"

"No. The men I just killed did."

"Janssen's men?" he asked stonily.

"Indeed. They killed your wife on his orders." The man behind Juliet seemed almost charming, as if they were gossiping about a couple of locals. "He sent them down here to kill all of us. Clean things up."

"Your real name isn't Conroy Fontaine," Brooker said.

"It's Poe. John Wesley Poe." He spoke proudly, the gun moving a few millimeters just below Juliet's ear. His tone suggested he was just waiting for anyone to contradict him. "My mother gave me the same name as the women who stole my older brother gave him."

President Poe? This son of a bitch had just killed two men in the backyard of the house where the president was raised, and now he was saying they were related?

Ah, hell.

Juliet felt a wave of dizziness. She couldn't breathe. She started to topple forward, tried to stop herself, then thought—why not? She went all the way, pretending to faint from her injuries, and fell against Brooker's knees. Fontaine. John Wesley Poe. Whoever he was, he grabbed her by the hair and pulled her off Brooker, throwing her aside. She landed hard on the gravel driveway, right on her road rash, and screamed out in pain, tried to yell to Brooker to duck.

But he'd gone over the edge of the bluff.

Who the hell is this guy?

Her mind was all over the place. Her body was reeling from the fresh waves of pain. Her ribs, her head. The damn road rash.

Fontaine jerked her to her feet. He looked awful. Her stomach lurched and she threw up on him, noticing that he had on green camouflage pants and jacket as she heaved. She was dizzy, reeling from pain.

He sneered in disgust. "I can kill you with my bare hands." There was no lilt to the accent now, no charm, however incongruous, to his tone. "Do you understand? I don't need a fucking gun."

Juliet nodded, then felt another wave of nausea and knew she really was passing out.

Thirty-One

Sarah loaded up a big wooden tray with glasses, a bowl of ice, a sugar pot, spoons and a pitcher of tea—regular tea, not tea punch—and carried it out to the porch. She abandoned the casserole. She wasn't hungry. Whenever she was stressed out, she'd tackle one of her grandmother's recipes. It wasn't just the comfort food, it was the inevitable images that came with it of her grandmother chopping onions, rolling out biscuit dough, cutting ripe peaches—losing herself, perhaps, in the ordinariness, the simple necessity, of putting a meal on the table.

But Sarah couldn't have concentrated on another recipe. Not now.

Joe Collins had called from New York. Again, her parents hadn't made their flight. He'd sounded faintly annoyed, as if the Dunnemores might be sucking him into some kind of drama unrelated to his investigation. Clearly, he didn't see what role a rich tax evader, even if he was a fugitive, could possibly have played in the shooting in Central Park.

Despite his obvious doubts, Collins had assured

Sarah that the FBI was leaving no stone unturned and promised to call the minute he heard anything.

Before his call, she'd found an inscription in her mother's freshman yearbook from Nicholas Janssen, telling her he would miss her and appreciated her for being his friend. Sarah had looked him up on the Internet and found the same picture Conroy Fontaine had—a wanted poster on the FBI Web site. But Janssen was just a tax evader, if a very wealthy one. He'd made his money in real estate and had homes in Virginia and south Florida. He was divorced with no children, the only child of a northern Virginia pharmacist and a homemaker. He was just eighteen when his father died—it was the reason he'd had to drop out of college.

Sarah doubted her mother had done anything illegal in talking with this guy at the Rijksmuseum. That he also knew Wes Poe had set off alarm bells, but nothing explained what had happened to her parents.

Where were they?

Nate came out onto the front porch. He'd taken a call on the living room phone. Sarah knew he was doing his own checking, with sources he had within the Marshals Service. That was where he got his sketchy information on Ethan. But he'd just finished with another call, and from his obvious impatience, she suspected the news wasn't good.

"Your pal Conroy needs to answer some questions. Looks like he might not be who he says he is. There's a real Memphis reporter named Conroy Fontaine, but he's sixty-four and just retired to Phoenix."

"Maybe the Conroy we know is his son? Why don't we just go over there and ask him?"

Nate leaned across the table and filled two glasses with ice, poured the tea, making his own attempt at normalcy, Sarah thought. She could see the butt of his gun under his open jacket. "I'm not leaving you here alone," he said, "and I'm not taking you with me. Juliet's flight got in almost two hours ago. She'll be here soon."

Having another armed deputy here would give him more room to maneuver. He handed Sarah a glass of tea, but she just stared at it. "I hope this all turns out to have nothing to do with what happened to you and Rob. It smells like politics and journalistic shenanigans to me. My mother—"

"Don't jump ahead. We have no idea what your mother knew or didn't know about Janssen, why he approached her at the museum—"

"Do you think he had anything to do with the murder of Ethan's wife?"

"I'm not doing the thinking on this one, Sarah."

Maybe not officially, she thought. She tried the tea. "I looked up Nicholas Janssen on the Internet. I'm sure you all have a thick file on him, but—" She'd known nothing about her mother's former classmate. "His mother died over the winter while he was on the lam. It was unexpected—he couldn't go home for her funeral. That had to be hard. I wonder if it's part of the reason he sought out my mother. Maybe he was just lonely."

"People don't think things through when they take off."

"I suppose if he'd been in prison serving his sentence—well, it can't be easy to lose a parent under any circumstances." She immediately regretted her words, remembering his own childhood loss of both parents. "Not that I'd know."

But his attention wasn't on her—she wasn't even sure he'd heard her. He set his glass of tea back on the table and started for the steps, drawing his weapon. "Brooker! What's going on?"

Sarah dropped her glass on the floor as she jumped up, tea splashing on her feet, ice cubes skittering under the chairs and tables. Nate charged down the porch steps.

Ethan was staggering past his cottage, soaking wet, half-drowned and in obvious pain.

He collapsed onto his knees in the grass.

Nate got to him first, Sarah just behind him.

Ethan was shivering from the chilly water and the cool breeze on his soaked clothes. Blood dripped from a swollen gash on the side of his head. "Fontaine's got Longstreet. The only reason I'm alive is because she distracted him." He was breathing hard, a thin stream of blood winding down his left temple and along his jaw. "She fell into me, pretended to faint. I went into the river. He dragged her off. I couldn't—" He tried to get up. "I hit my head on my way over the bluff. There was nothing I could do."

Nate helped him to his feet. "Did you see which way they went?"

"Into the woods between here and the Poe house."

That left hundreds of acres in which to hide. Sarah pushed back a stab of fear, dread. "It was Conroy? You're sure?"

Ethan brushed angrily at blood that had trickled into his mouth. "The fucker thinks he's the presi-

dent's brother or something. He killed two of Janssen's men.''

Nate swore under his breath. "Where?"

"Poe house. Maybe an hour ago. Longstreet and I
spotted the bodies—she was on her way back here to
make sure you two were okay when Fontaine ambushed us.'' His dark eyes settled on Nate. "She said
they were the men who attacked her this morning.''

Sarah slipped in the grass, heading for the back
door to the cottage. "I'll get ice and the phone, call
the police.''

"Wait," Nate said.

But she was already inside and grabbed the porta-
ble phone, ran for the freezer. Her mind was racing.
Janssen's men? What did *that* mean? She pulled out
an ice tray, hit the 9 for 911.

A hand came down hard over her mouth, a gun to
her right temple. "Not a sound or I'll kill you here
on the spot. Understood?"

She nodded, but the hand and the gun stayed in
place. There was nothing charming about Conroy
Fontaine now.

He kept the gun on her and dropped his hand from
her mouth, but she didn't scream, believed he'd kill
her if she did. He wrapped his free arm around her
middle and pushed her out the front door, moving
fast, half dragging, half carrying her into the woods
below the cottage, out of sight of Nate and Ethan.

"I warned you. I told you not to tell anyone."
Vines and brush slapped at her face and legs as he
concealed them within the thick undergrowth. "I told
you to wait. I told you if I could get to your brother,
I could get to you. Did you think I was joking?"

"I—"

"Don't talk! Now people will die because of you."

Her parents. Rob. Juliet. Sarah didn't breathe. It was as if she were in the treetops, watching what was taking place below her.

"You have one last chance to cooperate." His voice was low, his face close to hers. "Do *exactly* as I say and your parents might yet live."

Oh, God.

She landed hard back into reality.

Conroy Fontaine—whoever he was—had her parents.

"Juliet?"

"They have a chance. *If* you cooperate."

"What do you want me to do?"

He didn't answer, dragging her deeper into the woods, away from the river. He was obviously familiar with the woods, unintimidated by any thought of snakes, unworried about getting lost, stumbling into a sinkhole. He didn't seem to care if Nate or Ethan followed him. But Sarah knew she had to buy them time to contact the authorities, figure out their options—for them to come after her. They had to know by now that Conroy had her.

He drew her down a rocky slope, then into a shallow cave within the hillside. He let her go, keeping the gun on her, and she pulled up her knees and leaned against the cool rock. The cave was head-high but only a few feet deep, damp, smelling of the earth, its limestone sides crumbling in places. Sarah had played here with Rob as kids.

And Conroy—whoever he was—had lived here.

She knew now who he was.

"You want me to help prove who you are," she said.

"Money. I want money. The rest will come out. The truth."

Sarah stared up at him. "You're the boy Leola and Violet Poe talked about. Their Huck Finn."

"They wouldn't believe me when I told them that my mother was their boy's mother. That we're brothers." He was sweating, panting. "They called her a liar."

Sarah doubted they'd have been so blunt, not to what they'd obviously perceived as a troubled boy. "Times were different then. Leola and Violet did what they could to help you. I can, too, but my parents—"

"My man in Amsterdam has them."

"What—"

"He won't hurt them. He's waiting for word from me."

Sarah forced herself not to leap ahead. "And Juliet, where is she? Do you have her hidden in another cave?"

"That bitch."

He touched his neck, coughing, and Sarah noticed a swollen, bloody wound, halfway between his jaw and collarbone. "You've been bitten, haven't you? A cottonmouth got you. Conroy—"

"John Wesley."

It was what the Poe sisters had always called Wes. "John Wesley, I can see the fang marks. You're bleeding. The bite's on your neck, above your heart. That's not good if the snake released enough venom to harm you."

"I've been bitten before, lots of times. There's never been a problem."

"There is this time." The snake had definitely released its venom, obviously enough to harm him. Sarah knew the signs. The area around the wound was swelling, his mouth and eyes were twitching visibly, and he was perspiring heavily. "Do your face and scalp tingle, feel numb? Your toes? You're dizzy, aren't you? I'm guessing it's been over an hour since you were bit."

He screwed up his face as if he couldn't think, couldn't control what his body was doing to him. "Don't try to distract me."

"I'm not lying to you. I don't want you to die before you tell me where my parents are, where you stashed Juliet. John Wesley, listen to me. You need to stay still to keep the venom from spreading, and you need to get medical attention."

"I'll find some ice—"

"No. Ice isn't good. Did you cut yourself near the incision?" She squinted up at him and suspected he had. "That's a myth—it only helps the venom spread. I have an antivenom kit at the house. It can suck out the venom."

"No, we're not going back there!"

"It probably wouldn't do you any good, anyway, not at this point. You need medical treatment, a doctor. Your condition is going to get worse with time, not better." She started to get to her feet, but he gave her a menacing look and waved his gun at her. "Please. Let me help you. It's not too late."

"I want you to call the president. My brother. Ask him for a pardon for Nicholas Janssen, his old classmate. He'll do it.'' Conroy's eyes seem to bore through her. "He'll do it for you.''

"A pardon? My God, is that what this is all about?''

"It's about five million dollars.''

And recognition, Sarah thought. He wanted people to know he was the president's brother. "Nicholas Janssen is going to pay you five million dollars for a pardon?'' Sarah was stunned at the insanity of what he wanted. "Conroy—John Wesley—Wes would never agree to pardon anyone under these conditions.''

"Then your parents die. Juliet dies. Your brother. I can get to him, too. I'll ruin his reputation, blame his negligence for the shooting.''

"Central Park—that was your doing?'' She tried to keep him talking, agitated. But not so much that he shot her.

"Your brother had put a call into the Memphis paper where the real Conroy Fontaine used to work. I needed more time before he figured out I wasn't who I said I was." He smiled raggedly. "And I know you, Sarah. I've studied you. You wouldn't talk to the president just because I asked nicely. I had to pressure you, scare you badly enough that you'd cooperate.''

"The letter. The snake in the kitchen—''

"I'm glad you saved it. I saw you.''

His words hit her hard. Rob was suffering in part because this man wanted to pressure her—wanted her to use her influence with the president. She wrapped her arms around her knees, trying to keep herself from shivering. "You wanted Rob out of commission and me scared and off balance. Well, you've succeeded. What about Nate? Hector Sanchez?''

"I told Hector all he had to do was sit in Central Park with a gun and then disappear. It was so easy. I knew he'd be spotted, there'd be witnesses.''

"What did you do, hide nearby and do the shooting yourself?''

"I was a yard away from Hector. He never even saw me. No one did. And I didn't leave a trace for the feds. I'm that good.'' He tried to catch his breath, but the snake venom was making him pant. He glanced around the small cave. "It's because I grew up here. I know how to hide. People never believed Leola and Violet when they said they saw me out here because I never left a trail. It was like I didn't exist. I've used that to my advantage.''

Sarah's teeth were chattering now. Nerves, fear. It was damp in the cave, but she wasn't cold. "Did you give Hector the drug overdose?''

"That was the easiest part of all. He was an addict.''

"And Nate—''

"I meant to kill him. My aim was off. It would have been an easier shot if they'd stayed on the street. Your brother—'' He shrugged, wiping his palm over his swollen, bloody snakebite. "I didn't care one way or the other if he lived or died, so long as he wasn't asking questions for a while. Dead or alive, I knew I could use him to motivate you to help me.''

"Did Nicholas Janssen send you?''

He scoffed. "No, he thinks he can get a pardon on his own by manipulating your mother. Fool. He wants to come home to northern Virginia and visit his mother's grave. He's pathetic.''

"His men—why did you kill them? Aren't they on your side?" Sarah dropped her hands to her sides, leaning back against the cave wall, slowly edging to her feet. "Oh, I get it. Janssen didn't know what you were up to. When he found out, he didn't like it. Five million's a lot of money if he thinks he can get a pardon free from my mother. You're both crazy.''

"Janssen wants a pardon more than anything, but he put the hounds on me.''

"And when his hounds found out you were shooting federal officers in Central Park—'' Sarah shook her head. "Your guy Janssen wouldn't want that pinned on him. It's a much worse crime than federal tax evasion.''

"His men would have killed you, too. Don't think Nicholas Janssen is just your garden variety tax evader. He'll pay me. I'll blame your gardener for his men's deaths—Janssen'll have Ethan killed before the week's out. He should have done it weeks ago.'' Conroy was still panting, sweating from the snake venom coursing through his bloodstream. "The big dope wants to find his wife's murderer.''

"How did you get mixed up with Janssen?''

"You," he said simply. "I looked you up in Scotland to find a way to get the recognition I deserve. Then I went to Amsterdam. Your parents were there—I saw your mother meet with Nicholas Janssen. I saw her meet with Charlene Brooker. I put it all together.''

Sarah's stomach twisted. "But—''

"Your mother's old friend from college had Captain Brooker murdered because she was getting too close to uncovering his real crimes.''

Sarah couldn't speak. She watched Fontaine unraveling before her, sweating, slurring his words. If he'd just keep talking long enough, he'd weaken, and she could do something—get his gun, tie him up. Or Nate could find her. They could get him medical attention and keep him alive so he could tell them where he had her parents stashed in Amsterdam.

''Talk to the president,'' Conroy said weakly, passionately. ''He'll do anything for you. You know he will. No one can undo a presidential pardon. He has the sole right. It's in the Constitution. He *knows*.''

''There's a procedure.''

''He doesn't have to follow it. Presidents pardon hundreds of people.''

''Conroy—John Wesley, there's no way he'd pardon Nicholas Janssen just because I ask him.''

''Yes. He will. I know he will. So do you.''

She stood upright, the top of her head grazing the dirt and limestone ceiling of the cave. She couldn't breathe. ''You were there that day. With the snake. You saw.''

''Everything. You saved *him*, Sarah. You saved his life. He didn't save you.''

''It's not that simple.''

''It *is* that simple. What happened that day isn't what people believe happened.'' Some of the friendly charm had returned to his voice, but he toppled back slightly, dizzy, undoubtedly, from the snakebite. He managed to keep his gun pointed at her. ''Tell him about me. Tell him he has a brother. Once news of the pardon gets out, the press will be all over it.

They'll find out about me. I'll be long gone, living in luxury, but the world will know who I am.''

Sarah forced herself not to let her thoughts leap ahead. "I'll do as you ask. Just don't harm Juliet or my parents.''

He seemed relieved. "All right, then. Go. Call the president. You have one hour.''

"What? Conroy—John Wesley, I don't even know if I'll be able to reach him in an hour!''

"An hour. If my man in Amsterdam doesn't hear from me, he kills your parents and disappears.''

"You're asking the impossible!''

"I'll contact you. I'll know when it's done.'' He smiled at her, as if she were a student he believed in who was having a crisis of confidence. "Trust me. President Poe will grant the pardon if you ask him. Don't delay. Deputy Longstreet won't last more than an hour where she is.''

Without warning, he bolted, disappearing around the far edge of the cave. He was agile, fit, and he knew the land.

Sarah crept gingerly out of the cave. She couldn't hear him moving through the woods. A squirrel chattered at her from the branch of a cedar tree.

She had to find Nate, Ethan, get the police here, sort out what of Conroy's story and demands was real, what was bluff—what was pure fantasy. She made her way through the woods toward the river and the path that led between her family home and the Poe house. Conroy—John Wesley— hadn't shot her. He hadn't beaten her up. Physically, she was fine.

You can do this.

She didn't dare call out and risk Conroy hearing her, deciding she wasn't cooperating. How could he have her parents? He was a loner—that was what had so worried Leola and Violet, the idea of a teenage boy out here living on his own, alone. Who could he have working for him in Amsterdam? Was he bluffing about having her parents?

Sarah stumbled on an exposed tree root but managed to keep her footing.

The snakebite would kill Conroy. She wasn't sure if *he* had an hour. He had to get medical attention.

She pushed back the thoughts and kept moving toward the river, finally reaching the main path. She felt a burst of relief and started to run.

But she heard something and stopped, listening.

A mockingbird. More squirrels.

And something else. A muffled cry—or her imagination, turning the normal sounds of the woods into a human cry.

She was at the junction of the main trail that ran along the top of the bluff and a steep, narrow path, barely a foot wide, that curved down to a cave worn into the limestone above the river.

It had to be where Conroy had stashed Juliet.

Without hesitation, Sarah veered off onto the narrow path. One wrong move, and she'd be in the river. It was a vertical drop into the water, no real riverbank here. The path deteriorated into a foot-wide limestone ledge that led horizontally across the bluff to the cave, the same ledge where she'd come across Wes Poe that day with the snake.

The main path was twenty feet above her, the river twenty feet below her. If she fell, she didn't know if she'd fare as well as Ethan had.

As she reached the mouth of the cave she heard the muffled yell again. The cave was only about four feet high and twelve feet wide, a dark, dank, claustrophobic slit in the limestone bluff. She and Rob used to like to sit on the edge and throw stones into the river, catch the occasional snake off guard and release it unharmed. But caves weren't her favorite places.

With a quick intake of breath, she ducked and hurled herself inside.

Juliet Longstreet lay flat on the dirt and rock, in the shadows, her mouth gagged, her hands and feet bound.

Sarah scooted toward her. "You don't have a bomb or something tied to you that'll go off if I untie you?"

Juliet shook her head.

The bastard had used one of Ethan's bandanna's to gag her, so tightly the fabric cut into the sides of her mouth. Sarah carefully eased the gag down to her chin, until it hung loosely around Juliet's neck. "Fucking snakes," she spat. "Goddamn. There were two in here the size of Godzilla. I *hate* snakes. That bastard's been bit. I hope it was a poisonous snake."

"It was. I saw the bite. Are you okay? Were you bit?"

"I'm fine. Get these damn ropes off me, okay? Where's Nate? He send you in here alone? What the hell's the matter with him—"

"He's with Ethan Brooker."

"The gardener," Juliet said sarcastically.

Sarah worked on the tight knots that bound Juliet's wrists behind her. "Conroy thinks he's the president's brother. He used to live out here—he must have been a teenager at the time."

"What, you two sit and chat awhile?"

The knots loosened slightly, but Sarah realized she

wasn't going to get them undone. She pulled and pushed on the rope, stretching it, noticing the marks on Juliet's wrists that indicated she'd done the same. "He says he has my parents. He said you wouldn't last here another hour—"

"I wouldn't if another freaking snake slithered in here. Look, don't be gentle, okay? Just get the fucking rope off me so I can go after this bastard."

Using all her strength, Sarah clawed at the rope, felt it and her fingers digging into Juliet's skin, but, finally, managed to get it below her thumb joints.

Juliet shook the last of the rope off and tackled the one on her feet. She was deathly pale, her lip swollen and bloody, her entire body shaking from pain and exertion. "What does this son of a bitch want?"

Sarah stemmed her rising sense of panic. "He wants me to get Nicholas Janssen a presidential pardon. He thinks Janssen will pay him five million dollars and the world will find out that he's really the president's brother."

"Jesus Christ. The bite'll slow him down." Juliet freed her feet and gave a small, involuntary moan, then took a breath and turned to Sarah. "I'll get him. I thought he was going to throw me in the river after he tied me up. I swear, I'd just as soon he did as be in here with the snakes."

"Cottonmouths don't nest the way you see in movies. When they're born, they scatter. They're very solitary."

"Yeah." She grinned feebly. "A solitary snake is plenty for me. Look, Fontaine let you go, right? He thinks you're doing his bidding. You're safe out there. So you go on, get to Nate, and fill him in. Otherwise,

I'd have to stay and protect you, and I think we'll all be better off if I go find this bastard.''

- Sarah shook her head. "Juliet, listen to me. You're in no condition—''

She crawled toward the mouth of the cave. "I'm never living this down. The guys at my apartment, this Brooker character, tied up and left to die in a goddamn cave." She stuck her head out of the cave, into the sunlight, then rolled back. "Crap.''

"Is it Conroy?" Sarah asked, reaching for a loose rock, anything.

Juliet shook her head just as Ethan squatted at the mouth of the cave. "Nice little tea party you ladies are having, huh?''

"Oh, for God's sake," Juliet said. "Brooker, I've got a job to do. How did you get here? Why aren't you drowned?''

"I'm a good swimmer. I picked up Sarah's trail. The law's right behind me.''

"I *am* the law.''

"You don't look it. You look like a pretty lady who's had the shit kicked out of her.''

She groaned in disgust.

"Juliet, Ethan's right." Crouching under the cave's low ceiling, Sarah crept toward them. "Not about patronizing you, but about your condition. Ethan, tell me you have a SWAT team out there and not just—''

"No SWAT guys yet. Just Winter." He settled back against the cave wall, his eyes glassy in the dim light. He had to be in almost as much pain as Juliet. "I'm not going to be much good to him with my head beat in. It wasn't one of my smoother dives into the damn river." He managed a grin. "Guess I'll stay here and keep you womenfolk safe.''

Sarah suspected he was deliberately annoying them to cut through the tension, but Juliet gritted her teeth. "God, you're even more obnoxious when you're injured." But some of her initial energy surge was going out of her. "Concussion?"

He shrugged. "Probably. I hit my head when you pushed me off the cliff."

"I didn't push you. I should have."

Nate peered into the cave. "Juliet, Sarah—you two okay?"

Juliet nodded, but Sarah scooted to the edge of the cave. "Fontaine has my parents. He'll tell me where they are if I get Nicholas Janssen a presidential pardon. If I don't—if he doesn't get word to his guy in an hour—my parents will be killed. I have an hour."

Nate touched her hand. "We'll get him, Sarah. Just hold on."

She ducked out of the cave and stood up on the narrow ledge, pushing back a wave of vertigo at the steep drop to the river. "Conroy's been bit by a cottonmouth. He's not going to last long." She could feel her heart racing. "He might not even last the hour."

"Listen to me—"

"I have to find him before he dies and try to get through to him that I—" She placed a hand on the limestone layers to help keep her balance. "What he's asking of me can't be done. It's impossible."

"He could be bluffing," Juliet said from within the cave.

But Sarah couldn't wait any longer and moved as quickly as she could along the ledge. Nate could do what he wanted. Knock her into the river, follow her or stay put. It didn't matter. She was going after Conroy Fontaine, aka John Wesley Poe.

She heard Nate behind her and thought, he could also shoot her.

"Keep going," he said close to her ear. "I don't want to end up in the damn river."

"I know you're worried Conroy's hidden somewhere with a sniper rifle, but he's in no condition—and he wants my cooperation."

"Sarah."

She nodded. "I'm going."

Juliet figured that every nerve, muscle, vein and artery—every damn cell in her body—had been stripped raw. "If I don't get out of this cave," she told Brooker, "I'm going to go buggy. I have a cell phone in my coat pocket. My hands are too numb—can you get it?"

"No problem, Deputy."

He crept toward her, his clothes soaked, his head swollen and bruised. He had to have a concussion. But she could see the ripple of muscles in his arms, sensed his overwhelming masculinity and felt an urge to carve out her own authority. He reached into her pocket and retrieved her cell phone.

She licked her cut lip. "I should be pissed at you for being such a retro chauvinist, but right now, I feel like such crap that I'm going to let the 'pretty lady' stuff go."

He grinned at her, not moving back from her as quickly as he could have. "That was worrying me, you know," he said lightly, clicking on her cell phone. "Battery looks good."

"Any service out here?"

"Should be."

She eyed him. "What are you, some kind of spook? Secret Service?"

But he didn't answer, just handed her back her cell phone. She crawled out of the cave onto the narrow ledge, managing to sit with her legs dangling over the side. She stared at the readout screen but couldn't make out the dial numbers. "My eyes aren't working right. That bastard Fontaine—" She licked her lips again. "He smacked me on the back of the head before he left me in the cave. I think he knocked my eyeballs loose or something."

Brooker moved in next to her. "What number you calling?"

Her head was throbbing. She struggled to remember the number Joe Collins had given her in the E.R., then recited it to Brooker. He dialed without a word and handed the phone back to her. "Winter talked to some FBI type on our way over here. He's sending in the cavalry."

Juliet had expected as much. One of the FBI agent's flunkies answered. She told him to put on the big guy. She'd been smacked around one too many times today for anything approaching niceties.

Collins came on. "Where are you?"

"In a cave with snakes and some kind of spook who's been playing the Dunnemore gardener. Listen to me. This Conroy Fontaine character had someone snatch the Dunnemores in Amsterdam. He says they're his hostages."

"We're on it. We've got a team on the way to your location. Sit tight, will you?"

"I don't have much choice. Nate and Sarah Dunnemore—"

Collins cut in again. "Winter says you found the guys who ambushed you this morning—dead."

Juliet paused. "Don't start with me, okay? I didn't kill those men. Look, get word to the SWAT guys that Fontaine thinks he's the president's brother."

"Jesus Christ," Collins breathed.

"And he's been bit by a cottonmouth. It's bad. Sarah Dunnemore wants to find him before he dies."

"Winter's with her?"

"Yes."

"All right. You know what to do."

"Yeah. I'm getting out of this goddamn cave. Tell your guys I'll meet them at the Poe house. That's where the bodies are."

She hung up and glanced at Ethan. "You're armed?"

"Nine-millimeter Browning."

"Not going to share, are you?"

He grinned. "Not a chance."

She'd figured as much. "Well, are you game for getting out of here?"

"I had my fill of caves in Afghanistan. Let's go."

She grimaced at the river below her. "Fontaine told me the water's forty feet deep here. Strong current. I'm not the best swimmer."

"Relax." Brooker grasped the rock at the top of the cave and pulled himself to his feet, glancing down at her with a wink. "It doesn't matter if it's forty feet deep. You can drown in six feet of water."

Thirty-Two

Nate appreciated Sarah's spirit and determination and understood her fear for her parents, but he wasn't going to drag her through the woods to look for a killer. They were almost to the Poe house. When they got there, they'd wait for the SWAT guys. FBI, USMS Special Operations, Secret Service, local guys—whoever Joe Collins managed to get in there could go find Conroy Fontaine. For all Nate knew, they could be there now.

In the meantime, it was his job to keep Sarah Dunnemore alive.

She didn't see it that way. She walked just ahead of him, her energy not flagging even slightly. "You're not responsible for me. It's my decision to go after Conroy."

"You have your own way of looking at things."

"That's right, I do."

The trail had descended toward the river—they were only fifteen feet above the water now—and cut steeply back up toward the Poe house. Conroy Fontaine had the skills to hide in Central Park in the middle of a rainy early May day and pick off two marshals. He'd killed two presumably highly trained bodyguards. He'd wormed his way into the Dunnemores' lives. Nate had believed the guy was just another reporter looking for a story.

"Conroy wants the pardon so he can get his money and his recognition," Sarah said. "He doesn't want to kill me. That's not what this is about."

"Let the SWAT negotiators talk to him. They're the experts. What if you find Fontaine and end up screwing it up?"

That caught her up short. She broke her stride. She was in the shade of a cedar tree growing precariously up out of the limestone, between the path and the river. For a split second, Nate thought she was going to back off. He heard the rustling noise above them.

A huge black snake dropped from the cedar and landed on Sarah, latching its fangs onto the right side of her neck, its thick body writhing and wriggling. It had to be five feet long.

Simultaneously Conroy Fontaine leaped from the tree, its branches halfway out over the river, and made a sprawling dive into the water. Sarah screamed in shock and tried to pry the snake off. "Don't shoot it!"

The snake wrapped itself around her arms and was going for another bite. Fontaine had used it as a distraction. "I've got it," she said. "Trust me. *Please.*"

Nate jumped to the edge of the path and pointed his gun at the water, saw Conroy swimming toward a boat anchored in a small, shallow cove just downriver from the bluff below the Poe house.

Making his escape.

"Stop him," Sarah said. "Don't worry about me."

She staggered backward over the roots of the cedar tree and went feetfirst over the edge, wrestling with the damn snake all the way into the river.

Nate ran past the cedar and tore his way down an eroded section of riverbank, slipping on the wet rocks and dirt. He could see the snake scurrying away from Sarah in the water. She came up for air and waved Nate on as she swam toward shore. Her strokes were strong, determined.

She'd be all right.

Conroy was twenty yards downriver, climbing into his boat.

Nate had a shot. A difficult one, but he'd take it if he had to. He raised his weapon, feeling a jolt of pain from his injured arm. "Freeze, Fontaine."

Fontaine flopped onto the pilot's seat. "You won't shoot me." His voice was raspy, breathless, as he shouted across the water at Nate. "I know where the Dunnemores are."

The guy was in bad shape. But he was right. Nate didn't want to shoot. Keeping his gun pointed in the general direction of the boat, ignoring the pain in his arm, he ran up the short stretch of embankment to the shallow cove, positioning himself above Fontaine.

He had one chance.

Without hesitation, Nate jumped, landing on Conroy, knocking him down and sticking the HK in his face. "Don't move."

"I should have killed you when I had the chance."

His words were slurred, his body fiery hot even after being in the cold river water. "Where are the Dunnemores?" Nate asked quietly.

"Fuck you."

"Was it a bluff? Do you have them?"

Sarah was on shore, scrambling along the eroded bank, blood from her snakebite dripping down her neck. "My parents—"

"Get the pardon," Conroy screamed at her, trying to jerk his head up against Nate's hold. "It's not too late. Call President Poe. I'm his brother. He's never known his true family. I'll tell him everything about us. I'll share the money with you."

Nate had heard enough. The guy's condition was worsening from the snakebite. "You need a doctor."

Conroy vomited, what looked like mostly river water spewing out over the boat. He was shivering violently, panting, sweating. Nate got him to his feet. "The parents," he said. "Come on. It'll be a hell of a lot easier for you if you tell us where they are."

But he was unconscious, slumped against Nate.

Sarah splashed out into the river, water up to her waist. "John Wesley, don't die."

Juliet was behind her, looking as if the current would sweep her away. But her voice was steady, firm. "Ouch. God, you're a mess. Look at that neck. What happened to the snake?"

"He's okay. It was just scared." Sarah was hardly aware of what she was saying. She squinted at Juliet. "Ethan?"

"He's greeting the SWAT guys."

Sarah shook her head. "Nicholas Janssen had Ethan's wife killed. Ethan'll go after him." She reached into the boat and touched Conroy's hand. "Please, don't die."

Nate wasn't optimistic. He looked at Juliet. "You've got him?"

"No problem. I'm in rough shape, but I can handle someone unconscious."

He helped her into the boat and turned his weapon over to her, then climbed out. Blood flowed freely from Sarah's snakebite. He had no idea if that was good news or bad news. Above them on the bluff, he saw the first of the black-clad SWAT guys.

"Shit's hitting the fan," Juliet said unnecessarily.

Sarah clawed at him. "My parents. It's been an hour."

But one of the first wave of SWAT guys to reach them told her that they'd just got word from Joe Collins. The Dunnemores were safe. Dutch authorities had them in Amsterdam. One of Janssen's bodyguards had grabbed them at Schiphol Airport—Conroy must have offered him part of the five million to work on his behalf.

No Janssen. He'd apparently slipped out of the country.

As Sarah had predicted, Ethan Brooker hadn't stuck around to greet the SWAT guys.

He'd disappeared.

Sarah sat in Granny's rocker on the front porch of the log house that had always been home, a safe haven, and tried to drink some of her sweet tea punch. Her snake, though angry and frightened, hadn't released any venom, just left a single nasty bite on the side of her neck. She'd had it cleaned and bandaged in the E.R.

Conroy Fontaine—John Wesley Poe—wasn't so

lucky. By the time they reached the hospital, there was nothing doctors could do for him. He died fifteen minutes later.

He'd lied about so much, but not that John Wesley Poe was his real name.

When she was a teenager, his mother had heard about the Poe sisters and the baby they'd found on the doorstep. Pregnant, unmarried and broke, she created the fantasy that her baby and Leola and Violet Poe's baby had the same father. She named hers John Wesley—why she'd given her child the same name as the man she would later tell him was his half brother remained a mystery—and changed her name legally to Poe.

Agents searching out Conroy Fontaine's background in Memphis had dug up that story with little effort. Francine Poe was long dead. After Wes Poe was elected governor and then president, everyone who'd known her and her little boy remembered her crazy tale.

Nate came out onto the porch and sat on another rocker next to Sarah. His arm was freshly bandaged, and she'd overheard an E.R. doctor giving him a stern lecture about taking it easy for a few days. *You've been shot, need I remind you?*

Sarah sipped more of the tea punch, her snakebite aching, her mind fighting off the memory of going into the river with the fat, wriggling cottonmouth. Once it realized it was in the water, it released its grip on her neck and tore off to safety. "Conroy—it's hard to think of him as John Wesley—would have had a better upbringing if his mother had left *him* on Leola and Violet's doorstep, too."

"They were up there in age when he was born, weren't they?"

"They'd have seen to it he got to a good home."

"Why didn't they do that with the president? Not that there was anything wrong with their home, but two maiden sisters living alone out here on the river, World War Two raging—" He shrugged. "It can't have been an easy decision to keep him."

"They believed he belonged here." And Sarah left it at that, angled a quick smile at him. "You'll have to watch my documentary."

He smiled back at her. "Sarah Dunnemore, Ph.D." But he tilted back in his chair and hoisted his feet up onto the porch rail, a warm breeze bringing with it the smells of grass, flowers, river. Nate, who'd been in marshal mode for hours, glanced at her with those incisive, impatient blue eyes. "Why would our young John Wesley Poe think the president would grant Nicholas Janssen a pardon if you asked him? It's got to be more than your pretty gray eyes."

Sarah looked straight ahead, across the shaded lawn to the river and didn't answer.

"What do you have on the president?" Nate asked quietly.

"You have a suspicious mind, Deputy." She laid on the sexy southern accent but still didn't look at him. "The Dunnemores and Poes have been neighbors for a lot of years. I'm sure we can tell many tales about each other."

"Whatever it is, it's going to come out now. The media's descending. You've got the Secret Service crawling all over this place. The FBI, the marshals, the ATF, your local sheriff—they're all going to want to know why Conroy Fontaine/John Wesley Poe thought President Poe would grant a fugitive a pardon if only he could manipulate you into asking him.''

"And I could tell them I have no idea," she said. "I could tell them that Conroy never discussed his reasoning with me when he had me in the cave." She glanced sideways at him. "Here's a question for you. Should I have tried to scream when he grabbed me in the cottage kitchen and put the gun to my head?"

"You should have trusted your instincts, which is what you did."

"How long before you and Ethan realized he had me?"

"Seconds. We didn't want to get you killed." His eyes narrowed, darkened. "It was not a good moment."

She felt a rush of warmth, but warned herself against reading too much into it, too much into the sparks that had flown between the two of them for days. They both had so much to process. And yet, she didn't want him to go back to New York. She wanted to keep him right here, sitting with her on the front porch.

"I trusted you to deal with your snake," he said.

Back to what she had on the president of the United States. She was smart to remain on her guard. "I left you no other choice."

"I could have kept you from doing that kamikaze, feetfirst dive into the water, or I could have gone in with the two of you."

"And got bit, too."

"The point is that I trusted you to handle yourself."

"Thank you, and I trust you to do your job as a marshal and therefore tell your superiors if I tell you something about the president, who is, after all, your ultimate boss."

"So you're saying you do have something on the president?"

She groaned.

"All right. Don't tell me. I'll read about it in the papers."

He didn't seem irritated or even that curious, just satisfied that he was right and she did have a presidential secret.

He tilted back in his chair. "I'll bet it has something to do with snakes."

"You're like the cottonmouth that had hold of my neck. You won't let go, will you?"

"Ah, Sarah." He grinned at her, his tiredness evident underneath, but a light of humor and pure, deliberate sexiness shone in his eyes. "I'd love to latch onto you in about a dozen different ways right now. But don't compare me to a snake, okay?"

"You've seen more cottonmouths since being here than I've seen in the last ten years—" But she sighed, and set her glass down, gazing again at the river. "Wes was a self-made businessman when I was in high school, a millionaire with political ambitions and a desire to serve the public. Leola and Violet were still alive. He'd drive out here to see them. Evelyn, his wife, often didn't come."

"Sarah…"

She pretended not to hear him. "It was a hot day. Muggy. Rob and I were home from school. I didn't know Wes was here. As I told you, I'd been visiting

Leola and Violet—they didn't know, either. He and Ev had just lost their fourth child. Ev was very depressed. There were rumors she was suicidal." Sarah shut her eyes and rocked back into the chair, feeling herself at almost seventeen, practically skipping back from the Poe house. "Wes believed he was at fault, that his ambition, the pressures of his work, had hurt their chances of having a child. He came out to the river to pull himself together. It was the low point in his life, in his marriage."

"He told you all this?"

She nodded, opening her eyes, wishing she could slow her mind, stop the pace of the images repeating themselves. "He was standing on that narrow ledge in front of the cave where Conroy had taken Juliet. I heard him from the path. He was sobbing. I don't think—" She broke off a moment, searching for the right words. "He's not one to cry in front of other people."

Nate picked up her iced-tea glass and took a sip. "Think he was going to jump?"

"I don't know. I'll never know." She rocked back in her chair. "I don't think he intentionally went out to the ledge to jump. I think he just found himself there. It's not that much of a jump—there's no guarantee he'd have died even if he had planned to commit suicide."

"Water's deep there, current's strong."

"He's an excellent swimmer. Not that it matters if he'd wanted to die."

"Was he drunk?"

"Who's telling this story?" But he'd brought her back to the present, and that was where she needed to be to continue. "He surprised a water moccasin on the ledge. I saw it. It came after him—they can be very aggressive when they're startled. Wes panicked."

"And you?"

"I grabbed the snake and threw it in the water."

Nate smiled. "You and these snakes."

"The story got told differently than how it was."

"That's one way of putting it. He said he saved you from the snake. That he saw you on the ledge and you were the one who panicked."

"Ah. You've done your research. No, he said none of that. It was how the story got told. It was how people wanted it to be. A high school girl and a man who would be president—wouldn't you want him to be the one to save her from the snake?" She looked out at the river, smelled it on the breeze. "He simply never corrected it."

"Did he ever ask you not to correct it?"

"Never. Not once. I think if I hadn't been there, he'd have crawled into the cave and died. He wouldn't have jumped in the river and committed suicide, but he would have seen the snake as confirmation of all he'd thought and doubted about himself that day. I don't mind how the story's been told. Wes understands what it's like to be at rock bottom. He's brought that into his public service. His political enemies would say he was a grown man saved by a seventeen-year-old girl, but the truth is far more complicated."

"He'd never have granted Janssen a pardon on your say-so."

It was a statement, but Sarah shook her head.

"Never. He took an oath. He just wouldn't—no, never. That Conroy—John Wesley—believed he would was a fantasy on his part."

Nate took another swallow of tea. "This tea punch is growing on me. I still think it could use a pound less of sugar."

"Are you drinking out of my glass?"

He leaned toward her, skimmed his knuckles across her cheek. "If this place wasn't crawling with feds and you hadn't just been bit by a cottonmouth, I'd be carrying you upstairs right now and drinking—"

"You're determined to embarrass me, aren't you?"

"Uh-uh." He kissed her on her forehead. "Just to make you smile."

The Dutch authorities released the Dunnemores into the protective custody of a deputy U.S. marshal sent in specifically for the task, who in turn not only put them on a plane but sat next to them for the duration of their flight to New York.

Juliet figured it was the only way to get them to their kids without another damn drama.

She inched her way out to the porch after she'd talked her E.R. doctors out of sticking her in a Nashville hospital and got a ride back to Night's Landing from a very cute FBI agent with a southern accent.

She hurt all over. She figured she'd hurt until she was a hundred.

Sarah was still in her rocking chair. Nate had joined a million other feds down at Ethan's cottage. They'd already gone through the fishing cabin that Conroy Fontaine had rented. Apparently he'd left behind a considerable amount of damning information on

Nicholas Janssen, who was, allegedly, involved in illegal arms trading, extortion, murder, fraud—tax evasion was the least of his misdeeds.

"I thought you were being admitted to the hospital," Sarah said.

Juliet gave her a crooked smile. "I had to threaten to shoot my doctor to keep him from strapping me to a stretcher. I hate hospitals."

"More than most people?"

"Yeah. Probably." She changed the subject. "Did I see you and Deputy Winter smooching out here?"

Sarah sighed, looking smart and pretty and not blushing even a little. "Maybe it's the snakebite, but I think I'm falling for him."

Juliet grinned. "It's the snakebite." She glanced out at the cottage and wondered where Ethan Brooker was now. "I knew he'd take off."

"Ethan? Why didn't you stop him?"

"He was the one with the nine-millimeter."

Sarah put her feet up on the porch rail. "I hope someone gets to him before he does something he regrets."

"Like kill Nicholas Janssen? I'm not sure he'd regret it." Juliet eased herself slowly, painfully, onto a cushioned chair. "Joe Collins read me the riot act for not stopping him. Like I didn't have enough to do with two dead bodies, the snakes, you in the river, Nate going Tarzan on us, this Conroy Fontaine character foaming at the mouth."

"Collins is hard on you because he respects you."

"He's hard on me because he's a prick."

Sarah smiled. "And I suppose you told him that?"

Juliet realized that she'd come to like Dr. Dunnemore. "Yeah, as a matter of fact."

"Ethan's going after Janssen," Sarah said.

Juliet nodded. "That must have been some woman he lost."

Thirty-Three

Janssen cocooned himself in the fishy, salty-smelling woolen blanket and tried to stay warm deep in the bowels of the ancient trawler that was taking him to safety. Away from luxury, away from hope. He hadn't slept in hours, because when he did, he dreamed of his mother crying for him on her deathbed, of Betsy Dunnemore smiling at him at eighteen and making his heart melt. He'd let them both down.

John Wesley Poe.

Conroy Fontaine.

He was the psycho who'd interfered in his life and shot the marshals in Central Park. Who'd tried to extort five million dollars from him for a pardon that was even more of a fantasy—a flight of fancy—than Janssen's own dream of getting Betsy Dunnemore to intervene with the president on his behalf.

Conroy had weaseled his way into Janssen's life last fall and learned everything about him.

No, not everything. Too much, certainly, but not everything.

Not the location of his safe houses. Not his backup

plans once he knew there was little hope for a simple conviction on tax evasion charges.

Five years in prison? He'd be lucky now to avoid the death penalty.

Charlene Brooker, lowly army intelligence officer, had been pulling at the thread that would unravel everything and set him up for big trouble. Her meeting with Betsy—beautiful Betsy—was the last straw for Janssen.

But it was Conroy Fontaine with his crazy idea that he was the president's half brother who'd destroyed the careful life Nicholas had constructed for himself, all in an attempt to extort money from him for a pardon and manipulate the president of the United States into acknowledging him as his brother.

The crazy fuck.

Now the authorities apparently had the concrete information they needed to turn the suspicions of a murdered military intelligence officer into a full-blown investigation of all his activities.

He had become one of the most wanted criminals in the world.

But he was prepared. He had a plan for just such a worst-case scenario.

He would survive. He'd always survived.

The Dutch police, the Swiss police, U.S. law enforcement, Interpol—they all wanted his scalp. But at least with them, even with all he'd done, it was professional, not personal. They would capture him and bring him to trial. They wouldn't slit his throat in the night.

With Ethan Brooker, it was different. It was very personal.

The hatch creaked open. "Sir?"

"What is it?" Janssen asked irritably.

"I have news of the man you wanted me to—"

Brooker. "Yes, what?"

"The FBI and the U.S. Marshals Service want him for questioning in that mess that happened in Tennessee. He's disappeared."

Just as I feared.

Janssen had two choices. One, he could let Ethan Brooker come to him. Two, he could get to Ethan Brooker before Brooker got to him.

He pulled the blanket over him, shivering on the cold, skinny mat under him.

Those weren't any choices at all.

Thirty-Four

The Dunnemores reminded Nate of wizards. Eccentric, dramatic, full of secrets and magic spells, but fun and a bit removed from lesser mortals. It wasn't that they didn't make mistakes or were arrogant—they were kind, funny, generous and intelligent. And, despite their oddities as parents, they loved their twin son and daughter. Nate saw that when they finally arrived in New York five days after their son was shot in Central Park, one day after their daughter almost got herself killed in Night's Landing.

He hadn't flown up specifically for the occasion. He'd simply realized he couldn't hang around in Night's Landing and had decided to return to New York, his apartment, his work, his life.

Both Betsy and Stuart Dunnemore had thanked him profoundly for everything he'd done, but all he could think of was the night he'd made love to their daughter in their kitchen.

He didn't want to be thanked for anything.

He thought of his own family—Gus and his egg lady and his hole-digging dog, his sister Antonia and her senator husband, his sister Carine and her PJ husband. They were a different kind of family. Direct, argumentative, loud. Not much going on beneath the surface, not many secrets, except, these days, for the occasional deranged killer. It wasn't subterranean stuff that got them into trouble—it was their keen sense of independence, their reluctance to rely on anyone but themselves.

Carine had learned better, Antonia had learned better.

Nate wondered if he ever would.

He walked down the hospital corridor with Rob, markedly improved but still with a long way to go. The Dunnemores were off to some health-food store to stock up on vitamins and herbs to aid in his recovery. He was getting out of the hospital in a day or two. In another few days, he could fly down to Night's Landing. "Couldn't you have told them Sarah's snakebite wasn't nonvenomous? Then they'd have to fly down there to see her."

"She's cooking casseroles and putting them in the freezer."

"She's *alone.*"

"Not that alone. She's got the Secret Service camped out in the back yard."

President John Wesley Poe was coming to Night's Landing.

And so were the Dunnemores, just not soon enough to suit their only son. Sarah had urged them to stay with her brother at least until he was out of the hospital and give her a chance to get the house in order.

Wizards.

"I should have stayed on Conroy Fontaine," Rob

said. "I should have pushed harder. And Ethan Brooker. Nicholas Janssen. They were under my nose."

"We'll get Janssen. It's just a matter of time."

"Before Brooker does?"

"I hope so. Brooker's all right. I'd hate to see him go down for taking out that murderous bastard." Nate tried to smile. "Something about Longstreet seemed to get to him. Maybe he's not so far gone in wanting revenge that he can't make it back."

"I knew my parents had hired him. I should have—"

"It worked out, Rob. We all got out of this thing alive."

"No thanks to me."

"Don't do it to yourself. I was within yards of your sister when that sick bastard grabbed her. I was within *inches* when he threw the snake at her." Nate could feel his pulse begin to race and knew he had to stop or he'd be no good to Rob, never mind himself. "Your damn tulips might have saved my life. Fontaine would have had a better shot if we'd stayed on Central Park South."

"That's something, anyway. I don't know when I'll be back on the job." Rob shuffled another few steps. "Or if."

"Just concentrate on getting well."

He glanced at Nate with gray eyes that were so like his sister's. "You?"

"It's time I went home."

Wes Poe arrived in Night's Landing two days after Rob had made it home himself.

Except for the presence of the Secret Service, nothing had changed.

Visibly, at least. As he walked down to the dock and stared into the coppery water, Wes could feel the evil that had lurked here. He could taste the bitterness of how close he'd come to losing both Sarah and Rob.

He didn't even remember Nicholas Janssen from Vanderbilt.

Sarah joined him on the dock. He smiled at her, saw that the snakebite had almost healed. "You always get in trouble when you're between projects. Leola and Violet have been one huge, overarching project for you for a long time, but you broke it up into smaller projects—and every time you finished one, you'd get yourself into some sort of mess before you got started on the next one."

"This was a big mess."

"Nate Winter's accepted a promotion to marshals' headquarters in Arlington. He starts in a couple of weeks."

He thought she squirmed, but she managed a quick smile. "Now, why do you think that'd interest me?"

He didn't hesitate. "Because you're in love with him."

"I barely know him."

"Sometimes you fall in love with someone first. Then you get to know them. It happened that way with Ev and me."

"She's a wonderful woman, Wes."

Ev hadn't come to Night's Landing with him. This was his visit, his day of reckoning. "She's the best thing that ever happened to me. I think—" He slipped an arm over Sarah's slender shoulders. "You and the cottonmouths are a big story around here. All over the country. I'm going to set the record straight on what happened out here fourteen years ago. I'm going to tell people what really happened that day.''

''Wes—''

''I should never have let it stand that I was the hero—that I'd been bit by a poisonous snake saving your life.'' He squeezed her, holding her close. ''I was bit by a poisonous snake. But you're the one who saved a life that day. Mine.''

''You don't know what you'd have done.''

''I wouldn't have gotten medical attention in time. That I know.'' He glanced at her. ''You told our Deputy Winter?''

She nodded.

''That's good. That's very good, Sarah. You trust him.''

''I trust a lot of people.''

''But you don't let them in, do you? You and Rob are so accustomed to being on your own, emotionally, physically. But you let Nate Winter in.'' He didn't wait for her to protest and argue and analyze, go Dunnemore and Ph.D. on him. ''They tell me he's solid. I wouldn't want anything else for you. I remember that watery-eyed academic you brought home a few years ago—you rolled over him in two seconds flat. You need a man with backbone.''

''Wes! That was a perfectly nice man.''

''I'm sure he was.''

''Listen to those stereotypes. Never mind who saved whom from the water moccasin all those years ago, the media would skewer you for something like 'watery-eyed academic.'''

He grinned at her. "I'm not making generalizations about every academic. I'm talking about you and this—what was he?"

"A well-respected medieval scholar."

"Just what you thought you were looking for, hmm? I don't think so. Your parents are worried Rob's the throwback to Dunnemores of old. He probably is, but you—you are, too, Sarah, with a lot of Granny Dunnemore thrown in. You're full of adventure, curiosity, drive. You hate being bored. Your father's the same, but he managed to be a Dunnemore in a way that didn't upset Granny after all she'd lost."

He heard laughter drifting from the front porch. Stuart, Betsy, Rob. For a heartbeat, he thought he could hear Granny and Leola and Violet.

Sarah's eyes misted. "Dad's not as energetic as he used to be. You can see him starting to fail."

"Your mother wasn't tempted, Sarah," Wes said softly, knowing what was on Sarah's mind. "Not even for a second. I was here when she and your father met. I've been here all the years since. Nicholas Janssen was never a threat to what they have."

She nodded. "I know. Oh, Wes. Leola and Violet would be so proud of you. They never wanted you to leave Night's Landing, but the White House.…" She smiled. "They'd have liked that. They'd have taken the train to Washington and gone to all the inaugural balls."

He laughed. "Ah, yes, they would have." And he could see them, the two strong, loving, impossible women who'd raised him. "I never believed their story about a Huck-Finn-type boy living on the river, did you?"

"I could never corroborate it. I wasn't sure I never believed it."

"He was in the cave that day?"

"I think so. The snake might have left the cave because of him."

"Sarah…" He started back toward the house, the laughter of friends he'd taken for granted for far too long. "I'm flying back to Washington tonight."

"After supper. I'm thawing a prune cake."

Granny's prune cake. He adored these people. "I love you, Sarah. You are truly the daughter Ev and I never had. I'm convening a press conference tomorrow morning. Wherever you want to be is fine with me. I just wanted to warn you that the proverbial shit is about to hit the fan. The media's going to want to talk to you even more than they do now about our friendship."

"I think—" She walked next to him and hooked her arm into his. "If I get a move on it, I'll bet I could be in Cold Ridge tomorrow morning."

"Cold Ridge, eh?" He grinned at her, loving her as much, he thought, as he could love any daughter he'd had. "Take your woolens. It's still winter up there. Although from what I hear about you and Deputy Winter," he added devilishly, "you won't need any woolens to keep you warm."

Thirty-Five

Nate warmed his hands in front of the stone fireplace in the brick house Abraham Winter, an ancestor, had built and where his brother-in-law, Tyler North, had grown up. North had broken open a six-pack. He was on leave for a few days. Carine was off taking pictures.

North, a skilled combat paramedic, had wanted to know all about the snakebites. He was the sort of guy who understood catching poisonous snakes for fun. He'd already said—more than once—that he thought he'd like Sarah Dunnemore.

"Gus tell you?" North got two frosted glasses out of the freezer, which were his new wife's doing, since he was a drink-from-the-bottle type, and poured the beer. "Antonia's having a girl."

Nate hadn't heard, but it seemed so natural, his oldest sister as the mother of a baby girl. Yet, less than a year ago, she'd convinced herself that she and Hank Callahan would never make it. She'd immersed herself in her work for years. All three Winter siblings had.

"I don't trust myself," Nate said abruptly, staring into the fire North had started to take the chill out of the air.

Ty handed him an icy glass of beer. "With women or with babies?"

"Both."

"Who does? Just don't think too hard." North took a sip of his own beer and tossed another log onto the fire. "You wait as long to find the right woman as we have, it's easy to think too much."

"Where do you get the 'we'?"

North grinned at him. "Come on. You've all but carved little hearts onto the ridge over your Ph.D. in Tennessee."

"Jesus, North. Hearts." Nate drank some of his beer, not really tasting it. "You and Carine. Any regrets?"

"Yeah. Loads. She'd never have gotten that goddamn puppy if I hadn't gone and done it. Puppy's related to Stump. She digs. Carine insisted it was a Gus thing, but it's a Stump thing."

Getting a serious answer out of Ty North could be a chore. But he finally sat in front of the fire and got quiet as he stared into the flames. He'd grown up in the sprawling house with an eccentric, artistic mother who'd ended up leaving it, fifty acres and an unexpected trust fund to him. Nate had sat with him here, in front of the fire, countless times over the years, before North had decided to take up with the youngest of the Winter orphans.

Nate finished his beer. "North?"

"I keep telling myself if Hank can stand it, I can. He lost a child."

"What?"

North sighed. "Carine's expecting."

"A baby? Carine?"

"Yeah. A baby."

Nate thought of both of his younger sisters as mothers, thought of his own mother. Even now, more than thirty years after her death, he could hear her singing, feel her breath against his cheek as she'd kissed him good-night. And his father. The firefighter. The rock.

A wife, babies, puppies, a regular life—Nate had rejected them all for himself. He told himself it was because of the work he did, but that was an excuse. Half the reason he'd chosen his work—half the reason he'd started volunteering his first day on the job for the most dangerous assignments—was because it gave him a reason to skirt any kind of commitment to having a family of his own. He was the eldest of three orphans. That was enough.

"Congratulations," he told his brother-in-law.

"Thanks. Carine hasn't told Gus yet." North grinned suddenly. "He might kill me yet."

Sarah stood shivering in a freezing store with soft wooden floors and a very fit white-haired man who was piling a bench with everything she needed to hike Cold Ridge in the middle of May. It was a frightening amount. A moisture-wicking lightweight top, a fleece pullover, moisture-wicking hiking pants, a waterproof jacket, waterproof pants, wool socks. Day pack, water bottles. Boots. He dragged out six pairs of boots for her to try on while he added a flashlight, a compass, maps, waterproof matches, gloves and a hat to her pile.

"Why do I need a flashlight?" she asked. "I'm only doing a day hike."

"You never know."

"And the hat and gloves? It's spring."

He looked at her as if he just knew she was a mountain rescue in the making. "It's forty-one degrees on the ridge."

"Oh. Well. Make sure those are warm gloves." She chose the cheapest pair of boots that passed his suitability test. "But, honestly, if there are no poisonous snakes on the ridge, then I'm good."

He didn't crack a smile.

Only when she signed her credit card bill did she notice the name of the place. Gus & Smitty's. "Are you Gus Winter?"

Now he smiled. "Yes, Dr. Dunnemore, I am."

"Just Sarah is fine. How—"

"You've been all over the news." His expression softened. "Everyone in America now knows what historical archaeology is."

She'd skipped much of the media coverage of her family and their relationship to Violet and Leola Poe and the child they'd raised who was now president, and Wes and her mother's relationship to Nicholas Janssen—and what the media and authorities had pieced together on his criminal activities.

She'd learned all she wanted to know about John Wesley Poe, aka Conroy Fontaine. He'd disappeared from his home near Memphis after his mother died when he was sixteen. No one had any idea what had happened to him until he turned up dead of a cottonmouth bite in Night's Landing fifteen years later.

Sarah had lain awake one night, remembering a conversation she'd had with Leola and Violet about the Huck Finn boy they maintained was living on the river. *He won't let us help him. He won't let anyone help him.*

Every reporter in America was back to trying to find the one clue that would tell them who President John Wesley Poe's biological parents really were. There was nothing.

Sarah's relationship with him and the women who'd raised him was analyzed and dissected, her academic career and her various projects on the Poe house and the people who'd lived there were explored—but she'd refused all interviews. Her work on the Poes was now in the hands of the Poe Trust. When the house opened to the public as an historic site, she would visit it only as a tourist.

It was time for her to move on.

Gus Winter cleared his throat, pulling her out of her thoughts. "You don't want to climb the ridge alone, especially not this time of year. Nate's over at the house. He's been hiking every day since he got here. He's in good shape."

"They say he's good at tracking people. One of the best." Sarah handed over her signed receipt and gathered up the two big bags of gear. They barely cleared her chin. She smiled at Nate's uncle, the man who'd raised three orphans on his own. He was younger than her own mother. "Let him track me if he wants to."

She borrowed a pair of scissors and ducked into the changing room. She cut off all the tags of her new gear, then peeled off her travel clothes and put on the primary layer of her hiking clothes. She glanced in the full-length mirror. Not very attractive, but they'd do.

"Where is the ridge?" she asked Gus Winter on her way out.

He blinked at her. "It's above you."

She gave him a reassuring smile. "I mean the trail."

He gave her directions to a brick house out of town—Carine and North's place, he said—and told her to turn left past it and follow the signs.

She did, and within an hour of tramping up the trail, she'd decided spring took way too long to get to New Hampshire.

It was just plain *cold.*

But the rock formations, the tiny new leaves fluttering in the midday sun, the crystal-clear streams—and the views—were incredible. As she climbed higher, Sarah stopped every few feet to look out at the valley and the surrounding mountains. It was a clear, bright, cool, magnificent day.

When she got closer to the tree line, the wind picked up, whipping her face, blowing across the gnarled, squat evergreens and struggling new grasses. There were pockets of snow in the rocks above her. She put on her hat and her gloves and bundled up in her fleece, thinking that in Tennessee, she'd be on the front porch, having barbecue and strawberry pie with her family. Gus Winter had tossed a half-dozen power bars into her pack. They did not rival prune cake, fried apricot pies, squash casserole—

She stopped her train of thought and rested a moment on a rounded boulder in the middle of the trail.

When she'd left last night for New Hampshire, her mother had hugged her for longer than usual. It was enough. Nothing more needed to be said between them. If the Dutch police hadn't found them, she believed Conroy's man would have killed them. But he'd given up without a struggle. Authorities were still interviewing him.

Nicholas Janssen had intercepted her, courted her, stalked her. He had his own agenda, his own plan for obtaining a pardon—for wooing the girl he'd known in college.

Her mother had been horrified, shaken, when she learned that the army captain who'd told her Nicholas was facing prosecution in the United States for tax evasion had turned up murdered. That the man fishing on the dock that day in early April was Charlene Brooker's husband.

She simply hadn't known, she said.

Wes Poe had arranged transportation to the Nashville airport. Sarah's father had walked her to the car. "The worst part about being held captive was thinking not just that we'd never see you and Rob again, but that you'd have to live with the knowledge of what happened to us." He'd paused, his eyes shining. "I didn't want you to have that burden."

Sarah thought she understood what it was to want to spare someone else a burden, to want to ease a burden from someone else's shoulders—and that it couldn't always be done, not just because it was impossible, but because that experience was a part of who that person had become.

Which she didn't have to explain to her father. He knew.

She'd spent the night at an airport hotel, rented a car early that morning and arrived at Gus & Smitty's in time to spend a fortune.

She experienced a wobble of vertigo as she looked off one side of her boulder, down into the valley, much greener than it was up high. The wind whistled in the cracks and crevices of her granite surroundings.

She hoped Nate would get on with tracking her down.

But his uncle had outfitted her for the conditions, and she could scoot down the trail, back amongst tall trees, if the wind picked up and she really started to feel the cold.

She took another bite of her power bar and washed it down with water, but she'd noticed a pleasant-looking diner when she was in the village of Cold Ridge. She'd rather get off the ridge and eat there.

When she climbed down off her boulder and turned to resume her ascent, Nate was there above her, sitting on a ledge as if she'd conjured him out of the thin mountain air.

He leaned back against another boulder and didn't say a word as she made her way up to him. He had on scuffed boots, hiking pants, a black fleece—no hat, no gloves. And no gun, she thought. The horrors of the sniper attack and Conroy's manipulations were slowly receding.

"How did you get ahead of me?" she asked. "Did you drop out of a helicopter?"

"With an ex-pilot and a pararescueman in the family, I suppose I could have. But you'd have heard a helicopter.''

''I don't know. With this wind, I might not have.''

But he'd found a spot sheltered from the wind, still and quiet as she sat next to him.

''There's more than one way up here,'' he said.

''Then you weren't already here. You saw your uncle—''

''He said he did what he could to make sure you wouldn't be fined for recklessness when he had to come pluck you off the ridge. I told him not to underestimate you.'' He moved in closer, and she had the feeling if she scooted away from him even an inch, she'd fall off into oblivion. ''It's easier to track a woman who wants to be found than a fugitive who doesn't.''

''Well, I did narrow your options.''

He smiled and touched the corner of her mouth with his thumb. ''I've missed you.''

''Good, because I wasn't sure if I was crazy—'' She caught his wrist in her hand and slipped her fingers into his. ''Sometimes it's hard to know what of that week was real and what wasn't.''

He kissed her fingers. ''I was real.''

''My family—it's wonderful to have Rob home. He's doing well. And my parents are fine. They're resilient, already planning their return trip to Amsterdam so that Dad can finish his project there.''

''You Dunnemores and your projects.''

She laughed. ''Yes, it's true.''

''And the president?''

''He was in Night's Landing yesterday.''

''I saw on the news.''

"He's holding a press conference today in Washington. He's setting the record straight on the snake story and letting reporters exhaust every possible question they have about our relationship. Honestly, when the snake thing happened, I just wanted him to be okay. None of the rest mattered. I don't think it really did to him, either. People will think it did, but he had so much else on his mind besides who'd saved who from a water moccasin."

Nate withdrew his hand from hers and skimmed his fingertips along her jaw, down the right side of her neck. "How's your snakebite?"

His touch had her feeling warm again. "All healed."

"Wes Poe's surrogate daughter. I'll probably be guillotined for making love to you, almost getting you killed."

"You knew we were close when you threatened to arrest me that day in New York."

"That's different." He threaded his fingers into her hair and kissed her softly. "We can't make love up here. We'd kill ourselves on the rocks."

She smiled. "Always so impatient."

"Something we have in common when it comes to lovemaking, as I recall."

She stayed put, gazing out at the surrounding mountains. "I have something I want to tell you. Wes mentioned your promotion."

"He is the boss."

"He said you're taking it. I'm thrilled for you."

"Thank you."

"There's this historic house in northern Virginia.

Arlington, actually. It's not far from the Marshals Service headquarters."

He said nothing, just watched her with those incisive eyes, even bluer now, she thought, against the northern New England sky.

"It's like the Poe house," she went on, "a combination of private, state and federal interests. Pristine. Lots of history."

"They need an historical archaeologist?"

She nodded. "It's an exciting project. People say the house is haunted."

"Not by a president, I hope."

"Abraham Lincoln and Robert E. Lee, as it happens."

"Ah. Of course."

"I thought if I took on this project, then I'd be in the area and we could go on dates."

"We could have candlelight dinners," he said.

"That's right. And go to movies and concerts."

"How long do we have to date?"

Her heart jumped. "I do see why people say you're impatient."

"I'm patient. I'm being patient now. I'm not throwing you over my shoulder and marching down to the nearest shelter, am I?"

It was a delicious thought, but she forced herself to stick to what she'd come to Cold Ridge to say. "I have other offers. I don't want to crowd you in your new job. But I want to find a way for us to be together that's good for both of us."

"It's what I want." He got to his feet, no indication that he was concerned he could take one wrong step and end up in a heap on the rocks. He offered her a hand, pulling her to her feet, kissing her softly. "It's all I've been thinking about since I left you."

"Everyone was convinced I'd fall for a charming intellectual."

"I'm charming."

She laughed. "That's the other thing people say about you. 'That Nate Winter, he's a charmer.'"

"Do I detect a note of sarcasm?"

"Damn it, Nate, you know what I'm saying."

"You're saying that *you* thought you'd fall for some weak-kneed type. No one else did. They all thought you'd fall for—"

"A hard-driving, hard-ass marshal?"

"Yeah." He grinned. "That about covers it. Can we make love after our dates? Or am I to deliver you to your door with a chaste kiss?"

"I like a little mystery and drama. Surprise me."

They climbed back down to the trail. Sarah held his hand tightly in hers. "Nate—where—"

"Way out on the ridge." He'd understood her question. She wanted to know where his parents had died. "Carine took up nature photography partly as a way to make her peace with our parents' death. Her photographs of the mountains tell her whole story. Antonia went into healing. I went into catching bad guys. Get them off the street before they can hurt anyone else, themselves, the people who care about them."

"It's beautiful up here," Sarah said.

"It can be deadly."

"I'm glad I came. I've fallen in love with you in a very short time, and I can see now that part of the reason for it is here. Part of you is here."

"Part of me is about to freeze off." He winked at her. "Carine has a log cabin she uses as a studio a short walk from the trailhead. She's got her husband with her for a few days—she won't be using it. We can have a candlelit dinner there."

Sarah nodded. "It sounds perfect. I'll get to meet her?"

"Oh, yeah. If I don't bring you by, she'll sneak in on us." He lifted her backpack off her shoulder and slipped it over his, adjusting the straps, not looking at her. "Don't think I'm going repressed Yankee on you and ignoring that part about you falling in love with me."

"Well—"

He didn't let her go on. "Gus always said I'd fall like a rock for someone one of these days and I'd never see it coming." He looked at her now, his expression as soft, as tender, as she'd ever seen. "He was right."

"He'll love that, won't he?" She grinned at him. "About this log cabin. Does it have a fireplace?"

"Better yet, Miss Sarah. It has a bed."

A gust of wind pushed at her back, as if propelling her down the ridge, and Nate laughed—really laughed—and showed her his shortcut.

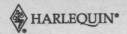 

Carnival Elation
7-Day Exotic Western Caribbean Itinerary

DAY	PORT	ARRIVE	DEPART
Sun	Galveston		4:00 P.M.
Mon	"Fun Day" at Sea		
Tue	Progreso/Mérida	8:00 A.M.	4:00 P.M.
Wed	Cozumel	9:00 A.M.	5:00 P.M.
Thu	Belize	8:00 A.M.	6:00 P.M.
Fri	"Fun Day" at Sea		
Sat	"Fun Day" at Sea		
Sun	Galveston	8:00 A.M.	

TERMS AND CONDITIONS

PAYMENT SCHEDULE:
50% due upon booking. Full and final payment due by July 26, 2004.
Acceptable forms of payment are Visa, MasterCard, American Express, Discover and checks. The cardholder must be one of the passengers traveling. A fee of $25 will apply for all returned checks. Check payments must be made payable to **Advantage International, LLC** and sent to: **Advantage International, LLC, 195 North Harbor Drive, Suite 4206, Chicago, IL 60601.**

CHANGE/CANCELLATION:
Notice of change/cancellation must be made in writing to Advantage International, LLC.

Change:
Changes in cabin category may be requested and can result in increased rate and penalties. A name change is permitted 60 days or more prior to departure and will incur a penalty of $50 per name change. Deviation from the group schedule and package is a cancellation.

Cancellation:

181 days or more prior to departure	$250 per person
121—180 days or more prior to departure	50% of the package price
120—61 days prior to departure	75% of the package price
60 days or less prior to departure	100% of the package price (nonrefundable)

U.S. and Canadian citizens are required to present a valid passport or the original birth certificate and state issued photo ID (driver's license). All other nationalities must contact the consulate of the various ports that are visited for verification of documentation.

<u>We strongly recommend trip cancellation insurance!</u>

For further details call 1-877-ADV-NTGE or visit www.GetCaughtReadingatSea.com

For booking form and complete information
go to <u>www.getcaughtreadingatsea.com</u>
or call 1-877-ADV-NTGE

Complete coupon and booking form and mail both to:
Advantage International, LLC
195 North Harbor Drive, Suite 4206, Chicago, IL 60601

Harlequin Enterprises Ltd. is a paid participant in this promotion.

Visit us at www.eHarlequin.com

GCRSEA2

MIRABooks.com

We've got the lowdown on your favorite author!

☆ Read an excerpt of your favorite author's newest book

☆ Check out her bio

☆ Talk to her in our Discussion Forums

☆ Read interviews, diaries, and more

☆ Find her current bestseller, and even her backlist titles

All this and more available at

www.MiraBooks.com

ROBYN CARR

BLUE SKIES

Nikki Burgess, Dixie McPherson and Carlisle Bartlett are three women who could seriously use a break. A fresh start. A shot at success and a chance to shine. Maybe a little romance—the kind that sticks. And some adventure wouldn't hurt.

So when they're presented with the challenge of joining a team starting a new airline in Las Vegas, they don't hesitate. With nothing to lose and everything to gain, these three friends are going in search of their own blue skies.

> **"Robyn Carr writes books that touch
> the heart and the funny bone."**
> —*New York Times* bestselling author
> Debbie Macomber

Available in May 2004 wherever paperbacks are sold.

CARLA NEGGERS

66923	STONEBROOK COTTAGE	___ $6.50 U.S.	___ $7.99 CAN.
66845	THE CABIN	___ $6.50 U.S.	___ $7.99 CAN.
66972	THE CARRIAGE HOUSE	___ $6.50 U.S.	___ $7.99 CAN.
66684	COLD RIDGE	___ $6.99 U.S.	___ $8.50 CAN.
66651	THE HARBOR	___ $6.99 U.S.	___ $8.50 CAN.
66971	THE WATERFALL	___ $6.50 U.S.	___ $7.99 CAN.
66970	ON FIRE	___ $6.50 U.S.	___ $7.99 CAN.
66969	KISS THE MOON	___ $6.50 U.S.	___ $7.99 CAN.
66266	CLAIM THE CROWN	___ $5.50 U.S.	___ $6.50 CAN.

(limited quantities available)

TOTAL AMOUNT $_____
POSTAGE & HANDLING $_____
($1.00 for one book; 50¢ for each additional)
APPLICABLE TAXES* $_____
<u>TOTAL PAYABLE</u> $_____
(check or money order—please do not send cash)

To order, complete this form and send it, along with a check or money order for the total above, payable to MIRA Books, to: **In the U.S.:** 3010 Walden Avenue, P.O. Box 9077, Buffalo, NY 14269-9077; **In Canada:** P.O. Box 636, Fort Erie, Ontario, L2A 5X3.

Name:_____
Address:_____ City:_____
State/Prov.:_____ Zip/Postal Code:_____
Account Number (if applicable):_____
075 CSAS

  *New York residents remit applicable sales taxes.
   Canadian residents remit applicable GST
   and provincial taxes.

MIRA®